Praise for

ANNE O'BRIEN

'O'Brien cleverly intertwines the personal and political in this enjoyable, gripping tale'
The Times

'[A] fast-paced historical novel'
Good Housekeeping

'Anne O'Brien has unearthed a gem of a subject'
Daily Telegraph

'A gripping story of love, heartache and political intrigue'
Woman & Home

'There are historical novels and then there are the works of Anne O'Brien – and this is another hit'
The Sun

'The characters are larger than life…and the author a compulsive storyteller'
Sunday Express

'This book has everything – royalty, scandal, fascinating historical politics'
Cosmopolitan

'A gripping historical drama'
Bella

'Historical fiction at its best'
Candis

Anne O'Brien was born in the West Riding of Yorkshire. After gaining a BA Honours degree at Manchester University and a Master's at Hull, she lived in the East Riding for many years as a teacher of history. After leaving teaching, Anne decided to turn to novel writing and give voice to the women in history who fascinated her the most. Today Anne lives in an eighteenth-century cottage in Herefordshire, an area full of inspiration for her work.

Visit Anne online at www.anneobrienbooks.com.

Find Anne on Facebook and follow her on Twitter: @ anne_obrien

Also by

ANNE O'BRIEN

VIRGIN WIDOW
DEVIL'S CONSORT
THE KING'S CONCUBINE
THE FORBIDDEN QUEEN
THE SCANDALOUS DUCHESS
THE KING'S SISTER
THE QUEEN'S CHOICE
THE SHADOW QUEEN
QUEEN OF THE NORTH

A Tapestry of Treason

ANNE O'BRIEN

ONE PLACE. MANY STORIES

HQ
An imprint of HarperCollins*Publishers* Ltd
1 London Bridge Street
London SE1 9GF

This edition 2019

1

First published in Great Britain by
Harlequin (UK) Limited 2019

A catalogue record for this book is available from the British Library.

ISBN
HB: 978-0-00-822546-9
TPB: 978-0-00-822547-6

MIX
Paper from responsible sources
FSC™ C007454

This book is produced from independently certified FSC™ paper to ensure responsible forest management.

For more information visit: www.harpercollins.co.uk/green

This book is set in 11.4/15.5 pt. Bembo

Printed and bound in Great Britain by
CPI Group (UK) Ltd, Croydon, CR0 4YY

With all my love, as always, to George, who immersed himself in this tale of medieval politics and high drama. A born Lancastrian, after reading of the devious exploits of the House of York, he remains a dyed-in-the-wool supporter of the red rose.

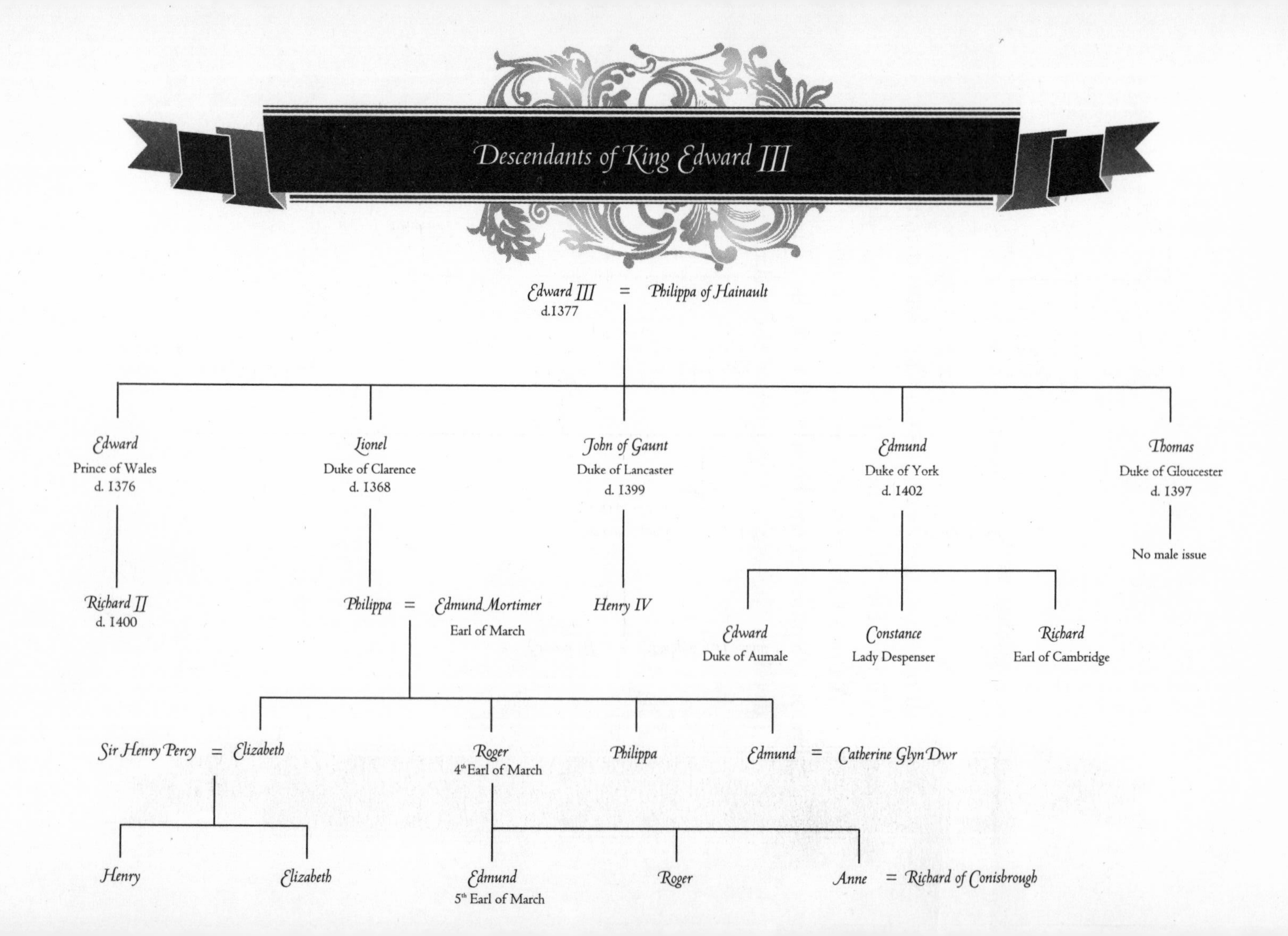
Descendants of King Edward III
Edward III = Philippa of Hainault
d.1377
Edward
Prince of Wales
d. 1376
Lionel
Duke of Clarence
d. 1368
John of Gaunt
Duke of Lancaster
d. 1399
Edmund
Duke of York
d. 1402
Thomas
Duke of Gloucester
d. 1397
No male issue
Richard II
d. 1400
Philippa = Edmund Mortimer
Earl of March
Henry IV
Edward
Duke of Aumale
Constance
Lady Despenser
Richard
Earl of Cambridge
Sir Henry Percy = Elizabeth
Roger
4th Earl of March
Philippa
Edmund = Catherine Glyn Dwr
Henry
Elizabeth
Edmund
5th Earl of March
Roger
Anne = Richard of Conisbrough

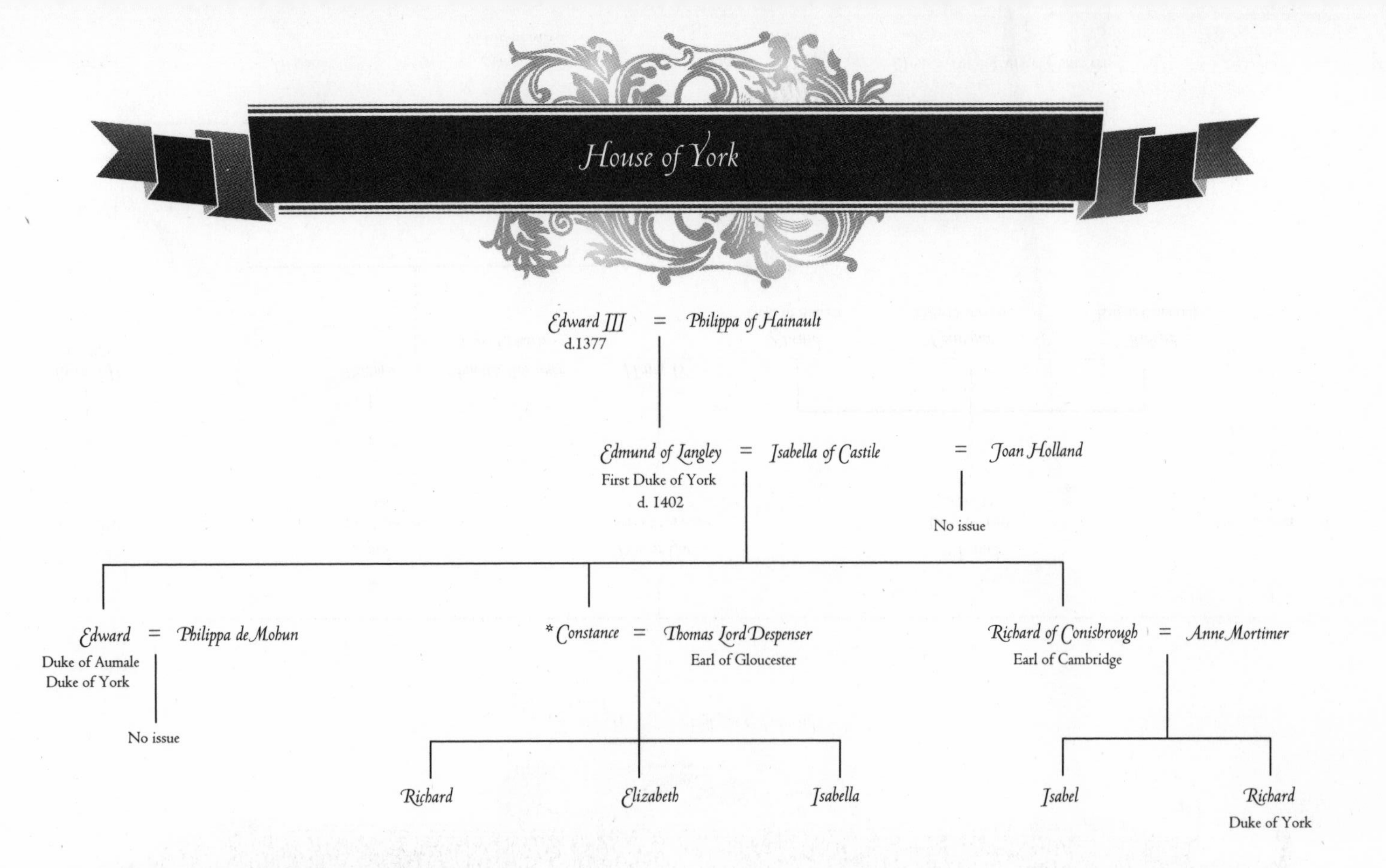
House of York
Edward III
d.1377
=
Philippa of Hainault
Edmund of Langley
First Duke of York
d. 1402
=
Isabella of Castile
=
Joan Holland
No issue
Edward
Duke of Aumale
Duke of York
=
Philippa de Mohun
No issue
*Constance
=
Thomas Lord Despenser
Earl of Gloucester
Richard
Elizabeth
Isabella
Richard of Conisbrough
Earl of Cambridge
=
Anne Mortimer
Isabel
Richard
Duke of York
*daughter Alianore with Edmund Holland, Earl of Kent.

Chapter One

February 1399: Westminster Palace

'Entertain us, sir.'

Since my invitation caused Friar John Depyng to step aside in a display of speed impressive for so corpulent a figure, I smiled a brief show of teeth to soften my command. 'If it please you, sir. We desire to take a glimpse into the future.'

Friar John, not won over to any degree, dared to scowl. 'Divination is not for entertainment, my lady.'

Unperturbed, my brother Edward, forcefully large, grasped his elbow and drew him along with us. 'You would not wish to refuse us. It would displease the King if your being disobliging happened, by chance, to come to his ear.'

The quality of Edward's smile lit fear in the cleric's eyes.

At my behest, we were borrowing Friar John, one of King Richard's favourite preachers who had the gift of soothsaying, to while away an otherwise tedious hour after supper. Weary as we were of the minstrels and disguisers, my two brothers and my husband were not averse to humouring me, for here was a man famed for his prophecy. Was he not held in high regard by our cousin King Richard? Why not allow him to paint for us the future? I had said. All was in hand for the campaign against the treacherous Irish, waiting only on the King's final command for embarkation. Why not enjoy our victory before it was even won?

We took occupation of a chill room in the Palace of Westminster, a room that looked as if it had once stored armaments but was now empty, save for stools and a crude slab of a table more fitting for some usage in King Richard's kitchens.

'Tell us what you see of the future,' I demanded as soon as the door was closed, lifting the purse at my girdle so that it chinked with coin.

Yet still Friar John looked askance at me and my companions: my brothers Edward and Dickon, and Thomas my husband.

'I will not,' Friar John said. He lowered his voice. 'It is dangerous.' He glanced at the closed door, through which there was no immediate escape.

'You will. I am Constance Despenser, Countess of Gloucester. I know that you will not refuse me.'

'I know full well who you are, my lady.'

I pushed him gently to a stool, with a little weight on each shoulder to make him sit, which he did with a sigh while I leaned to whisper in his ear, the veils, attached with jewelled clasps to my silk chaplet, fluttering seductively. 'We will reward you, of course.'

'He's naught but a cheap fortune teller.' Thomas drew up a stool with one foot and sank onto it. 'A charlatan who would tell any tale for a purse of gold.'

I did not even grace Thomas with a glance; to mock our captive priest would not warm him to our purpose. 'The King goes to Ireland,' I said. 'Tell us of his good fortune. And ours.'

'But not if you see my death,' Edward grinned. 'If you do, I expect you to lie about it.'

I passed a coin to Friar John who, suitably intimidated, took from a concealment in his sleeve two golden dice, placing them on the uneven surface of the table.

'I like not dice prophecy,' Thomas growled.

But Friar John, now in his métier and with the prospect of further coin, was confident. 'It is what I have used to give the King a view of the coming days, my lord.' Picking up the dice, with an expert turn of the wrist he threw them. They fell, rolled and halted to show a six and a six.

'Is that good?' Dickon asked, leaning his weight on the table so that it rocked on the uneven floor, until I pushed him away. He was Richard of Conisbrough when formality ruled, which was not often in this company. He was my younger brother by at least ten years.

'Too good to be true.' Thomas was scowling. 'I recall the King had a pair of loaded dice, a gift when he was a child, so he could never lose. Until his friends refused to gamble with him. They were gold too.'

Friar John shook his head in denial, but more in arrogance. 'There is no sleight of hand here, my lord. This is the most advantageous throw of all. The number six stands for our lord the King himself. It indicates his strength. This shows us that England is a paradise of royal power.'

'Excellent!' Edward said, arms folded across this chest. 'Throw again.'

Friar John threw again. Each one of the die fell to reveal a single mark.

'Is this dangerous?' I asked. 'Does this single mark then deny the royal power?'

'Not so, my lady. This means unity. There is no threat against our King.'

'None of this has any meaning!' Thomas slouched on his stool, his chin on his folded hands, his solid brows meeting above a masterful nose, marring what might have been handsome if heavy features. 'I swear it's all a mockery. Don't pay him.'

'Again,' I said. 'One more time.'

Another throw of the dice to show a three and a three. Friar John beamed. 'Excellent: the Trinity. And three is half of six. So to add them – three and three – means that the King remains secure. The campaign in Ireland will bring nothing but good.'

He collected the dice into the palm of his hand and made as if to secrete them once more into his sleeve, relief flitting across his face.

'Not yet.' I covered his hand with mine, for here, to my mind, was the true purpose of this venture. 'Now throw the dice for us. What will our future hold?'

With a shrug, he threw again. A two and a three. The three was the first to be revealed, then the two to fall alongside. From Friar John there was a long intake of breath.

'What is it?' Edward demanded. 'Don't stop now . . .'

'When two overcomes three, all is lost.' The friar let the words fall from his tongue in a turbulence, with no attempt to hide his dismay. 'When two overcomes three, disaster looms. Two reveals disunity. Disunity threatens the King. It threatens peace. It is necessary to unite behind the King to prevent so critical an attack on the peace of the realm. Sometimes it is necessary . . .'

He swallowed, his words at last faltering.

'Sometimes what?' I saw Edward's fingers tighten into talons on our friar's shoulder.

Friar John looked up into his face. 'Sometimes it means that the King is unable to hold the realm in peace, my lord. It means that the lords of the realm must unite to choose a new King. One more fit for the task.'

'But we don't need a new King,' I said. 'We are content with the one we have. We will unite behind King Richard to . . .'

Thomas pushed himself to his feet with a clatter as the stool fell over. 'Is that it? Is that all you see? It makes no sense.'

Needing the answer, reluctant that Thomas should break up the meeting, I grasped his arm. 'Does seeing it make it so, sir? Is this what will occur? Disunity?'

'No, my lady. Not necessarily . . .'

'So it is all nonsense. As I said.' Thomas, freeing himself, was already halfway to the door. 'Pay him what you think he's worth and let's get out of here. It's cold enough to freeze my balls.'

His crudity did not move me. I had seen the anxiety in Friar John's eye. But before I could question him further: 'Do you see me in the fall of the dice, Master Friar?' Dickon asked.

'I see no faces, no names, sir. That is not the role of the dice.'

'Then where will you see me?'

Friar John was unwilling to be drawn by a question from a mere youth, not yet grown into his full height or his wits. 'I cannot say. I might see it in a cup of wine, but there is none here to be had.'

He looked hopeful, but indeed there was nothing of comfort in the room, except the heavily chased silver vessel that Thomas had brought with him.

'Then you can take yourself off, Master Dissembler. You'll get no more from us, neither coin nor wine.' Thomas held the door open for him.

But Friar John was staring at his hands, laid flat against the wood, fingers spread. His eyes stared as if transfixed by some thought that had lodged in his mind.

'What is it, man?' Edward asked.

The tip of the soothsayer's tongue passed over his lips, and his voice fell as if chanting a psalm at Vespers, except that this was no religious comfort.

'*When a raven shall build in a stone lion's mouth*
On the church top beside the grey forest,
Then shall a King of England be drove from his crown
And return no more.'

A little beat of silence fell amongst us. Until Dickon laughed. 'Do we have to kill every church-nesting raven, then, to save King Richard's crown?'

Friar John blinked, looked horrified. 'Did I say that? It is treason.'

'No, it is not,' I assured, hoping to get more from him before he fled. 'Just a verse that came into your head from some old ballad from the north.' I pushed Thomas's abandoned cup in his direction.

Friar John drank the contents in two gulps, wiping his mouth with his hand, and when we made no move to prevent him, he left in a portly swirl of black robes. He forgot to take the dice with him.

'Well! What do we make of all that?' I asked. A sharp sense of disquiet had pervaded the room, as if we had stirred up something noxious.

'I have no belief in such things,' Edward replied. 'Do we not make our own destiny?'

I could not be so dispassionate. 'Cousin Richard has opened the doors of power for us. It will not be to our advantage for that power to be threatened.'

The Friar's uneasy prediction was not what I had wanted to hear. We had been given a warning, enough to get under the skin like a winter itch.

'Do you want my prophecy, sister?' Edward was irresponsibly confident. 'Without any need for golden dice, I say all will be well. I say we will return from Ireland with music and rejoicing. To whom will Richard apportion land in Ireland once it has fallen to him? I doubt we will be overlooked.'

'And our authority will be greater than ever,' Thomas concurred. 'Let's get out of here and find some good company.'

Edward punched Dickon on the shoulder. 'And if we see a raven nesting near a grey forest, we set Dickon here to kill it.'

We laughed. Our tame soothsayer was indeed a mountebank, yet a discomfort remained with me beneath the laughter. Friar John had been disturbed. It had been no deliberately false reading. And to what purpose would it have been, to prophesy unrest and upheaval? There had been terror in his flight.

I scooped up the dice that the magician had left behind, before Edward could take possession. Out of cursory interest, I threw them, without skill. A three and then, a moment later as the second die fell, a two. The three overcome by the two. A warning? But to whom? I had no power to read the future.

I kept in step with Edward and Dickon as we strolled back to the Court festivities where the practised voices of the minstrels could be heard in enthusiastic harmony.

'Did you learn what it was that you wished to learn?' Edward asked.

I avoided his speculative glance. 'I do not know that I wished to learn anything.'

'Oh, I think you did. It was not merely a frivolous entertainment, was it? It was all your idea.'

I smiled, offering nothing, uncomfortable at his reading of my intention. I had learned nothing for my peace of mind but I would keep my own counsel, Edward being too keen to use information, even that given privately, to further his own ends. Not that there was anything for me to admit. As a family we were at the supreme apex of our powers. I merely wished to know that it would stay that way. Now I was unsure.

'Give me the dice,' Edward said, holding out his hand.

'I will not,' I replied, 'since you have no belief in their efficacy.'

I would keep them. I abandoned my brothers when Edward lingered to demonstrate for Dickon a particular attack and feint with an imaginary sword, their breathless shouts and thud of feet gradually fading behind me.

Thomas had not waited for me.

Since there was nothing new in this, it barely caught my attention.

Early June 1399: Westminster Palace

At last the campaign was under way; King Richard was leaving for Ireland where he would land in Waterford and impose English rule on the recalcitrant tribes. It was an auspicious day, and as if Richard had summoned God's blessing, jewels and armour and horse-harness glittered and gleamed in the full brightness of a cloudless sun. An accommodating breeze lifted the banners of the magnates who accompanied him so that the appliquéd motifs and heraldic goldwork rippled and danced. As did my heart, rejoicing at this creation of majesty on the move, as I stood on the waterfront to bid them farewell and Godspeed. Richard's previous invasion, four years earlier, had not ended on a sanguine note, the settlement collapsing as soon as the English King's back was turned. This time Richard's foray would bring lasting glory to England.

'I should be going with them.' Dickon's mood was not joyful.

'Next time I expect you will.'

'I am of an age to be there.'

He was of an age, at almost fifteen years, even if he had not yet attained the height and breadth of shoulder that made his brother so impressive a figure on the tilting ground or in a Court procession. One day he would be so; one day he might even achieve some coordination of thought and action. But even though that day was still far off, Dickon should have been a squire, riding in his lord's entourage. Comparisons on all sides did nothing but intensify his dissatisfaction with life. Brother Edward had been knighted by King Richard at the ridiculously young age of four years. Yet here was Dickon, without patronage, without recognition, a mere observer in the courtly crowd. What could I say to make him feel better about his lot in life? There were things no one talked of in our family.

'Enjoy this grand moment of celebration,' was all I could offer. 'You'll get the chance to go to war soon enough.'

I understood the grinding need in him to make a mark on the world, to make a name for himself, even as it baffled me that men were so keen to go into battle and risk their lives.

'Talk to the King, Con. Ask him to take me as one of his household. Or even Edward.'

I shook my head. It was too late. No one had in mind a younger son with shadows surrounding his birth. Instead I pinioned Dickon to my side. There was much to be enjoyed in the image of royal power set out before us, the walls of Westminster Palace providing a stately if austere backdrop. This would be the campaign to coat King Richard's glory in even more layers of gold. The horses, commandeered from the monastic houses of England, glowed with well-burnished flesh. A dozen great lords paraded their own wealth and consequence. And then came a large household of knights, of bishops and chaplains, even foreign visitors who accompanied the King with dreams of victory.

King Richard stood at the centre of this Court of his creating. Clad in eye-catching red, his most favoured colour, his bright hair curling beneath his brimmed hat, he drew every eye. The knowledge that he had made his will was thought to be no detriment to the success of this venture, nor that his holy relics and regalia were packed up to accompany him. Now he raised his hand in farewell, so that we might admire the ring that blazed red fire from a ruby that he had once granted to the Abbot and monks of Westminster, on condition that he could resume it when he left the country. Worth the vast sum of one thousand marks, the gem once more graced his hand as he mounted and took his place in the procession.

The forthcoming victory, as predicted by the golden dice, would shower us, the royal cousins, with even greater power. King Richard smiled on us, his hands open with generosity. And how important we were to the whole enterprise. My brother Edward, Duke of Aumale, fair and well-favoured, riding at the King's side, noted by all as the King's most beloved companion. Then came Thomas Despenser, my husband, Earl of Gloucester, in comparison dark and sallow-skinned, one of the inner circle of Richard's friends and companions. Two of the Holland connection, John and Thomas Holland, the Dukes of Exeter and Surrey, joined to us through my father's recent marriage to Joan Holland, rode in close company, forming a buttress around our King.

We had not always been so ostentatiously dominant. Until Richard's reign we had wallowed in obscurity, thanks to my grandfather King Edward the Third. My father might be his fourth surviving son, thus rich in Plantagenet blood, but he had been much neglected in the handing out of titles and land and royal office. It was not until Richard became King that my father was created Duke of York. Until then he had been simply Earl of Cambridge, poorly endowed, without the estates and wealth appropriate to an earldom. He might have hoped for an endowment from marriage to an English heiress, but instead my grandfather saddled him with Isabella, who, foreign and disinherited, brought no dowry.

Nor was my father blameless, doing little to remedy his lack. With no noticeable ability in military ventures to bring home a fortune in ransoms, with no interest in the manoeuvrings of the Royal Court, my father did not shine on the political stage. He had no ambition, but we, his children, who would inherit these meagre offerings, were driven from the earliest age by naked desire to match our influence to our royal blood.

How superbly successful we had been. We were now power personified, for with the titles had come land and castles, vast estates and the wealth of gold coin from royal patronage, all these recent ennoblements bestowed by King Richard himself. To whom did the King turn when he needed advice? To Edward and Thomas. With whom did King Richard converse at royal masques when the child-Queen Isabelle grew weary? With me, the newly created Countess of Gloucester. We were the bedrock on which Richard's power rested, the foundation and fortifications of England. We were pre-eminent, holding dominion within our new lands, and we would serve Richard well. It might not be for me to own political influence, a woman in a world where decisions were in the hands of men, but the promotion of my family was strong in my heart.

'The King makes a brave show. Pray God the Irish are impressed.'

A laconic comment from the man at my side; stooped with years, his face seamed with unpleasant experience, my father and the King's uncle, Edmund Duke of York. He was to be left behind in England to uphold firm government in Richard's name as Keeper of the Realm. Another golden stitch in the tapestry of our value to the King.

I nodded, watching the pattern of the final leave-taking as Richard consigned his wife into the care of her ladies-in-waiting; Edward bid farewell to his wife Philippa with a gesture of the rich folds of his chaperon, intent primarily on catching the interest of the crowd with his smile and his handsome flamboyance. As for Thomas, he managed a brusque inclination of his head which might have been in my direction. Dickon had taken himself off to who knew where. My father, without a word, abandoned his young wife Joan at my side when summoned by the King to receive some final instruction. Joan, now alone, made no attempt to converse with me. Likewise, I had nothing to say to her.

All told, the day had been an exhibition of absence of familial affection. Fortunately, we were bound fast together by raw ambition.

Chapter Two

31st August 1399: Palace of Westminster

'If you are going to keep me company, I could wish you would not fidget.'

Two months. Two short months during which all the glamour of King Richard's departure had collapsed into disaster. I could make no pretence that my mood was anything but heavy, unease sharpening my tongue. Indeed it was not an unease; by now it was rampant fear. If Dickon expected tolerance from me he would see the day pass without even a gnat-bite of it. I was held in chains of a grave anxiety.

We were still suffering the sultriness of high summer, but the heat did not penetrate to where we stood, Dickon and I, carved emblems of royal power pressing down upon us from above, enfolding us from left and right, from every angle. Such symbols of royal authority, King Richard's authority, should have soothed and reassured. I frowned and Dickon continued to twitch and shuffle, a mess of angular limbs.

'How can I not fidget? How long have we been waiting? You don't even know that he will be brought here.'

'I do know. He will come.'

'There are twenty-six of them,' Dickon informed me inconsequentially, squinting at the angelic band of heavenly angels, carved at the end of each hammer-beam above our heads. He had been passing the time in mindless counting, but I was not prepared to engage in ineffectual conversation. It seemed to me that my family and I were balanced like angels on the head of a pin. All we had achieved was about to be thrown into chaos.

'How much longer?' Dickon groaned. 'Will he be shackled?'

When his large feet continued to scuff against the Purbeck stone, his shoulders hunched in a perpetual slouch, I pinned him with a stare of displeasure as I dug my fingers into the fine weave of his sleeve. I cared not that it was detrimental to the raised pattern.

'Whether he is shackled or not, you will award him all courtesy. He is your godfather as well as your King.'

'And the only source of any wealth that will come to me. I will be all courtesy, as *douce* as a girl, because if I'm not I'll be cut off without a silver groat.' Dickon's glance was sharper and more calculating than it had a right to be. 'Except that he may no longer have any groats to lavish on me. Will he be a prisoner?' Dragging his sleeve from my grasp, he moved so that he could see through the carved arch of the doorway where they would eventually make an entrance.

'I do not yet know.'

But I could not see this charade, this exchange of power from King to Invader, ending in any other fashion.

A servant entered, one I had sent on a mission, now hot from riding. He approached at a jog.

'Well?' I asked.

'They are here, my lady, two miles outside the city.' He bowed then wiped his face on his sleeve. 'They'll be closer now. The King is here with them.'

'Who is in command?'

The servant shrugged. He was not one of mine or he would not have dared to shrug in my presence. 'The Mayor and aldermen have met with them, my lady. It was their decision that the King should be brought here to Westminster. The King had no choice in the matter, I'd say.'

'And the Duke of Lancaster?'

'He rides at the head of his army, my lady.'

'Is he in control? Does he have an air of authority?' I was curious. What was the demeanour of my cousin Henry of Lancaster? Had he returned as supplicant or conqueror?

Richard had banished Henry from England, ostensibly for treason. Now Henry was returned on the death of his father, to reclaim both his title and his inheritance, choosing the opportune moment when Richard was in Ireland. I had to admire his perspicacity. Many would say that Richard had been far from wise in condemning Henry to banishment for life at the same time as he confiscated all the Lancaster wealth and lands for his own use. Our cousin Henry was unlikely to accept such wilful destruction of his true inheritance with a head bent in obedient acceptance. Cousin Henry would demand what was his by right. He had landed at Ravenspur to the north in the first week of July, collecting an army which included the puissant Percy Earl of Northumberland, and now he was here in London with King Richard firmly tucked into his gauntleted fist.

The messenger broke into my thoughts. 'The Duke of

Lancaster's armour is very fine, my lady. Italian and worth a King's ransom, so they say. He looks like a man who knows what he wants and intends to get it.' His face split in a wily gap-toothed grin. 'There'll be much changing of allegiances, I reckon, now that the King is under Lancaster's heel.'

Heel or fist, the result could be the same. Disliking his humour, I dismissed him without further coin than I had already given. King Richard's crown was under threat, but we would wait until all was made clear. Dickon drifted away again.

'Do you know what I think . . .?' he called across the vast echoing space.

I was never to know. The repetitive beat of marching feet intruded, the clatter of horses' hooves, and not least the rancorous shouts of the crowd. My sole concentration was focused on the great doors, now dragged back, stirring the air. In marched an armed guard; at the centre of their protection, or perhaps their containment, walked Richard. King Richard, heir of King Edward the Third, our cousin and God's anointed King of England, all hedged about by bland-faced soldiery. In the face of such military might, Dickon and I retreated once again to the feet of a carved and unimpressed statue.

The guard came to a halt and so did the King.

I could not take my eyes from his face. Never had I seen him so unkingly, whether in demeanour or in apparel. Pale, dishevelled, his soft lips pressed hard together, Richard stared round him as if he had still to accept where he was and why he was here, hemmed in by soldiers not in his own livery. Then he was plucking at his tunic, a garment that he might have been wearing for the whole of the journey from Wales, so travel-worn and stained as it was. His boots were covered in dust, as were his hose to the knee. Eyes wild and uncomprehending, he was hollow-cheeked, implying that he had not eaten a good meal since he had fallen into Lancaster's hands. This man was so much changed from the crimson-clad ruler who had left London a mere few weeks ago that all I could register in that moment was shock. His youthful beauty and vibrancy had been beaten out of him. Even his hair visible beneath the plain felt cap had lost its lustre. He wore no jewels. The ruby ring had gone from his hand. There was no sword at his side. Degradation, as rank water in a thunderstorm, dripped from him.

Richard's vacant gaze fell on me, so that I stepped forward and, through a lifetime of duty and custom, curtsied. The King might have been robbed of all royal grace, but I, clad nobly in deep blue damask with gold stitching at cuff and hem, would uphold it for him. We owed him so much. Was he not my own cousin, my own Plantagenet blood? Unfortunately so was Henry of Lancaster. As I rose to my full height, I foresaw a complex future, troubled by bonds of conflicting family loyalties.

At a glance from me, Dickon bowed.

'Constance?' The King's voice trembled.

'Yes, my lord.'

'Have you come to petition me?' His tone was querulous.

'No, my lord.'

I was distracted, for into the Hall had marched an escort in livery that was my own by birth, the same lions and French lilies as were carved onto Richard's shields, and then came the Mayor and aldermen, self-important in their red robes despite having walked the distance from their first meeting with the

King. It was the man at the head who was in command, a man who once had the height and bearing to be an imposing figure. Now his hair was grey, his face marked by years, his shoulders no longer braced beneath the armour plating. My father, Edmund of Langley, Duke of York.

'My lord.'

I curtsied dutifully again. He nodded to me, ignoring Dickon, concentrating on dealing with the immediate problem.

'Take the King to his chamber,' he directed his serjeant-at-arms. 'See to his comfort there, but post a permanent guard at door and window. We need no more attempts at escape as at Lichfield.'

I thought that Richard, standing silent and unresponsive in our midst, would not have the wit to escape. The Mayor nodding his approval, we watched as the King, with a light touch to his arm, was led unresisting, uncomplaining, away in the direction of the royal apartments.

My father approached, forehead thick with lines. 'What are you doing here?'

Why would I not be here? What I found difficult to understand was why Richard's Keeper of the Realm was acting in the role of captor, and thus I wasted no words in courteous greeting. Fear was too strong in me.

'The King is a prisoner and suffers humiliation, sir,' I observed. 'Could you do nothing to stop it?'

'It was not possible.' My father, perhaps unaware of my peremptory demand, slapped his gloves against his thigh, raising a cloud of dust which made him cough, his gaze tracking to where Richard had just departed. 'I am merely following orders.' Then he added: 'As will every one of us, if we have any sense.'

'Whose orders? Are you not Keeper of the Realm?'

'For the moment.' He returned his gaze to me and it was uncompromisingly bleak. 'Lancaster plans to ride to St Paul's to pay homage at his father's tomb. From there he will stay at the Bishop of London's palace overnight, before returning here. All will be settled tomorrow. I advise you to keep your opinions to yourself meanwhile. What is loyalty in one breath becomes treason in the next.' Which I decided was a surprisingly apposite warning from my father who was not known for his keenness of wit. I too looked to where the guard had disappeared, taking Richard with him. 'Tomorrow I expect he will be moved to the Tower.'

'And no good will come of that.'

He raised his brows in reply. 'He is still King. That has not yet changed.'

Then he turned away to discourse with the importunate Mayor, before signalling to his entourage to depart.

'Where is my brother Edward?' I asked before he was out of earshot.

My father halted, looked back. 'Aumale is with Lancaster, of course. Where else would he be?' I detected more than a breath of cynicism.

'Making himself indispensable, I expect,' Dickon added sotto voce as the Duke of York was swallowed up into a crowd of loitering soldiery and aldermen. 'And your most noble husband? Where will he be? You did not ask.'

I overlooked the sneer that Dickon had been practising of late. 'I know where he'll be. Following in our brother's footsteps, so close that he treads on his heel. As he always does. They'll both be waiting on the commands of the Duke of Lancaster. If Lancaster is in the ascendant, why would they throw in their lot with Richard?'

'Why would they?' The sneer did not dissipate. 'I doubt you need to worry. Thomas will be polishing his armour to make the best impression in the ceremonial entry, at Lancaster's side.' But then his grin robbed his comment of too much malevolence. 'And what will you do?'

I thought for a moment. Power seemed to hang as insecurely as a bees' nest in a wind-tossed sapling. 'Stay here at Westminster. I'll be here when King Richard's fate is decided, one way or another. You should do the same. It may be vitally important to us.'

Was all not still in the balance? If my father, brother and husband were cleaving to Lancaster's cause until we were certain that Richard's crown was lost, it might be good policy for me to show my loyalty to the man who was still the anointed King. If that was to be cunning within a cunning family, then cunning is what I would be. A York foot in both camps could prove to be advantageous. I made to follow my father towards the rabbit warren of apartments in the Palace of Westminster where the Duke of York's family could always command accommodations. Dickon elected to accompany me.

Recalling the King's sad humiliation amongst this regal display that he had created, I realised for the first time the enormity of what had happened. Halting at the end of the Great Hall, I took a moment to inspect the row of Kings, thirteen fine statues of Reigate stone set in carved niches, each one representing one of our past Kings from Edward the Confessor to Richard himself. Their crowns were gilded and their robes painted red and green, giving it the air of a reredos in some great church, an altarpiece to the glory of God. And before it all, there was set in place the new throne that Richard had had carved, complete with a gilded cushion. I considered whether he would ever again sit on that throne. There had been cries for his execution from some of the aldermen.

'All will be decided on the morrow,' I said aloud.

It seemed to me that the only hope for Richard was if some high-born family with military strength was willing to lead a resistance against Lancaster. Who better than our own? We could surely command support. But was it too late? How firm were Lancaster's hands on the reins of power?

I walked, to halt before the finely executed statue of Richard himself.

'Where is our loyalty?' I asked Dickon who had come to hover beside me, not really expecting a reply.

'Where do you think? You saw Richard. All was lost for him. I'll stand with Edward and Thomas. I expect you will too.'

'Are we so fickle?'

I must discover how far my family, and the Holland lords, had committed themselves to Henry of Lancaster, and how much Lancaster was prepared to forget our past allegiances. If he was unforgiving, our position at Court would be untenable, our humiliation as great as that of the King, which led my thoughts into a different path, an unpleasant one edged with thistles. If our future lay with Lancaster then we must bow and scrape. How I despised such a plan, even as I accepted that sometimes the despicable must be adopted for the future good and because, indeed, I was given little choice in the directing of my fate. I grimaced lightly. Much as in my choice of husband, where I had been given no choice at all and found him more than despicable.

I remembered Friar John, wondering where he was now. The warnings of his golden dice had proved to be more than accurate. We should have taken heed. But what could we have done?

'If you're going to upbraid your lord and husband for abandoning Richard, I might just come along,' Dickon, still shadowing me, suggested in a spirit of devilry.

'No, you won't. I'll see Thomas alone.'

It was early evening before the brisk tread, easily recognisable after so many years of sharing the same less than amicable space, announced the arrival of my husband. The latch on my chamber door was raised and he entered.

'Thomas,' I said, with a smile that could be interpreted, by the uninformed, as a welcome. 'I expected you a good four hours ago.'

'Constance, love of my life. They said you were here. I knew I would receive a wifely tribute to my survival.'

'You receive the words due to you, my lord.' The smile remained pinned to my lips. 'They said that you had returned in Lancaster's train.'

'Are you going to take issue with that?'

'Should I?'

My hours of solitude had given me no respite and my temper was warm. Thomas, only now discovering the time to visit me, had seen a need, despite the critical events afoot, to change his well-travelled garments for a figured silk-damask tunic and velvet cap. Insurrection might threaten the realm but Thomas must dress to proclaim his rank. As he closed the door behind him and leaned his compact figure against it, his chin was tilted in defiance.

I chose not to rise from my chair where I knew the light from the high window would enhance my beauty in this richly appointed room, the perfect setting, as carved gold enhanced the flawless jewel in the brooch at my breast. Moreover I had freed my hair from its confinement. The Earl of Gloucester was fortunate in his bride, both in her looks and in her royal connections. Unfortunately, Thomas would have wed me even if I were the most ill-favoured Plantagenet daughter in England.

'A picture to welcome any man home from the wars.'

'What have you been doing?' I asked, continuing my cold appraisal.

'I had matters to attend to,' he said, walking slowly forward.

'As I see.' I made a languid gesture to the furred garment and the costly shoes before firing the obvious arrow. 'To whom are we bowing the knee today? King Richard or the Duke of Lancaster?'

He was annoyed. He bent, elegantly, to raise my chin with one finger, scanning my features, as I returned the regard. Not an unattractive man with dark hair, flattened into seemly order beneath his cap, and eyes the colour of brown agates, I thought for the first time that it was unfortunate he roused no heat in my blood.

'And good day to you too, Constance.'

'Is it? It is not a good day for Richard.'

Thomas caught my gaze, held it. 'Have you seen him?'

'I have. He was under guard.'

'So you don't need to ask where our allegiance must be.'

I remembered Richard as I had seen him in the Great Hall. Bewildered at his change in circumstances, all his glory dimmed from his dirty shoes to his vacant expression. Yet here was Thomas, very much undimmed as he dropped his gilded gloves and chaperon onto my lap. In a little spirit of spite I allowed them to slide to the floor, ignoring Thomas's silent snarl.

'Have you seen York?' Thomas asked.

'Yes. My father was keeping guard on the man who may or may not still be King. He says he's following Lancaster's orders. I understand my father did not even engage with Lancaster, despite the strength of the army at his command.' I made no attempt to hide my disgust. 'Surely Lancaster could have been stopped when he first landed in England,' I suggested.

'I expect that he could, but he wasn't, and now he's strong enough to order up and pay the piper and we all dance.'

'And you are garbed for dancing, my love. Lancaster cannot fail to be impressed.'

I stood and ran my hand down the length of his embroidered sleeve, but when Thomas moved away, I deliberately softened my mood, knowing from long experience that I would get nothing from him unless I appeared compliant.

'All we can do, then, is wait,' I offered.

'Wait for what? For Lancaster to decide that I and the rest of your family are as culpable as King Richard for robbing him of his inheritance? Is there wine in here?' he demanded.

I fetched the cups and a flagon from the cupboard and poured as he flung himself into the chair I had just vacated.

I chose my words carefully.

'I know so little, Thomas, and my father was too busy with

the Mayor. Put my megrims down to spending too long alone with no certain knowledge.'

Not quite true but he would enjoy informing me of his own experience.

Thomas took the cup of wine, raising a little toast at last with a show of grace. 'I'll tell you what I know, for what it's worth, but it's not pretty. York headed to Gloucester, we thought to join up with Richard when he returned from Ireland, and together they would deal with Lancaster.'

Thomas scowled.

'But that didn't happen,' I prompted.

'It didn't happen. York went to Berkeley Castle where he just sat on his arse. When Lancaster advanced west against Richard, when your father could have stood in his way, York did nothing other than meet him in the church outside the walls of Berkeley Castle.'

'And what was the outcome?' I took a low stool at his feet and sipped.

The damask rippled in a shrug. 'York agreed to let Lancaster proceed against Richard. And by doing that he sealed Richard's fate.'

I watched him, absorbing the underlying anger which in effect matched my own. Beneath the brutal self-seeking that governed his every action was a man of some ability, acting as one of Richard's trusted lieutenants in Ireland. At Court he had been one of Richard's close coterie of friends. Now his past loyalties had put him in danger; his whole future could be in doubt unless he was clever enough to extricate himself from the coming conflict of Lancaster against Richard. From Lancaster's inevitable victory.

My future would be in doubt too.

'So you are saying that all we can do is wait.' I was becoming as repetitive as a well-trained popinjay.

'But we will use the waiting well, and make plans.' Thomas leaned forward. 'Are you going to welcome me home?' His hand closed around my wrist to pull me to my knees, close enough to plant a kiss on my lips, a possessive gesture rather than an affectionate one. 'I could have died in Ireland. Did it cross your devious Yorkist mind that today you might be a widow?'

I was well used to retaliation. 'Yes, it did. But you obviously survived to return to my welcoming arms.'

'Would it have been a blessing if I had fallen into an Irish bog?'

I considered his polished presence. 'There are no signs of battle on you. Did you actually fight?'

'Do you brand me a coward?'

I did not flinch from his regard. No, I would never so condemn him. Lacking courage he was not. Thomas had been given command of the rearguard of Richard's army. And not only was he capable with sword and lance, but he had proved to be equally skilled in negotiation. He had been sent to bring the King of Leinster to terms. It had not been his fault that he had failed, so I understood.

'Would I openly brand the father of my children as coward?' I replied in all fairness. 'Don't judge me. I don't wish your death, Thomas. It would not suit me to be a widow, nor our children to be left fatherless.'

'Your dower would keep you, as a widow, in silk under-tunics.'

'So it would. My dower has kept you in well-bred horse-flesh,' I responded in similar style for the value of my father's gift to my husband had been a prime attraction from the moment our marriage contract was signed. I was a woman of affluence and worth a marriage, with estates and castles in Glamorgan as well as scattered throughout England. I knew my value, as did Thomas.

Yet he was clearly feeling aggrieved. 'If I were dead on a battlefield, you could wed again, a knight of your own choice.'

'My father might have something to say about that. And better the devil you know . . .' I smiled at his grimace, twisted my wrist from his grip and sat back on my heels. 'Tell me: what have you been doing since the Irish campaign came to so abrupt an end? I presume you fought with your usual panache?'

'Of course.' Preening came second nature to him. 'I returned with Richard – although what your brother Aumale was thinking in dripping poisonous advice into Richard's ear . . . Doubtless he'll have some good reason. He always does. And I'll wager it smacks of some outrageous scheming.'

My ears pricked up at my brother's involvement in something nefarious.

'What did Edward do?'

Thomas was not inclined to be informative; his smile was feral. 'Oh, he'll tell you himself, full of self-vindication which no one will believe. As for what *I* did – Richard sent me to rally the men from my estates in Glamorgan. They refused.'

The crease in his handsome brow suggested some unfortunate clash of will, which he had lost.

'How hard did you try?' I asked, giving no quarter since he had been unwise enough to suggest that I might wish him dead.

'Hard enough to know there was no moving them.'

Which did not surprise me. Thomas had no interest in estate management and made no effort to win the goodwill of his people through fair husbandry. I considered the jewels on his hands, the gilded leather of his soft boots. All he did was rake money from the rents for his pleasure. He took with one hand, then took again with the other. His tenants despised him, and if I were in their worn shoes, I would have refused to march north for him. What was the point in abandoning the harvest, with possible death on a battlefield as the only incentive, for a lord who had no thought for their well-being?

Thomas must have seen the derision in my gaze before I could hide it.

'Oh, I tried, whatever your opinion of me might be. I know as well as you where our interests lie and a small force of our tenants rallying to Richard might have made a difference. But then Richard abandoned his army at Carmarthen and fled north, so it would have made no difference at all.'

'And you fled with him.'

'Yes. I did.'

I frowned, taking the empty cup from him, handing him mine which was almost untouched. 'And so?' I enquired.

Thomas's voice was as flat as a boned herring. 'I left Glamorgan to return to fight for Richard but I was taken into custody with him at Conwy. God rot those cold and draughty Welsh castles! There were eight of us. Richard asked for guarantees of our safety from the Earl of Northumberland, who has thrown in his lot and his Percy troops with Lancaster, which to my mind makes Lancaster invincible.'

'So your life was never in danger.' I did not wait for a reply. 'You changed sides. You abandoned Richard and gave your allegiance to Henry of Lancaster.'

At that moment I disliked him more than I had ever done in my life. He had been my husband since I was four years of age. I did not like him then; I liked him far less now.

'I did. I'll not lie to you.' His eyes narrowed in some bitter memory. 'The cause was lost by the time Richard was taken from Conwy to Flint under restraint. The Holland Dukes of Exeter and Surrey had tried to negotiate with Henry, but they had already relinquished their freedom. What value would there be for me – for us – in my remaining at Richard's side to join your Holland cousins under lock and key? If I had, I'd be locked in the Tower with Richard now. Is that what you would have me do?'

I shook my head. In truth that would not have been to our advantage. Nor to Richard's. If there was any hope of his rescue, he needed his friends with freedom to conspire, not comrades sharing his incarceration. Moreover I understood the ambition that drove Thomas. To stand with Richard at the eleventh hour, without an army, without friends, faced with the overwhelming power of the Percy retainers, would have been politically inept and personally destructive. But I suspected that there was little compassion in Thomas's planning for Richard. Thomas would do whatever would best suit his vision of Despenser aggrandisement.

'What do you suggest that we do now?' I asked with the sweetness of autumn honey. 'You know that I dislike sitting on my hands when all is to fight for.'

For the first time in our exchange of hostilities Thomas

laughed, although the edge was plain enough. 'Thank God He never put a sword into your hand and sent you out onto a battlefield!' But the laughter died. 'I don't think we have any choice in the matter. The momentum is against us. Lancaster is proving to be a driving force with an iron will to batter all into submission.'

'But what we don't know, of course, is whether Lancaster will accept your change of heart.'

'No, we do not. And I dislike the possibilities if he decides that we are too much of a threat to his plans, whatever they might be. He executed the rebels who stood against him at Bristol fast enough. So we must keep our heads below the parapet.'

'As long as we have heads to protect.'

His glance was sharp. 'What we have to ask ourselves is – what is Lancaster's intention towards Richard? Does he want him alive or dead?'

I saw the cold judgement in his face, heard it in his voice. Would he actually care, as long as his own neck was safe? Ambition aside, I hoped that I cared.

'Do you actually like Richard?' I asked, without thinking.

'Like him?'

'You have lived in his palaces, eaten the food provided by him, worn the clothes and jewels he has given as gifts, enjoyed the patronage and the title of Duke of Gloucester. You have enjoyed Richard's recognition of your family and its reinstatement after the Despenser treasons of the past. You have been grateful to him. But do you like him?'

'Does it matter? I swore my oath of loyalty to him.'

'That is not at all the same thing.'

He considered, prepared to answer my question after all. 'Like is too innocuous a word. Yes, I am grateful. Without this upheaval I would have remained loyal to him. But I don't trust him, if that's what you mean.' And I thought that for once I could accept Thomas's honesty, for there was no one here for him to impress except myself. 'He is fickle. He can turn against his friends as quickly as he can turn against his enemies. Any man foolish enough to make an enemy of Richard might risk the kiss of an axe against his neck.'

We all knew it well. When Richard was still young and untried as a monarch, giving power and patronage to unsuitable favourites, a group of magnates had taken issue with him. His favourite, de Vere, was beaten on the battlefield and hounded into exile. Richard was forced against his will to promise to take advice from those who knew better. Thus the Lords Appellant had become a force to be reckoned with.

But Richard would not accept this curb rein on him for ever. Three years ago now, he had taken his revenge on those five Lords. His uncle Thomas of Woodstock had been smothered in his bed in Calais. The Earl of Arundel had been executed on Tower Hill, the Earl of Warwick imprisoned. The Earl of Nottingham had been banished for life. And Cousin Henry, then Earl of Hereford, the youngest of the Appellants, had been banished for a treason he had probably not committed. We all recognised that Richard had a vengeful spirit.

'He carries grudges. He is self-absorbed in his own powers. No, I do not like him. I do not trust him.' Thomas finished off the cup of wine. 'Now we have to see what happens with the disposition of the crown, since it has been snatched from

Richard's fair head. We will act accordingly. I will not willingly give up what I have achieved.'

He tightened his hand into my hair, curling his wrist into its thickness, and bestowed another kiss, harder, surer.

'The question is, my lovely, ambitious Constance. Do you stand with me or against me?'

My loyalties to my family were strong, yet I would stand or fall with my married Despenser fate. Indeed, were they not so completely intertwined, as Thomas's hand in my hair, that there was no need to make a choice? York, Holland and Despenser would fight as one to keep their pre-eminence, whoever was King, be it Richard or Henry.

'With you, Thomas. Are you not my devoted husband?'

His kiss deepened. His hands tightened on my shoulders.

'Then show me.'

'Do I not always?'

'No. Of course you do not.' His hands slid to encircle my wrists and he pressed his mouth against the soft skin there, where my pulse beat, slow and unaroused. 'I missed you.'

'Which I do not believe.'

'If only for your sharp tongue.' His eyes softened, warning me of his change of mood. 'But not only that.' He lifted the ivory-backed mirror from the coffer at my side. 'What do you see?' He held it before my face. 'What do you see, my lovely Constance?'

'What should I see?' I asked, determined not to respond to his cold-blooded wooing.

'I'll tell you.' The curve of his lips became sardonic, his chin tilted, as he surveyed me. 'I see a profusion of hair as fair as that of any angel painted in a missal, a face which is a perfection of shape and fine bones. Eyes lustrous enough to entrap any heedless man. A straight nose, lips indented at this moment with displeasure, an unhandsome crease between elegant brows.' Thomas stroked the brows with the tip of one finger. 'Is that sufficient to express my heart-felt admiration?'

'How unexpectedly chivalrous,' I observed as the crease became deeper and thus even less handsome.

'Smile, Constance.'

Obedient to his command, I smiled, knowing that my face would be lit as if with an inner light, even though it was a mockery.

'If your unholy mother gave you nothing beyond a love of duplicity, at least you inherited the handsomeness of your Castilian forbears. Why should I not miss you? A lovely woman at his side is a gift of value to a man of ambition.'

The mirror was cast aside regardless of its fragility. His chaperon and gloves were abandoned where I had left them on the floor, the damask garment shrugged off to join them, while I was efficiently dutiful if not enthusiastic as he led me into the inner chamber where the great bed with its Despenser hangings, all sumptuous gold fretwork on a red field, dominated the space. I knew the words to say, the caresses to give. I knew what duty meant within a loveless marriage. We had a son and a daughter, healthy evidence of my wifely attention. I gave him ease and obedience. If he wanted ecstasy he could employ one of the Court whores and pay her well in coin and compliments. He paid me in neither and awoke no desire in me. Nor did I expect it. I would live out my life with no experience of love, be it the soft caring gestures within a family or the blazing passion of lust. Life, I accepted, would be far more equable without. My mother had felt the hot breath of such a lust, with raw repercussions when she took a lover. I would never follow in her scandalous footprints. Political aspiration for my family would serve me well enough.

Thomas fell asleep at my side with no more than a grunt of exhaustion while I lay awake and considered the dangers in which we found ourselves. For what was treason? Treason depended on whose brow bore the crown. At the moment it seemed that the crown of England lay in the gutter.

And then as I fell into sleep, I wondered what was the advice that Edward, in Ireland, had given Richard which had awakened Thomas's suspicions. I sighed a little. Whatever it was that Edward had set his hand to must wait.

From where had my enmity to my husband stemmed? It had always been there. I had never found anything to like in Thomas, Lord Despenser, as he had been titled since the day I had wed him at the age of four years. There were some elements of that event that clung to my mind, to make a lasting impression on the woman I was to become. I was told what to say during the ceremony and spoke the words, although I did not understand the questions asked of me by the priest. The boy of six years at my side, gloomy-faced, without a glance in my direction, said the same. We were word perfect, and there was much indulgent laughter when our hands were joined and the boy was instructed to kiss my cheek, which he did, a peck worthy of a cock pheasant.

I was his wife, I was given to understand. I looked at him with some interest, for he was a handsome boy. He looked at me, fleetingly, as if he would rather I had been the gift of a new hawk or hound. I don't think that he looked at me again, except when I asked him:

'Where is your father? Is he not here?'

'My father is dead,' he said.

'I am sorry.'

'I don't need your sorrow.' His lips twisted. 'I don't like you. I am here because my mother commands that I must wed you.'

The only words we exchanged on that auspicious occasion. I would never forget his utter lack of interest in me, not that I would ever allow him, then when I was a child, or in later years when it mattered more to me, to see how much his indifference had wounded both my pride and my desire to be liked by this boy to whom I was tied by oaths and religious ceremony. Nor could I forget the overheard heat of ill temper between my father and mother as we sat at the culmination of the feast.

'Could we not have done better than this?' my mother asked under cover of a ceremonial blast of a trumpet as King Richard arrived late, but still to grace us with his presence.

'The lad is a ward of the King. How much better do you want?' My father was trenchant.

'Despenser! His family is mired in past scandals. There are still treason judgements against his ancestors for corruption and misplaced ambitions. Are we not worth a more advantageous alliance?'

My mother's voice was still heavily accented from her Castilian birth, but her words were clear to those who eavesdropped, as I did while I washed my hands in a silver bowl.

'*Your* mother was a whore,' my father said. 'Before your father made her respectable and married her. How much scandal do you lay claim to, Isabella?'

It meant little beyond the shock of his use of that word in polite company.

'But a royal whore, and to your advantage. You only wed me because of my royal Castilian blood.'

There was no love lost between them.

'I wed you, Isabella, because my father the King insisted on it and for no other reason,' was the brusque reply. 'Both Castilian heiresses married to two of his sons. As my wife, no one can use you to make a claim against your sister Constanza, who as the elder has the claim to the Castilian throne. If anyone will be King of Castile it will be my brother John of Lancaster who had the privilege of wedding her. I will not challenge him.'

This was not new to me, that my uncle John of Lancaster hoped to lay hands on the Kingdom of Castile for himself in his wife Constanza's name, although then, in my childhood, it was beyond my true understanding. My mother and her sister were the heiresses of King Pedro of Castile, recently stabbed to death by his half-brother Enrique of Trastámara. Through their blood ran the claim to the kingdom even if their mother Maria de Padilla had been Pedro's mistress, her secret marriage to Pedro repudiated in favour of a more well-connected legitimate bride. Thus the legitimacy of the two girls was open to dispute, but my mother was a woman of some importance, particularly in her own mind.

'You have water in your veins,' she announced to anyone who wished to hear. 'I would have liked you better if you had refused me.'

They detested each other.

My mother caught me, now patting my fingers dry on a length of fair linen, at the same time watching and listening.

'Go and sit with your husband.'

Thomas was engaged in fighting imaginary battles or tilting at famous opponents, in company with some of my cousins. He had not turned his head in my direction for the whole of that interminable feast.

'He has no interest in me, madam,' I said.

She leaned and whispered, lips thin: 'You will do well to make him have an interest in you, child.'

'Why, madam?'

'Don't question everything, Constance.' She was always impatient. 'You'll learn soon enough. Just do it.'

But how to achieve the impossible? Thomas Despenser regarded me as a possession to stamp respectability on his name.

'What does mired in scandal mean?' I asked my brother Edward, for with two more years than I, he would surely know.

He wrinkled his nose. 'Nothing good, I'd say.'

So I asked my nurse.

'Nothing you will ever be accused of, Constance. You will be the perfect daughter. The most acclaimed wife. Look how pretty you are. And how pretty your young husband is.'

'Will I see him again?'

'When you are a young woman grown.'

'When will that be?'

'When you have reached your fourteenth year.'

It seemed an age away. 'I don't think he will miss me.'

'No, I don't think he will.'

'It doesn't matter, does it?'

'No. You are royal, my child. And he is not.'

'Will he like me?'

'It matters not whether he does or does not.'

It was an unsettling day after which I returned to my life of prayer and learning and skills appropriate to a daughter of Edmund, Earl of Cambridge, fourth son of the old King Edward the Third and soon to become Duke of York. My parents returned to their own interests which, with deliberate intent, did not often bring them into each other's company, nor into that of their children. We had no memory of maternal love during our childhood years. If we had, it might be that we would have become a less rancorous brood.

As for Thomas Despenser, Lord Despenser, I had wanted more than the hostility that sparked between my father and mother, whether he was worthy of me or not. It was not to be. I might have loved him. I might have experienced at least an affection for him, but Thomas admired my dowry and my Plantagenet blood far more than he admired me, and for the most part ignored me except for the need to produce an heir. In the end, it did not matter. We were man and wife and, as many another ill-matched pair, we would live out our days together.

Chapter Three

Early September 1399: Tower of London

'Where is Mathes?' King Richard demanded as soon as I set foot within the confines of his room. 'What have you done with Mathes?'

'Who?' For a moment I was nonplussed. Of all the opening commands or pleas I might have expected from Richard, this was not one of them.

'Mathes. My greyhound. I wish him to be here with me. Where is he?'

'I don't know, my lord.'

It seemed to me that there was far more serious content for this discussion between us than the whereabouts of Richard's favourite greyhound.

'Bring him to me. I command it.'

But how could I?

I had awoken that morning, Thomas long gone on his own affairs, with one clear thought leaping fully fledged into my mind. I must go to Richard. Waiting for Henry of Lancaster to show us the length and breadth of his ultimate goal toward

Richard and the kingdom was all very well, but I could not rest. The one memory I could not shake free from my mind was that of Richard standing in the Great Hall, alone, isolated, even though he was surrounded by my father's retainers. It had touched my heart with a deep compassion of which I had thought myself incapable. I could not abandon my cousin.

Richard commanded our duty and our loyalty. He was our King, anointed with holy oil, crowned and invested with the sacred regalia of kingship. Casting off such a loyalty was not a simple matter. Nor, for me, was it only a matter of loyalty to my King. Thomas would not understand, but Richard was my cousin. I had known him from birth, enjoyed his hospitality and his patronage, but also his kindness, which had not been merely an extension of his power. Were we not close by blood?

I recalled him drawing me into the intimate circle around his first much-loved wife Anne. I had clear memory of his dancing with me when my steps were still unsure. A collector of fine jewels, he had given me the heraldic brooch of a white hart, bound with gold and rubies, that I pinned to my bodice every morning.

With no need to inform anyone of my movements, for the Countess of Gloucester was beyond criticism, I arranged to travel by river from Westminster to the Tower in my father's barge. Enjoying the luxury of the scarlet-cushioned seats with their gold-embroidered lions, I made good time for the tide had just turned, the strengthening current aiding the oarsmen. Once there, entering by the Watergate, I acknowledged, as I often did, that the bulk of the Conqueror's White Tower would intimidate any visitor, its shadow causing me to shiver despite the warmth of the autumn sun reflecting from the stonework.

There was an immediate obstacle to my plan, all six feet of him standing in my path before I had barely stepped beyond the wharf. Will Plimpton, knight, my father's Captain of the Guard. He had known me since I was a child and still had the habit of addressing me as he had when I held no status other than my father's daughter.

'If you have come to see the King, then you can't. He's kept under strict confinement, Mistress Constance.'

He had read my intent well enough.

'I am not here to manage his flight to safety, Will. I am here as a friend and a cousin, to give comfort.'

'There's an unconscionable number of cousins in this affair. And be that as it may, mistress, he is allowed no visitors unless sanctioned by the Duke of Lancaster himself. Those are my orders.'

He was an old ally of mine. 'Do you not serve my father?' I asked with terrible innocence, smoothing my knuckles over the Yorkist livery that covered his chest with fleurs-de-lys and Plantagenet lions.

'Not when Lancaster is occupying the royal apartments.'

I changed direction. 'I am a mere woman, Will. I am no threat. I will not stay long and none need know that you have given your permission. Certainly not my father or Lancaster. I promise I will not speak of it. Besides, my father does not object to my being here, so why should my cousin of Lancaster? Indeed, I believe my father discussed my visit with Lancaster on his arrival in London.'

My father had done no such thing; he had no idea of what I was about, and would have forbidden it out of hand if he had been aware, but what was not known could not be grieved over.

The serjeant grunted, patting my arm with appreciation, his eye gleaming at my attempt at subterfuge. 'I don't like it, my lady. And I know your ability to twist the truth to your liking.'

Which made me smile. 'You will be rewarded in heaven for your compassion to the man who is still your King.' My own words struck home, a sharp little pain against my heart. 'We must not forget that. The crown still belongs to him. How can it be removed, except by God?' At that moment I meant every word I said.

'As you say. Come then, Mistress Constance. But don't blame me . . .'

There was a guard outside the door. When the captain opened it with a key at his belt, I saw that a guard also stood within the room, beside the window, as if my royal cousin would consider an escape by that means, unlikely as it might seem. Richard was not given to feats of strength or endurance or climbing through windows.

'May we be alone?' I asked. 'I would speak of family affairs to my cousin.'

On a gruff sigh, the captain beckoned the man to wait outside the door.

'Not too long, mistress.'

And there was Richard standing in the middle of the room. Yesterday he had been bewildered. Today he all but crackled with anger.

He had been allowed to change his garments, so that he looked more like the man I knew in a deep red full-length tunic embellished with fur and gold stitching at neck and cuff. His hair cleansed and curling against his neck, shining in a ray of sun that had crept in through one of the high windows,

Richard was restored to some element of kingliness, except for the shocking hollowness of his cheeks. On the coffer behind him was a platter of bread and meat and a dish of fruits, all untouched. The flagon of wine was still covered with a white cloth. I thought again that this was not the first meal that he had refused.

'I want my dear companion, my greyhound. Where is Mathes?'

'I don't know.'

Richard's lips set in a line of bitter self-pity. 'He went to fawn over Lancaster. Even my dog loves Lancaster more than he loves me. Will you return him to me? I would like him here.' But before I could speak again, Richard's temper flared across the room. 'Where is my authority? Why are my orders not carried out?' And then, as he focused on me perhaps for the first time: 'Constance. Are you come to release me?'

'Of course I am not. How would I have that power?' I replied to my cousin rather than my King. 'There is a lock on the door, and you may have noticed that I do not have the key.'

Richard scowled. 'They have no right to keep me here. By what right do my subjects keep me in confinement in my own realm?'

While Richard flung away from me to hammer his fist on the stonework of the window surround, I considered an answer to his question. What gave a man, a subject, the right to keep a King imprisoned? In this case the power of the sword. The support of the great magnates of the realm. Henry had the power to do as he pleased.

'Why are you here?' Richard was facing me again, eyes wild with displeasure. 'Are you here to argue Cousin Henry's cause? Do you like him more than you like me?'

It was the accusation of a child. 'No, I am not. I am here to give you company. Are you well treated? You have food, I see.' The muscles in his face twitched under the strain, but he had been well accommodated in the King's Great Chamber in St Thomas's Tower. No sparsely furnished dungeon here, but a room with every comfort. The walls, smoothly plastered, were painted with leaves and flowers, candle-sconces aplenty offered light in the darkest corners, and, on a carved and polished coffer, books had been left to help him pass the interminable hours. They were still unopened.

'Will you take a cup of wine, my lord?' I asked.

But he waved it away. 'I will not. I will not be won over by food and fine cloth.' He tugged at the furred collar. 'I demand my freedom.' His eyes narrowed on my face as he beckoned imperiously: 'Come and talk with me.'

He sank onto a stool and pointed at one beside him. I sat in obedience.

'I am afraid,' he said.

'There is no need. Our cousin will treat you fairly.'

'Is it fair to take what is not his, what is mine and beyond his taking?' He leaned close to speak in almost a whisper. 'He will make me abdicate,' Richard fretted. 'How can I? How can a King abandon his sacred anointing at his coronation, in the sight of God and his subjects? I cannot renounce it.'

As he suddenly gripped my hand, crushing my fingers, I felt the weight of sadness that bore him down.

'They will say that I must give my power into hands stronger than mine, Constance.' He looked at me, a world of suspicion in his gaze. 'Your royal father, my uncle of York, is my designated heir. Not Henry of Lancaster. Will your father take the throne from me? Is that why you are here? To plead his cause so I will hand it over, weak as a kitten? Your family always had ambition above its position.'

So we had become the accused also. How easy it was to slide into the pool of Richard's enmity.

'I am not here to persuade you to give up your crown, Richard. My father does not seek the crown.'

But Richard was on his feet again, driven by unknown terrors, his fingers tugging his hair into disarray before covering his face.

'I trust no one. My people do not love me, I am told. They cry out for my blood, my head. I must believe it. I heard them.' And then, voice still muffled: 'What do I do if I am not King?'

I allowed myself to reply cautiously to his irrationality. 'What do you wish to do?'

He thought about it, hands falling away so that his reply came clearly. 'If I were not King? I would live in a place of my choosing. With friends and servants and enough resources to maintain myself in an honourable state.'

Rising, I gathered his hands, more gently than he had gripped mine. 'You must not give up hope, Richard.'

His answering smile was wan. 'Will you have your family speak for me? We were always friends. Aumale and Gloucester, Exeter and Surrey. And my uncle of York.' He had forgotten that they had done nothing to prevent his falling into Lancaster's hands.

The minutes were passing. 'Do you need anything? I cannot stay long.'

'Better you here than the guard who watches my every step.' The anger had gone, replaced by desolation. 'Will you give my dear wife Isabelle this from me?' He made to take a ring from his hand, as if he expected to see the great ruby gleaming in the sunlight, only to find his hands naked of jewels. 'Where is my ring? They have taken it from me.' It was almost a sob. 'I can do nothing. They have taken all my treasure. And Mathes.'

I knew that they had confiscated all of Richard's wealth, all the forty thousand pounds of it hidden away in Holt Castle so that he was stripped down to a man of absolute poverty. Again there were tears in his eyes, which coated my compassion with irritation, not for the first time. It was important now for me to give counsel.

'You must listen to me, Richard.' And when he nodded, seeking any consolation, still holding fast to my hands: 'You must be strong. Do not give in to Lancaster. Offer to negotiate with him, but do not agree to relinquish your crown without promises for your safety and your future.'

'Will he listen?'

I thought not, but I must give this man hope. 'You have friends. Friends who will not desert you. I am your friend.'

'What can you do? I am deserted. I think he will have my head. Henry was always my rival.'

'He will not.' How difficult it was to implant into this man a backbone that would carry him through the next days and weeks. 'Listen to me, Richard. Be strong. Tell Lancaster that you will discuss terms. He is a fair man. He does not desire your blood.'

'If I offer to reinstate his land and inheritance, will he allow me to go free?'

'Yes, that might do it.'

Oh, Richard. Lancaster wanted far more than his inheritance.

By taking up arms against the King, Henry had proved that he desired more than the reinstatement of his title of Duke of Lancaster and the Lancaster acres. I could see no glory for Richard, but he should be allowed to keep his dignity.

'Don't forget. The family of York will not abandon you. Do not sign any document that robs you of your royal authority. You must not abdicate unless Lancaster listens to your conditions.'

'But what are my conditions?'

I tried not to sigh.

'Your freedom is the main one. Demand that you be set free.' Then I delivered the most vital piece of advice, for all of us. 'Demand a guarantee of a pardon for all your counsellors, so that Lancaster cannot punish them for any perceived fault in your reign. You must think of the men who supported you, advised you. They must not be threatened by Lancaster. Do you understand me?'

'Yes, yes, I can do that.'

'Promise me that you won't forget. Otherwise Henry will have his revenge on all of us.'

'I promise. You will not suffer for your friendship to your King.'

He was smiling at me, although a watery affair as I saluted him on his cheeks and walked to knock on the door to summon the guard to release me. I had done all I could, for Richard and for my family's uncertain future, but Richard's utter weakness appalled me.

'How can I live, if I am not King?'

His final despairing words as I left him standing at the window, looking out on the realm that was indeed no longer his, remained with me as I returned to the barge, the oarsmen who would need to flex their muscles against the drag of the Thames, aiding their wait with leather jugs of ale. My family and the Hollands owed so much to Richard, our present Dukedoms of Aumale and Surrey and Exeter a precious gift after our support in his campaign to punish the Lords Appellant. We could not abandon the giver of such costly patronage. We had been the jewels in Richard's crown, but it was clear to me that Henry might prise those jewels out and replace them with new. And then where would we be? I had no confidence in Richard's promise to win Henry's compliance, that we would be free from any revenge if Henry decided to take it.

Thomas said we should wait.

It seemed to me too dangerous to wait.

'You've company, mistress.' The captain broke into my thoughts, nodding towards the gilded prow where a familiar figure sprawled on the cushions, regaling the rowers with some tale that had them laughing.

'How did you get here?' I asked as I stepped aboard and the oarsmen took their positions.

Dickon pointed at a wherry that was heading towards the opposite bank. He came to sit beside me.

'What does the King say?'

I shrugged. 'He's concerned about his ruby ring and his hound.' I caught the slide of my brother's eye. 'What is it?'

'A man might wonder whether you came here for Richard's sake or for ours.'

How true. I had not been completely altruistic, but I would not deny my loyalty to Richard. Equally I would not reveal to my brother the content of my advice to him. 'A man should keep his inquisitive nose out of my affairs,' I said, and turned my face towards Westminster, where all was to play for.

A little time after dawn on the following day I met with my family in my father's private chamber at Westminster, summoned by him with unaccustomed stringency. Even the timing was unusual. My father, ageing rapidly week by week, rarely broke his fast before the day was well advanced. There were six of us all told. It had, I decided, although I would never have been allowed to attend such a meeting, the semblance of a council of war. The room might be familiar with its solid stonework and hunting tapestries, but the atmosphere was as sharp as that first sip of newly brewed ale.

'You are late,' my father observed as I entered.

I curtsied, watching my tongue. I suspected that this would be a long and acrimonious exchange of views.

Here we were, my father lowering himself awkwardly to a cushioned chair. His lips were pressed hard against the pain that these days never left him. The stiffness in his back was now permanent, exacerbated by any attempt to ride or walk far. It made his temper chancy. Joan gave him a cup of ale and took a stool at his side.

And then my brothers. First in importance as my father's heir, my brother Edward, indolently stretched on a window seat, a hawk on his fist, a smoothly brindled greyhound at his feet. Dickon lounged against the ribbed stonework near the door as if to escape at the first opportunity, fidgeting with a knife he had taken from his belt. Thomas, my husband, seated on the only cushioned stool, glowered with some silent discontent.

And I? Why was I tolerated in this convening of male minds? Because in this household we talked politics and power. We always had, from dawn to dusk, assessing friend and enemy, alliances and allegiances. Such were the subjects of most importance to us. I stood behind my husband, my hand lightly resting on his shoulder, seemly as any wife. Joan was present because everyone had forgotten about her. She had a gift for drawing no one's eye. My mother, the Castilian princess who had caught everyone's eye, had been dead for seven years. My father's second wife, Joan Holland, was young at nineteen years to my father's fifty-eight. I watched them together as she stood to stuff another goose-feather cushion behind him, remarking not for the first time that the famous beauty of her grandmother, Joan of Kent, had left only the faintest imprint on her. She was a sparrow here, amidst a flock of goldfinches, yet however unmemorable her brown hair and pale, plain features might be, my father smiled his thanks. He treated her like a daughter, with far more affection than he had ever shown to me. Sometimes I found it difficult to tolerate Joan's presence, much less her meek subservience.

Thus the house of York, the noble family of the fourth son of King Edward the Third. Some would say a family to be reckoned with given our rank and royal blood; others would deem us a family to be wary of, a family driven to snatch at wealth and power. Beneath the unity of our name seethed rank ambition and sour suspicion, in no manner alleviated since the day that our gifts had caught the wayward eye of King Richard, when our present and our future had gleamed with gold. Now that golden gleam hung in abeyance. After my meeting with Richard, I would not wager a silver penny on any golden future.

Nor, it seemed, could my husband.

'Why could you not keep Richard safe and at liberty?' Thomas demanded, unconsciously echoing my own thoughts, voicing the concern that had clearly eaten away at him since Lancaster had taken his royal prize. 'Was it beyond your powers?' He turned his eye on my father. 'You were Keeper of the Kingdom with an army at your command. Surely it was not beyond the wit of man to defeat a traitor who landed in the north with only a handful of misguided supporters? It wasn't that you did not know Lancaster was coming.'

Thomas stood, shaking off my hand, as if he could bear to sit no longer.

My father replied promptly. 'I knew he was coming, but I did not know where he would land. How can we gauge the tides and the winds? By the time we met, it was my judgement that Lancaster's following was too powerful to be stopped.' His gaze narrowed against the attack, his response blisteringly formal. 'You had your own role in our failure, Despenser. A man who could not get his own tenants to arm and march to the succour of their King is in no position to denigrate others. You are not innocent in this debacle.'

The room, from carved roof beams to painted tiles, churned with rancour. I could do nothing to halt the accusation and counter-accusation, and indeed knew better than to try. Joan withdrew circumspectly to the far end of the chamber, as far from the imminent conflagration as possible, signalling her distance by picking up a length of girdle that she proceeded to stitch.

'At least I stayed with him to the end.' Refusing to be silenced, Thomas's eye swept on to land on Edward. 'Unlike some of us here. And it wasn't me who advised Richard to remain in Ireland, when we all knew Lancaster was already in England. Why in God's name did you do that?'

Edward merely smiled, eyes as hooded as the hawk's whose neck he scratched, causing it to bob its head in pleasure. 'No one wanted all-out war, and one we would have lost.'

My father was reining hard on his temper. 'Sit down, Thomas. You knew the situation as well as I. Lancaster was stronger. The Earls of Northumberland and Westmorland were riding with him and more than half the northern magnates, not to mention the Cheshire archers. If we had taken it to a battlefield we would have been beaten out of sight and Richard would be in a worse position than he is now.'

Thomas sat, hands planted on his knees, but was no more amenable to reason. 'Is that possible? He's a prisoner under Lancaster's brutal justice. If you had met with Lancaster near Ravenspur, before he joined up with Northumberland, you could have swept him back out to sea. But no, you marched west and—'

I replaced my hand on Thomas's shoulder and pressed down hard. No point in inflicting wounds here that could never be healed. The past could not be changed, even though every accusation he made against my father was undoubtedly true.

My father continued to explain his lack of effective action. 'I marched west to meet up with Richard's army and present a united front. That was the plan.'

Thomas had no intention of being silenced, since by now we were all aware of the flush of guilt along my father's cheekbones. 'Which didn't happen.' Thomas twitched free of my hand once more, a rough gesture. 'By the time Richard landed on the Welsh coast,' – once more he glared at Edward – 'you were comfortably holed up in Berkeley Castle. You had an army of three thousand men. Surely you could have made a good resistance.'

My father's face was still flushed, but his reply held the quality of ice.

'I made a truce with Lancaster at Berkeley because I believed that his claim for justice had much weight. He is my brother's much-loved son, and as such he should be answered. Besides, my army was breaking up. My best troops were those of John Beaufort. When Beaufort made his peace with his half-brother of Lancaster, he took his troops with him. I would not have expected otherwise.'

Thomas continued to accuse, ignoring the increased pressure of my hand as his tone became increasingly insolent. 'God's Blood! So you had sympathy with Lancaster's cause?'

'I did,' my father acknowledged. 'Richard treated him shamefully.'

'I don't deny it, but Richard was our road to power.' Thomas's reply lacked pity for either Richard or Henry of Lancaster. 'Now the goose that laid the golden eggs for all of us is shut up in the Tower, impotent and likely to stay there. I don't expect Lancaster to be liberal in casting largesse in our direction. We were all too close to Richard for Lancaster to trust us.'

Edward had been as silent as I throughout Thomas's torrent of invective, but I needed an explanation for the insinuation that he could not ignore if he was guiltless.

'Why did you advise Richard to delay his return from Ireland?' I dropped the question into a pause in the hostilities. 'It smacks of rank stupidity, but when were you ever so careless of battle tactics? You could be accused of collusion with Lancaster.'

Edward, totally unmoved by any of the arrows fired in his direction, stood to place the hawk on the stand against the wall. The hound followed him, sticking close to his heels when he returned to take up a stance in the centre of the group. On my left Dickon slid to sit on the floor, arms around his knees, forehead resting there as if he might sleep through sheer boredom.

'I am neither stupid nor careless,' said Edward. 'It all depends whose poisonous tongue you prefer to believe, dear sister.'

I remembered Richard's utter weakness. Was Edward truly to blame?

'Lance the venom, Edward,' I responded. 'We'll all be interested in your explanation.'

'By God, we will.' Thomas leaped once more to take up the attack. 'All was ready in Ireland. We knew Lancaster had returned. The ships were loaded, even down to the horses being on board with all the trouble that takes. And then what? Then you whispered in Richard's ear and all was unloaded again. We sat and waited in Waterford for another two weeks – two weeks! – by which time Lancaster was well and truly embedded in the country. Whether you were traitor or just incompetent, it was ill-managed, Aumale.'

My father grunted his displeasure, but Edward merely returned to his seat, stretching himself out again in unruffled good humour.

'There is no mystery. It was neither incompetence nor treachery, but supremely managed. Since we were short of shipping to embark as a major force, I considered it impossible to transport the whole army home again. Where was the incompetence in that? What *was* possible was an advance guard to land in Wales and head north to take Chester for the King. That is what was arranged, so no treachery there. The fact that Salisbury, who took the command, failed to fulfil his orders, and most of his force either joined Lancaster, or simply went home, was no fault of mine.'

'But why did we not fight for Richard? Why did we go over to Lancaster so fast?' Thomas refused to retreat, his voice sharpening in petulance, his hands closing into fists against his thighs.

Edward shrugged. 'The Welsh gentry said they believed that Richard was dead, so it would be good sense for them to join Lancaster. Your troops in Gloucester would not heed the call to arms.'

Thomas, rigid with fury, returned Edward's regard. 'I've never seen any man change sides as fast as you. It was a miracle of deceit. When I had last seen you in Ireland you had been a King's man. When our paths crossed again at Flint Castle you were part of the delegation dispatched by Lancaster to discuss Richard's future.' The sneer hung in the room like a plague miasma. 'The Lancaster livery was most becoming on you.'

'It surprises me that you would wish to remind us of what happened at Flint.' Edward accepted the contempt and returned it in full measure. 'When you, Despenser, said not one word to the King. You kept as great a distance from him as you could, other than standing in the bailey. You threw Richard to the Lancaster wolves just as effectively as I.'

Thomas shifted uneasily. Edward continued with perfect poise.

'Had we not all seen which way the royal banners were flying in the wind by then? When Bristol fell to Lancaster, he made it more than clear what would happen to those who stood by Richard. Scrope, Bussy and Green, royal counsellors all, lost their heads fast enough. I had no intention of my head joining theirs on some distant gateway. My new livery was a light cost to pay to escape beheading. But at least I stayed with Richard until there was no more hope. You couldn't get out from under his shadow fast enough.'

'Enough!' My father raised his hand, but Thomas's ire was in full flow.

'You have all the perfect explanations, like honey on your tongue.' Thomas showed his teeth in the leer of a wolf before attack. 'We can't wait to hear. How did you explain to Lancaster, when you knelt before him with promises of fealty, that you had been given a large part of his Lancaster inheritance, which Richard had confiscated and portioned out to those he loved best? Have you actually told him? He might not be so keen to have you as an ally if he knows you've been living richly off his land.'

'Of course I've told him. I said that I would happily restore all his inheritance to him. I said that I had drawn no money from it.'

Edward's response was fast and smooth, without decoration, punctuated by a yawn as if it were all of no importance. I could not resist the accusation – if only to ruffle his magnificent feathers.

'Only because you did not have the time to get your hands on it,' I said.

'Whereas you, dear sister, would have made all speed to spend a good portion of it, would you not? All that wealth at your fingertips? How could you have resisted?'

He was not ruffled at all. I waved away the presumption of my extravagance as I looked at my father. Someone must make an attempt to untangle all these threads that were being woven into a tapestry of mutual hatred. 'Why are we here, sir? We have heard much discussion of loyalty and treachery, but what is our position now?'

'We are here, as must be obvious to you all, to decide what we will do next.'

'Do we have a choice?' Edward asked but needing no answer since he supplied it himself. 'We do what we must. We become unimpeachable supporters of the new order of things.'

A silence filled the room, broken only by the hound scratching for fleas. Joan remained at her chosen distance, silently stitching as if none of this was her concern, stabbing the linen with her needle. A grey kitten had joined her from some previously hidden refuge to entangle her embroidery silks. Her trivial occupations continued to irritate me beyond measure.

'You say that we give our allegiance to our cousin Henry,' I said.

'Yes. Is it not obvious?'

'Will he accept it?' I was unsure. 'He might consider our loyalty suspect.'

'It will all hang in the balance. But I fear Richard's days are numbered.' My father's face set in doleful lines. 'There have already been cries for his execution.'

'Lancaster will not scatter patronage in our direction with the same easy hand,' Thomas repeated. 'With four sons and two daughters of his own, and a drain on his finances if the kingdom is uneasy, his purse will be empty soon enough. I doubt he'll look to us for friendship or counsel. He's more likely to banish us to our estates, as soon as he gets his lands back from you, Aumale.'

'I think you are wrong. He needs all the friends he can get.' Edward stirred himself so that the hound took its chin off his foot and sat up. His advice was the epitome of fair reason. 'I for one see nothing to be gained by opposing him and much to be lost. And yes, I will willingly restore the Lancaster estates to him. And you, Despenser, will be a fool if you do not meet him at least halfway. Richard can give us nothing, but Henry can and must be persuaded that we have his best interests at heart. Who will be closer to him than us? No one. We are his blood and his family. You, my lord,' – he bowed his head to my father – 'are the only royal uncle he has left, the only connection with his royal forebears. He might, if encouraged, see you in the role of his own father. Of course he will not turn us away. He needs to win us to his side, and we must be willing to be won.'

During this masterful speech, I became aware of the dog, its eyes fixed in canine adoration on Edward's face.

'I recognise that animal,' I said.

'So you should. It's Richard's.' Edward laughed. 'Or was Richard's. Mathes.' He snapped his fingers and the hound subsided once more against his feet. 'It transferred its allegiance to Lancaster. Clever animal, I'd say.'

I remembered Richard, his pining for this creature that had been quick to betray him. Were we not following in its footprints?

'Will Lancaster take the crown?' I asked Edward, already knowing the answer.

'Of course. I would, in his shoes.'

'I don't like the thought of leaving Richard to Lancaster's tender mercy,' Thomas stated.

'What would you do?' For the first time Edward's patience seemed worn. 'Launch an attack, snatch him up out of the Tower, and get him to France?'

'I could think of worse.'

'What do we have with which to launch such an attack? No one would be willing to commit to such a hopeless scheme, and your retainers won't do it.'

Thomas flushed. 'Better to try than to turn traitor!'

Without further comment, Thomas marched from the room, the door thudding behind him. I watched him leave. Wifely duty might suggest that I accompany him but I was not inclined, choosing to stay with my family by blood despite some antagonism, much hostility and all fair planning for the future now in pieces.

'Is it impossible to rescue Richard?' I asked, again with that sense of guilt that we had abandoned him in his hour of need.

'From the Tower? Under guard?' replied Edward. 'You know better than that.'

'He misses the hound.'

Immediately I had spoken I realised that it would drop me into a morass of explanation that I could well do without. Not for the first time I wished that I had been born another Yorkist son, my participation accepted, weight given to my words, at the centre of events rather than on the edge of it all like Joan, unless I fought to make my voice heard.

'And how would you know that?' Edward asked.

I could have lied but I was not in the habit of dissimulation. Instead I raised my chin in a challenge. 'I have been to see him. I felt sorry for him.'

'Sorry you may be, but stay out of this, Constance.' My father's response was unequivocal. 'It is no business of yours. If you wish to be useful, go and talk some sense into your husband.'

'How do you know that I do not agree with him? We seem to have abandoned Richard as fast as that hawk would relinquish a mouse for better prey. At least Thomas sees that we owe him some fidelity.'

'You are a daughter of York. We are masters of the art of pragmatism.' Edward stood again, clicking his fingers for the hound to join him, which it did. He had a gift for winning the affection of both animals and men. 'Let us prepare to smile and bend the knee on all occasions.' His eyes touched on mine, held them in severe discourse. 'For what other can we do, in the circumstances?'

'Nothing,' I admitted.

So it was decided.

'Not one of you has talked of my position in all this.' Dickon, who had been silent and motionless throughout all the previous exchanges, so that we had all but forgotten his presence, now lurched to his feet. 'What will be my future? You don't speak of it. I have nothing and we all know why.'

'We will continue not to speak of it.' The Duke of York was emphatic in his denial.

'I will speak of it.' Voice breaking on a croak, it was rare for Dickon to be so openly dissenting in the Duke's company. 'It is only thanks to my mother that I have anything at all to my name.'

Which was true enough. It had been left to our mother, in her will, to persuade King Richard to grant Dickon an annuity of five hundred marks. With great foresight she left all her jewels to Richard, to aid her cause, and thus Dickon received a royal annuity but nothing more. Our father had settled neither land nor title on him. He was merely Richard of Conisbrough, to denote where he was born.

'I have not even been knighted, which is my right,' Dickon growled. 'Am I not worthy of a title of my own as a son of York? Without Richard's acknowledgement I am destined to penury. What happens to me now?'

'You had nothing much to lose in the first place, little brother.' Bitterness was beginning to drip through Edward's earlier facade. 'Do you think I have enjoyed this change of fortune? By God, I have not. All I had achieved, all I had worked for at Richard's Court, flattering him, winning him round to see me as the most loyal friend he had ever had. And now with Lancaster's victory, even though the crown is not yet his, most of those gains are already lost to me.'

Edward flung out his arms in pure performance.

'Do you think that I enjoy the consequences of this usurpation? I am no longer Constable of England. That position was stripped from me at Flint. Now I am called upon to surrender the Constableship of the Tower of London. I doubt it will be my last loss unless I can match Lancaster guile for guile.' Irritation was a river in spate to sweep away any good humour. 'And you, Dickon, complain about a paltry sum of an annuity that might dry up. I am still Admiral of England, Constable of Dover, Warden of the Cinque Ports, Warden of the West March.' He ticked the offices off on his supremely capable fingers. 'All in the gift of King Richard. How long will Lancaster allow them to remain with me? I am Earl of Rutland, Duke of Aumale.

Much of the Arundel lands came to me after Arundel's execution two years ago. Will Lancaster allow me to keep them? I would have been heir to the English throne, after my father. I can say farewell to that! And you think you have all to lose? You don't know the half of it.'

Dickon, face mottled with pent-up rage, was not to be diverted. 'But you are our father's heir. Even if you lose all the titles Richard gave you, one day you will be Duke of York. You will never remain in obscurity, while I will be invisible until the day of my death.'

Hearing the disenchantment, seeing the rank fury glitter in Edward's eyes, watching my father struggle to rise to his feet to take issue, I grasped Dickon's arm and drew him, still protesting, from the room, pulling him into a deserted window embrasure in the antechamber, where I constrained him to face me, my hands on his shoulders.

'Listen to me, Dickon.' At least here was a role I could play.

'Why should I? You cannot help me.'

I shook him, fingers hard in his young flesh. 'No, I can't, but still you will listen.'

'And will you give me fair advice?' His lips curled in very adult mockery.

'All is not lost for you, Dickon.' I stared down the challenge in his eye. '*You* did not raise arms against Lancaster. *You* had no influential involvement in Richard's Court. Your position is more secure than for any one of us.'

Dickon's eyes narrowed. 'You did not raise arms either.'

'I, my foolish brother, will stand or fall with my husband's decision. If Thomas is punished, then so will I be.'

A thought that might just keep me from sleep, if I allowed it.

'I may not be called to account, but I have no call on Lancaster's patronage or his good will,' he snapped. 'As Thomas said, he has four sons to provide for.'

Here was the old problem, yet I put my arm around his shoulders as I guided him from the embrasure and through the connecting antechamber, all but dragging him when he resisted.

'I'll never allow you to become destitute.'

'My brother wouldn't care.'

I felt the line of a frown develop between my brows. Did it never strike Dickon that, unless Edward produced an heir, which appeared more and more unlikely as the years passed and Philippa aged, that he, the younger brother, would inherit the Dukedom of York? Dickon's future was not as black as he frequently painted it.

'Your brother suffers from intense disappointment,' was all I said, adding in an attempt to lighten the burden on my brother's brow: 'Edward will have to abandon his plans to build a new house outside Temple Bar, paid for with coin from Lancaster's inheritance. A house of some ostentation, for I have seen the plans. It will hit him hard.' I hugged Dickon closer, even when he resisted. 'I will not leave you to beg in the gutter.'

'Unless you are begging in the gutter at my side.' Sometimes he was percipient beyond his years. 'Most likely we will all become so.'

What none of us had mentioned was the looming danger from our past, a threat to us that could not be buried in obsequious language and actions. The attack on the Lords Appellant, two years ago, when Thomas and Edward had received their new enhanced titles in reward for their participation in the bloody events, was sure to raise its head when parliament met again. We were all involved to one extent or another. We might try to be pragmatic; Lancaster, who had suffered exile in that clash of power, might have no intention of allowing us to be so. It was an anxiety that rumbled constantly, a sign of a brewing storm.

'We will try to be optimistic,' I advised laconically, since there was no good reason to encourage Dickon's dissatisfaction. 'We are Lancaster's noble cousins. We will make the new kingdom our own and come out covered with glory. He will realise that he cannot do without us.'

'And God help us if he rejects us.'

'God help us indeed.'

And God help Richard, I thought, for we could not.

Chapter Four

'It's like juggling with a set of priceless goblets,' snarled Thomas, never amenable to direct orders, after he had been sent by Lancaster as part of a deputation to visit Richard in the Tower. He was dragging on a high-necked, calf-length garment, soft as a glove, fixing a jewel in his cap.

'Then I advise you to learn to juggle. And fast.'

What could we do in the forthcoming days when Henry of Lancaster took control? We could play the most prominent role, whether it be a heavy decision or a light festivity, as if our loyalty to Lancaster was not, and never had been, in question.

All through those weeks of September, weeks that were tension-ridden and full of latent anxiety, we had learned to step to a different rhythm, a more complicated dance tune played at his behest by the personal minstrels of Henry, Duke of Lancaster. It was not difficult. We were masters of concealment, adapting to political necessity like a goshawk flirting with wind patterns. We accepted the change with slick acumen, even Dickon keeping his complaints to himself. So that our commitment could never be questioned, we were evident at every step of the way. Even if I in person was not. There was no public role for me except as a silent and smiling witness, but I could dance as well if not better than any one of them. I had danced with Richard; I would dance with Henry. Nor would I always be that silent witness, for it was not in my nature to allow such crucial events to flow past me, unacknowledged.

And so I did dance, when Henry occupied chambers in the Palace of Westminster, summoning the magnates who had accompanied him to London to join with him there in an informal evening of wine and music, of dancing and celebration to mark his return to don the mantle of his hereditary dukedom. If I was uneasy at being invited, I masked it with flamboyance in my execution of the stately promenades. After all, there was no need to exchange any dangerous conversations; no need to even voice the perilous words 'crown' and 'throne'. I would play my unusual role of peacemaker with all the subtlety that my mother had never learned at the English Court.

Henry smiled. 'You are as comely as ever, Constance.'

'I am honoured to meet with your approval.'

His gaze was flattering. *Wear the yellow damask*, Thomas had ordered. *It's guaranteed to win Henry's approval.* But in perverse fashion, and since I disliked the ochre hue and the quality of the pale vair, I had chosen instead a new gown of Burgundian cut with trailing hem and high waist. The deep-patterned azure-blue silk and sable furs at cuff and neck was far more becoming to my fair colouring. It was not difficult to ignore Thomas's displeasure.

'You don't need my approval,' Henry said. 'You, of all women in this room, know your own worth.'

More flattery. 'We are pleased to welcome you back, Henry.'

'It is good to see so much welcoming. I have need of good friends.'

Henry exhibited every quality lacking in the imprisoned Richard. Assurance blended with authority. Any observer might be drawn into the mummers' play that Henry would be the better man to wear the crown. Moreover I sensed no hostility in him. Confidence fell gently over me, a silk veil. Until, that is, when, the slow steps of the measure bringing us together, Henry observed with gentle insouciance:

'I am told, Constance, that you visited Richard.'

I inhaled slowly. 'I did.'

'Against my orders.'

'What harm could I do?'

We parted, reunited. My heart began to beat as if the dance were an energetic one. Henry's sword-calloused fingers were firm and rough around mine, destroying all semblance of urbanity.

'I trust that you will not make a habit of it, cousin.'

I smiled self-deprecatingly. 'Habits can be hard to break, Henry.'

The music died away. He bowed. I sank into a curtsey. When I stood, he was looking at me, his expression uncommonly stern.

'My advice: break this one, for your own good.'

To visit Richard or to obey orders? It was a warning and I would be a fool not to heed it.

All we had to do, when not dancing, Edward had advised, was keep our shields raised, our daggers honed and our swords sharp. There were enough enemies around us to take the opportunity to blacken our name and defile our reputation in the eyes of the one man who now dictated the order of events.

But Thomas, unconvinced, continued to expand on the

unfortunate resemblance of our present status to the frailty of precious vessels. 'One mistake, one fumble, one twitch, and they all crash to the floor and shatter into pieces.' He considered the prospect. Then changed the image. 'Our security is as fragile as a pheasant chick in the jaws of a fox. Its neck can be snapped before we can blink.'

'Then we must ensure that we bear no similarity to either priceless vessels or chicks,' I said. 'We will be the sure and certain underpinning to this new power that Henry's building. We will be as watchful as raptors.'

It began with much negotiation with Richard in the Tower, to encourage him to resign his crown to his cousin to make the transition easy and legal. My family of York, Aumale and Gloucester were part of that august gathering who presented themselves before him in a spirit of solemn persuasion.

And Richard?

Richard signed away his birthright for a mess of political pottage, becoming once more Richard of Bordeaux. My advice to him to sign nothing, to agree to nothing, had fallen on deaf ears. What choice did he have, when it was as clear as dawn that the majority of magnates and clerics stood solidly behind Lancaster? So we must stand behind him too. If Lancaster became the new King, how blunderingly inept it would have been if the family of York had resisted. It would have been to cut our own throats.

If there was any regret, any fear for the future at Lancaster's hands, we hid it behind a screen of fluent knee-bending and hand-kissing.

Thus the Duke of York and his heir and his son by law were part and parcel of the procession through the streets of London on the thirtieth day of September when Lancaster took his place in the Great Hall at Westminster. Richard's Great Hall, but what good repining? Richard's empty throne was draped in cloth of gold, ready for its new occupant who was led in by the two Archbishops and Sir Thomas Erpingham bearing a new sword of state, the jewelled Lancaster Sword that Henry had carried at Ravenspur on his landing. Behind him marched the two Holland Dukes of Exeter and Surrey as well as my brother Aumale. Thomas played his role as one of the seven commissioners appointed to witness the pronouncement of Richard's deposition. When Lancaster was ultimately proclaimed King of England by the lords and clerics in the Hall, it was our father of York who committed us to the new regime by leading Lancaster to the throne to take his seat.

Thus we were shackled and bolted to the new King for all time. Thus we disavowed Richard. Thus we were all brought neatly into the Lancaster fold, a little flock of important but impotent sheep, chivvied by the sheepdog named Ambition.

'Can we all breathe easily again?' I asked in a hiatus between signing documents and celebrating the auspicious events.

'We have cut our cloth to suit the occasion.' The Duke of York might regret the outcome but he had embraced his nephew with admirable fervour when Lancaster had acknowledged him, as we had hoped, as a father figure.

'And a fine cloth it is, too,' I remarked, and indeed nothing could have heralded our pre-eminence at the coronation more than the cost of our garments. Clad in silk damask and satin and sumptuous fur, provided for us by the new King as befitted our Plantagenet rank, we gathered in a little smoothly expensive knot as the feast was drawing to a close, to raise our cups of fine wine in private recognition of what we had achieved. At the beginning of August we had been the most loyal of subjects to King Richard the Second. By this day, a mere two months later, we had made the transition to supporters of Lancaster. The connections of the past could be forgotten, masked in the well-seasoned dishes and outward show of this royal feast. The future of Richard, still in the Tower with the prospect of a trial hanging over him if our new King gave his consent, must not be considered as we gorged on roast cygnet, venison and a multitude of game birds, the subtleties, fantastic creations sculpted from hard sugar, stuffed and enhanced with preserved fruit, their carved crowns and eagles sending out the pertinent message to all who dipped their spoons. King Henry the Fourth demanded our fealty and obedience and we gave it with much flamboyance.

Why had we ever doubted our ability to step unchallenged from one loyalty to the next? We allowed a collective sigh of silent relief.

'I did think that at the eleventh hour he might order the arrest of the lot of us,' Thomas remarked. 'Even when I knelt to take the oath, I could feel the kiss of an axe against my neck, but it seems that we are still in possession of our titles, and our heads.'

I could not be so sanguine, but masked the persistent fear. 'Edward says that Henry needs us, and thus our future is secure.'

'Edward says whatever suits him best. He's as slippery as an eel resisting being dropped into a pot of boiling water.'

'Are we not all carved from the same wood? Self-interested to the last?'

Thomas emptied his chased and enamelled goblet with some satisfaction. 'Of course. We'll all perjure ourselves if necessary.'

Our thoughts, which it seemed were for once in unison, were interrupted by a great crash of wood against stone, as the doors of the feasting chamber were flung back and a knight in full gleaming armour, on horseback, rode in. Around us many voices were raised, but no one seemed too perturbed. There was some laughter, some groans. Thomas sighed as the knight lifted his visor to announce his name: Sir Thomas Dymoke. His voice, raw as a jackdaw's croak, bounced from the stonework.

'I am here by right of inheritance through my lady mother. I am the King's Champion. I challenge to a duel any man who doubts King Henry's right to the throne.'

Spurring his horse to a brisk walk he made a circuit around the hall, brushing against the tapestries to release clouds of dust. The preparations for this festivity had been hasty. One circuit and then another. And another, by this time raising some ribaldry.

'Is there no one here who will challenge the right of our King to wear the crown? If there is any such, then I will fight him, sword against sword.'

'For God's sake, someone challenge him and put us out of our misery.' Thomas had no patience, while Edward, who had been dispensing wine to the new King from a silver flagon, strolled over to replenish our cups with what remained in the vessel.

'A more pompous idiot I have yet to meet,' Edward observed.

'So will you not answer his challenge?' I needled gently.

'Not I. I am firmly in the royal good books. And I will make sure that I stay there.'

The greyhound, no longer following obediently at Edward's heel, was restored, hale and hearty, to the company of King Henry. It lay beside him, its head on the royal foot as once it had rested on Edward's, and probably before that on Richard's, reminding me that all dogs could be fickle creatures.

Edward followed the direction of my gaze. 'And there's the truth of it,' he nodded in a moment of whimsy. 'Henry the greyhound putting to flight the white hart of Richard.'

'I dislike omens. And I've more care for my dignity,' Thomas said, 'so don't look at me. Public challenges only bring ridicule to all concerned, whoever wins.'

My father grunted his disapproval but acceptance of such levity. It was tradition.

'I'll do it.' Dickon spoke out, his face aglow. 'I'll throw down my hood.'

'You'll do no such thing,' I said, suddenly made alive to the inadvisability of drawing attention to our ambiguous position at this dangerously new Court.

'But I will.'

And he did, his fur-trimmed hood flung to the floor in formal challenge as Dymoke rode past. Before anyone could see and comment, I stooped, picked it up and pushed it into his hand.

'Be silent!'

'Why should I?'

'Such ill-considered chivalry could be noticed. And lower your voice! You are a fool, Dickon.'

'At least I am loyal.'

'Then you will perforce learn a new loyalty. As we all have done this day.'

It was Henry who brought the display to an end.

'I shall personally relieve you of this onerous duty, Master Champion, since no one seems to be prepared to pick up your challenge.'

I wondered if he had seen Dickon's defiant gesture. Cousin Henry was sharp-eyed. He would need to be if he was to carry this reign to success. I allowed my regard to sweep across the assembled throng. How many here were as ambivalent in their loyalty as we were? As the dregs of the feast settled down around us, the Champion retiring with much unkind laughter, Dickon subsiding, we exchanged a grim smile and raised a toast. To the future. To a new beginning. To inscribing the House of York with gold.

'He has called for parliament to resume tomorrow,' my father reminded us, as if we needed the reminder. It was the poisonous fly in the ointment, the occasion when all past enmities just might be stirred into life. Seeing the fine line between his brows, I asked:

'Do we fear it?'

'No. I expect it will be a discussion by the Commons of what to do with Richard, and by the Lords how we might curtail the powers of the new King by restricting his finance.' The line disappeared. 'Nothing for us to fear there.'

I said what was hovering over all of us. 'I am thinking that the affair of the Counter-Appellants might not be quite dead and buried. There are those in the Lords who will see an opportunity for revenge for what was done two years ago in Richard's name.'

Edward grimaced; clearly it had not been too far from his mind. 'Then it would be good policy, Constance, if you could offer up a prayer that we are all too busy with Richard's fate that no one thinks of it.'

It could indeed be dangerous. 'I will. In absentia,' I added. 'It is my intention to leave you to your parliamentary deliberations. There is no more for me to do here.'

I allowed my eye to continue to travel over the gathering. The faces, the heraldic symbols, all familiar to me. The rich aroma of meat and spices, the songs of expert minstrels. The inbred wealth and traditions and ceremony. Here was my future. Nothing had changed, except for the wearer of the crown. It was a belief that I must hold to, even though my deepest apprehensions could not be dispelled. We did not yet know what changes King Henry might set in train, nor would we until those changes were in place. Whatever they might be, even if they undermined the very foundations of my family, we were powerless to prevent the excavations.

Meanwhile there would be no event to demand my involvement at Court, when this first meeting of parliament would take precedence over all things. I knew what I must do with my time.

'Do you go to Elmley?' Thomas asked as the feast drew to a close and we made our way to our own accommodations. His interest in my whereabouts was mild at best; he would readily find female company, in bed and out. I was resigned to it, almost relieved that his demands on me were light. He already had his heir. 'If you do, take a look over the rent rolls and send me what you can. My purse is to let.'

'So soon?'

I knew he had drawn heavily on his estates to equip his expedition to Ireland, and not merely to pay for men and horseflesh, which had been costly enough. Intent on gallant display he had purchased new spurs, rich cloth to fit out his entire entourage and two new gold and appliquéd standards to exhibit the Despenser presence on any battlefield. His annual income of something near two thousand pounds had been stretched.

'What is it to you?'

'It matters nothing to me, except that your extravagance could beggar us all.'

'I don't have to answer to my wife.'

'Of course you do not.' I smiled winningly, which did not enchant him to any degree. 'All you have to do is enjoy the proceeds of my dower lands.' And then before he could retaliate on this well-worn theme: 'You don't wish to accompany me? You might become reacquainted with your son and daughter. They see little enough of you.'

He shook his head. Thomas would take his seat in the Lords, and the thought intruded as he left me at my door. 'Do you fear that Richard's decision over the old Despenser arraignment will be reversed by Henry?'

His eyes narrowed. 'No. What would be the value for Lancaster in doing that?' But I thought there was a vestige of fear buried in his mind.

'Only revenge,' I mused. 'Be watchful.'

'When am I not?'

He made no effort to embrace me in a fond farewell, and I did not encourage him. Already he was striding away towards who knew what liaison. Then he stopped and spun on his heel.

'You could take Dickon with you. Keep him out of mischief.'

'I doubt he would come. And before you order him to do

so, I would rather not travel with a sullen youth with an axe to grind. You keep an eye on him here.'

There was nothing to be concerned about other than Richard's fate. I would offer up prayers for King Henry's compassion. Yet why had I found a need to warn Thomas? Who was it that had helped Richard in his scheming to have his revenge against the Lords Appellant? We had. We had been the Counter-Appellants. We had aided, abetted and benefitted beyond all imagination, hoarding titles and lands from those who had fallen under Richard's displeasure. We had reaped the harvest grown from the blood of others. A bitter harvest it might prove to be too, planted in tainted soil. There were indeed many at Court who would seize this opportunity to wreak their revenge on a family perceived to be greedy and self-seeking.

On the following morning I began my journey west to Elmley Castle, if for no other reason than to see my children. Richard, called for the late King, was almost three years old, Elizabeth still an infant. Not that they were neglected: cosseted in their own household of nurses and waiting women, employed to rock the cradle and encourage my growing son in his games and lessons, they lacked for nothing. Soon it would be time to appoint a tutor for my son so that the future Earl of Gloucester would be literate in words and figures as well as confident in the use of arms. Soon it would be necessary to discover a future husband for Elizabeth. Daughters were valuable. Alliances were of vital importance to every noble family.

I rode west with a light heart. In some ways it would be a relief to leave the high tensions of Westminster. I must rely on the good sense of my father, brother and husband as well as Joan's Holland relatives, when parliament opened. It was not easy to do so. My father leaned towards choosing the easy path if he sensed that he was under threat. Edward was as tricky as a cat. Even I as his sister knew that it was best not to place complete trust in a man who beneath his polished exterior had only one interest at heart. Edward would fight for himself.

He had never explained why he had counselled Richard to remain over-long in Ireland, nor would I expend the energy in asking him, even though it smacked of treachery.

As for Thomas, who knew? At the moment he was resentful of the new King. Could he overcome that for the ultimate good of our family? I was sure that he could, particularly if Henry proved kindly disposed over the whole question of past Despenser treasons. Thomas's ancestors had been driven by more sly ambition than Thomas would ever lay claim to, resulting in their horrific executions. With an old judgement of forfeiture still hanging over them, Richard had been generous enough to remove it, thus giving Thomas the satisfaction of an ancestry wiped clean and smooth as a newly baked egg blancmange. If Henry was inclined to uphold Richard's reversal, the Despenser name thus reinstated, then Thomas would be effectively won over to the Lancaster cause. I could see no real reason why Henry would not, even though I had warned Thomas to beware of the royal dagger between his shoulder blades.

So much for Edward and Thomas, but then there was Dickon.

As I and my escort left the sprawl of London behind, I wondered what Dickon was doing, left at a loose end as new loyalties were stamped out. Perhaps my father would find him a place in King Henry's household, where he could impress with his soldiery skills, if he had any to impress with, and earn the patronage he so desperately desired. Dickon needed a sponsor with some authority to foster his talents and keep him in line.

The morning was cool and crisp, providing good travelling weather, with many on the road, mostly merchants who were drawn by a new Court with its need for food and cloth. I wondered if Henry would have the money to satisfy them. Meanwhile I would enjoy a brief respite from devious doings in the tranquillity of Elmley Castle, one of the Beauchamp properties of the Earl of Warwick that had fallen into our hands when the Lords Appellant were swept away. It was a pleasant place, set like a jewel in its deer park.

The sun was only just beginning to move past its noonday height when the rattle of hooves of a single, fast-moving horse beat upon my ear. Without my intervention, we drew to a halt, my escort with hands to their swords, the recent potential violence in the country still making all travellers wary. My rank was obvious from my Despenser device of silver, red and gold, on tabard and pennon. I signalled to move on. A rider alone could be no threat to us, and indeed my escort visibly relaxed as the rider closed the distance.

'It's Master Dickon.' My serjeant-at-arms allowed the grip on his sword to ease.

'Dickon . . .' I rode forward, a little trip of concern as he hauled his mount to a halt beside me. It was sweating, and so was he. He grabbed hold of my bridle and pulled me a distance away from the soldiers, his strength surprising me, as did the severity of his eye and the lines that deepened the corners of his mouth. He was short of breath.

'You must come back with me.'

His voice broke on the hard consonants. His hair was wild, his garments dust-plastered. All his youthful flippancy had been stripped away, replaced by a raw anxiety.

'Henry's new parliament is out for blood,' he said. 'Our blood.'

So short a statement, so savagely delivered. It was enough. Without a word I turned my mare, indicating that my escort should follow. Suddenly it was no longer merely a matter of our losing land and title, of patronage and office with this change of monarch. Now it could be that our lives were truly in danger if parliament was pursuing revenge.

We had been far too complacent, expecting that the threats were over with the placing of the crown on Lancaster's head.

I kicked my weary horse on, urgency a vital spur. Of what value was my return? What could I do? Not a thing, but I knew that I must be there because, before all else, we must present an image of unity and loyalty, so that Henry could never question our demeanour in the coming days of unrest. What I did not know, what none of us knew, was whether our new King would allow his parliament to have its vengeance. Henry had been vocal about the empty state of his coffers. What price would parliament demand for granting him future finance and a peaceful existence?

Furthermore, Cousin Henry might see this as an excellent opportunity to kill two plump partridges with one arrow. To remove his relatives whose loyalty was suspect at the same time as he made a favourable showing with parliament and obtained the promise of a hefty coffer of gold.

Surely he would not.

But how many enemies did we have?

It was late, well into the evening, when I arrived in the York apartments in Westminster Palace, my father struggling from his chair, until held firmly back by Joan. She welcomed me with a rise of her mouse-brown brows, before withdrawing to sit with her back to a tapestry depicting a conspicuously bloody hunting scene, all bared teeth, rent flesh and gore, as if she had nothing more to say or do in the affair that was developing elsewhere in this vast palace. Yet what a complication of family connection there was for Joan through her marriage to my father. The executed Earl of Arundel, most influential of the five Lords Appellant, was her uncle; the Duke of Surrey, hand in glove with my brother and husband in bringing Arundel to his death at King Richard's behest, was Joan's eldest brother. The equally complicit Duke of Exeter was also her uncle. Noting her retreat, I felt nothing but mild contempt for her complacency. How could I admire a woman who was so inexplicably unperturbed by the events around her that touched her family so closely? I would not be complacent. I might adopt a serene mask but every sense was tuned to the latent threat to my family.

'Dickon says we are in trouble.' I had sent Dickon to procure spiced wine. I thought we would need a strengthening draught before this night was out. Judging from the deep seams between nose and mouth and his white-knuckled clasp around the arm of the chair, it was one of my father's bad days.

'So it seems. And I can barely move from this room.'

His hands closed again on the arms, the tendons stark beneath the mottled skin.

'Have they accused Edward of Thomas of Woodstock's death?' I asked, seeing here the real threat.

'Yes. So I believe.'

'Is he arrested?'

'I think not. I hope I would have been told if my heir was at this moment under lock and key.'

'And Thomas?'

My father shrugged, a grimace of pain tightening his features. 'I know not.'

'What about Surrey and Exeter?'

'I fear for them all.'

'So it will be a witch-hunt to clear us all out.' There was only one man who might have prevented it. 'You did not think to be there, sir.' It was a statement rather than a question.

'My lord, your father, has been unwell.' Joan had risen and interceded in his defence, quiet but firm. 'The pain has kept him abed until an hour ago. He has only risen at the prospect of your return.' Her quick glance toward me was a surprise in the challenge that it held, daring me to say more. 'As you can see, he has had much to trouble his mind.'

'I am aware. So have we all.'

Accepting the challenge with a nod, for indeed my father looked drawn as if with a winter chill, I approached to touch his arm, the nearest we got to affection, as Dickon returned with a servant and a flagon and cups. I waved Dickon away. He went reluctantly, and I wondered if he might listen at the door.

'It is that worm Bagot who is stirring the pot, so I am told.' My father gripped my hand, which was signal enough of his anxiety. Sir William Bagot, one of Richard's close associates, perhaps the closest other than Edward, had fled smartly back to Ireland when Richard had fallen into the hands of the Earl of Northumberland, rightly fearing for his life. It had not been a successful flight, for he had been taken prisoner and brought back to London in chains. I imagined him scattering accusations with the ready hand of a hen-wife feeding her chicks in an effort to deflect the blame of evil counsellor from himself.

'A pity he could not have escaped more successfully,' I said. 'Or someone could have applied a knife to his throat when he was first captured. It would have saved us a deal of time and worry.'

'Sometimes your vindictiveness concerns me, Constance,' my father said. 'It must be the Castilian blood in your veins.'

'They were quick to deal with traitors in Castile.'

'If we in England were to copy them with summary executions, my son might already be dead. Your Castilian grandfather King Peter was stabbed to death by his half-brother who coveted his throne. Do we wish to emulate such an example?'

Which effectively silenced me.

And then all we could do was wait. The time passed. My father sipped morosely from some potion supplied by Joan, who picked up her endless stitching. I turned the pages of a book of poetry without focus, conscious of my dusty dishevelment that for once meant little against the approaching storm. If Dickon was listening he would learn nothing.

'What are you thinking?' Joan asked eventually, quietly. She had moved to sit at my side as my father's eyelids closed and he fell into a light sleep.

'I am wondering what we should do if they are already all locked in the Tower with Richard,' I replied with brutal honesty.

She looked horrified. 'Surely not. Surely the King would not be so precipitate . . .'

Footsteps, more than one set, approaching. It could be a deputation of royal soldiers to arrest all of us. Edward and Thomas might already be in chains along with Bagot. The tension in the room became the twanging of an ill-stringed lute. I stood, closing the book, facing the door. My father sat up.

'Surely the King would not stain his new kingdom with blood so soon,' Joan whispered. 'Would it not be bad policy to give in to parliament at its first meeting?'

So Joan was better informed than I had expected. All I could do was concentrate on the latch, which was lifted without a formal knock.

The door opened to admit Edward, followed hotfoot by Thomas, who closed it and leaned against it. I might have felt relief, but stark fear walked into that room with them, touching my nape with ice. Thomas's face was without expression, while Edward was as pale as if his blood had been drained in a fatal wound.

'Thank God! Thank God!' My father, awake with the noisy intrusion, managed to stand, taking Edward's arms in as firm a clasp as he could. 'Thank God you are returned.'

'Too soon to thank the Almighty, sir.'

Seeing the pain in his face, Edward led my father back to his chair while Thomas regarded me with complete lack of warmth.

'I thought you were gone to Elmley Castle.'

I swallowed hard against the creeping terror. 'I have returned. I understand that we are under attack.'

Edward came to my rescue. 'Let her be, man.'

It was then, as Edward took a cup of wine from Joan, that I saw it was not fear that held him, but a heat of fury that was banked around him. I could smell it, rank with incipient danger. Gone was the smiling insouciance, the habitual self-confidence of a man who saw his future painted in clear lines. Now Edward had had the solid rock as heir of York mined from under his feet.

'Under attack?' He picked up my comment and embellished it. 'Before God! It's more than an attack. I am on trial for my life.' He gulped the wine, eyes fierce with the humiliations of the day. 'Don't be under any illusion. I'll be fortunate to come out of this with my head still attached to my body.'

He tossed the now-empty cup in his hand, catching it neatly, and for a moment I thought that he might hurl it against the recessed fireplace, but before the unwavering gaze of his father he steadied himself and handed it to me.

'Will you tell us?' I asked. Best to know the worst of it.

'Oh, I'll tell you. As soon as the Speaker asked for all evil counsellors to be arrested, I knew it.' His lips thinned into one line. 'I could see it written on the faces of those lords who had not been as fortunate as I under Richard's hand. The desire for revenge could be tasted, like sour ale lodged in my gullet. It was Bagot's doing,' he confirmed, 'trying to save his own skin by smearing the blame elsewhere. It seems, in Bagot's weasel words, that I was the principal evil counsellor at Richard's Court. I am accused of two treasonable acts. Two! I am an accessory to the murder of our uncle Thomas of Woodstock, and as if that were not enough I have expressed a desire that King Henry should also be murdered.' He snatched back the cup and refilled it in two fluent actions, replacing the flagon with a force that almost buckled the metal foot. 'I am accused of sending two yeomen to Calais to do the mortal deed against Woodstock. To smother him in his bed. Could Bagot destroy my name any further? I've never heard him so voluble in his own defence, while I am the one to carry all blame for Woodstock's death.'

It was indeed damning. The cold hand around my throat tightened its grip.

'But you were involved in Woodstock's death,' I ventured, seeing the true danger here.

'Of course I was,' Edward snarled. 'As were we all.' He gestured towards Thomas who still leaned, silent as a grave, against the door. 'It was Richard's wish that the deed be done, to punish his uncle for curtailing his power. Who was brave enough to withstand Richard's wishes? He was volatile and becoming more so, like a bed of rushes swaying in a high wind. To refuse a royal order was to sign my own death warrant.'

'He would not have had you executed,' I suggested.

'He would have had me stripped of all he had given me! I'd not risk it. We all knew what was in our best interests.' He swung round. 'Did we not, Thomas? You, if I recall, were as culpable as I.'

Thomas straightened and strolled forward, nudged at last into voice. 'Yes, we knew what we must do. But I had no hand in Woodstock's murder. I was not there when the pillow was held to his face. I'll not accept any blame for Woodstock's death . . .'

There they were, facing each other like two sharp-spurred cocks, goaded in a fighting pit. I might not trust my brother overmuch, but here was Thomas sliding out from under a political murder in which they had both been complicit.

Thomas Despenser would sell his soul to the Devil to keep the power he had.

'You will not tear each other apart. Our enemies will do that willingly enough,' the Duke intervened. 'What was the outcome? You are clearly not imprisoned.'

'No. Not yet.' Edward continued his furious complaint. 'I said I would prove Bagot false through personal combat. I threw my hood at his feet and challenged him to a duel. I'd force him to eat his words. But what did King Henry do? Calm as you like, he ordered me to pick up my hood and return to my seat. So the accusation still stands, Bagot is free to continue his poisonous complaint against me and throughout the whole, the King's face was as much a stone mask as the statues around us. I'll not have confidence in his mercy.'

'You are his cousin. He'll not have you executed.' What an empty promise that was, yet I attempted to pour cooling water on this explosion of vitriol. We needed Edward to be cool and calm, capable of careful planning, not alight with a fire of self-righteousness. 'Tomorrow all will be well.'

'Tomorrow all will be far from well,' Edward growled. 'You were not there. You did not read the magnates' delight, gleaming in their eyes, in the opportunity to be rid of me. Once I might have thought them friends. There are no friends where power is concerned.'

'I see you are not concerned with my safety,' Thomas added with terrible petulance.

I had neglected him, when usually I was careful in my response to him, a man who was easily stirred to selfish anger. Now was not the time for him to sink into sullen recrimination.

'Be at peace, my lord. Indeed, I recognise your danger.'

I went to him to refill his cup, to soothe with a formal kiss of greeting to his cheek, which he accepted with ill grace.

'I think you do not. Bagot wasn't satisfied in attacking Aumale. He went on to accuse the rest of us involved in the removal of the Lords Appellant. We are all incriminated as evil counsellors.' I became aware of Joan stiffening at my father's side. This was the news she had not wanted. 'Bagot named Surrey and Exeter too, as well as Salisbury.'

Thomas was not finished. 'He also named me.' He glanced at Edward, prepared now to concede a point. 'I was not directly involved in Woodstock's death, but I was one of the Counter-Appellants and reaped the rewards. The Earldom of Gloucester as well as Arundel and Beauchamp estates and castles. It will not be easily forgiven by those who thought Arundel died a martyr's death. I foresee no pardon for Surrey or Exeter. Or for me. As for the rest of you,' – his gaze swept us all – 'the King might decide to rid himself of the whole hornets' nest of potential traitors.'

'I thought—' I began.

'If you think we had persuaded him that we could be of value to him as supporters of the new reign, then you are wrong. We were all wrong.'

It is exactly what I had thought. But here was violent death lurking on our threshold. Joan looked as if the dread angel sat on her shoulder. My father was stricken to silence, a hand, shaking, covering his eyes.

'What do we do?' Joan asked helplessly.

It was as if no one cared to answer her. Perhaps they thought her question fatuous, as I did.

'This is what we do,' I said, for there was only one choice to make. What could we possibly do to pre-empt the next step by the King? 'We do nothing. We keep our temper. We preserve a good humour. We challenge no one. We answer all accusations, or not, as required. We admit nothing. We discuss it with no one. We do not allow temper to cloud our judgement.'

I had their eyes and their ears. I did not hold back. In this black void of fear they would listen to me.

'We do not beg for mercy from the King until we need it, if we need it. And we wait. Nothing to be gained by doing anything else. We will conduct ourselves as if we were innocent. Any accusation against us must be proven. Will the King listen to Bagot before his own blood?'

'He might not.' Edward's fury had subsided somewhat into a mere rumble of falling rocks. 'But the Lords would gladly do so.'

'Then we trust that the King sees sense and dismisses the Lords. He cannot afford to lose you, Edward.' I glanced at my husband. 'He can't afford to lose any of us. Meanwhile, we'll add nothing more to the danger we are already in.' Then to my father: 'Have you been threatened to any degree, my lord?'

He shook his head.

'Surely Henry dare not,' Edward said, equanimity restored at last as some degree of clear thought came into play. 'Our father played kingmaker at Berkeley, by negotiating rather than directing his army to fight. Without that, Henry's struggle against Richard would have been twice as difficult. He owes our father an incalculable debt of gratitude.'

'Then let us hope that he realises it,' I agreed. 'And that to reward the Duke of York for past services, he must pardon the Duke of York's family.'

But Edward was frowning down into the empty cup. 'Bagot said that John Hall should be questioned,' he admitted.

'And who is John Hall?'

Edward's eyes met mine, and there was deep concern still alive and well.

'John Hall was one of the valets involved in the death of Thomas of Woodstock in Calais. Bagot says he should be questioned because he knows who was involved. Who sent the order and who carried it out. Hall is in prison in Newgate. I expect he'll be in the Lords' clutches by tomorrow morning.'

'Will he incriminate you?' I asked, knowing the answer before I asked the question.

'Yes. This could all be much worse than we think.'

It had to be Thomas who pointed out the obvious: 'Worse?' He rubbed his hands over his face. 'How can it be worse? I can see death writ large for all of us.'

Chapter Five

Doom kept us all company through the hours of night and into the morning, when Joan and I converged on what had become the women's chamber, our embattled menfolk already on their way to attend the meeting of parliament. This was no day for any one of them to be absent, not even my father, still in pain but determined. Only a ministration to his limbs of the roots and leaves of hound's tongue and marjoram, steeped in warm oil, to dull the pain, together with the strong arm of his body servant, got him through the door; his discomfort could not be disguised but he would stand beside his family. The Dukes of Surrey and Exeter joined them to put on a brave face. The fate of all would hang together.

Which left the womenfolk, as ever, to await the outcome while the royal greyhound fretted outside the door. For some reason beyond my guessing, it had returned to Edward's care, which seemed absurd when the King had rejoiced at its change of loyalty. I refused to allow it entry. It was enough to tolerate the sickly sweetness of the marjoram which hung in the air, strangely at odds with the stench of alarm.

'It is one of the few times when I wish for a squint, to spy upon what parliament might be doing.' I pressed my cheek against the almost opaque glass, to peer through the window in the direction of the Great Hall, considering the value of the narrow aperture in a church to allow the host in the side chapel to be elevated at the same moment as the miracle occurred at the high altar. I wanted to know what was being said, what challenges were being issued and by whom. Ignorance was a cruel word and most pertinent. Infuriatingly it was my lot, and that of every woman, never to know of pertinent events within parliament until informed at some later date, if at all. 'I fear this day will prove interminable.' I paused, considering the worst scenario, in spite of my brave words on the previous night. 'And of course, they may not return.'

'Better not to know,' Joan observed, her head bent over her stitches. She had recovered her composure since hearing that her brother and uncle too would face the Lords' vengeance, but that probably her husband would not. A treasonous husband could mean any number of difficulties for his wife, however innocent she might be, not least confiscation of all the family estates, including her dower. Joan was unlikely to suffer. I would not be so fortunate. The promise of hours of uncertainty scratched at my temper.

'Better not to know? Until they are condemned to death?'

Her head snapped up. 'I cannot believe that of Henry. He owes my lord the Duke a debt of honour.'

'I am not so hopeful. I would like to know that my family is to be sent to join Richard in the Tower before it actually happens.'

'But you can do nothing to prevent it. As I can do nothing to safeguard my brother and uncle.'

I could not answer that, for it was true. I paced. Joan

continued to sit and stitch at some linen garment, until I could bear the silence no longer. I watched her needle flash in and out of the fine material. I resented her stillness, her acceptance. Did she not care? Finally I stopped in front of her. The linen was particularly fine.

'Are you breeding?'

'No.' She did not even look up. 'This is an altar cloth. Not that it is any of your affair if I was carrying a child. And what's more, I despise stitching. I would that I were a man and could wield a sword rather than a needle.'

Which confounded me. She and my father had been married for seven years now but I had made no attempt to become acquainted with her, nor even questioned why my father should choose to marry a girl so much younger than himself. It was nothing more than an alliance between two powerful and interrelated families, the Hollands and Plantagenets. Could he not have done better if he had wanted a wife for companionship in his last years? I had thought her insipid, self-effacing. Whereas I was incapable of remaining aloof from the events that would impinge so keenly on our future, my stepmother was weakly accepting of her lot in life. I studied her still-bent head. Where was all the fire and duplicity of her Holland family, her notorious grandmother? It had dissipated into insignificance in this young woman. Recognising the complete lack of affinity between us, I had no desire to know her better than I did at that moment.

And yet this barbed response with its new insight into Joan's mind grasped at my attention. Perhaps I had been wrong. Here was a young woman who felt as constrained as I.

'I was merely enquiring after your health,' I said curiously. 'Do you resent my doing so?'

'No, you were not merely enquiring.' Now she did look up and her gaze was a forthright stare. 'Yes, I do resent it, and no, it is not your affair, Constance. You were delving into my relationship with your father.'

Which I suppose I had been, my query born out of impatience rather than compassion, which made me deserving of the rebuke. No, she was not lacking in confidence, and I had been wrong. But then a granddaughter of Joan of Kent would be unlikely to be a wilting flower, choked by the pre-eminence of those around her. The Fair Maid of Kent by both character and reputation had never been intimidated. I was ten years old when she died and recalled a woman with a sharp tongue and little patience for royal children who got under her feet.

Perhaps my stepmother, ridiculous as it might seem to have such who was younger than I, deserved my attention. I studied her profile as once again she turned back to her work. Not the beauty of Princess Joan, nor her flamboyant choice of style and colour, but she had inherited her caustic tongue when she allowed it free rein. It was regretful that Joan still favoured a sideless surcoat in dull autumnal hues rather than a houppelande, and her silk chaplet with a short veil was plain to a fault, but it might be worth my while to make better acquaintance of her, given that we were destined to spend considerable time together in the circumstances.

'Do you remember your grandmother?' I asked.

'Barely. I was little more than six years when she died, and she had lived most of her final years as a recluse at Wallingford.'

'She was a remarkable woman. I remember her visits to

Court at New Year.' I continued to regard her. 'Have you been satisfied in your marriage, Joan? Until this upheaval?' Some conversation was better than none.

'Life could be worse.'

'Your grandmother wed where she chose.'

'And I did not.' She was quick to pick up my implication. Once again she fixed me with a stare that was a challenge. 'I would never have chosen a man almost forty years older than I as my husband.'

Here was plain speaking. I could not imagine why I had been used to refer to her, in my thoughts at least, as 'poor Joan'. I paused in my perambulations. 'Was your heart given elsewhere?' I was surprised to find that she had my compassion if it was so. I had no experience of such. My heart was quite untouched, either within marriage or without.

'No.'

'Does my father hold an affection for you?'

'Yes, he does. I am grateful.'

Again there was the warning, in the flash of an eye, that I should not intrude too far. I considered, reluctantly liking her spirit.

'I imagine he has more thought for you than for Isabella.'

'He detested Isabella. So it would not be difficult.'

'Has he told you that?' Now this did surprise me. They must be closer than I had imagined for my father to bare his soul.

'Yes. He disliked her face, her character and her morals. He only wed her because he was instructed to do so by your grandfather.'

So they did converse. Which is more than Thomas and I did.

'Did he tell you that too?'

'Yes. If he hadn't wed her, Isabella would have been prey for any man who had an eye to the kingdom of Castile. Better if both daughters of King Pedro, Constanza and Isabella, were safely shackled with English princes. John of Gaunt had little affection for Constanza, but at least she did not act the whore, whereas he was not averse to flaunting his Swynford mistress with appalling immorality before the whole Court. Isabella had no thought at all for her reputation, only for her personal satisfaction.'

She paused, colouring faintly. 'Forgive me. I should not have said any of that about the lady who was your mother, or about your uncle. There may have been extenuating circumstances, I suppose. I might have done the same as Isabella if I had been trapped in such a marriage.'

'Whereas you can see widowhood at least hovering on your horizon.'

'Yes.' Her gaze was again formidably forthright. 'I'll not lie to you. Being Duchess of York is all very well, but I'd exchange it for my freedom. Or the hope of a child.'

Which made me laugh. I had not expected to find a confidante so plain-speaking, or so close to my own heart. I decided to repay honesty with honesty.

'I am as aware of my mother's reputation as you appear to be, and I had little affection for her other than that demanded by duty. As little as she had for me.' My thoughts deflected from the present chaos. 'I know my father spent as little time with her as he could. Enough to get himself an heir. And myself.'

'But not your younger brother.'

I felt my brows rise. 'So he told you that as well.'

'Of course. He makes no claim that Dickon is his.'

'And, since you are so well informed, I presume you know who rumour says is Dickon's father?'

'Yes.' She appeared quite unmoved. 'My uncle has a reputation.'

Indeed he had. It was whispered in kitchens and royal bedchambers that my mother Isabella had enjoyed a lengthy and fiery liaison with John Holland, Duke of Exeter, the result of which had been Dickon. My father's lack of interest in the child merely added fuel to the flames. So Dickon was born a York son, but raised under sufferance. I frowned. My younger brother was the only one of my family who roused my compassion.

'Sometimes I think it would be better for Dickon if my father was more compassionate of his circumstances. It is not his fault and it does no good to treat him as a bastard. There is a bitterness in Dickon that worries me.' I took a cushioned stool beside Joan, thinking of my own children. 'Is there no hope for you, for a child? Do you and the Duke never share a bed?'

'Again it is not your concern. But no.' At last her hands fell unheeding to her lap, crushing her despised needlework as her cheeks flushed stronger with bright colour. 'His pain is too great, and his hope is in Edward. He regrets that Edward has no children of his own to carry on the line.'

'Nor is there any likelihood,' I observed.

Edward had married Philippa de Mohun, a lady a good decade older than he who had already been twice wed, twice widowed. She bore her first two husbands no children, nor was there more success with Edward. Where the fault lay would be impossible to say. Perhaps Edward should have chosen more wisely. He was said to have married for love but I saw no evidence of it in their calm demeanour and frequent partings.

'She may yet be fortunate.' Joan was condemning of my cold judgement.

All I could do was give the lightest of shrugs. 'Your one consolation is that my father is almost into his sixtieth year and in ill health. You will be a young widow. And a desirable one.' It sounded callous, even to my own ears, but it was true, and no more callous than Joan's own opinion of the whole affair. 'His brothers have not proved to be particularly long-lived.'

'Particularly when murdered.' She flinched her apology at the reference to my uncle of Woodstock's unfortunate demise. 'I will probably wed again at the dictates of my family. You know what it is like.' Her bitterness, I realised, matched that of Dickon.

'I'm not sure that my situation matches yours.'

'It does not take great intellect to know that you and Thomas barely tolerate each other. Is that not so? Does he have any affection for you?'

'No.'

'Do you have an affection for him?'

I considered replying that it was no concern of hers, as she had warned me. Instead: 'No.'

'You were married young.'

'We were children. Another political marriage.' Why not admit it? 'Yes. I know what it is like to be wed for an alliance. I know what it is like to find no union of spirits in a marriage. We tolerate each other. We are also able to live apart. He has his heir.'

'But would wish for another.'

'What man does not?'

'I think you suffer more than I. Your father never neglects me.'

'Then you are fortunate.' I kept my tone without inflexion. 'It is perfectly possible to live without love. Those of our status do not expect it.'

'Do you have no regrets?'

How persistent she was. 'How do you regret something of which you have no experience? Life is far more comfortable without. I do not have to consider the state of Thomas's emotions, as he does not have to consider mine. He never has, he never will. It is as good as any foreign alliance based on pragmatism between two parties who have nothing in common, and they work well enough.'

'It sounds a cold existence.'

'Cold, yes. He gives me the status I desire.'

Why was I indulging in confession to Joan Holland? It was not my intent to engage her pity. Still frowning, I stood and began to pace again, turning the conversation into a different yet no-less-painful path. 'I need to know what is happening.'

'Why don't you go and find out? I am not dependent on your company for my contentment.'

Which was uncommonly sharp as she returned to stabbing her needle into the cloth. I responded in kind, since she had forced me to face my isolation, to acknowledge my ignorance of affectionate emotion. I had not enjoyed the experience.

'How fortunate for you,' I replied. 'I doubt anyone is dependent on my company.'

'I did not mean . . .'

'Yes, you did. Here we are, two bitter and powerless women trapped in marriages we did not want. No matter.' I turned my back on her, looking down again from the window. 'I cannot go. I would be too obvious.'

'Then send a servant to discover and report any developments.'

'I'll not open the coffers of our family affairs for servants to riffle through.'

'They will know anyway. They know everything. They know that I am still a virgin. I expect they inspect the sheets regularly and inform the whole household.'

I looked back across the room with just a breath of pity. 'I am sorry.' Then turned away from the sudden sadness in her face. Her advice had given me an idea. I might not go. A servant was unacceptable, but . . .

'I could send Dickon to be my messenger.'

'An excellent idea.'

It was suddenly comfortable to be standing on less personal ground. 'But Dickon, as ever when needed, is invisible. It is below my dignity to stand at the door and shout for him. Nor is he always amenable to orders when he sees no personal advantage.'

'If you smiled at him, and offered a bribe . . .'

'A bribe?'

'What would he like most, that you could give him?'

'I have no idea, other than an estate, a title and a chest of gold. As well as a mission to fight someone, somewhere in Europe. There are ten years between us. Our thoughts do not keep company.'

'Does that mean that you have no knowledge of him? I suppose my family is closer than most. I always knew what my younger brother Edmund was thinking although, of necessity, we have now grown apart.' Her eyes sharpened. 'What I would say is that Dickon is a young man of interest. He might be useful to you one day.' She paused. 'I will ask him for you, if you wish it. I do not find him unamenable. He makes me laugh, when I don't have much to laugh about.'

A day of revelations.

'I think I have misjudged you. I thought you were a mouse.'

'I think you have. A rat, more like, but I hide my teeth and choose not to engage in battles which I will never win.' She regarded me with some speculation. 'But then I think you often do misjudge those around you. I suppose it is easy for a woman with royal blood to consider herself superior. Even though my own blood is as royal as yours through my grandmother.'

Joan left the room to send a message to bring Dickon to us, leaving me discomfited. She was right, I admitted, even though I might not like the picture she painted. And why had I not been aware of Joan's keen intelligence and wit? Because I had never made a true effort to know her beyond a superficial acquaintance. That was my fault, too. But now was not the time to consider any blemishes in my character.

Within a handful of minutes Joan returned with Dickon; he was dragging his feet, but at least he had been open to persuasion.

'Constance.' He looked wary. 'What do you want? I was busy.'

It did not bode well. 'Busy doing what?'

'Whatever will allow me to keep out of the royal eye. Today might not be the day to advertise my connection with the families of York, Holland and Despenser.'

Succinct and accurate, he had had an ear to some closed doors.

'We have a favour to ask,' Joan said with an encouraging smile before I could hack at his lack of loyalty.

'What's that?'

Joan glanced at me.

'I need an ear to the ground,' I said. 'An ear that is less obvious than mine. Go down to the Great Hall . . .'

'They'll hardly let me in!'

'As I am aware, but you can merge with the hangers-on and question those who have knowledge. I want to know what's happening. I want to know if John Hall has been questioned and if any of our family is in danger. If there is a threat to our lives or our freedom. I want to know if any one of our enemies dares to push for single combat. I want to know before Edward and Thomas are put under restraint.'

He opened his mouth, I presumed to refuse, but Joan stepped in, gripping his arm with both small hands.

'My brother is in danger too, Dickon. Ask about the Duke of Surrey. And my uncle the Duke of Exeter. Will you do that for me?'

He looked unapologetically hostile as only a thwarted youth could. Then shrugged. 'I'll do it.'

'I would also like for you to discover the King's mood, as far as you can,' I said.

Dickon grinned. 'You mean will he throw us to the snarling dogs? I'll do what I can, though I don't see why we can't just wait for the outcome.' He caught the sharpness of my glance. 'But I agree it might be best to know sooner rather than later. Are we planning a flight to the Welsh Marches if King Henry proves hostile?' He paused, then grinned again. 'I may need coin for bribes.'

At last Dickon's eyes shone with the light of conspiracy.

'I have none to hand,' I said.

'Then I won't do it.'

But Joan discovered some in the purse at her belt and handed them over in a little clinking stream into his palm.

'Thank you, Dickon,' I said. 'I will be very grateful.'

'I'll remind you of that.' And when the greyhound, which had followed him into the room, showed a willingness to accompany him, he pushed it back. 'Keep it: it might be the only bargaining tool that we have. The greyhound in exchange for Edward's life.'

Which might have seemed horribly prescient.

'Let us hope,' I said as Dickon's footsteps faded into the distance, 'that it's all like one of Henry's subtleties at the end of the feast. All decorative wizardry and no substance, that collapses at the first breath of wind.'

Joan came to stand beside me at the window.

'Nor should we forget that Richard is still under constraint. And his future so uncertain.'

No. We must not forget. It was easy to do so in this maelstrom of personal attack. While we awaited Dickon's return I had visions of flight to one of our distant estates if Henry showed any leaning towards the ultimate punishment. Joan and I could make our escape, perhaps to the staunch walls of Conisbrough, before the royal guards reached us. Or, as Dickon had so flippantly suggested, to my estates in Glamorgan. How extreme this all sounded, fleeing for our lives. Meanwhile Joan returned to her sewing. Her wrists were thin and fragile, but she wielded her needle with energy, despite her professed hatred of it. The greyhound settled down at her feet since, for once, Joan was not accompanied by one of her grey cats. I remained at the window, watching the busy ravens, waiting for some sort of sign of good or ill fortune. Until Joan looked up at me, addressing me with an unsettling question.

'Does your brother of Aumale ever consider his own closeness to the throne? Richard recognised the Duke of York as his heir, which would make Aumale next in line after his father. An excellent reason for Henry to rid himself of your brother.'

'My thanks, Joan. You have just stoked my anxieties threefold. So it will matter not whether John Hall gives evidence against Edward. Henry will sign his death warrant.' I bared my teeth against the awful prospect. 'As long as he does not sign mine. You know that I'll fight to the death to save us all from ignominy.'

When Joan at last abandoned her altar cloth, folding it, then placing her hands neatly on top, she tilted her chin and smiled at me, a sharp-toothed little smile.

'I think I would not like you as my friend, Constance. But I would like you even less as my enemy.'

I bristled, on the defensive. 'It is fortunate then that you are unlikely to have me as either.'

'Who's to say, in the future, you might even need me as a confidante?'

'Why would I?'

'You have no female friends, I think.'

No, I had not. A little silence fell between us, broken only by the hound twitching in its dreams and a soft fall of ash in the fireplace. I had never had female friends, nor had I felt the lack of them. Why would I need to bare my breast to another woman who would gossip and prove less than trustworthy? Better to keep my own counsel.

'I have no need of them.' I eyed her, resenting what could

only be criticism. 'Nor do I see you surrounded by a flock of admiring Court women.'

'Ah, but I have sisters.'

Her smile was infuriatingly complacent, and I would have responded with even more astringency. But I did not.

'Listen,' she said.

I realised that every one of my senses had been held in tension. Throughout all our conversational meanderings I had been straining for the first intimation of Dickon's return.

Chapter Six

The door was flung back and Dickon entered, bringing with him an excitement that caused the greyhound to leap up and bark as our spy gathered enough breath to announce:

'It's not good news. Not for any of them.'

'Then tell us . . .'

He paused to gulp in air. Now beneath the excitement and flush of exertion I could see the suppressed horror, the pale skin around his mouth as if his lips had been pressed hard into silence. Whatever it was, it had been enough to shake Dickon's engrained shallow heedlessness. His words fell over each other.

'It's this. The valet John Hall has been brought from Newgate, on the King's orders. He is being questioned about the death of our uncle, Thomas of Woodstock, about what he knows and what he saw. But that's not the worst of it. The King has summoned the Lords to meet with him.'

I shook my head, unable to dispel the dull beat of fear that Dickon's news had delivered. 'To what purpose? I presume that our family is still safe.'

'You might say that. But not for long, I'd say.' A feral expression twisted his face into that of a malign imp. 'The King's excluded from his audience with the Lords those accused by Bagot. The Counter-Appellants. So our Dukes of Aumale, of Surrey and of Exeter are all left to cool their heels in an antechamber while the rest give their counsel.'

The fear roared back into life with the agility of the hound that still leaped up against Dickon as he pulled its ears.

'What about Thomas?' I asked. 'What about our father? Are they too banished from the King's presence?'

'I don't know.' Dickon subsided to sit on the floor almost at my feet, his back against the window seat, arms clasped around the hound, chin tilted. 'What I do know is that the King is asking the Lords for advice. Should these maliciously evil counsellors named by Bagot be put under arrest?'

Worse than I thought, but Edward had warned me.

'Who tells you this?' I demanded.

His grin widened to accompany a self-deprecating shrug. 'I have my informants.'

'And what does your informant say? Will the Lords push for imprisonment?'

'It's still being discussed, but voices in the chamber were raised. Even I could hear them. There is much throwing down of hoods, I was told, which is bad, but no one has yet drawn his sword, which is good. The King is being circumspect and has made no decision so far but tempers are high.' Dickon's eyes gleamed. 'I can go back, if you give me more coin.'

I considered a sharp refusal, but with this unforeseen twist knew that I must send him. The axe falling on our combined necks might just become reality.

'Try not to find it all so enjoyable, Dickon. The outcome here can endanger us all.'

'I know. But the atmosphere in Westminster buzzes like a beehive disturbed by a badger's claw. Do I go back?'

Joan allowed a second stream of small coin to fall into Dickon's outstretched hand, watching it disappear into his clenched fist. By now, as Dickon departed, Joan's stitching was abandoned on the floor.

'I don't think there is any hope that the Lords will lean towards mercy,' I said. There was nothing to be gained from wishing for the unobtainable.

'But we don't know,' Joan fretted.

'I think we do.' And no point at all in trying to bolster her spirits when all pointed to a disaster.

But Dickon, who returned before the end of the day, flushed with his efforts, eagerly snatching the cup of ale from me and gulping it down, seemed on the surface to be more hopeful.

'They're still free. But that's all I can tell you.'

'Is that not good?'

The question was drawn from me, because for the first time there was a crease between the lad's brows to match my own. 'It all hangs in the balance, as I see it. It's being said that the Counter-Appellants were charmed foster-children of King Richard, and they had incited the King in his vengeance. Since the foster-father was now locked in the Tower, so should his foster-children be condemned to join him there. There are those who are demanding execution.'

I ignored Joan's intake of breath. This was no time for excess emotion. 'So it is revenge.'

'Not revenge. Not in the eyes of the Lords. To them it's common justice.'

And so it would be in the eyes of many, as I knew.

'I must pray,' Joan announced. 'I will be in St Stephen's Chapel. Will you come?'

'No. What good will that do?'

'How do we know? Better than standing here, watching the prospect of an agonising death unfold before us!'

'Then you go and pray. I will do the standing and watching.'

Rosary in hand, she left the chamber. I could not pray. It needed some political intervention to save my family. My prayers of thanks to God would come when our position was secure.

They returned. At last, before the sun fell below the horizon, they came to us, including Joan's brother, a desperation hanging over them like a pall, but still free. Joan, having returned from an hour on her knees, was no less anxious despite her recourse to the Almighty.

'We know what has been advised by the Lords,' I said as I helped my father to his chair, Joan relieving him of chaperon and heavy cloak. 'Dickon has played the spy for us.'

'It was a terrible day.' My father, ashen, drawn with pain, his jaw tight, groaned as he settled his limbs. He looked older by a decade as I poured him wine and pushed it into his hand, tightening his fingers around the cup as he looked up into my face. 'As bad as any I recall. If you will lock the door, I will be grateful. If the King decides to take us prisoner, it will not be tonight unless he is of a mind to break it down. Lock the door, boy.'

Dickon obediently turned the key in the lock.

Wine was poured but the food I had ordered to be brought sat in a congealing mess of grease and sauce, the aromas of roast meat pleasing to none. No one had an appetite.

'But not one of you is restrained.' I tried to delve beneath the bleakness.

'Not yet, we are not, but the Lords in our absence were in damnably unanimous agreement.' Once again anger overlay anxiety for Edward as he took up his habitual stance in the centre of us all. He would not lounge at his ease today. 'We should all be imprisoned, they advised. Myself, Surrey and Exeter. I, of course, head the list of undesirables. I am accused of being midwife to Thomas of Woodstock's murder, desiring it and giving birth to it to further my own ends. Thus saith the Lords. The Commons too demand that all the evil counsellors should be arrested.'

'Which will include me,' Thomas added. 'I was not banished. I was in the Lords to hear the venom. It suffused the whole chamber like a stench from a midden in high summer. They're after our blood and won't rest until they get it.'

Joan, white-faced, was enfolded in her brother Tom's arms. Prayer had brought her no relief. I could have told her, but momentarily I envied her the solace of Surrey's embrace. Thomas was not so moved to reassure me, but then I would have rejected his comfort as a cynical ploy.

'What is the valet saying?' I asked. For I knew that all might rest on this one testimony.

'All that he could to incriminate me,' Edward replied. 'John Hall says that it was *my* valets who were foremost amongst those sent from England and who smothered our uncle to his death in Calais. It's damning and it's horribly accurate.' Then: 'I should have silenced John Hall,' he added, 'by one means or another, when I had the chance.'

'Since you did not,' Thomas accused, 'all is lost. You have

no evidence to give to prove your innocence. If they make their charges stick against you, Aumale, then the rest of us will soon follow.'

'No. All is not yet lost,' Tom said. 'Nothing is yet clear.' I thought he was adamant for the sake of his sister. The odds were weighted impossibly against us. 'The King has warned the Lords against taking extreme measures. I don't think he wants a bloodbath so early in his reign.'

'But he might want justice for his uncle. He might find this the perfect opportunity to rid himself of those who were party to his exile,' I said. What use was being full of hope when there was so little hope to cling on to?

'Perhaps.' Tom released Joan with a final embrace and a smoothing of all the laughter lines in his austere Holland features, flexing his soldierly shoulders as if he would protect her from whatever Fate had to drop at our feet. 'All we can do is support each other. Since our future, for good or ill, will hang together, we must support Edward.' He gave Thomas a warning glance.

'I'm hardly likely to give evidence against him,' Thomas responded.

'For which we must all be relieved.' Edward, too, caught Thomas in his stare. 'If we do not stand together, we will fall.'

'I never said that we wouldn't stand together—'

Against the backdrop of antagonisms, our danger seethed and boiled like a deadly quicksand. But I could not allow myself to be drawn in, and interrupted Thomas before he could begin another liturgy of complaint:

'Stop snapping at each other and listen. We know the argument we must hold to. We were under the King's power and we were not in a position to disobey him. Richard wished to be revenged on the Lords Appellant, who curbed his power before he grew to his full strength. As loyal servants we did what he bade us. There is our proof, that we did nothing that was not demanded of us by the King himself.'

I paused, and when there was no rejection of this as a plan: 'What man would have dared disobey Richard? There is not one member of the Lords who can deny Richard's determination to bring the Lords Appellant to their knees. There is not one of them who can deny Richard's fury when he was thwarted. And since our present King also suffered at Richard's hands, he must see the rights of our argument, if you hold fast to it.'

'God's Blood, it's a specious argument.' Thomas was not convinced. 'Will Henry accept our obedience to Richard as a reason for the murder of his uncle? And if the Lords and Commons are in agreement against us, then what value in our supporting one another?'

'Because you are all guilty,' I said. 'And you as much as anyone, Thomas. We will do nothing to undermine each other. That would only be a monumental stupidity.'

My father grunted and struggled to his feet, a hand on Joan's shoulder as he headed towards the door, gesturing for Dickon to unlock it.

'I'm for my bed. We can do nothing but wait on the mercy of my nephew of Lancaster.'

I watched him go, considering the strong possibility that he might be the last of our family to bear the title of York. Henry had removed Richard. How difficult would it now be for him to remove the families of York, Holland and Despenser as well?

*

The days in which my family continued to remain at liberty, a blessing in itself, passed with the slowness of winter ice-melt, agonising in the manner in which each one crept from hour to hour, from sunrise to sunset, Dickon continuing to fulfil the role of informant for Joan and myself. It was a relief to know that the Dukes were all once more allowed to take their places in the Lords, but the atmosphere there did not improve. The demand for revenge, or justice, continued unabated, coloured by much throwing down of hoods in challenge for personal combat. Even without Hall's testimony, many of our erstwhile friends were convinced that we had been party to royal murder.

'Nothing's happening,' Dickon reported on the third day, looking disappointed. 'There's a general thought that no one would have dared disobey Richard, but the blame for our uncle's murder is still being batted back and forth. We are to blame. Brother Edward is to blame. I fear they'll get him in the end.'

'What's the King saying?'

'That all must be done within the letter of the law. But it's my thought he might just go along with them to shut them up.'

Which was as mature and as jaundiced as I had ever heard him.

'But if he will cleave to the law, it is in our favour,' I remarked to Joan, even going as far as to hold her hands for she was in dire fear for her brother. 'All we did was follow royal commands. It was not treason. He cannot execute Edward for that.'

'But it was murder.' She clung to me for the briefest of moments, fretful. 'I pray that you are right.'

'Of course I am.'

*

'It's Hall. The Lords have found him guilty.'

Our hopes were devastated, Dickon the bearer of the worst news. My mouth was dry with it.

'But he was a mere witness, was he not?' Joan asked. 'And against his will, if he is to be believed.'

But I understood, and found no pleasure in telling Joan why it had been done. Hall was a commoner, involved in the death of a prince of royal blood. The King might hesitate before condemning the Dukes themselves, but this man had no birth or rank to protect him. Dickon confirmed my worst fears.

'He's condemned as a traitor and will be sent to Tyburn. He'll be hanged, drawn and quartered.'

Joan covered her face with her hands.

'Don't weep,' I said. 'If you must, pray that the thirst for blood will be quenched by the death of Hall.'

'At least if Surrey is condemned, it will be death by beheading,' Dickon said, lacking pity with the brutal callousness of youth. 'It won't be pleasant but at least an axe to the neck is quicker than a traitor's death at Tyburn on the end of a rope and the executioner's knife.'

'We can do without your observations.'

'But true.'

I opened the door and ushered him out.

It was all too true. It was horrifyingly true. Dickon might have a self-interest worthy of a Venetian merchant haggling over a bolt of Byzantine silk, but he had summed up our predicament perfectly. If Hall's confession was enough to send him to a traitor's death, what hope for us, as the perpetrators of that deed?

*

On Sunday, when there was no meeting of parliament, despite a layer of exhaustion covering us all we attended Mass in St Stephen's Chapel with all the sangfroid of a truly loyal family. Even John Holland, Duke of Exeter, put in an appearance with his wife Elizabeth, King Henry's own sister, bidding for familial support. We acknowledged all with nods and bows and an exchange of polite greeting, as they acknowledged us. We knelt and prayed. We gave our responses to the liturgy in firm voice, accepting the priest's blessing. Until the King had pronounced otherwise, we were still the descendants of King Edward the Third, royal blood demanding recognition. We were still innocent and owed our allegiance to Henry.

'There is no overt hostility here,' Joan murmured as the magnates I had known all my life bowed and acknowledged us in return.

'No one is inviting us to sup with them,' I remarked.

'Thank God,' Joan admitted. 'What would we talk about?'

'Also thank God, because some might consider adding belladonna to the wine.'

I thought they were all capering mummers, biding their time until the King's ultimate decision allowed them to fall on us with claw and fang to rend us to pieces.

'No one is effusive,' Thomas said, after exchanging a handful of words with the Earl of Warwick, one of the lords who had managed to come out of the affair of the Counter-Appellants with his life after two years of imprisonment. Warwick's unfathomable expression as he turned away was impossible to read. I inclined my head with dignified grace.

'You can hardly expect Warwick to fall into your lap, offering lifelong friendship. He was incarcerated in the Tower because of you, and you were the beneficiary when his estates and castles were handed out to his enemies.'

I wondered whose prayers God would listen to as Mass drew to its completion.

The King's greeting to us was brief but amiably enigmatic. Had he truly decided that the ties of Plantagenet blood were stronger than taints of treason?

'I don't trust him,' Thomas said, again in a sour aside.

'You don't trust anyone.'

Edward smiled and conversed with all, ever-confidant, ever-graceful, as if nothing were amiss.

Sunday moved on into Monday when Henry took his ceremonial bath, one week after his coronation, to wash away the remnants of the sacred oil which until then had remained greasily on his flesh. With no meeting of parliament there was not one whisper of treason or vengeance to strike terror in us. And we began to move a little more easily, to breathe a little more freely. We met for supper with, for the first time for days, some appetite to do justice to the cook's fried fig pasties, much loved by my father. There was amongst us, and we allowed it, the faintest sense of relief, which blossomed with the cups of wine with which we toasted our good fortune when the meal was at an end and the servants dispatched.

'I think we might have weathered the storm,' Thomas said, cup lifted. 'If Henry has not been convinced of our guilt by now I think we can safely assume that Hall's blood will be enough to satisfy Lords, Commons and King. Let us drink to our future under this new King, whether we like it or not.'

The toast was made with some laughter. Could we not now look forward?

No, I decided. We could not. Not yet.

'What of Richard?' I asked, since no one had seen the need to mention him. It was as if we had banished him to his imprisonment because that would be the easiest for us all.

'I would like to think that he can be rescued,' Surrey mused.

'I don't advise it,' Edward replied. 'I'll have no part in any foolhardy plan to fight our way into the Tower. I say we accept what we have been given. We are not condemned. Rumours and antagonisms will soon die a death when it's clear that Henry will give no substance to them. My part in my uncle's murder will be conveniently forgotten. All we have to do is to slide quietly into the new Court, to stand at Henry's right hand and give good counsel. Henry is no fool and knows what is needed to settle an unsettled country, when his claim to the throne is not accepted by all. To achieve that he must reward us, whatever the unpleasantness of the past.'

Which seemed to sum it all up perfectly, even if it condemned Richard to a permanent incarceration. He would be the one to pay the real price, I feared.

'Then let us hope that Henry continues to feel grateful to us,' I said. 'And that he continues to owe you a debt for caring for his lice-ridden hound. I hope that you will deliver it back to him now that the crisis is past.'

Edward laughed, jovial once more. 'Tomorrow, I promise. Not that it has more lice than the King, if rumour is true.'

Henry's ceremonial bathing had removed much hair and

a whole plague of lice, according to bright-eyed gossip. It pleased us in our victory to show little respect. My father, a flush of celebration along his cheekbones, confirmed what we all wished to believe:

'When the Lords and Commons meet again, this unfortunate matter will be closed. We will work for Richard's future comfort, of course we will, but we will give our allegiance to the House of Lancaster. Let us drink to our success, for King Henry and for the House of York.'

We raised our cups once more.

'Are you content?' I asked Thomas, seated beside me, as the evening drew to a close.

'How should I not be?' His expression was benign with the reassurance of the good food and wine. 'It is the best we could have hoped for. A few days of terror followed by years of royal appreciation. As for Richard . . .'

A tread of booted feet in the antechamber.

'That's probably Exeter, come to celebrate our good fortune,' Edward said.

But then we heard the issue of a brisk command. A solid knock on the door that brought us all to our feet, as if we were infused by the same presentiment of the future.

We were wrong.

How deliberately blind we had been, how desperately misled, to believe that our once wholehearted support for Richard, our supremacy at Court, our delight in wielding power, our unquestionable involvement in the punishment of the Lords Appellant, would go unpunished. Or that Henry of Lancaster would not ultimately feel a need to be revenged for the death of Thomas of Woodstock. His newly bathed feet set on the path to his new power, King Henry, impatient with parliament, irritable with the never-ending demands for punishment, took his own retribution.

We were the sacrifice on the altar of political necessity.

There we were, toasting the future, prepared to embrace a smooth transition into the new reign, yet all our hopes were already undermined. After the ritual bathing, Henry, cleansed and sanctified, had issued the order for this remarkably discreet escort to arrive at our door. And with the escort came the order for the arrest of the Counter-Appellants. For Aumale. For Surrey, and for Gloucester. For Joan's uncle, the Duke of Exeter. And for the Earl of Salisbury and even Henry's half-brother, John Beaufort, Marquis of Dorset.

'How fortunate to find three of our quarry here, all under the same roof,' Henry's Constable remarked with all the ease of royal authority on his shoulder. 'Only three more to collect. Exeter, Dorset and Salisbury.' His smile was thin-lipped. 'You are to remain incarcerated at the King's will. I hope you have dined well. I warrant there'll be no venison in fancy pepper sauces where you're going, my lords.'

No violence, no manhandling. No argument. No parting sentiments. We all recognised the inevitable. Had we not, in our hearts, expected it? My brother, my husband and Joan's brother were surrounded by their escort and ushered out.

Cold revenge or even colder justice, the result was the same.

Chapter Seven

Late October 1399: Palace of Westminster

I sank into a faultless obeisance. I had prepared my speech and must now deliver it as persuasively as I was able, without stirring Henry to further political retribution. My pride flinched, but there was no one else to do it. I had left Joan once more on her knees, trembling in horror. My father had not yet left his chamber.

'My lord . . .' I kept my head bowed.

I was given no opportunity to make my case.

'Stand up, Constance. I know what you want. You can say nothing that I do not already know.'

King Henry had his back to me and did not turn. I had not seen him since the coronation, since when his hair had been cropped short, giving weight to the rumour of an infestation of lice. At his feet sat the returned greyhound. I could not read his mood but the set of his shoulders and the timbre of his voice were not encouraging. I had been shown into one of his private chambers which was littered with books and documents, a prie-dieu in a corner with an open missal beside it. I had found myself hoping that Henry's prayers had moved him to reconsider. His greeting destroyed any such hope.

Anger was a hard knot in my throat but I would not be deflected. There was only one reason for my being here in the royal apartments. Who would plead for mercy, if I did not? I had chosen formality rather than cousinly warmth, my over-gown enclosed to the throat and severely undecorated. My veiling was almost nun-like, more worthy of Joan's choice of all-confining crispinette, as I continued smoothly, despite the uneven thump of my heart.

'I know that you have many demands on your time, my lord. But I would ask, I would *beg*, on your mercy . . .'

'I have no mercy.'

At last he turned, casting aside the document he had been perusing, and I inhaled at what I read in his eyes. They were uncompromising, bleakly unemotional. Henry was now King of England and had my life in the palm of his hand. I must remember that. I could not afford flippancy or levity, or even casual assumption. He might be my cousin but his power over my life had become supreme at the precise moment that the holy oil touched his brow.

'It is my duty to ask, my lord.'

'We'll dispense with duty on this occasion, Constance.'

He was short on patience. Well, of course he would be. The whole question of Richard's future was hanging over him. Now that the Counter-Appellants had been swept away into incarceration, quite probably to await their execution, the Commons were vociferous in demanding that our late King be brought before them, to be given a trial of sorts. Henry did not agree, for this would be to hand the future of Richard over to others. If I knew anything of this man it was that he would keep Richard's person securely under his own dominion. He would grant Lords and Commons as little power as he could.

Once more on my feet, folding my hands lightly at my waist over my girdle, I selected the man most effectively damned by the evidence. If Henry would listen, there was hope for the rest of them.

'But my lord, surely my brother does not deserve imprisonment.'

'Your brother is accused of being – what was that incomparable phrase used by Lord Fitzwalter?'

I knew it, as well as he.

'Midwife to the murder of our uncle Thomas of Woodstock, my lord,' I said.

'I am surprised that you would remind me of it. It is damning.'

'My brother of Aumale denies his involvement, my lord.'

'Of course he does. He was rewarded for his foul deed with the title of Aumale and more land than is fit for one man to hold. I suppose you will say the same for your Despenser husband. That he was entirely ignorant of the murder as well. When he conveniently became Earl of Gloucester.'

'No, my lord.'

'No? So he would accept his guilt?'

Henry's attention was sliding back towards the rejected document. I used the argument that I had used before because it was the only one that held some credence.

'No to that, too, my lord. They would all reject their guilt, but how could they deny knowledge of it? They knew of the plan to remove our royal uncle. King Richard desired it. We were merely the tools that were used to accomplish it. It was dangerous to disobey King Richard. As you yourself discovered.'

I acknowledged that I sounded disgracefully glib. And so thought Henry.

'You are as crafty-cunning as ever, Constance. And dressed for repentance. Seemly as a nun. From whom did you borrow that gown?' But there was no amusement there.

'Merely well informed, my lord.' I disliked his malice. 'Disobedience led to your banishment from England and the confiscation of your inheritance. Any man who dared to defy Richard suffered the consequence.'

An argument he would be unable to deny.

'Be that as it may,' – his features had set in granite, knowing that I had hit the truth – 'I trust neither your brother nor your husband. Nor any of the Counter-Appellants, if truth be told.'

'They bear you no ill will,' I said, fighting what I hoped would be a good rearguard action. 'They supported you in your coup against Richard.'

'Only when the future became self-evident. They were all hand in glove with Richard, until they saw his cause was lost, when they decided to exchange his gauntlet for mine.'

There was no moving him, but at least I had his attention again.

'They have sworn to be loyal to you, my lord.'

I hoped that he could not hear the growing despair that thundered in my head.

'Of course they have. They had little choice.' He raised his hand in a sharp gesture of denial. 'I'm in no mood to listen to platitudes. Murderers they might not be, though I'd not argue so thin a line. Evil counsellors they most certainly were. I'm in no mind to treat them with any generosity. Imprisonment will provide the Counter-Appellants with the opportunity to search their souls.' His mouth twisted in what was not a smile.

'Will my father too suffer the same fate?'

His chin was tilted as he considered. 'Perhaps not. I have a debt of true gratitude to the Duke of York. His conciliation at Bristol was beyond price to me. He could have stood against me but saw the right of my claims. It will please me to recognise that debt.'

'Thank you, my lord.'

At least there would be some good news to carry to Joan, although Surrey and Exeter remained prisoners somewhere. She had wanted to accompany me, abandoning her prayers, but I had refused. I did not think we would gain anything by her weeping on the King's shoulder. But perhaps I had been wrong. Female tears might have won the day. My reasoned arguments were having no effect.

'I would still ask for clemency, my lord.' I could not let it go. I must not. Holding out my hands, palms up, I adopted a sorrowful expression, even though the requisite tears were beyond my summoning. 'You had John Hall disembowelled as a traitor at Tyburn. Is that not enough?'

'Enough? No, it is not enough.' The spark of anger in the royal eye exploded into blistering heat of rage. I had not expected it, nor could I truly understand it. 'I can do the same with the rest of the rabble, common or noble, traitors all. Go away, Constance. Look to your own household.'

'My family deserve your thanks, not your condemnation,' I persisted, my recognition of his royal status disintegrating. Yet still I worked to preserve a persuasive mien. Probably as a capon cheeps on seeing the axe in the cook's fist.

'Do you say? The whole lot of them would sell their souls to the Devil for office and status.'

'And you would not?'

'I would not. God's Blood! You were always confrontational, Constance.'

'Why not? When your family are in danger, you fight for their lives.' He was no longer my King but my cousin. 'Will you listen to the bloodthirsty, self-seeking Lords with their rabid accusations, who would happily sweep us all away?'

'Who I'll listen to is not your business. I'll discuss it no more.'

'Because you know you are wrong. My menfolk will be loyal if you will give them cause.' I fought a last-ditch stand. 'They are audacious men, and audacity can be dangerous, but they are gifted both on and off the battlefield. They will use those gifts for you.' I ignored Henry's jaundiced expression, concentrating on my eloquence. 'I know you have the allegiance of your Beaufort brothers and the Percys, but Plantagenet blood is stronger than you know, and a wise man would not consider casting aside such skill. What will you need for the future? Diplomats, administrators, leaders in battle. You can't afford to lose such an array of talent as we can provide.'

'I can't afford to place these apparently gifted men in positions of authority. I don't trust them. I don't trust you.' Unmoved, Henry drew a breath. 'You have said enough, Constance. Go back to your father.'

I had pushed him beyond tolerance. I had failed. I curtsied and turned to go, my spirits tumbling into the depths of hell.

'Or even better, cousin . . .'

The King's voice, softer now, stopped me. It might be soft

but there was mischief in the slippery cadences when he strode past me to the door, opened it, and raised his voice to summon some distant minion.

'Even better, I'll have you escorted to the Tower. You can spend some time there with your husband. Whatever it was that Despenser was involved in, I cannot believe that you were ignorant of it. How fortunate that you came here, Constance. An opportunity I would be unwise to ignore. A neat matter of two Despenser birds in one secure cage.'

My respect for him as my King died an instant death and my spirits revived. 'You would not!'

'Oh, but I would.'

'I am innocent of all charges. No charges have ever been brought against me.'

'So you say, but do I believe you? You can discuss your past sins and examine your souls together.' And when I opened my mouth to deny the need: 'What's more, if your younger brother was of an age to have been involved in the ignominy of our uncle's death, I'd send him too. You are all as devious as a basket of ferrets.'

'Unfair, Henry!'

'And it would be unwise of you to forget that I am your King.'

'How could I forget!'

The minion had arrived, one of Henry's household.

'Robert. Arrange for me if you will the escort of the Countess of Gloucester,' – the curl of his lips disparaged the title that we had achieved from Richard on the death of his royal uncle – 'to the Tower.' He returned to the table, where he scribbled a note and signed it with a flourish and his seal pressed into a gout of soft wax. 'Give this to the Constable. The Countess is to be lodged with her husband. At my pleasure.'

'Yes, my lord.'

'And Robert . . .'

'Yes, my lord?'

'Lady Despenser has a persuasive tongue. Do not listen to it.'

'No, my lord.'

I could not believe what I had just heard.

'How long will you keep me there?' I demanded.

'As long as it pleases me. Until I see fit to release you. Or not. Good day to you, Constance. You may inform Thomas Despenser that I am considering his future. At this moment it looks bleak. I might even gain pleasure from being certain that he will enjoy your company far less than I have just done. It will add to his discomfort.'

Good sense fled. 'You know well how to turn friends into enemies, my lord.'

'Perhaps. But I do not know as yet that I can count you and your family as my friends.'

'They are your family, too.'

'Will that stop them seeking my blood? I think not. After all, who is closer to me in blood than Richard? He would gladly have enforced my permanent banishment from England. There is no love lost there.'

He turned his back on me, returning to the document, stooping to run his hand over the greyhound's head.

It seemed to me that Richard's royal barge was a fitting conveyance, all crimson velvet and gilding and sumptuous cushions, as I was escorted by river by the minion who finally handed me from barge to quay. When I had last been here, I had known that I would depart within a matter of hours. Now my stay was limitless, my freedom curtailed in this formidable bulk that housed both Richard and my husband Thomas. I must make of it what I could. No one would know that beneath my cloak I was shivering with fear. The tide had been running against us, which smacked of an unpleasant omen.

I turned my eye on my escort. In fact he was no minion, but Sir Robert Waterton, a trusted friend of the King who, with Thomas Swynford, had been given the care of Richard. He was a close ally who had helped bring Henry to the throne, an important man in Henry's household. On dry land, with the most winning smile I could muster, I did not hesitate in sending him about my bidding. I might be his prisoner, but I was still royal.

'Tell my household at Westminster that I wish my women to bring what I will need for a short stay.'

'Yes, my lady.'

'And I wish for books.'

'I will tell them of your needs, my lady, and that your stay is at the will of the King. Short or long.'

Unfortunately true. I could not afford to antagonise him as my future comfort might be dependent on his good offices.

'The King will soon see the value of our release, Sir Robert.'

'Yes, my lady. Everything is possible. It will be my duty to make your stay a comfortable one.'

I nodded briskly and followed him. After the events of the previous weeks I was no longer sure. Now I too had joined the prisoners; once I would have laughed at the unbelievable foolishness of it all. Now I dare not. The future was a dark vista with nothing clear to be discerned.

'Where is my lord Richard?' I asked, looking up at the solid stone that dwarfed all who stood within its shadow. Was he in the same chamber where I had visited him? I could not imagine how he would spend the long hours alone, a man who revelled in company, flattery, laughter.

'My lord Richard's whereabouts are not your concern, my lady.'

Which put me in my place. Sir Robert bowed and left me to the hands of the Constable of the Tower.

Royal palace. Royal prison. For all of us.

I could not stop the shivering.

I was escorted into the White Tower. A door was opened into what were royal apartments and I was bidden to enter. There, supine on the bed at the far side of the chamber against the wall, lounged my husband, fingers linked behind his head, ankles crossed.

'Constance?' He pushed himself slowly to a sitting position as his foot swung round to the floor, a frown descending with a rapidity I recognised. 'Why are you here? Have you brought me a change of garments?' His eyes flickered to note my lack of baggage. 'No, of course you have not . . .'

His self-interest was a thing to marvel at. I had had enough of opinionated men for that day.

'No, I have not. If you want a change of clothes, send a servant. And don't disturb yourself.' He had not actually managed to stand up to acknowledge my arrival. 'It will delight you to know that I have come to stay.'

The door was already closed at my back. I heard the key turn in the lock.

The line between his brows had deepened. 'I thought you would plead for my release.'

'I tried.'

The frown had become a scowl, although he stood, but not to help me remove my cloak. 'Not hard enough, it seems.'

He had no idea of how I had fought for his freedom, nor would I tell him. He would give me no praise for it, even if I had need of it. This was going to be a long and unpleasant sojourn together.

'Our new King was not prepared to listen to any arguments I might make. He considers me as guilt-ridden as the rest of you. We await his mercy or condemnation. It seems that we are destined to await it together.'

A bark of disbelieving laughter.

'He sent you here to stay?'

'Unfortunately, yes.'

My shivering had stopped. I swung the cloak from my shoulders and cast it onto a settle beside the door as again he laughed, the harshness deliberately cruel.

'Did he know that it would enhance my penalty, to spend my incarceration with my sharp-tongued wife?'

'I expect that he did.' I lifted my hands, palms raised in some degree of supplication. We must make the best of this. 'As you see, I am here. It is no better for me than it is for you.'

The thought of spending endless days with Thomas in these confined quarters appalled me. He had been here barely two days and was already harsh-featured with impatience. I hoped my household would send sufficient books to while away my time.

'Where is Edward?' Thomas demanded.

'Incarcerated at Windsor.'

'And Surrey?'

'I think he is somewhere here in the Tower. And Exeter too.'

'To Hell with Surrey and Exeter. It's your brother that worries me. He could be our downfall. He's in it up to his neck. If he confesses, he might implicate us all.'

'He could also be our saviour.'

'He could also buy his own release by incriminating the rest of us with evidence of our complicity. I wouldn't put it past him.'

'He could. I doubt he would deliberately send me to the gallows.'

I surveyed the room where I was destined to spend who knew how many days or weeks, then walked through the doorway to the chamber beyond. Our quarters were comfortable enough, well furnished with stools and coffers. They were also spacious enough with windows which although narrow let in sufficient light. Here was no prison cell or dungeon to force us into despair or even confession. The bed on which Thomas had been – and was still – lounging had a fine mattress as I discovered when I pressed down on it to test it, running my hands over the coverlet and hangings, all well stitched, well matched and in fine condition. There was a fireplace with logs laid against a cold night. An abundance of candles was comforting, as was a platter of food that had been left for us, a flagon of ale or wine and expensively chased cups. I ran my finger along the edge of a carved settle. It had been cleaned recently; there was no dust. It could be worse. Our imprisonment was not intended to humiliate us.

Except for the lock on the door and the key that was in the possession of our gaoler.

'We must believe that Henry will listen to whatever apology

Edward makes. All we have to do is remain silent and allow Edward to make amends for all our past sins. He has a belief in his own immortality and in his ability to charm any creature to his hand. He's the only one of us who can coax the Lords to soften their demands.'

To my mind, he was the only hope we had. Henry would not listen to me, and a glowering Thomas would do more harm than good.

'Well, he's pretty much failed so far.'

'Are you going to pour me a cup of wine?' I asked, seating myself on the edge of the bed that he had just vacated, spreading my skirts around me.

'Pour it yourself.'

I allowed my brows to rise, upon which he poured me a cup but without any noticeable grace. By now I was in no mood to be gentle.

'Be honest with me, Thomas. Were you involved in the business of my uncle's death?'

He was watching me over the rim of his own cup. 'Why? Would you despise me more if I was up to my wrists in his blood?'

'No, I could not dislike you more than I do at this moment.' I chose my next accusation with great deliberation. Not that his reply would make any difference. 'Tell me this. Were you also involved in the death of my uncle's son, Humphrey, in Ireland?'

His hand froze with the cup halfway to his lips.

'Who says that?'

'It is talked of. Did you think I would not hear? On his father's death, the boy would claim the title of Gloucester that was given to you. You might be encouraged to get rid of him.'

My cousin Humphrey, heir to my murdered uncle, had been taken to Ireland in Richard's household as a royal ward, but then had mysteriously died on his way home.

'And you believe that I did? That I would have a child killed?'

I gave an elegant little shrug. 'I only ask because that is what will be asked of *you*, if the King decides to send you to trial. And if you admit that you were involved in the sad demise of poor Humphrey, we are both dead, for who would believe that I was innocent?'

And, I decided, it did matter. This would have been a very personal and vindictive attack on a defenceless boy.

Thomas's shrug was less elegant than mine, his expression sour. 'I was involved as much as we all were. And we both benefitted. You are a Countess as a result.'

'I'd rather not be a dead one.' I sighed, suddenly weary of half-truths and evasions after a morning of failure. Faced with the locked door and the prospect of long imprisonment, despair came swiftly and I struggled to make amends.

'If we are to spend time together, you might try for a more equable mood,' I suggested.

For a moment he merely stood, deep in thought, before he came to sit beside me on the bed, taking my hands in his and his mouth curved in what might have been interpreted as affection if I did not know him better. 'What do you suggest that we do now, dearest wife?'

'Just hope that Edward is careful with his confessions.'

For that little seed of doubt had been effectively planted; Thomas's reading of Edward's character was not without strength. Would Edward throw us all to the ravening wolves in exchange for his own release? Edward with an eye to all possibilities and an ability to grasp any opportunity for his own benefit. I had seen it happen. When Queen Anne had died, and Richard cast into deep melancholy at the loss of his wife, who had come out of it with rewards beyond belief? Edward had become one of the three feoffees of her estates, administering them together with the Archbishop of York and the Bishop of Salisbury. At the tender age of twenty-one years, the extent of patronage that had fallen into his hands through this lucrative office had been remarkable. Edward always fell on his feet.

Pray God that he would not bargain again, at my expense.

Meanwhile Thomas had released me, left me, to hammer on the door.

'What are you doing?'

'If we are to be here for any length of time, I need clothes. And shoes.'

As I looked at the garment he was wearing, one of his Court houppelandes, pleated into a gilded belt, the elongated over-sleeves almost brushing the floor, his capacity for the frivolous never failed to astonish me. He issued orders for his garments to be brought from Westminster, for new shoes and hose. Money changed hands.

'I like your priorities, Thomas.' He cocked his chin. 'Here we are in fear of our lives and you send a servant to buy you new linen and hose and shoes.'

'I may yet need to impress Henry.'

'The shoes will certainly do it.'

'They might very well. And now that's done. . .'

Thomas was in strangely celebratory mood, my accusations momentarily forgotten as he returned to join me on the bed, removing my veil before pushing my skirts aside with well-practised efficiency but no finesse.

Silently I sighed. It would prove to be a long imprisonment.

I was fortunate in that his satisfaction was swift, greedily fuelled by nothing more than male lust that was effective but brief. Through long practice I tolerated his attentions, complying with every demand. I had learned well the lesson of submission within marriage. Love? I knew not what it was. I had never taken a lover. I had never met a man who aroused even the smallest spark of desire in my cold heart. Moreover I had never regretted the lack of so uneasy an emotion. Was it love that had drawn my mother into that disastrous liaison with John Holland? Or had it been mere lust, since she had been quick to cast him off when her desires had waned? Isabella was no example for me to follow. Love made a woman weak and vulnerable, and I would do well enough without it.

Thomas's celebratory mood was short-lived. It became a time of a permanently underlying fear, of an apprehension that never abated. Eventually a time of terror that made my stomach roil with nausea. The days passed in which, every morning, Thomas was summoned to be questioned before parliament, and returned every evening, each time more dour than the last despite his new garments and shoes. He might make a flamboyant, confident display but no one was prepared to release us on the strength of it. The key clicked in the lock with a terrible certainty.

'Same questions, same answers,' he grumbled. 'We circle around like carrion over a rotting carcase.'

I gave up asking, except for: 'Have you seen Edward? What about Surrey or Exeter?'

'I have seen none of them. We are questioned alone. So that we do not collaborate in our answers.'

'What do you think?' In the end I had to ask.

'What should I think? How would I know what's in Henry's head? If it's up to the Lords, we're dead men. I can already see them sharpening their knives.' He scowled down at his hose that were covered with dust from his journey from the Tower to Westminster. 'They are talking about what to do with Richard. They still hope to put him on trial too.'

The horror increased.

'Will Henry allow it?'

'He's too busy receiving ambassadors from the French Court. As a usurper, he has to make a good impression at regal fitness. I hear they are feasting nightly.' He eyed the meagre offering brought to us on a platter, selecting an unrecognisable piece of seared flesh and biting into it, explaining as he chewed, while I moved the platter to cover the worst of the stains. What should have been a fair cloth had not been changed for some days.

'He might let the Lords have their way. I think they want the accusations against Richard to be made known so that when they condemn him to death there will be no backlash against them. They are saying that he had planned to sell Calais back to the French. Which is sure to stir up London against Richard.'

'I've heard nothing of that. Is that true?'

Thomas licked his fingers and flung himself down beside me, in a mood to be eloquent. 'I don't know. From the gossip, Surrey's case is not looking good. It is said that Richard had intended to make him King of Ireland. It's possible. The Lords resent it.'

I let my thoughts run on, despairingly, eventually speaking them aloud.

'They're intent on finding any and every bit of evidence they can against us. It doesn't look good for any of us.'

'While Henry is being righteous,' Thomas admitted, 'and has decided that God is on his side.'

I feared he was right.

I read and reread the books that had been sent. I had no appetite for the romance or the courage of King Arthur's knights. They could not keep my mind from our fate. I thought that my father might be allowed to visit, out of compassion, but he did not. Henry was not open to compassion.

One night, on a Monday as I recall, when I was lying sleepless, I was disturbed by more than the usual night-bound noises of this great fortress. Drawn to the window by a coming and going below, I strained to look down into the courtyard.

In a moment Thomas was at my shoulder, struggling into a tunic to cover his naked flesh, grimacing at the chill of the room. He was as sleepless as I.

'What is it?' he asked.

'Impossible to see. But look . . .'

Figures came into view below. There was enough moonlight. Then there were lanterns, brought to illuminate a small escort. No horses. No carriage.

'It is someone who will travel by water,' I whispered, as if I too was drawn into the conspiracy. 'Someone who needs to travel with a degree of secrecy.'

'Richard?'

'Would they take him elsewhere to his death?' I asked, knowing that there was no possible reply. 'If that is what Henry wants, why not send him to Tower Hill, as Richard sent Arundel?'

'Or he could simply be tipped into the river and his body lost until washed up somewhere beyond Greenwich. It might solve Henry's problem for good.'

The escort with its lanterns moved out of our sight. Who might be in its midst we had no means of knowing, or of what his fate might be.

That same day, with dawn breaking, a note was pushed beneath our door.

'Dickon,' I said, recognising the writing which always surprised me in its neatness. 'He has bribed someone to deliver this. His capacity to be resourceful astonishes me.'

But the fact that he had gone to the trouble to do so made my heart plummet.

It was short.

A letter has been received by the King. The source of it I do not know. It threatens insurrection throughout England if he does not immediately give the order to execute the Counter-Appellant Lords responsible for the death of Thomas of Woodstock.

What he will do is still uncertain.

I thought you should be warned.

Terror throbbed between our four walls like a new wound, although neither of us spoke of it through a night that brought us no rest.

Chapter Eight

Thomas was collected by his glum escort.

'You will not be returning to the Tower, my lord.'

In the light of Dickon's warning, Thomas and I exchanged a glance, for once robbed of any ill humour. For the sake of peace with his parliament, Henry might well be busily signing death warrants. Thomas said nothing, merely donning chaperon and gloves, but his face was ashen and he had given no thought to the effect his garments might make on the beholder.

'Where do I go?' I asked. 'What is expected of me?' If Thomas was not returning, what provision had been made for my future?

'We are instructed to take you to the Duke of York's chambers at Westminster, my lady. If you will make ready . . .'

No, I did not want that. I would not be shuffled away while judgement was given.

'I will keep company with my husband.'

'To what purpose? Do what they tell you,' Thomas advised. 'This is no time for you to be interfering.'

'To sit in yet another chamber while events unfold that will have a bearing on my whole life? I will not. I will be there when Henry commits himself. The outcome involves me as much as you. I'll not sit with Joan and her stitching while you are all condemned.'

I watched the Constable consider this blatant disobedience, but then decide it did not greatly matter where I was, which merely built the fear of what might await us. Thus we were escorted, once again by the crimson-and-gold-cushioned barge, from the Tower to the Great Hall at Westminster. Thomas was led in. I was indicated to stand within the door, from where I could see the full complement of the Lords as well as the accused who had been brought forward to hear their fate. Their backs were turned to me, but I knew every one of them. Aumale and Gloucester. Exeter and Surrey. Salisbury and Dorset.

They had all had the political acumen to be wearing the Lancaster collars, glittering like a chest of New Year's ornamentations, so much so that I was stirred by an absurd desire to laugh at such deliberate outward show. And there was my father, seated with his peers, equally girded by heraldic chains. His head turned as we entered, his eyes meeting mine down the length of the hall. My fear was his fear. We would not escape this unpunished. All thought of laughter obliterated, I turned away, unable to tolerate his anguish as his beloved heir stood to accept his fate.

Light and shadow enhanced the occasion, moving and shifting so that the floor was criss-crossed like bars in a prison cell. This was Henry's space, no longer Richard's. The vast chamber with the eyes of the stone kings of the past looking down on us waited in a silence of expectancy. How long would it take to denounce them all and proclaim a sentence of death? Would I die, too?

At last Henry arrived to a rustle and murmur amongst the ranks of the Lords, to take his place on the throne, magisterially garbed in blue damask and ermine, a fine gold circlet enhancing his brow. My throat was dry, my nails hard-pressed into my palms as Henry then stood and proclaimed in a voice that could carry the length and breadth of a battlefield. Would it be life or death?

'After much deliberation and questioning of the accused, parliament has asked that the decision over the fate of the evil counsellors who brought Richard of Bordeaux to his knees be given into my own royal jurisdiction. I have agreed. The decision has been made.' Henry allowed his regard to move over the assembled ranks, over the accused, even resting momentarily on me, perhaps with a degree of surprise. Then he gave the nod to Chief Justice Thirning. 'If you would deliver my judgement, sir.'

The Chief Justice rose to his feet, cleared his throat, lifting the sheet of parchment although I could swear that he did not need it. He paused, surveying his audience. He would know exactly the wording of Henry's decision.

How hard it was to remain impassive. There was Aumale, Surrey, Exeter. My husband of Gloucester. The Montagu Earl of Salisbury and the King's half-brother John Beaufort, Marquis of Dorset. All men of rank and previous power. Would the King truly give his consent to the death of his cousins and his own half-brother? I could read nothing in his expression. If he weighed the death of these Counter-Appellants against parliament's warning of a looming civil war, he might just make the harshest of decisions.

As Chief Justice Thirning cleared his throat yet again, as

if the words gave him difficulty, there was a cold fist of dread lodged below my girdle.

And he spoke.

'My lords. My lord the King in his mercy, out of the love he would bear to you and the trust he hopes he might yet instil in you, has agreed to grant you pardon for your past offences and spare your lives.'

I breathed out slowly, trying to absorb what I had just heard.

So it would not be death. In spite of their undoubted conniving in the untimely death of Thomas of Woodstock, it would not be death for them. But would it be imprisonment for the duration of their lives? Banishment, as Henry had suffered banishment? There must be a limit to the royal magnanimity. And another thought, entirely selfish. Surely he would not commit me to a life of incarceration with Thomas. We would be at each other's throats before the first month was out. I could barely swallow at the prospect.

The Chief Justice once again addressed the accused.

'Your lives are spared at the mercy of the King. But there must be a penalty for your association with such crimes. The titles that were accrued by you since September of the year 1397, when the false judgements were made against the Lords Appellant, which resulted in the death and unfair punishment of noble subjects – these titles will be stripped from you. The lands and estates and positions which you acquired will no longer be yours to enjoy. You will not benefit from the counsel that you gave to the man who was then King.'

So the dukedoms were gone. Aumale and Surrey and Exeter would revert to being Earls of Rutland and Kent and Huntingdon. Thomas's earldom was stripped away and he would once more be Lord Despenser. Henry's brother was reduced to Earl of Somerset.

It could be worse. It could be much worse. But were we to be imprisoned?

The Chief Justice continued over the murmur that swept the Hall:

'My lord the King has decided that this will be punishment enough, that any unwise involvement in the death of Thomas of Woodstock was carried out at the behest of Richard of Bordeaux, whom you were right to fear.'

Still we did not know. Since it was not to be death, would it be banishment? Henry knew all there was to know about the misery of banishment, loss of family and home. Loss of status, reduced to eking out a living on the tournament field in a foreign land.

Chief Justice Thirning took a breath.

'My lord the King has in his mercy decided that you are now free to go. That will be the end of the matter. There will be no more recriminations. It is the King's will that the country settle into peace and prosperity for the good of all. His pardon is absolute.'

A silence hung over the Hall. Then the murmur of comment began again, to grow into a wash of sound. As the accused gripped hands, relief clear on each face, I felt the fear drain away, leaving me strangely empty after the days of high emotion. Whereas I might have been swamped by a mood for rejoicing, I felt nothing at all. Living with terror for so many days had left me unable to accept its final obliteration.

And here was another concern as I surveyed the assembly. What would be the reaction of the Lords who had wanted

Edward's death? I could not divine from the voices in the Hall. They had given the judgement over into Henry's hands, and he had made it. No mention had been made of Richard's fate or his present domicile.

Briefly I closed my eyes, wishing I could block my ears from the layers of resentment and jubilation that built around me, grasping at what had been made plain. We were free. No execution. No incarceration. But we had suffered significant demotion and loss of influence. We were no longer trusted counsellors.

When I opened my eyes, they were drawn to Henry's face, stern and implacable. We had been punished and pardoned, but it had been done out of cold necessity. As family we had been rejected.

What was there now for York, for Holland and Despenser?

'So he has been merciful. Should we be thankful?' Thomas was demanding, his voice recklessly loud, as I forced my way through the crowd towards him.

Should we not have been full of breathless gratitude that the King had deflected the vengeance of the Lords? There was neither relief nor gratitude in Thomas, who was using his breath most unwisely.

'He has stripped us naked, by God!'

The King had retired, the Hall begun to empty, and we had gravitated towards one end, because after the tensions of the hour, of all the hours imprisoned, it seemed to be the only thing to do, to join together as a family and take stock of the past tumultuous days. All demoted, except for my father who was leaning on Edward's arm. We stood close at the feet of Edward the Third, his stone eyes focused on some scene beyond our heads. No one else joined us, to wish us well. There were few who would have agreed with Henry's decision. They would not defy him, but on this day of justice they were still too raw to welcome us back into the fold. We were given a wide birth.

'I think you should be more circumspect,' Exeter said. Huntingdon, I reminded myself. It was still impossible to think of them reduced to their previous titles. 'I think we all should. You are not dead. You are not in chains. And it does no good to announce your dissatisfaction quite so loudly. Most would consider all of us fortunate indeed.'

'No good? We have lost our power. We have lost our titles.' Thomas made no attempt at discretion. 'The powers that Richard invested in us have been snatched by greedy hands. The lands we worked hard for are declared confiscate by this King. Do I show him gratitude?'

'Yes.' Tom Holland, once more Earl of Kent, was equally lacking in compassion. 'The fact that you have breath to make your complaint. Is that not worth a single drop of gratitude?'

'I think we should all acknowledge that this is neither the time nor the place to shout our refusal to accept the judgement . . .' There was a glint of warning in Huntingdon's tone, which Thomas ignored.

'Well, I am not—'

'Take care!' Huntingdon repeated, a hand on Thomas's arm.

Thomas snatched his arm away.

And I? I said not a word. I made no gesture. This was not my métier, and I knew it, having already been the recipient of critical glances. I should not be here. Moreover the voice of a woman in this impromptu conference would not be acceptable even though I might have added my words to the warnings. Their pride had been attacked; their status, their rank as royal counsellors. Even their manhood as leaders of the realm. The threat on their lives had been all too real, and I suspected it would take many days of careful handling to subside. For once, sensitive to this male enclave, I remained an onlooker, on the periphery.

'Keep your mouth shut!' Huntingdon's voice echoed over the general chatter of the departing Lords.

'I'm not beholden to you!' Thomas equally pugnacious.

The air might have become more vitriolic, except that Edward stirred himself from some deep thought. 'It is realistic to look ahead, Thomas. If you are so steeped in rage at your perceived mistreatment you will achieve nothing. If we continue to plot our own campaign, which we have always done, we will see that what has been lost can be regained. But we must be guarded. And vigilant.'

Thomas's expression was an essay in scorn. 'So we retire to the estates left to us?'

'No. What would be the sense in that? We remain at Court. This is where the power lies.'

'And do what? Dance to Lancaster's piping?'

The words leaped into my mind. *You are indeed a fool, Thomas. What choice do we have?* But I did not speak them.

Edward's smile was without humour, picking up my thoughts as he could often do. 'If we have to, then we do it. You are the fool, Thomas. Have you no vision? All is not lost. Not by any means, as any clever man will know.'

'Are you saying that I have not the wit to see what has been done?'

'If you wish to read it that way. You are making no sense.'

'And you are?'

'More than you.'

Edward's smile took on a faint mockery. Thomas glared, making me grateful that they were not wearing weapons. There had been enough challenges over the past days. Edward could usually be relied upon to be equable, but not today, and Thomas was beyond reason.

'I'll not take criticism from you, man . . .'

Thomas turned to walk away, but Edward seized his arm.

'Hush. Be careful what you say.'

We should have been celebrating our freedom, but the atmosphere had a strange anticipation in it, as if we were on the battlefield, awaiting the signal to charge the enemy. As if the final conflict still awaited us. As if Henry's decisions had not been the end of this particular game but merely giving the office to begin some future conflict. Looking over my shoulder I saw the expressions of those who still remained and could not help but overhear. We were standing in a hostile presence, despite Henry's judgement.

'I'll not hush; I'll not be chivvied like a woman! The title of Gloucester should be mine! I am descended from the great Earl, Gilbert de Clare.'

The loss of his title of Gloucester had hit Thomas harder than I had expected. His de Clare ancestor, now dead more than a hundred years, had been Earl of Gloucester. For Thomas, the title's restoration to him by Richard on Thomas of Woodstock's death had been a matter of pride. It was a shame that he had more pride than intellect.

I saw Edward's knuckles whiten as he gripped harder, even

as Thomas jerked his arm for release, but it was my father who replied. 'That is old history. The title of Gloucester when held by de Clare died out without male heirs. It was recreated for my brother. It would be wise of you not to open up the death of my brother, or my brother's heir in Ireland.'

Thomas had denied his involvement to me. He would do so again whatever his guilt, his mouth stretched in denial, but then he huffed out a breath as one of the royal Pursuivants of Arms, Bluemantle, approached, formal and magnificent in blue tabard and staff of office. With a bow he handed over four scrolls, to Edward, to Thomas and to Kent and Huntingdon. They were the same, all replicas bearing the royal seal.

'My lords, here are the wishes of my lord the King.'

Thomas snatched his open, tearing it, the red wax of the seal scattering in pieces which clung to his sleeve. Edward unrolled his with precision. Kent turned away to peruse his in silence, while Huntingdon eyed his with cynical contemplation. So what was it now? I almost asked. Henry had said there would be no further punishment.

Edward re-rolled the scroll, thrusting it roughly into the engraved and gilded panels of his belt. Now his smile was one of genuine amusement.

'Perfect. Did I not say that we would make good our losses on this day?'

And at last, seeing my frustration, Edward took pity, although the mockery was still a haze over his comment.

'And here is Constance, more silent than I have ever known her, all but dying of curiosity. We are appointed – all four of us, I imagine – to meet as members of the King's Royal Council, called for tomorrow. Did I not say? We are no longer ostracised. This is the first rung of the new ladder of our climb to power.'

Kent was uncertain. 'He's more short of friends than I could have believed, if he chooses to have us in his Council.'

'But he is short of friends. How many capable men are there whom he can trust to take hold of the administration or lead men into battle?' Edward's eyes were alight. 'We are proven in government and on the battlefield. Henry can't afford not to have our loyalty. This is his first attempt to win it. You don't have to like it, just take it and enjoy the power when it comes to your hand. My advice for those of you who wish it – let us swallow our principles and our pride and bow to the new monarch. We took our oaths of loyalty to him at the coronation. He will never see more loyal supporters of the Lancastrian crown.'

Looking at the faces around me, the truth was there for me to read: my father believing that all would be well, Edward smilingly serene. What underlying plots were fomenting in that clever brain? Kent resigned, perhaps hopeful. Huntingdon sardonically in agreement. And Thomas. Of them all, he was restless, discontented, unconvinced, his pride humiliated. I thought he would never accept. It would make him an uncomfortable ally, and unpredictable.

'I'll attend his damned Council,' he said. 'I'll make the gesture. But not yet.' The scroll was crumpled in his fist. 'It sticks in my craw. I'll not stay. I'm going to my lands in Glamorgan.'

He marched towards the door. Then stopped, looking back, for the first time addressing me.

'Are you coming? I'll not wait for you.'

And I made to follow. I knew better than to create dissent

in public. But Edward stepped in my way, voice lowered, head bent towards my ear.

'I would like you to do something for me.'

'If I can.'

'Get your irascible husband to return to Court. Or even stop him from leaving it in the first place.'

'I doubt I can do either.' I looked up at him, wondering why the urgency. 'Why would it matter where he is?'

'As I said. This is where all will be worked out for the future.'

There was a familiar gleam in his eye.

'So you have a plan.'

'I might.'

'You have to give me more to stir Thomas to action.'

'I don't think I will yet. But it may interest you to know that Richard is safe and well in Pontefract Castle.'

So that was where he had been taken, to the great Lancaster fortress in the north.

I felt a frown hovering. 'From which he can hardly be rescued.'

'Who's to say? Come back to London as soon as Despenser has licked his wounds.' And then a final comment. 'Don't say a word of this to him. Let him think it is his own decision. If I do have any plan – if I do – I don't want Despenser to be aware of it.'

'Don't you trust him?' I asked.

'Do you?'

I could make Edward no promises. One image remained with me as I followed Thomas through the Great Hall.

On the one side as I left, there were my father, brother and the Hollands, already making an attempt to talk to the

Lords who lingered there. Nor, strangely, were they rebuffed. I heard Edward laugh aloud, the men who had demanded his execution responding without overt hostility to his winning assault. They were already smoothing their future paths, winning friends where there were friends to be won, and these magnates were once again closing ranks, taking my family back into their midst. Hypocritical, some would say. Carefully pragmatic would be my opinion.

But there, in front of me, still marching towards the door, was Thomas. Charmless, refusing to hold out a hand of reconciliation to any man. His face, although it was hidden from me, would exhibit nothing but black anger. I knew why, all mired in past history in the reign of King Edward the Second. Thomas resented his long-dead ancestors' degradation, Hugh Despenser, father and son, who both came to a gruesome end. I doubted he would ever accept that their reputations for double-dealing and raw ambition were truly earned. Thomas admired them and the pre-eminence they had achieved for the Despenser name. Now his own humiliation at Henry's hands would be to his mind an unforgivable slight.

Edward had demanded too much. I had given myself a hard task.

November 1399: Cardiff Castle

Richard was in Pontefract Castle, as mighty a stronghold as the Tower of London, yet Edward would seem to have some plan in mind, although it was difficult to ascertain exactly what it was. On the one hand he was encouraging us all to fall into line behind the new Lancaster throne; on the other suggesting that

Richard might be rescued. Unless I had misunderstood him. Since Thomas was a morose companion, both on the journey to Cardiff and once we were in residence, it allowed me the opportunity to consider the future.

Yes, with our restoration to the Royal Council, it seemed that we could regain a portion of our influence at Court, but was it not a short-term plan? As Henry's sons grew they would dominate the positions of power. The Princes Hal and Thomas were already showing their precocious skills that would doubtless make them soldiers of renown. Of course, they would eventually take the reins from their father, to be joined by the two younger boys, John and Humphrey, as they too grew into maturity. There was only one hope for the true restoration of the House of York. Richard would be a safer, surer route to our dominance. Our hold would be pre-eminent if we could rescue and restore him, until he produced an heir with Isabelle, which, given her young age, would not be for some years.

If it were to be true inheritance, after the death of the old King Edward, it must be Richard. And if he had no heir of his own body he would choose my brother Edward, heir to the Duke of York, as he had in the past. Edward was the obvious choice, since Henry, after Richard's restoration, would pay mightily for his usurpation. He would be fortunate to keep his head. It would, I decided, assuage my conscience. For in all the granting of pardons, there was that one unsatisfactory element not addressed: Richard's fate.

But how to rescue Richard?

Would it not take a major rebellion to rouse the whole country? Or some secretly devious plot to undermine Henry and snatch Richard away? I decided to leave the conspiracy to my brother, but I would ensure our return to London. Thomas would soon grow weary of life in the country amongst his tenants. In fact, he might decide to return without any intervention at all from me.

But then I was distracted from Edward's plots and Thomas's ill humour.

'May the Blessed Virgin come to my aid!'

I did not know whether it was a curse on my tongue or an offering up of prayers.

Since settling into our apartments at Cardiff I had been stricken by all manner of ailments, mild but enough to disturb me from my habitual strong health. Considering each one, irritated by their persistence, I made my excuses.

An intense lethargy: understandable after my confinement in the Tower with fear as a constant companion.

A lowering of spirits: equally understandable since so little was resolved to our liking. We were Despenser again, Thomas was shouting orders to his steward, but Richard, without hope, was captive.

An ache in my back, both waking and sleeping: no doubt product of the fast travel from Westminster to Cardiff that Thomas had insisted on. Even my bones ached.

A debilitating nausea: nothing of a lengthy nature, nor was it difficult to explain. The eel pie with its rich sauce of almond milk, crushed walnuts, herbs and chopped dates had laid me low. Perhaps the eels had not been the freshest, or our cook had been heavy-handed with the spices. I must speak with him about who was catching our eels.

I could make an excuse for all of my maladies.

Within a week I knew the true cause. The pie was quite innocent.

My enforced sojourn in the Tower with Thomas had had a result that I would rather it had not. I had taken no precautions to prevent such an outcome and Thomas, in his boredom and with no mistress at his beck and call, had been enthusiastic. A knowledgeable woman should have been able to prevent this, but my circumstances had not been of the best, without resource to known remedies for an unwanted conception. I did not even have in my possession my paternoster beads fashioned from the black stone called jet, which if held by a woman desiring to protect herself would be most efficacious. To hold one of the beads in my mouth for a short time would have been even better. The carrying of a weasel's testicles wrapped in goose-skin had been even more unthinkable in the circumstances, not that I altogether believed my women's advice on this remedy.

When I missed my courses, I sat and pondered what I knew for certain even though it was early days. My body's rhythms being as regular as the sun's rising, I knew beyond doubt. I was carrying another child.

I sighed a little.

My pregnancies had been an inconvenience rather than an event to fear, but I was not filled with joy. Joan would have fallen to her knees in blissful thanks to the Holy Mother. I found myself hoping that when this child was born, Richard would once more be King of England.

I supposed that I must inform Thomas of the repercussions of my dutiful obedience in the Tower. It might drag him out of his chancy mood. If it was a son, another male in line to the inheritance, it would give him a sense of fulfilment. He might even prove to be better company. When he returned from his morning's hunting I would tell him; meanwhile, I kept my discovery to myself. My women would be aware, but, on pain of dismissal, they knew better than to gossip about my private affairs.

It promised to be an eventful few months. A conspiracy that might stir the whole country, Richard's rescue, and the birth of a new Despenser child. At least Thomas might find some reason to rejoice.

'Where is my lord Despenser?'

'In the muniment room, my lady. He has work to do there.'

Sir John, our steward, managed to look scathingly disapproving beneath the polite reply. This was the chamber that Sir John used for his business affairs, full of scrolls and tally sticks and the distinctive reek of wax and ink. Full of records of tenants: who did and who did not pay their dues into Despenser coffers. The balance was on those who did not. It was a surprise to hear that Thomas had chosen to be there and for so long a time. Such intricacies were usually left to the steward.

'Are you sure?'

'Yes, my lady. My lord has been there since dawn.'

So he had not been hunting after all. Another surprise. Thomas spent as little time on the day-to-day administration of his estates as he did on the dishes produced for his pleasure from his kitchens. Others were paid to do both. What would keep his interest all morning?

Nor, it had to be said, was the muniment room a chamber

that I much frequented, but at least I knew my way around Sir John's system of keeping his documents in order.

I entered quietly, standing just within the door. Thomas did not hear, for he was surrounded by opened coffers, with piles of documents and scrolls. His hair was awry and he was humming softly some bawdy tavern ballad, tapping his left hand on the desk as he wrote, rapidly covering a page with a scrawl of handwriting. Sunshine gilded his hair. It was a peaceful scene, one of diligent husbandry, yet a presentiment crept under my skin that he had a notion in his head, and one that I might not like.

The presentiment grew when I noticed, in the corner of the room, its lid thrown back, the coffer which contained carefully wrapped pieces of armour. This was the engraved and incised body armour that Thomas wore when intent on appearing at his best in some noteworthy tournament. There were no tournaments, to my knowledge, in the approaching penitential period of Advent.

For a little while I watched him. The lines of discontent were more heavily marked than ever, but his brisk actions had a life to them that had been lacking since the King's pardon had set him free.

'What are you doing?' I asked when he cast the pen onto the desk and drew his hands down his cheeks. He looked up. With the thin winter sun shining through the high window to illumine his face, I could see that he was flushed. Excitement? Guilt, I thought. But his reply was without hesitation or guile.

'I am putting aside the documents that no longer appertain to me since the estates are no longer mine.' He lifted one and threw it, so that it winged its way to the floor. 'Such as

Elmley Castle. And the castle at St Briavels.' Another document followed the first. 'And Gloucester.' A third fluttered down to join its companions.

A reasonable answer. Except that Thomas had shuffled those he had been writing into a neat pile, so that I might not read them.

'Do you not employ someone to do that for you?'

Of course he did. I walked to his side, intending to peer over his shoulder. The announcement of my pregnancy was shelved.

Thomas dropped the leaves of parchment into a small travelling coffer and turned the key. Except for one that escaped his attention. Before he could stop me, and he tried, I turned it round to read, lifting it out of his reach.

'What is it? A list of necessities for travel, if I'm not mistaken.' I skimmed quickly down, then placed it once more before him. 'You have forgotten to add extra under-tunics for cold weather, more than one pair of gauntlets, and I doubt you would be willing to travel far without your collection of enamelled cups . . .' When he attempted to snatch the list from my sight, I smiled at him, or at least my lips curved. 'Are you considering embarking upon a long journey, Thomas?'

'What if I was?'

'And when were you going to tell me?'

He stared at me.

'And where were you considering? A return to Court? But you wouldn't need so much provision for your horses, for so short a journey.' My smile had gone. 'Nor would you need to keep it secret from me.'

His gaze on mine was quite fierce as he smacked his hand down over the list. 'I plan to go further than London. A crusade is in my mind.'

'How noble of you.'

'If it is of any interest to you.'

'Of course it is.' I moved to sit opposite him, leaning with my elbows on the desk. 'I am wondering why. When you have just been readmitted into the King's inner circle . . .'

He grunted.

'. . . and you are now a member of the Royal Council. I am wondering why, given the fact that the King is holding out an olive branch, you would throw it all away and go crusading?' I tried not to let my cynicism colour my words. 'And I thought you were a man of *ambition*, Thomas.'

My heart was beating fast. Would he truly break this olive branch and head for Europe, to fight and make a new reputation for himself? I feared that he would. I could not see any good in such a plan.

'I am not a man of complacency, like your father, if that's what you mean.'

'True, you are nothing like my father.' The Duke was seemingly at ease with the Lancaster hold on power since Henry had proved generous to his ageing uncle. His possession of the castle and Lordship of Rising in Norfolk had been confirmed to him and he had been granted the Lordship of the Isle of Axholme in Lincolnshire. My father appeared to desire nothing more, but then advanced age was a great leveller of ambitions.

'Oh, I have ambition. What I do see, unlike your brother, is that there's no chance of it here in England. Whatever Aumale says – or Rutland as I must call him – promotions will go to those who returned with our new King. The Earls of Northumberland and Worcester and Archbishop Arundel have the royal ear. His Beaufort brothers. Not Despenser.' He closed another little coffer with some force. 'I have a fancy to go crusading. I'll make a name for myself on the battlefield.'

'I suppose crusading is in the blood,' I agreed, my mind working furiously, trying to raise some plan to keep him from vanishing into the battlefields of Europe.

'It is,' he agreed with a lightening of his expression as he recalled past glories. 'My father, my uncle, my cousin. They all adhered to some foreign cause to fight for, to achieve. To make a name of renown for themselves.'

'And where will you go?' I asked.

'You are mightily interested, Constance.'

'Why would I not be?'

He lifted a shoulder. 'I thought of Rhodes, perhaps. Or Prussia.'

So his plans were not in a full state of completion. It might never happen, of course. I placed my hand over my girdle where the new child grew. If Edward was plotting Richard's release he would want Thomas in England. He might not have much admiration for him, but Thomas was a leader of men on the battlefield as he had shown in Ireland. If we were to re-establish ourselves in this kingdom, he needed to be here. If it ever came to a battlefield. My heart jolted at the prospect.

'When were you going to tell me?' I asked again, gently. This must be handled carefully. Thomas was a man to be cajoled.

'When I had finally decided. Now, if you have nothing else to say, I am busy . . .'

I remained where I was. How to keep my husband here? *Persuade Thomas to return to Court*, Edward had urged. It seemed to me that there was only one obvious path. It was dangerous, in that it placed some treasonous material within his keeping, but

I must trust him to keep it close until we returned to London. I thought that I could since it would be to his advantage, but would it sway him? *Don't tell him*, Edward had warned. To do so might be the only route to keeping Thomas in England.

I sat up and placed my hands palm down on the board, selecting how I should speak.

'And what about Richard?' I asked.

'What about him?'

He was stowing away the keys in the purse at his belt.

'Have you given him any thought at all?'

'Other than that he is in Pontefract, no.'

I leaned forward. 'Will you go on your crusade and abandon him? When the country is so unstable, perfect for an uprising, will you abrogate the oath you took to Richard?'

'I took an oath to Lancaster too, if you haven't forgotten.'

I forgot to be calm and wifely.

'Have you no sense of duty to anyone?'

Thomas leaned and pinned my hands with his, using a weight that spoke of the passion of disappointment that ruled him.

'What is it that you are asking? If you mean Lancaster, then no. I'll not spend the rest of my life as a mere cipher in his Council, a man with little power, little influence, and what I have all hanging on Lancaster's whim.'

'Then what of your duty to Richard? If you need a war of the cross, why not consider rescuing him? Restore him to his rightful throne. It is a war worth fighting, surely.'

'It can't be done.'

'Are you saying there are none who would join with you? I could give you the names of those who would. Now there's a campaign for you, if you need a glorious cause.'

I hoped that he would not ask for the names. It would be speculation at this stage.

His face darkened. 'Has Edward sent you to me with this idea?'

'No.' I had no hesitation in lying, knowing that he might spurn any initiative by Edward out of hand. 'This is between us. You and me. For now. Are you not capable of planning and launching a bid for rescue? Take up God's banner and fight for Richard. Restore him and regain your land and your title of Gloucester. Are there not enough men in England who will rally to Richard's name?'

He looked at me. I could see the ideas blossoming in his mind. I could almost see the gloss of pride settling once more over him.

'Can it be done?'

'Why not? But not here. We need to return to London. To Westminster.'

His fingers released me. I could see their imprint in my flesh.

'I suppose the crusade could wait.'

I stood, walked round the table and placed a hand on his shoulder in what might have been interpreted as a caress.

'*This* should be your crusade, Thomas. I am sure that you will inform me when you have decided. And by the by, if you are going into Prussia, you must ensure that you add fur cloaks and boot linings to your list. It will be a cold winter when you are there.'

I smiled and left him. I did not tell him of the coming child. Time enough for that when Edward's intriguing had been made clear.

Thomas kept me waiting for two days. On the third, rising

early, he had abandoned his crusading plans; his armour was restored to the armoury and we were on the road to London.

But what was it that Edward had in mind? Even if the rescue of Richard were possible, did he plan to secretly smuggle our erstwhile King abroad, to Scotland or even France? But what good would that do? I could see no value in it, for Henry would still be King of England. A banished King would be as valueless as an incarcerated one. It gave me much food for thought to take my mind off my pregnancy.

Chapter Nine

Early December 1399: Palace of Westminster

This was the night we planned it, all laid out as sumptuously as the banquet I arranged to be set before us. This was the night that we signed our names to treachery. This was the night that set in motion all that would shadow us in the coming days.

'Let us raise this cup of finest Bordeaux to the honour of King Richard.'

Which was a treasonable statement in itself. I cannot recall which of our company made that first declaration of intent.

We raised our cups.

'We wish him a long life.'

'We drink to his freedom.'

Would any man here say it? There was a pause. So I made the toast.

'We pledge ourselves to his release and restoration to the throne that is his.'

An exchange of glances around the table, as redolent of intrigue as the air was fragrant with the dishes that had been set before us. Heat prickled over my skin, a dangerous anticipation. I saw it mirrored on every face.

'God aid us.'

'Amen.'

And so we drank. Edward and Thomas. Joan's brother Tom and their Holland uncle, John of Huntingdon. Not our father: we decided it would be better, for his health, to keep him in ignorance. Nor Dickon, who could not be trusted to hold his tongue, and would play no part in the outcome. Joan was present, choosing to accompany her brother.

Despite it being Advent when indulgence was discouraged, I had arranged a feast of Richard's favourite dishes, a symbol of his presence in our midst as well as in our thoughts. Roasted swan and venison in frumenty as a first course; roasted herons and pheasant for a second; potage of almonds and roasted larks for the third; ending with a rich *Crustarde Ryal.* It seemed fitting that we enjoy the culinary masterpieces that so pleased him, fashioned in his own kitchens. It made us remember that while we feasted, he was restrained, under what privations we had no knowledge.

This was a council of war, in effect, which allowed me to observe the unspoken roles in the seating. The armed chair at the head of the table remained tellingly empty. The Duke of York might be kept in ignorance, and so absent, but no one chose to step into his shoes, however ineffective he might be. My brother of Rutland, as heir, automatically took the stool to the right, Huntingdon facing him. Next to him Tom and then Thomas, present but worryingly morose. Four dispossessed lords, seeking restitution. Joan took a stool at my brother's side to face them.

And I? I took the stool at the foot.

There was no drunken euphoria, no careless planning. The servants were dispatched after delivering the final array of sweetmeats and marchpane, the door locked; then the conspiracy began. How clear the lines of our planning. There was no dissent. We would remove Henry of Lancaster from the throne on which we had helped place him. We would remove his sons who could pursue the Lancaster claim. We would rescue Richard from his imprisonment in Pontefract Castle and restore him to his rightful inheritance.

And when would we achieve this? On the occasion of a great festivity for Twelfth Night, to be held at Windsor, at the Epiphany tournament to which all knights of renown were invited. With Henry and his sons all in the same place it was the perfect time.

'If we remove Henry, and his sons, the Lion of Lancaster is without its head and claws. How difficult can it be for us to call on the country to rouse itself in a burst of fervent loyalty to restore Richard?' Edward asked.

There it was, spoken at last, the treasonous words hanging in the room with the smoke from the fire. Treason indeed. I looked round the faces that I knew so well, all imprinted with dissatisfaction. Their restoration as members of the Royal Council had not proved to be sufficient recompense. Not one of them was averse to taking revenge, as revenge had been taken against them. Even the Bishop of Norwich, Thomas's Despenser uncle, was with us in spirit if not in episcopal body, to give us clerical recognition.

'And what could be a better time to choose?' I added, breaking a piece of marchpane into crumbs as Joan refilled our cups. 'The Epiphany is the day to celebrate Richard's birth.'

There was only one problem remaining. How to persuade the country that Richard was worth fighting for, that he was worth the risk of an uprising. Foreseeing a lengthy discussion, I decided to leave them to their deliberations of troops and rescue attempts.

With Joan deciding to join me, as we walked to our rooms, making no comment on what we had set our hands to, we passed a young man who bowed and wished us good eve. I nodded, then turned and stood still, watching him disappear across the room and through the far door, his figure caught up in shadows as he stooped a little to lift the latch.

'Who was that?' Joan asked.

'Just a clerk.'

'So what caught your attention?'

'Nothing at all.'

Some hours later I tapped on Edward's door.

'I thought you might return. Come and bend your devious brain to our problem.'

There was only Edward, seated with his feet on a footstool, hands folded on his stomach around a cup of wine.

'There was no point in my staying to discuss troop manoeuvres. Was anything decided?'

I pushed his feet off the stool and sat on it myself.

'Yes.' He crossed his ankles instead. 'Much as you heard before you left.' He allowed his chin to drop on his chest. 'There is one weak link in this chain we have forged. It will all depend on the country rising to our call, particularly London. If it won't, no matter how many soldiers we can raise in our own names, then we lose and Henry wins.' Edward frowned. 'And if Henry wins there will be no second chances for any of us.'

'I have an idea.'

He groaned. 'You always do. Why not tell Thomas?'

'Thomas has a weakness in him. He rarely listens to me.'

Edward's face creased in a sly grin. 'So tell me.'

'What is it that will get the Londoners to rise to your support, without question, and overthrow Henry?'

'Richard, of course. They were quick to turn from him, but they might just welcome him back. As you said, Richard, free and in our midst, is the one factor that could secure us the following we need. But Richard is not available until we can rescue him. And that will not be until Henry is overthrown. It is one of those chicken-and-egg riddles much loved by mummers, without start or end.'

I took his cup of wine from him and sipped.

'We could play a mummers' trick, of course . . .'

'It will have to be a believable one.'

'I think it can be. Imagine if you will the young man who was clerk to Richard, whom you took into your household, Richard Maudeleyn.'

'What of him?'

'Tall, slender, fair of hair, pale of skin. Now think about Richard.'

A gleam slowly grew in his eye.

'It might work. A clever subterfuge.' A smile grew. 'Yes, I can see it. Why did I not think of that?'

'And some more advice, if you wish to take it,' I continued, seeing what could be achieved. 'Give the task to Thomas, to discover our clerk and make preparations.'

'Why? I can do it myself. More efficiently.'

'Do you not trust my husband?'

'Do you?'

I sighed. 'Thomas is fallible. He has been talking of going crusading because there is nothing for him here.' I waved Edward to silence. 'I doubt he will, but he needs to be committed. He needs to be inveigled into this plot to restore his pride and his vision of success.'

'So you tell him.'

'And he will listen to, and answer to, his wife? I managed to get him to return to Court, which was as much as I could do. Now it is up to you. Your confidence in him will tie him to your side. Once he is involved, then he will not retreat.'

'Then we will do it. My clerk will become King Richard overnight and we will restore the real Richard – who will then restore us.'

'And Thomas will bathe in the glory of what he has achieved.' I restored Edward's wine cup to him and stood. 'And we will not mention that the idea was mine.'

'Are you at ease with this?' Edward asked as I reached the door.

'Why would I not be?'

His regard on my face sharpened. 'You are not in your usual good looks.'

I had no intention of telling Edward that this pregnancy was wearying. I must have recourse to my cosmetic pots and potions.

'Thank you, Edward. A woman enjoys being told that she has blemishes. I am in excellent health and temperament.'

He regarded me over the rim of his cup, not yet finished with me. 'Are you at ease with what will undoubtedly be a bloody outcome?'

It was nothing that I did not already know.

'Yes,' I replied. 'I must be at ease. What choice do I have?'

'To cleave to Henry.'

I did not deign to reply.

Within the turn of the sun and moon, Thomas sent a page to find me and bring me to him.

'Where are you taking me?'

'Not far now, my lady.'

It appeared to be one of the antechambers used to receive foreign dignitaries in the days of the old King but now, since it had not met with Richard's vision of grandeur, there was much dust and cobweb even though the tapestries were very fine. I could not recall ever being present at a Court occasion there. I was bowed in, to find Thomas waiting for me to the right of the door.

'What is so urgent?' I feigned lack of enthusiasm and ignorance but my blood had begun to race. Thomas had been busy. Now he pulled me with him into the light from one of the decorative stone-traced windows and turned me to face the dais where the King would have stood to welcome his guests.

'What do you see? Whom do you see?'

When I took a breath of apparent surprise, Thomas, standing behind me, closed his hands hard on my shoulders.

'A miracle,' I murmured, disgracefully astonished.

'Of course, it is not what it seems. But here's a mummers' trick.' So Edward had used that phrase to him and Thomas adopted it fast enough. His eyes on the distant figure, he could not see my smile. 'How well does it seem to you?'

'It seems to me to be Richard.'

King Richard. Surely, to any brief assessment, it was King Richard standing on the dais, fair hair covered by a soft cap. Tall and slight of figure. His garments were fine damask, richly bejewelled, his shoes as extravagant as any that Richard might wear. And yet it could not be him, as we both knew. It was a clerk named Richard Maudeleyn, formally one of King Richard's household. And as I walked slowly forward, I saw that he was barely twenty years of age, his hair fairer, his face with little similarity except for the roundness of cheeks and chin. Yet at a distance . . . How right I had been to think of him. He was perfect. Dressed in armour and heraldic achievements he would fool the Londoners into believing that here was King Richard restored. The chain, its golden links resting heavily on his shoulders, gleamed with cabochon rubies.

'Remarkably good,' I said. 'Who is he?' My expression was all innocence.

'Richard Maudeleyn. Some household clerk or other. Your brother found him.'

'So you will dress him as Richard.'

'In armour, with the royal standard flying above his head. Londoners will see their King come again into their midst and march against the man who mistreated him. Meanwhile, we will organise the rescue of the real Richard.'

'Clever.' Thomas glowed with his achievement, all his ill humour dispersed.

Our false King was eyeing us with some wariness, his hands clasping and unclasping.

'Does he know what is expected of him? And the dangers?'

'There will be no danger. And yes, he knows what we will do. We will teach him a few words to address the rabble in the street. He will be given coin to distribute with a liberal hand if necessary.'

How confident he was. Was he too confident? Thomas sometimes needed a restraining hand.

'It's dangerous his being here,' I suggested. 'If we were interrupted, this would be impossible to explain away.'

'I needed to know if he would pass muster.' Thomas fisted his hands on his hips. 'We will not be interrupted or discovered. I will remove the jewels and the ostentation fast enough.' And as I re-surveyed the regal figure I laughed, for did I not recognise the ruby-set chain as my own, a Despenser jewel given to me to celebrate some event in the past? 'I'll muffle him in a cloak and deliver him back to your brother's household. Is that a good enough mummers' ploy?'

'Excellent.'

Walking forward, I curtsied deeply before our mock prince. The clerk, having lived for much of his life in Richard's presence, bowed with regal grace. Yes, it would work. He had been well taught. Here was the figurehead for the rebels and encased in a closed helm this subterfuge would not be detected. The rebels would cheer as they marched behind their King into London. What could go wrong? Then the true Richard would be restored to us, and Thomas, hand in glove with the plotters, would think no more of crusading. How easy Thomas was to manipulate. I felt a brief moment of affection for him.

I was not there when on the seventeenth day of December, our conspirators met in the Jerusalem Chamber in the Abbot's lodging at Westminster Abbey, but I was with them wholeheartedly in spirit. I knelt in St Stephen's Chapel, not too far from the plotters, imagining the unfurling of the plan, the discussion of who would do what and when. It would, I imagined, all be military might and swordplay from which I would, by my sex, be excluded. Unless I donned armour and rode with them, which would be entirely unacceptable, I was superfluous and must accept my demotion to the role of obedient woman. But I would be in London to welcome the return of King Richard. I would make it a celebration such as London had not seen for many a year, unlike his last entry into Westminster Hall.

I knew well those who signed their participation in blood. Thomas and Edward, Tom of Kent and Huntingdon and the Earl of Salisbury, all the Counter-Appellants, except for John Beaufort, as had been agreed. All men with an axe to grind on the whetstone of Lancaster's retribution. With them there was a group of interested parties who could be trusted. The deposed Archbishop of Canterbury who had no love for King Henry or the new Archbishop Arundel. Richard's physician Master Pol. And the clerk so essential to the plot, Richard Maudeleyn. Sadly not the Despenser Bishop of Norwich, who claimed some diplomatic ill health, but we had his blessing.

Here it was, the plot that we had devised between us, without any obvious complications or dangerous pitfalls as far as I could see to gnaw at my nerves. Our little company of plotters would give orders to cause their troops to be assembled at Kingston on the first day of the New Year when Henry and his family were oblivious to anything but the festivity of gift-giving. These troops would make their way to Windsor on the fourth day when Henry was busy with arrangements for his tournament on the sixth day. The plotters would take Henry and his four sons and the Arundel Archbishop prisoner, then give the signal for their forces to seize leading towns across the country, for we would all have called out our tenants to our support. The clerk would play the role of King Richard: the Londoners would march under the royal banner and take control of the city. Richard would be set free from Pontefract and restored. We would be his friends and be made welcome into his open arms, restored as royal counsellors, our lands and titles intact.

What could go wrong?

King Henry was oblivious. No one would talk. The anticipation of victory ran sweetly through my veins. All that I had to do was withstand the Court festivities before bidding the conspirators farewell and good fortune. Nothing that any one of us said or did must awaken any suggestion that a plot was afoot.

We hunted in fine style. The gathering in a fair meadow surrounded with trees in the park at Eltham was a perfection of ceremonial in the hands of Edward, Earl of Rutland, who played out his role as Master of the King's Game. His expertise was second to none when creating a display on the hunting field. The grass was spread with rich tapestries, while braziers were set to burn red to keep at bay the bitter cold of this first January day. And there we gathered, the great and the good of England, to drink hot spiced wine and eat meat and sweet pasties from gold platters. We stood or sat, conversing lightly while the lymerers and grooms returned with their stately lymer hounds to report on the close presence of deer that we would hunt.

And I was honoured. The Master chose me as the Lady of the Hunt since Henry had no wife to be so honoured. Bowing before me, Edward discussed the deer, their size and their probable speed, allowing me to give the decision of which direction to take to the finding.

It was a fine chivalric moment as I listened, assessed the scenting, and gave solemn judgement, enjoying the status afforded to me. And then as the morning wore on and the thin sun warmed the ground, we set forth. How magnificently at one we were. How richly clad, how brilliant in the clear winter light as the running hounds, greyhounds for the most part, ran, swift as water over a millrace, and we urged our horses in pursuit to be there at the finding and the ultimate kill.

When the horns called us to a halt to draw breath as the sun made its low progression to begin its descent, servants brought cups of ale and wine. We toasted the King and each other, voices raised in the still air in self-congratulation that the new reign had settled into what would be embraced as normality. No one could have guessed that beneath the satin and wool and leather of a significant number of those present beat hearts drenched in betrayal. Edward was at the forefront, directing the hounds. Thomas and Tom Holland passed the time of day and swapped hunting anecdotes with those who clustered round the King. The Duke of York, in blissful ignorance, stayed close to the King and gave advice whether it was needed or not. Huntingdon surveyed all with knowing dark eyes, while King Henry watched his Court with complacence. The usurpation had been an unprecedented success. Not a breath of treason, not a glance that could be misinterpreted beyond one of loyalty. No suspicious cliques of men who might be discussing a perilous outcome for this Court. All was high-spirited celebration of the good hunting to be found in these royal preserves.

But no, all was not as it seemed. Soon it would be Richard bidding his huntsmen to direct the hounds.

The smooth-skinned greyhounds and the alaunts loosed, a good fast run brought us to a covert where they brought down a fine-tined buck which was duly dispatched, the best parts reserved, the rest, the offal and the head presented as a reward to the hounds. A scene I had been party to all my life since the day my father deemed me capable of staying on my horse without embarrassing him. Joan, who had been riding towards the rear, had pushed her mare beside mine.

'Why is it that men enjoy the spilling of blood, whether it be in a tournament, or the blood of that fine animal?' she asked with a wrinkle of her nose.

'It is in their nature.'

'I care not for it . . .' She turned her face away as the alaunts gorged on the remains of the buck, snarling over possession, their muzzles red and dripping. 'I wish I had not come.' Her face had paled above her furs.

'You are rarely so squeamish.'

'Not of this.' She gestured to where the carcase of the deer was being loaded onto the back of a sumpter animal, the ground red with its blood. 'It was just a thought . . .'

I waited. She leaned across to whisper: 'What is it that is planned, in the coming conflict? Will it be as . . . as bloody as this?'

'Hush!' At least she was relatively discreet. 'What do you think?'

She looked aghast. 'I suppose it is the only way.'

'Yes, it is the only way. There can be no doubt of it. Did you suppose Henry and his sons would be allowed to go free? That would solve nothing. You must have talked of it with Tom.'

'Not in such detail . . .' She shortened her reins to draw her mount away from the carcase, swinging lifeless.

I liked the thought of bloodshed as little as she but Henry could just as easily have had all our menfolk executed without a qualm. Would he not have Richard murdered if he thought it in his best interests? Richard's release and safety could only be secured by Henry's death, and his heirs with him. There was no room for squeamishness.

I turned my head to watch Henry . . . my cousin, a man I had known all my life. There was a cold weight on my heart, but we would not pretend, not even for Joan's sensibilities, that Henry would be allowed to live, that the terms of his exile could be restored and he dispatched once more to a permanent sojourn in some distant country. It must be a complete and final denouement to bring Richard home and destroy those who threatened him.

'Will Henry be put on trial?' Joan asked.

Yet even I knew that this would never be. The King and his sons would be removed during the conspiracy.

'No.'

'So they'll be put to death at Windsor.'

'It is the only way.' I repeated my previous thought.

Joan paused, staring at me. Then: 'Have you no conscience?'

Conscience? It struck me like a blow from a hunting whip, fine and cutting. What was conscience? A jackdaw, picking up one shiny object, then discarding it for another, whatever would suit the occasion. Or haphazardly collecting one bright stone after another, until it had a whole array of glittering trivia in its nest. My conscience urged me to be loyal to Richard. How easy it would be to exchange that for an obeisance to Henry. How simple to replace one with the other. Conscience was all very well when it offered soft choices, bolstering fear with feather-filled cushions. Mine was all hard edges predicting pain and grief. All I could do was what seemed right.

Was that being without true conscience? Perhaps it was.

'Have you no conscience that within a matter of days your cousin and those young boys will lie in blood, hacked to death?' Joan whispered, the delivery as harsh as the accusation.

'No, I have not,' I said, of a mind to be obtuse since the image was so terrible, the stench of blood raw. 'Edward has none either. Huntingdon certainly has neither conscience nor morality. As for Tom, only you know about your brother.' I turned to look at her, reading the condemnation in her lips, thin-pressed as a summer coverlet. 'And what about you? You are quick to condemn me. You were there when this was planned. Are you regretting it? I did not hear your voice raised in denial.'

'What use in regret? I think you are beyond redemption. I will leave you to your bloodletting . . .'

'Joan . . .'

But Joan yanked on her bridle and set herself to return home. I did not. I would see this hunt out to the end, as I would see out the conspiracy. There was no turning back for any of us. Whatever the dice were foretelling, we were well on the path to insurrection, and who could blame us? We had almost been thrown to the slavering wolves by Henry. Now we were the wolves, and we were hunting. Yet even I turned away from the blood-soaked ground, with the faintest shiver of distaste, or even guilt. It was not something I could enjoy, this leap from chivalric ceremonial to violent bloodlust.

I watched them, the men of my family. Did I believe them capable of killing in cold blood? The evidence was here before me as I turned every page of the past years. Thomas of Woodstock smothered in his bed, his son Humphrey done to death in Ireland. Huntingdon had killed the Stafford heir in a roadside brawl due to some misunderstanding or family feud. No, they would have no compunction. And were they any different from the rest of these great lords who would have shed our blood, if Henry had allowed it? All guilty.

Here was our one chance to remake our power. And if our phoenix must rise out of the flames of bloody murder, then so be it.

'You look very severe.' Edward loomed at my shoulder.

'I find that conspiracy has that effect,' I replied before touching my spurs to my horse's side.

On the third day of January we made our farewells at Westminster. Ostensibly the men were en route to participate in the jousting at Windsor, their equipment sent on ahead with their households, apart from a small escort. Nothing to draw attention from the approaching ceremonies, they were clad in festive raiment, a splash of bright colour and rich cloth to clash against the tapestries.

'It is all arranged as we planned,' Edward said, enveloped in gloom, as thick as the velvet that proclaimed his rank, a strange melancholy for a man who had worked so hard to divert the course of this new reign. 'God be with us in this venture. It's a parlous undertaking that we have set our hand to.'

'Are you not satisfied with what you have done?' I asked, not understanding.

'Yes.' He pulled on his gloves with sharp gestures, as if there was nothing more to say.

'We can't lose.' Thomas, already hatted, booted and gloved, was keen to be on the move, his eyes fierce with the prospect of action now that the waiting was over. 'Our associates can be trusted to rouse their tenants across the length and breadth of England, and keep their mouths shut until the signal is given.'

Edward was already striding to the door, tugging the swathes of his chaperon low on his brow so that I could no longer read his expression.

'You are in a hurry.' I followed him.

Edward's eyes did not quite touch on mine even though he halted and took my hand in a grip that crunched my fingers so that I winced.

He released me. 'Forgive me.' The hard lines in his face softened into a smile. 'All is urgent now, and I have said that I will dine with my father before I leave.'

'Will you tell him?' I asked, curious as to whether he would keep our father in the dark.

'No. I'll not burden his ageing soul with this project.'

I could find no fault with it. 'Then God speed and good fortune.'

His habitual placid humour was restored. 'Good fortune indeed.'

I was left alone with Thomas, who surprised me when he wrapped his arms around me as if we were the young lovers we had never been, parting for many months. I had no recollection of his ever saying farewell with such emotion. He kissed me on the lips.

'Do you wish me well, too?'

'Of course.' And I returned the salute. 'I will pray for your success and that you will bring Richard home.'

Lightly, he touched my cheek with his fingertips. 'We have not always been a tender couple. Perhaps I have neglected you.'

'Perhaps you have.'

'And you are very beautiful.'

'And you have only just become aware?'

He tilted his chin, part challenge, part admiration. 'No. But usually I am more aware of your sharp tongue. Today I see your lovely face.'

In spite of everything, I felt the seductive warm breath along my cheekbones, but I would not be wooed by a man who had treated me with such casual disdain for all the years of our marriage. 'The prospect of success is making you emotional, Thomas.'

'Say that to me when I return.'

'I doubt that I will.'

'So do I.'

I felt a brush of affection when he smiled and I saw the handsome man behind the raging ambition. No, we had not done well by each other, but Thomas had never shown any interest in what I might think or desire. Yet I would not condemn him for it now.

'God go with you.'

'And with you. What will you do?'

Which made me return the smile, but without humour, that at last he thought to ask. Any softness was swept away.

'I will remain here. Huntingdon will stay in London too, until he hears of your success at Windsor. Then he can put in hand the seizure of London. I'll do what I can to help, if necessary.'

'There'll be no need. An army of six thousand men, we

are promised. Henry will not be able to withstand us. When they see our strength, the Londoners will clamour to join us. I wager the Mayor and aldermen will rue the day they opened the gates to Lancaster. When we return we'll have Richard with us, I promise it. Our fortune has turned, sweet Constance. Our fortune has turned.'

I changed the angle of his russet-felt cap, pinning its jewel more securely, planting a kiss on his forehead. 'Then go and seize it and we will rejoice at your homecoming.'

I walked with him down to the courtyard where his horse and escort were waiting, steaming in the cold air. I raised my hand in farewell, not a little moved when Thomas bowed low over his mount's withers. It crossed my mind as he rode out that I had still not told him of the expected child.

What was left for us, Joan and I? What was always left for women. We took refuge in one of the side chapels of Westminster Abbey where we knelt to offer up prayers. A long moment of silence fell between us. The hunting episode had left a few unhealed wounds.

'For whom do I pray?' Joan asked.

I looked sideways at her, noting how the light through the stained-glass window of the Assumption of the Blessed Virgin turned the colour of her own gown to a deep blue, as if she were the Virgin herself. Yet over Joan's veil and face, the reflection of the blood-red Rosa Canina that encircled the Blessed Virgin's feet, shifting as the clouds covered the sun, was unnerving.

'Pray for the King,' I said.

'Which one?'

'Pray for the King, and God will decide, in his mercy.'

Joan's fingers clicked over her rosary and her lips moved in endless petition.

My thoughts were impossible to control. Would God listen to a foresworn traitor? Surely He must since Richard was His chosen one. I prayed for the King, for all those involved, for this child that had been conceived in captivity. I tried not to notice as the blood-red hue crept over my own gown and hands.

Back in my room, I gave in to temptation and tossed the gold dice, distressed when, again and again, a plethora of mismatched numbers tumbled onto my bedcover, offering me no consolation when I commanded the dice to show threes and sixes. The recalcitrant dice were beyond my interpretation. There would be no consolation until Richard was restored.

Chapter Ten

January 1400: Palace of Westminster

And so it began, and London was awash with rumour and noise that surged and eddied like a spring tide. Joan and I went to the Great Hall, ostensibly to discover what was afoot, but for me to be there at the centre of it all. We had conspired with great exactitude, had we not? I must be there to welcome the victors, even though I must acknowledge that it would be some days before Richard could be escorted all the way south from Pontefract. Our lords had set out as early dusk was gathering, intending to arrive at Windsor under cover of the night and do the deed, leaving London in the control of Huntingdon and the Mayor. What I did not expect was the vast milling of crowds in the streets. Or the rumours rife with truth and untruth. I knew not where Huntingdon was. Should he not be evident in his coordination of events in the city? The crowds in the street, surging back and forth on the bridges, were more mob than army.

And yet it held an air of excitement in the fervour, the clamour, enough to stir the blood with hope. Would Henry be escorted into London as a prisoner, as Richard had been forced to suffer that indignity? I thought that he would die where he faced the assassin's blade at Windsor.

Black night fell. Torches flickered; a brave sight, but anxiety increased within me. Yet why be full of fear? I chided myself. All had been so well planned, the details known to so few.

Joan and I could find nothing to talk about, beyond:

'Will we hear tonight?' she asked.

'Edward will send a courier with news.'

At last, there was Huntingdon appearing beneath the door-arch, confident and impressive, sword belted at his side as he conferred with the Mayor who wore his robes of office even at this late hour. They seemed undisturbed. Then they were gone.

A clatter of approaching horses, being driven along at some speed.

'Constance . . .' Joan turned to face the great door.

'I hear it.'

Was it Edward's long-expected courier come to report that all was well? Surely not. He could not have covered the ground from Windsor so quickly. And this was a troop of horsemen, not a single rider. We moved to the door to catch the first glimpse, Joan pushing ahead.

'Can you see the heraldic devices?' I asked.

Joan shook her head.

Something whispered a warning in my mind as the horses halted. This was wrong. It was pure reaction to some unseen danger that made me draw back into the shadow of the wall where the lights could not reach us, my hand closed around Joan's arm, pulling her with me. Now there was no need to struggle to see the device on the pennants, all royal lions and fleurs-de-lys. Henry. It was Henry striding in. Henry here in the Great Hall with the four boys. The Mayor, last seen in Huntingdon's company, was suddenly at Henry's side, bowing and scraping. Huntingdon was nowhere to be seen.

I drew Joan further into the angle beside the door. Henry was issuing orders, gesturing as he did so to send out messengers, who departed at a run. His voice was loud enough and crisp enough that we could hear as the commands were issued.

'Take the Princes to the Tower and lodge them there. Fetch someone from my Council. My brother Somerset if you can find him. Tell him to get the Council to meet and send out instructions to close the ports. I want no foreign interference on behalf of the plotters. Go and bring me pen and parchment. I'll issue writs for the arrest of the rebels.'

What terrible fear those instructions lodged in my stomach. What had gone wrong? If Henry was here and in command, the whole plot had collapsed with the conspirators on the run. Joan and I withdrew further. Now was not the time to be seen, with Henry full of life and fury. Or was it? Perhaps this was when it would be politic to display our ignorance of any insurrection. If there was any hope of proclaiming our innocence and wresting something from this fiasco, now was the time. If our plotting lords were in danger, one of us must remain to plead their cause.

And where, in God's name, was Huntingdon? An apprehension whispered, a chill wind, across my skin. This was not how it should be.

Henry was still issuing orders, now to the Mayor who had committed a complete volte face. 'I need a proclamation, sir. To be read throughout the city immediately.' How his voice echoed with authority. The ride from Windsor had filled him with life and energy, as if he had returned as victor from the battlefield. 'Tell them this. Whoever will ride with me tomorrow to flush out this nest of vipers will be well paid. And if they need an incentive to support their King, tell them that an archer will earn ninepence, a mounted man with a lance eighteen.' Even at a distance I could see his mouth twist in scorn. 'That should get them to think of the future at my side. What do the rebels offer? Nothing but chaos and disturbance.'

'They offer the man they call the rightful King, my lord.' The Mayor, smoothly, gave no indication that he would have supported Richard. 'They said that my lord Richard is at liberty and will take up his crown again.'

'That is false. I know where Richard of Bordeaux is, and it is not in London.'

'There are rumours, my lord, that he has been seen . . .'

'Rumours! Rumours that are flawed. What have the rebels done? Got some scapegrace clothed in majesty? A mockery of majesty! And against the prospect of coin in hand that will weigh little with the populace. I am the rightful King.' He looked round. 'I expected to find Huntingdon here. Where is he?'

The Mayor chose not to answer.

'When I find him he'll hang, with the rest of them.'

'And we too are inhabitants of the nest of vipers,' I whispered. 'God help us. Follow me, Joan, and look innocent.'

I walked out from the shadows. To say that I was unafraid would have been a lie.

Henry's eye fell on me. The Mayor, absorbing the expression on Henry's face, vanished circumspectly.

'I did not expect to see you here.' Then when he saw Joan emerging from the shadows, he bowed: 'My lady.' But his question was directed at me: 'I suppose you know nothing of this?'

'About what, my lord? Joan and I were brought here by the noise in the streets. We have been with my father the Duke, who is suffering pain tonight.'

'Very noble of you both. And where is Thomas Despenser? Am I to believe that he allowed you to walk unaccompanied through these noisome streets? I'll not believe it.'

'It was my understanding that he intended to travel to his estates in Wales but would be returning for the Epiphany tournament, my lord. I expect him daily.'

'A surfeit of travel, it seems. I am inclined to be disbelieving.' Henry's mocking eyes moved from me to Joan. 'And your brother of Kent, my lady?'

'I know not, my lord. Is he not at Windsor?' Joan had acquired a remarkable equanimity when faced with the banked royal fury.

'And I suppose that you have no knowledge of where your uncle of Huntingdon will be either?'

'No, sir. Is he not at Dartington with your sister and his family?'

We could all play at innocence. Henry might not believe us, but it might sow some seeds of doubt into his mind. The plot had gone awry and we must escape from its toils if it were possible. Joan would be safe since the Duke was not involved, but I saw my own future as a tangled web, and a bloody one at that. A memory of the blood red in the Abbey windows, creeping across my gown, my hands, all but choked me.

'Has there been a disturbance?' I asked.

'A disturbance? There has, by God. And if I find that you too are involved, Constance, I will punish you with the rest of the plotters. Those who seek my death and that of my sons can expect no mercy. I suggest that you take that as a warning. Now I advise you to return to your chambers – or to minister to the Duke my uncle. I trust he will be restored by the morn when I will require his services. Now go, both of you, before I forget that you are members of my own family. As you obviously forgot when you hatched this plot against me.'

We made haste, but I stopped at the far door to look back. Henry was once again busy sending couriers.

'How did Henry know? Who whispered in the royal ear?' Joan whispered in mine.

My mind was running over a litany of those involved. Not Huntingdon. Not Edward or Thomas or Joan's brother Tom. The old Archbishop hated the new one too much to undermine the plot. Thomas's episcopal uncle? I could not believe it of him. Nor of Salisbury . . .

'I have no idea.' Who would have told enough to enable Henry to escape? 'Let us be mindlessly obedient and go to the Duke of York's chambers. He will vouchsafe for our innocence tonight. Or at least yours . . .'

I had barely taken a step when 'Look!' Joan hissed. 'It cannot be.'

I turned, impatient with her over some triviality that could be of no importance whatsoever, and then I saw.

'No . . .'

As the centre of the Hall emptied around Henry, coming to stand at his side was the one man I would never have believed possible. Together with the Earl of Somerset and Sir Thomas

Erpingham. Three men who were clearly in collusion with the King. A long conversation ensued that I could not hear. There was an exchange of sharp laughter. Then all three acknowledged some command from Henry and walked out.

'Did we see that?' Joan's voice climbed to a high pitch with astonishment.

'Before God! We saw it. The question is . . .' I did not know quite what the question was.

We retired to my father's rooms, where, since he was already abed, we sat beside the dying fire in uneasy association.

'I cannot believe it,' Joan repeated.

I felt no compulsion to reply. It was so. The man who had appeared with Henry's brother Somerset and Erpingham was my own brother Edward. The man who had departed to fulfil some royal command was Edward. The man who had laughed with Henry's friends had been Edward. The last I had known, he was to be at the centre of the group sent to kill Henry and his sons. Now here he was in close collusion. He had laughed with the King. Was he the source of Henry's knowledge? Could that be true?

I covered my face with my hands so that Joan could not see my expression. I feared that it was one of total despair, if Edward had foiled the plot. But why would he engage in such a betrayal? And if that was so, where were Thomas and Joan's brother Tom? Where was Huntingdon, last seen in the Great Hall in the moments before Henry had walked in? Did they already know that the plot had disintegrated and that they were being hunted like wild boar with spear and hounds? And where was Richard Maudeleyn, glorious in my jewels and counterfeit royal garb?

'What do we do?' Joan asked. 'Do we tell my lord the Duke?'

I had not given my father a moment's thought.

'No. There is no doubting his innocence. Let him sleep.'

'Henry might believe that he knew, even if he did not act.'

I shook my head. All ideas escaped me, my mind in turmoil. 'We remain here until we know more. If we can do aught to help the rest of the plotters to escape then we will do it.'

'What will you say to Edward?'

Edward. What was there to say to him, if he was the one who betrayed us?

'I will damn him to hell and back.'

We sat on until daylight began to lighten the January sky and I could send a trusted member of the Duke of York's household to discover what Henry was about. He had already marched out of London, we were told, with an army at his back with the sole purpose of taking control of the plotters and the country. He clearly did not consider us to be of any danger to him. Why would he? We were women. There was no restraint on our movements.

My father's chamberlain returned, stiff with news and royal slight against his veracity.

'My lord the King asked where you were, my lady,' he announced. 'I informed him that you had been here with your father and Lady Joan. That my lord the Duke has been suffering from an ague. My lord the King said that it was a very useful ague.' The ducal chamberlain inhaled thinly. 'I assured the King that my lord the Duke's health is not at its best, but that his loyalty is as assured as any man could wish for.'

I rewarded him with thanks and a coin. Henry had seen a need to discover that we had obeyed him. What Edward was doing I could not even imagine. I stopped the chamberlain before he had closed the door.

'Has the Earl of Rutland ridden out with the King?'

'I do not know, my lady. He is not in his chamber.'

I decided we must wait, for there was no means of contacting him. And what would I have said to him if I had? He had been hand in friendly glove with the King. I could think of no other logical reason for his being with Somerset and Erpingham. He would cast the dice for Henry and hope for preferment, seeing it as a far safer wager than rescuing and restoring Richard. Edward was a man with ambition oozing from every pore of his body, but I would not have believed what I had seen in the Great Hall. I would have denied it utterly. But seeing was believing.

I could only hope, bitterly, foolishly, that there were extenuating circumstances. Would his double treachery spill the blood of his erstwhile friends and family? It could well spill mine.

'I am afraid,' Joan said.

'So am I.'

There was no point in creating an untruth that Thomas and Tom and Huntingdon would be safe. I feared for their lives. Only Edward appeared to have fallen, perfectly balanced, on his feet.

What interminable hours they were, that hunted us down, whatever it was we set our hand to. Nothing made them memorable but absence and a terrible brooding anguish. Henry did not return to Westminster and neither did Edward. As for Thomas, I could discover nothing of any reliability.

'What would I do in their circumstances?' I asked, not expecting a reply.

'Flee for safety,' Joan said.

It was the best idea that I could think of. 'Perhaps they are already in France if the winds are favourable. Thomas might indeed be forced to go crusading.'

'Is there any possibility that they can make their peace with Henry?' Joan fretted, face drawn with sleeplessness.

I thought the question did not deserve a response. There was no possibility. Henry had forgiven them once; Henry had treated them with astonishing leniency. He would not do so again. I doubted he would even give time for a trial before parliament. They had plotted his death and he had evidence of who and how and where. Their deaths were assured if they fell into his hands.

I too was sleepless. Edward had betrayed us. There could be no other explanation. But how would Edward have explained to Henry his own knowledge of the plot? I doubted even his plausible tongue could persuade Henry that he had never been involved, simply being an eavesdropper with a heaven-sent opportunity to lay the plot bare.

My father the Duke did not emerge from his chamber. Had he too known of the conspiring? I thought not, but I would not have taken an oath on it. I remembered that Edward had gone to dine with him before the whole edifice collapsed.

And then the news began to arrive, bad for us in its telling. How bad could it get? The chamberlain, venturing forth again at my behest, was close-lipped, bleak-featured, on his return. When Joan entered the chamber behind him I raised a hand to still anything he might say.

'You may not want to hear this,' I advised her, suddenly dragged from my own concerns at the sight of her pallor.

'Am I so weak? I will hear it.' She raised her chin with true Holland fortitude. Nor did she sit, but stood straight-backed as if a prisoner awaiting sentence. 'It is my right.'

I indicated that our messenger should begin.

'The Earl of Huntingdon took ship for Holland, my lady.'

I heard Joan sigh softly at my side, in relief that her Holland uncle had escaped Henry's revenge.

'The Earl of Kent is fled west, with the Earl of Salisbury. It is said that they hope to take refuge in Cheshire where they will join forces with the followers of my lord Richard.'

'God pray that they will.'

But I was hardly satisfied.

'And Lord Despenser? Where is he?'

'Fled, my lady, I'd guess. But I could find no news.'

Probably to Glamorgan, I surmised, to his own estates.

'And the Earl of Rutland? Is he still with the King?'

'I know not, my lady.'

So we knew little more.

Joan and I once more retired to the chapel to offer up prayers that the flight of the plotters would carry them far from Henry's reach, although I had little confidence in their efficacy as one day passed into the next. Flight to France or the Low Countries was the only remedy for this disaster. Even if we had perforce to accept that they could never again return to England, it might be better than facing Henry's wrath. The extent of his ire was already being spoken of in all corners of the Court where both servants and lords met to gossip. In Oxford, where a number of the minor plotters were brought before him, twenty-seven were relieved of their heads as a warning to others.

'Perhaps he will be satiated,' Joan said, still clinging to empty hope.

'And perhaps he will not.'

She gathered up her missal and her skirts. 'I will try to be optimistic, even if you will not.'

'I, dear Joan, am practical.'

When the news came, as it did, as it must, Joan's optimism was fated to crash to the ground. I considered keeping it from her, but to what purpose? She must be strong, as must we all.

She was not. Joan wept without restraint.

'We always knew this was a risk,' I chided, but gently. She had suffered grievous loss.

'We might, but I never faced it. I hoped that it would all come to fruition as we had planned. I was foolish, but so it is.' She smeared the tears across her cheeks, only to weep afresh. 'And then I suppose I presumed that they would escape across the sea. It could not happen, could it?'

They were dead. Both brother and uncle. Huntingdon had indeed fled, taking voyage for France, but his ship had been driven aground in a storm where, in Essex, he was put under restraint and delivered to the Countess of Hereford, Henry's mother by law at Pleshey Castle. Whatever her delight in having Huntingdon under her control, she handed him over to the mob who hacked off his head. I did not tell Joan the detail, merely that he was dead.

And then Tom, who had got no further than Cirencester in his bid for freedom.

'Tell me how he died,' Joan insisted.

So I did, with brutal clarity. When he took refuge with the

Earl of Salisbury in an inn in Cirencester, they were surrounded by townsfolk. Imprisoned in the name of the King, they might have lived to tell the tale but, it was said, they started a fire to cover an escape attempt. The townsfolk, furious at the destruction of the inn and the threat to the rest of the town as the flames roared and spread, had them summarily beheaded without trial or justice.

'Is that it?' Joan wailed when I had finished the tale. 'Will I never see him again?'

'No.' I was out of all patience, ravaged with worry. 'If you wish to see Tom again, his head has been sent to Henry in a basket. Huntingdon's head is on Westminster Bridge at this very minute, where I expect Tom's will join it. Go and see! But I advise against it. I'll not come with you.'

Blood drained from her face.

'I will not.'

'You can hardly complain of Henry's heavy-handedness. You would have supported his death. We could not say that we had not known what was intended from the beginning. Even you could not pretend that he would be dispatched back to exile. Of course he would not. It was always planned that Henry and his sons would be slain. So Henry lives and your brother and uncle die.'

She turned from me, from my vicious words.

'You are very cruel.'

'I am accepting the outcome of a plot that was leaked.'

'I will mourn on my own.'

'While you do so you might pray for those whose whereabouts we still do not know.'

'Before God, we know that your brother Edward is safe enough!'

The door slammed after her.

Why had I been so callous? I did not know of Thomas's fate. I might not love him but I had a care for him as the father of my children. As for Edward, I could not encompass what he had done. Or what I thought he had done. There was a suspicious silence around his deeds and his present service. In the dark times before dawn I feared the worst, another head delivered to Henry to increase his tally of traitors, but Thomas might have fled successfully into the heart of Wales where he could take refuge until a ship could be found. I prayed that he would.

When I heard that Edward had been one of those to lead Henry's forces at a minor skirmish against rebels at Maidenhead Bridge, the little episode sealed his fate as the traitor in our midst.

'Forgive me,' Joan sought me out. 'I should have known that you were concerned for Thomas.'

I rejected her apology. I could not bear her compassion. It merely compounded my guilt that I too had been one of the plotters, and so far I had escaped with my life when so many had not.

I could not bear to face the Holland heads, mutilated by carrion.

Thomas must be in Cardiff. Since there was no other news to the contrary, and much to suggest that that was where he was riding when last seen, I decided to abandon Joan to her tears and prayers and the somewhat guilty compassion of my father, and journey to Cardiff myself. Would I accompany him if he decided to leave England and settle in the Low Countries or in France? I thought that I would, except that there were our children to consider. It might be good policy for me to remain at Court, even in Thomas's exile, and argue for the security of their Despenser inheritance.

My thoughts circling hopelessly through what might and might not happen, ordering a horse and an escort, packing some necessities for a rapid ride, I went to bid farewell to my father only to see him coming to find me, leaning against the door jamb as he caught his breath. His face was seamed as deeply as a dried damson, and I thought his skin had the pallor of impending doom.

'Constance, my dear.'

The intimacy surprised me. His eyes did not quite meet mine, but slid to my travelling garments and the thick cloak that I had donned.

'I am going to Cardiff,' I said.

'No. You will not.'

I tilted my chin. 'No?' I rarely heard him so dogmatic and wondered why. Not that it mattered. 'You have no authority over me. If Thomas is there, then . . .'

'Do I not know it? You have always been wilful, as a child and as a woman, as your mother was before you.' He caught his breath, perhaps regretting his lack of affection, for both of us. 'I will tell you why you will not go. Why you will have no wish to go.' Pushing past me, he entered my room and sank into a chair, unable to silence a groan. 'Before God, my days are surely numbered. Joan weeps over me and over the memory of her dead brother while my body lurches from one day to the next.' Now his eyes held mine with a purpose that jolted my heart. 'Sit down, Constance.'

'To what end?'

I dared not sit at ease. Did I not see what was coming? I could already hear the words hovering on his lips.

'Sit down. I will tell you why there is no reason for your going to Cardiff. Despenser is not there.'

'Then where is he? Everything I can discover says that he has gone to Cardiff where he will take ship for France.'

'Not so.'

And at last I sank to the adjacent stool as I read the lack of hope in my father's face. When he held out his hand, obediently I placed mine there.

'He made good his escape to Cardiff, and once there he took ship. You would have missed him even if you had gone to Cardiff. And yes, it was his intent to reach France.'

I would indeed have missed him. 'So he would have left England without informing me.' I should not have been surprised, but then what choice did he have in the circumstances? My father had not told me all. I found that I was studying the stitching on my gloves, clenched in one hand in my lap. I dared not look at the warning in his face. His hand was cold around mine.

'I doubt he thought of it,' my father was agreeing. 'I did not choose him as your husband for his compassion.'

'No. You did not. How could you? We managed a desiccated tolerance for each other, for which I must be thankful. It was more than you had with my lady mother.' At last I raised my head. 'Are you going to tell me?'

My father gave no quarter, as if my reminder of his own first marriage was unbearable. 'You need tolerate him no more.' Which could have only one meaning. It hung in the chamber, sere as poison. 'I presume you wish to know how?'

I felt strangely empty, as if it had no bearing on me or on my life. All seemed at a strange distance. I recalled informing Joan of the dread details of her brother's death, and now here it was for me. I gathered my courage. Had I not anticipated this for some days?

'How did it happen?' I asked.

'The captain of the ship he sailed on had decided at the eleventh hour that he had no wish to be associated with those who rebelled against King Henry. He resisted all Despenser's attempts at persuasion to sail to France and took him instead to Bristol where he handed him over to the Mayor. I understand they had to overpower him first, when he threatened to jump overboard. I find that hard to believe.' My father's lips twisted. 'He would not risk the damage of salt water to his finery. He tried to bribe his way to freedom, which sounds more likely, but he failed. He was not well loved.'

I replied automatically. 'No. He was not. Not even by his own tenants.' What a trite observation. I breathed out slowly. I knew what was coming.

'In Bristol the citizens gave him what they saw as his just deserts. A quick execution by a frenzied mob. It was a lynching without trial. They refused the gold and jewels he was carrying, with which he tried to bribe them. He should have learned from the ship's captain.'

I could imagine Thomas, glittering with chains, a brooch fastened to his cap, his fingers be-ringed even though he was in flight. He would never be less than Lord Despenser. But then my mind shifted to his execution, balking at the violence, the blood, the disfigurement of his features. How he would have detested that, at the hands of a violent mob, his body desecrated;

the terrible humiliation, the loss of dignity, almost worse than the pain and the ultimate death.

'Is this true?' I asked.

'Yes. There is no doubt.'

'I might ask why he was in flight wearing jewels,' I said. My mind seemed to be incapable of absorbing the full detail of what I had been told, latching instead onto this trivia.

'He would have hoped to make an impression, as a lord worth saving. And he would have needed money wherever he ended up. It is immaterial.'

'Yes. It is immaterial. My thanks for coming to tell me, my lord.' Standing, releasing his hand, for a moment I suffered a roil of nausea, as if the babe had moved – the child Thomas would never see – then my father's words brought me back to the present horror.

'Sit down again, Constance, before you fall down. What you should know is that this afternoon it is planned that Despenser's head will be paraded down Cheapside at the command of the King. Then set on the south side of London Bridge.'

I thought about this.

'So you tell me this to encourage me to go and watch the royal victory?'

I sat, my legs weak.

'No. I think it would be ill advised. The greater the distance you can place between yourself and Despenser, the better. How much were you involved in this venture? But why do I ask? I am sure you were in it up to the hilt, along with the rest of them. Along with my son.'

'Then why ask at all?'

'Because I have no wish to see us all dragged down in the gutter. I will support you all I can.'

'Will my dear brother Edward support me?'

'I cannot tell you what he will do. I am not in his confidence.' He looked up at me, willing me to obey. 'Stay here, Constance. Wait on the King's pleasure. Flight will do you no good.'

There was a question I needed to ask.

'Did Edward tell you of the plot that evening at supper before he left London?'

The slightest hesitation, but not too long. 'He did.'

'Did you tell the King?'

'I will pretend that you did not ask that. It was mightily disrespectful.'

'All respect in me has died. Let us pretend that I did ask it. I think I deserve to know. Someone told Henry. Was it you?'

My father's face was as lacking in colour as whey as he stood at last to face me.

'You might deserve to know, but not from me. Consider carefully whom you will speak with and what you will say. We could all be branded as traitors. Do you understand?'

'Yes, my lord.'

I was not sure that I did, but he held out his hand so that I must curtsey and salute it as a good daughter. Then he limped towards the door while I sank back to the stool where I considered my reaction, sifting through the blur of emotions. Thomas was dead. Regret was there, at the manner of his end, hacked to death by a mob who would not be impressed by his gold or his jewels or his title, but I could detect no grief. My heart was not broken. It was never sufficiently engaged during our marriage to shatter. I could not imagine what a broken heart would feel like.

'One question.' I had not thought to ask before. My father, hand on the latch, looked back over his shoulder. 'The clerk, Richard Maudeleyn. The man who was dressed as Richard. Did he escape?'

'He is dead. He was discovered in London. Henry had him hanged.'

'Thank you.'

For him I could feel guilt. He had not asked for the role we had forced him to play. So I sat as the early dusk fell around me, furiously attempting to command my thoughts and emotions into line. By the time Joan came to grieve with me I had decided what I must do.

'I will not weep,' I warned her as she trod cautiously into the room. 'Don't expect it of me.'

'I don't. Have I ever seen you weep? You did not care enough for him. But you must fear for your freedom. Surely that will stir your emotions.'

'I do fear what Henry might have in store for me, but empty tears and wailing will have no effect. They will not melt the King's anger. I expect I'll become penniless and homeless, a poor widow of no use to anyone. Where will he place me? Not in Pontefract with Richard, I hope.'

She clicked her tongue at my apparent levity, but stayed with me.

Every sense was frozen. I could not weep. Nor was my mood improved by a visit from Dickon. I should have been expecting it, but the events of past days had driven him from my mind. He entered my room like a winter blizzard, his fury just as cold.

'You did not tell me. Why did you not tell me? Am I not capable of keeping my tongue between my teeth? While all this was going on, as usual you shut me out, as if I were a child to be cosseted and protected.'

'It was thought to be for the best.'

'Whose best?' he spat. I did not know whether the anger was engendered by his not being party to the plot, or through fear that he too would be implicated in treason not of his making. 'And don't tell me that our esteemed brother Edward was not thigh deep in the conspiracy. And if so, why is he now licking Henry's boots?'

I did not try to reason with him. What could I say that would not stoke his anger, or his fear, further?

'At least you are not dead.'

'And you do not seem to be in mourning!'

He stormed out, having achieved nothing but a further disruption to my self-control. I picked up a precious beaker, its pale glass translucent, banded with blue and sinuous detail around the bowl. It had belonged to Thomas and at some moment in the past, when moved by unlikely sentiment, perhaps at Elizabeth's birth, he had given it to me. I considered its beauty, its Venetian perfection. Then allowed it to fall, to smash on the tiles, the pieces showering my hem with hard-edged sparkle. It seemed a fitting end to the day when lives and ambitions had been shattered. However many glasses I broke, it would not heal the wounds that we had inflicted.

Chapter Eleven

January 1400: Palace of Westminster

Edward avoided me like the plague, but I stalked him until he could escape no more and I took up a stance at his shoulder like the dread Angel of Death, demanding an account of his days of sin and betrayal. I entered his chamber without knocking.

'Dismiss your servants.'

He did not look up from what he was writing. 'I am busy,' he said.

'I would say that you have been more than busy.'

At least then he put down his pen, gently, on the document.

'We have a crisis looming so all personal matters can wait.'

'A crisis? My husband is dead. Joan's brother is dead. Huntingdon is dead. I am waiting for Henry to decide to lock me up. How much more of a crisis do you need?'

Edward's face remained ominously blank. 'The King of France has refused to recognise Henry as King. He intends to break the truce between England and France. Already he has gathered a fleet at Harfleur and plans to invade the southern reaches of Wales. Which should be of interest to you, if your

Glamorgan estates come under attack.' Upon which he retrieved the pen, dipped it and began to write again.

I would not be dismissed so ungraciously. Edward's clerks, engaged in clerkish activity, waited with baited breath and a slide of glances for the next revelation.

'I care not. Do you wish me to reveal how the details of the Epiphany plot were made so conveniently available to King Henry? Do you wish your servants to gossip of your part in it? I will speak openly if you demand it.' Leaning, I plucked the pen from his hand and dropped it on the floor, grinding the expertly prepared goose-quill under my heel. 'After all, what have I to lose?'

Edward's brows drew together, as aware of servants' ears as I.

'I advise you to be more circumspect in your speech and in your dealings.'

'Circumspect?' I held out my arms, the black cloth of my recently donned widow's weeds rustling in the movement, my veils shimmering. My women had completed some hasty stitching, altering a severe houppelande I had last worn to honour my dead mother. 'What need for me to be circumspect? I am the widow of a traitor, as everyone at Court knows, and I swear you had a part in his execution.' My voice creaked with long-repressed emotion, for here were matters I had been unable to discuss with anyone. 'Does King Henry know that you were involved in the plot against him, from the moment of its conception?'

Edward calmly selected another pen and continued to write, although I had seen the flash of warning in his eye. Had he always been so prone to treachery and betrayal? Perhaps he had, and I had been willing to overlook it as an unfortunate trait in my brother, a deplorable trait suffered but tolerated by many families, but it had never been so pertinent to my own future as it was now. 'And you are so certain that I was the one to inform him?' he enquired. 'I swear you have no proof, and I have nothing to say on the matter.'

But, after a short moment of my silence, he raised his left hand and dismissed his servants.

As soon as the door closed I launched my accusation: 'I have much to say, and Blessed Virgin, you will not shut me out. Shall I tell you the gossip on the tongues of whores and drunkards in the taverns?'

During my verbal attack I had taken stock of my brother, so handily going about the King's affairs. His garments were formal, as if he had had an interview with Henry. His outer clothing, layers of rich silk damask, lay piled on a stool, his sword neatly balanced on top. Beside him as he wrote rested a velvet cap and a pair of gold-stitched gauntlets. Thus I surveyed the wealth of a man who had earned royal patronage. The glint of an intricate chain, half hidden at his neck, confirmed it, shouting it from the pinnacles of the Abbey.

'I swear that you know the truth better than I,' I challenged. 'I hear it whispered, where servants gather, that a noble lord, of some renown, enjoyed the favours of a London slut who frequents the gutters of the Court where she offers her wares. And, once sated in lust, this noble lord talked in his sleep. He talked enough to outline the whole intricate planning. Does that sound feasible to you?' I did not wait for a reply. 'Then this slut hopped from his bed to that of some other royal minion, entertaining him between one sexual advance and the next, with the juicy piece of information. And this royal minion, after an hour of dalliance and gossip, ran hotfoot to the King and spilled the detail of the plot into his lap. Beware men who talk in their sleep. They make unreliable plotters. Particularly when they have an itch to be scratched by some common whore.'

I smiled at him.

'Was that noble lord, who inadvisably talked in his sleep, you, Edward?'

Well, that made him look up although there was nothing in his fair face that I could read. 'You accuse me of seeking out some common woman of the streets.'

'No, I don't. I don't believe a word of it. I could even forgive you if you had. At least it would be human weakness, not a callous destruction of all we had planned. I think it's a neatly constructed piece of slander, to take the nasty taste from the mouths of those who might not like to be associated with a man who plotted in one breath, and then informed on the plotters in the next.' I leaned close, my breath stirring the closely cropped hair on his brow. 'Bringing them to their inglorious deaths at the hands of a mob.'

Edward sat back. I had all his concentration.

'So what is it that you accuse me of?'

It was the only possible answer to account for our failure.

'You told Henry, didn't you? I thought it might be our father who informed, but I don't think so. He no longer has the strength of will to do so, if he ever had. But you have, my dearest Edward. *You* acted informer and told Henry of what was going to happen.'

And when he made no reply:

'Why would you do that? Could you not stand the thought of the spilling of Lancaster blood, in your name? Were you so nice in your principles, or so great a coward? Yet you would commit Richard to lifelong imprisonment, if not his death. How could you do it? Where is your loyalty?' I laughed, a harsh sound in the room. 'Where is your conscience?' I gripped the trailing edge of his fine sleeve, careless of the stitching. 'And before you lie to me, I saw where your loyalty rests. I saw you with Henry in Westminster Hall. I know you were used in destroying those who rose in Richard's name in the skirmish at Maidenhead Bridge.'

I flung the sleeve from me in disgust, striding as far from him as I could go.

'Your soul is drenched in blood, Edward. So many familiar heads severed from their bodies. Can you live with that?'

Now he replied.

'My *conscience,* as you put it, would have been drenched in blood whichever way I had leaned.'

From a wary distance I watched his shoulders stiffen, but not in denial. What point in his hedging around the truth? He had been there with Henry, laughing, convivial, a trusted counsellor. He was the only one of all the plotters to keep his head and his freedom. Indeed to be taken into royal circles again. The rest had been dispatched without mercy.

I felt like striking him, dislodging the layer of self-satisfaction. I did not. I would not touch him.

His voice, unrepentant, unruffled, reached me across the room. 'Why did I do it? It became clearer to me by the day. There was never any hope of our success when the country remained loyal to Henry. London would not turn against him for some charlatan tricked out in royal armour. We were carried away with our own enthusiasms, even when we were condemned to failure. We would have failed whether I had told Henry or not. Our plotter associates lost their heads to the fair citizens of this land who stayed loyal to Henry.' He shrugged, at last standing to walk towards me, the soles of his well-crafted shoes scuffing softly on the tiles. 'We misread the situation.'

'No, we did not misread it. There was nothing to misread until you unwrapped the whole package for Henry. The country would have risen for Richard and he would have been restored, as is his right.' An even worse thought came to me. 'When did you actually tell Henry? And afterwards, full of royal grace, did you return to your friends – to our friends, our family – to encourage them to continue the plot and so dig their own graves?'

He made no attempt to either assent or deny. Instead he walked back under my assault to shuffle the sheets of orders together.

'Was it conscience or greed, Edward? What did he promise you? God's Blood. You have robbed Joan of her brother and uncle. What will you say to her? Can you live with that?'

'I can live with it.' He stopped fussing with the documents and looked up, but not at me. His focus was far distant. 'Did you know what the ultimate plan entailed, Constance? Henry and his sons and the Archbishop were to be killed. Murdered. All of them. Cut down, their bodies removed. There would be no mercy. Did you know?'

I realised that it had never been spelt out in so many words, but we had all known how it must be.

'Yes. I knew.'

His eyes narrowed. 'You were content with that?'

'I accepted it, however much I might not like it. Am I to

believe that you acted out of tender-heartedness for Henry, because you could not stomach his death and that of his children? You lie, Edward. What did he promise you? I hope it is worth it, for there is a stain on your soul.'

He sat again, in a cushioned chair beside the fireplace where flames leaped in cheerful counterpoint to his confession, and leaned his arms along his thighs, staring at the tiles between his feet, the documents forgotten.

'I changed my mind. As simple as that . . .'

It took my breath.

'If you foresaw disaster, why did you not advise that we retreat?'

'Because Huntingdon would not listen. In the end I could not comply. It seemed to me that England would be a stronger kingdom with Henry at the helm.'

'And you would enjoy the proceeds.'

'If you wish. Yes.'

Bitterness choked me. 'You have robbed me of my husband.'

'Yes.' Now he looked at me. 'Do you care?'

I could not believe that it was said so brutally. Did I care? The initial shock of Thomas's untimely death was gone from me, yet he remained in my mind when I retired at night. Did I miss his presence? No, I did not. Did I respect him in death? No more than I had in life. Yet Thomas had fathered my children. He had never been overtly cruel, as was the lot of some wives. We had engaged in verbal conflict, but had both accepted the demands of duty to each other. I had disliked his temper and his dogmatic nature, but I would never have wished him dead. I disliked the consequences of his death beyond measure. I was aware that Edward, expression speculative, was awaiting my reply.

I inhaled slowly, speaking the clear truth, though admitting none of my complex feelings to Edward.

'I cared not for him, as you know, but he died because of your perfidy, leaving me a penniless and disinherited widow. That I do care about.'

From the purse at his belt Edward took a chain, lifting it high so that the gold caught the candle flame and glittered. He let it spin alluringly.

'What is this?' he demanded.

'A Lancaster livery chain. I'd consign it to the midden.'

'Not so fast, Constance.' He snatched it away as I swooped and would have ripped it from his hand.

'Is it yours now to wear?' I sneered. 'A royal gift indeed, a token of Henry's ownership of you?'

Abruptly he stood, as if at last I had stirred some emotion in him, so that I took a step back.

'Stand still.' He cast the chain over my head so that it lay on my breast. Its weight was heavy, making me balk at the impression I imagined it making against my flesh. 'Yes, it's a gift, a royal gift. My advice, for what it's worth. Wear it.'

'I will not.'

With one hand he prevented me from wrenching it off, while with the other he pulled aside the neck of his own outer tunic. There, bright on his breast, lay the chain I had spied, glittering with similar links. I had been right. Another Lancaster chain of 'esses'. He had indeed been bought. What's more, Edward's chain bore a cunningly carved and enamelled white swan, a magnificent piece of workmanship, Henry's personal heraldic symbol; only given to those of the closest blood, as Richard had given us the crowned and chained white hart to display our ultimate allegiance.

'Do we not match in our loyalties?' Edward asked, his hand still firm on the chain on my shoulder. 'Wear it, Constance. Wear it for the duration of this reign, however long it might be. We failed. Oh, we failed desperately. Our only hope now, if we do not wish to lapse into obscurity, is to become essential to Henry's Court. Do you want to spend your life in the distant shadows of your Welsh estates, even if Henry allows you to keep possession of them, or the French do not seize them? You do not. Or would you prefer to be wed to some northern magnate who never sets foot south of Pontefract? That will not suit you.'

'No.' It was a bleak picture. 'It would not.'

'Then broadcast your allegiance. It is a chain, a mere trinket. It does not shackle your heart or your soul. If any one of us can play that role, you can do it. You have done it all your life in your role of obedient wife. And you might even, in the fullness of time, be able to pretend to forgive me. I did it because I could see no other way.'

'But Thomas is dead. Tom and John Holland are dead.'

'We're all callous when the occasion demands. All I ask is your honesty. And I will say this too. Watch your tongue. Don't say anything to any man that can show your knowledge of the plot. Our only way out of this is to cleave to Henry. He'll not harm our father, or Joan; too much close family there. I have bought my place at his side. He'll not touch Dickon who was not involved.'

Which opened my eyes to a few things.

'So I am the weak link in all this.'

'You are if you vent your anger or your knowledge in Henry's hearing. You have to be innocent, ignorant and regretful. As pure as driven snow. Play the grieving widow's role, as you are now. Black becomes you magnificently.' And as I made to remove the collar: 'Wear the collar. Even in bed if you have to, to proclaim your Lancastrian allegiance.'

My fingers closed around the chain, but I left it in place. 'You make it sound so easy, so cold. I am the widow of an attainted traitor. My land and title will be forfeit. And my children. Do I lose them, too?' I placed my hand on my belly. This unborn child would also suffer. What would be its inheritance?

'Has Henry told you that your Despenser lands are forfeit?'

'Not yet. But don't pretend that he will not.'

'You can survive that. If he sees you as the regretful widow you will soon be forgiven.' He focused on my hand, flat on my belly, then held my gaze with his own. 'Are you carrying Thomas's child?'

'Yes.'

'Even more reason for you to make your peace with the King. Wear the chain, admit your pregnancy and plead for royal understanding. How could you have known what your ambitious husband was planning? You are, of course, distraught.'

All so carefully thought out. So plausible. So thoroughly dishonourable.

'God damn you, Edward.'

'He probably will, but that is on my conscience. Look to your own.'

I twisted my fingers in the links, hating his advice, detesting it, but seeing its value when the alternatives were so dire.

'Does it not shame you that Richard Maudeleyn was executed for his part in the plot?' I asked, hating our guilt in his death.

'No.' Once more his hands were engaged with the documents, applying a seal to one of them. 'He knew what he had signed his name to. He was quick to don royal robes and become our counterfeit Richard.'

'Have you no regret?'

'No. Nor do you. Only anger. You were in this up to your splendidly elegant neck, Constance. You can pretend neither innocence nor ignorance with me. You are as guilty and drenched in blood as the rest of us.'

I stalked to the door. What point in staying longer? All he accused me of was true. My soul was as black as his.

'Wait.' He stopped me by the simple expedient of stepping in front of me.

'For what? So that you might berate me again?'

'As you berate me? No. This was sent, directed to you. It came into my own hands. You should read it.'

From one of the coffers he lifted a letter, well thumbed. I took it from him, reading the inscription in a hand I did not recognise. The seal was already broken.

'Did you do this?' I ran my finger over the sharp edges.

'Yes.'

'You have no right . . .'

'Just read it, Constance. It contains good advice that you might accept from a priestly hand, even if you will not from me.'

I opened it, a letter penned to me from Bishop Henry Despenser. It was brief and explicit, from a cleric who had absented himself from our conspiracy from the beginning;

his heart might have been in it but his head had not. I would suffer for my part in this morass, he warned. If I wished to salvage anything of value of the Despenser inheritance I must submit to reason.

'Reason . . .!'

'He makes a good argument for applying a heavy coat of gilding to the past.'

He did indeed. A true wily priest. It would be a sin, he argued, to question God's will, which it undoubtedly was, that Henry should emerge from the recent debacle with his skin in one piece. I felt my jaw clench – for did I not already know that it would be most urgent for me to recover what was recoverable in property, as well as in the restoration of the status of the Despenser family. They had suffered for the misdemeanours of past Despensers. It would be unfortunate if all that Thomas had achieved to reinstate them should be consigned once more to oblivion.

'Which our family Bishop would say,' I observed, 'since his own bishopric is probably coming under Henry's scrutiny. No Despenser is a good Despenser in this climate.'

The Bishop of Norfolk offered to do what he could for my profit, honour, comfort and pleasure.

'You will have found satisfaction in reading this,' I said to Edward, not enjoying his faintly malicious air. 'Our concerned Bishop vows to be father, uncle, husband and brother to me, to the best of his ability. I suppose, in exchange, he expects me to plead his innocence as well as my own.'

Oh, he did. The Bishop understood my predicament, but for everyone's sake I must control my emotions and be pragmatic. It made me choke with venom.

'Did I not say that it was good advice?'

It burned in my gut. But it was the truth.

'Do you wish me to weep on Henry's shoulder?' I asked. 'I can do that.'

'It might be as well if you do. But in moderation. For his cousin Constance to be too lachrymose will simply rouse his suspicions further.'

'I can be moderate in all things.' How hard it was to force the words from my lips.

'Look, Con . . .'

He would have placed an arm around my shoulder in consolation, except that I took a step away.

'Don't!'

'Constance, then.' Edward's advice surprised me, although it should not have. 'I would further advise, dear sister, that you do not attend the interment of Despenser in Tewkesbury Abbey. If you wish to mark his grave with prayers and grief, do so later when the savagery of the Revolt of the Earls has ceased to issue from every man's mouth.'

It would be no hardship. 'His mother has undertaken it,' I said. 'I left it to her, as she would have wished.'

There was nothing more to be said. I must cut my ties with the past.

My final words to Edward as I left the room, the Bishop's advice ringing in my ears: 'I don't think I can ever trust you again.'

The documents, not unexpectedly, were carried directly to me. They came by the well-tended hand of Ralph Ramsey, one of the King's esquires, a thin, angular young man of much dark hair, who admired his own importance as well as his appearance. There they were, held out for me to take, official, heavily sealed with Plantagenet devices. They reeked of revenge.

It was to be expected, in the circumstances.

Keeping the esquire standing in the centre of the room, I carried the documents to the window and read through them, or at least the pertinent phrases. It was exactly what I had expected. Oh, but they hurt, like the heat of a fire against unprotected flesh. I breathed in silently, slowly. Henry had done his worst, and I disliked the insolence in Ralph Ramsey's eye.

'Don't turn round, Constance, but I think you might need to see this now. Before you have to face the King . . .'

Joan, without embarrassment, was herself staring at something beyond my shoulder as, lips parted, her words dried in astonishment.

'Where must I not look? Is someone staring at me?'

I did not turn. I was well used to hostile eyes boring into my undefended back. I did not wish to know which of the noble lords saw me as his most detested enemy.

Strangely Henry had not forbidden me the Court, and so I attended as I had always done. I might raise my chin in defiance but it was not a comfortable experience. My presence could not prove my innocence. I was met with speculative glances on one side, hostile silences on the other; some merely wanted to gossip. I found it wearing, humiliating, but necessary. Nothing would be settled until Henry made his move.

And as everyone knew, I was not innocent. I could imagine the prurient interest in me and my future, even though I wore the Lancaster livery chain. I despised the clink and slide of every link against the black silk of my demure high-necked cote-hardie.

'You could remain in your chamber, in mourning. It is what would be expected of you,' Joan had suggested. 'You don't have to step into the lions' den of Henry's Court.'

'When do I ever do what is expected of me? I know I should retire from the world but I cannot. Do I spend my days in stitching and weeping? I have a need to be seen. I want no condemnation in my absence, and if you can do it, with your Holland reputation in rags, then so can I.'

'Ah, but I am considered beyond reproach,' she said demurely, if I ignored the spark in her eye. 'My husband is still an object of King Henry's favour.'

'Then you are fortunate indeed. I am surprised that you consent to be seen with me.'

'So am I.'

I smiled thinly. How had I ever thought her to be an insipid woman with no opinion? It seemed that Joan and I were to become allies in a hostile world for, whatever the future held, we must not be seen hiding away in corners. Having through necessity to admit to Edward's good sense, here I was at a reception for a group of self-important courtiers arrived from Brittany, along with Joan whom I suspected had been sent by my father to keep a high Court presence. Or simply to keep an eye on me. Joan was the one to be astonished by some occurrence, when, after the mounting horrors of the past days, I had decided that nothing would astonish me.

'Turn slowly and look at the youth standing to the right of the King,' she murmured.

So I did, if only to enliven the proceedings. There was

Edward in his sycophantic presence at Henry's side. My eyes moved on. For there was a dark-haired swarthy courtier, a confident elegance in his stance, head bent as if to catch some royal order.

'Ralph Ramsey, one of the King's esquires,' I said. 'An impertinent young man with whom I have had recent communication, not to my advantage. What of him?'

'Look again.' Joan nudged me, eyes wide in disbelief. 'Look at what he is wearing.'

I looked again. A showy garment to catch every eye, one that hung inelegantly, if extravagantly, on his sharp-shouldered figure. And I frowned. My heart thumped against my ribs.

'I doubt there is another in the kingdom quite like it,' Joan murmured. 'I remember the occasion on which it was stitched, when you said that once seen, never forgotten.'

I remembered well enough. How could I not have recognised it? Widowhood had made my mind unreceptive of all but my own dissatisfactions. Here before me was an impressively short hanselyn, loose-sleeved, decorated all over from collar to hem, with silver-gilt spangles in the image of whelks and mussels. King Richard had given one such to his cousin Roger Mortimer, Earl of March, before he had fallen from royal favour. Thomas had been much taken with it and had one made to mirror its ostentation. If a royal favourite could wear such a garment, then so would Thomas.

'You said it was vulgar,' Joan commented as we looked.

'It is still vulgar. I dislike the blinding glitter every time he takes a breath, and even Henry must admit that Ralph Ramsey has not the stature for such a garment.'

Had Henry done this deliberately to punish me? No, I

did not suppose that he had. If he had wished to make me fully aware of my treachery he would have dragged me to see Thomas's head paraded along Cheapside. No, Henry would not have given this garment a second thought after handing it over as a sign of his generosity. I recalled how much the garment had cost.

There was no doubt of its provenance. I looked again, my thoughts taking an unfortunate turn. Was Thomas wearing this garment when he was imprisoned? Did he wear it for his summary execution? My belly clenched nauseously until I called my emotions to order. If Thomas had been wearing this hanselyn it would have been stiff and black with his blood, the brilliants dimmed for ever. It would have been torn to pieces by the Bristol mob, the pearls picked over by the guttersnipes.

'At least Ramsey did not wear it when he brought Henry's orders to me,' I said. 'I would have stripped it from his back, using a dagger.'

Joan was not listening. 'And there. Look at that.' Her disgust continued to wax.

I did. William Flaxman, another Court minion, resplendent in a heavily furred gown of motley velvet and damask. Another garment made to be noticed.

'Thomas wore that at Christmas. He said he liked the weight of the velvet and would have another made.' I watched as Will Flaxman stroked his hand over the fur cuff. 'So the division of spoils has begun. Henry has seen fit to reward his household with garments from my lord's back.' Bitterness welled up, fierce as a storm wave.

'That's the way of the world of treachery.'

Joan flushed when I turned my regard on her. 'Treachery is too close to you for such flippancy.'

But her return gaze was steady. 'You mistake me. Unlike you, I am rarely flippant, particularly when I am in despair over my brother's death.'

'While I am merely full of wrath. Let us take ourselves out of sight of those monstrosities. I am of a mind to accost Henry and demand their return . . .'

'Don't do that!'

'I am not so lacking in judgement.'

Many would say that I was. The consequences of the Revolt of the Earls had proved vast and humiliating.

There were to be worse repercussions for me than seeing Thomas's garments gracing the King's esquires. The burden of Henry's revenge, delivered to me by the obnoxious Ralph Ramsey, returned daily to haunt me, as was the intention. It coloured every nook and cranny of my life in black rage, for the whole range of Despenser estates, the length and breadth of England and Wales, was declared forfeit. Every castle, every manor, every tract of land. My dower rights were taken from me. Every item of value that I owned, from jewels to silver and gold plate, was confiscated. In effect I was penniless and landless. Even King Richard's reversal of the sentence delivered in 1326 against the Despenser ancestors was revoked. The tarnished Despenser name, with all its old guilt of greed and uncontrolled ambitions, had been explicitly and deliberately resurrected.

Henry's revenge. My name was likewise diminished.

That was not all, for I had lost control of Richard, my son, now named as a royal ward who would be raised under the auspices of King Henry.

Nor could I hope for any support from my Despenser tenantry over this loss. There had been no outcry against Henry's decision. Thomas's tenants changed sides as fast as an arrow could be delivered at the hand of a master bowman. It was prudent for them, this seamless changing of allegiance. They saw no reason to die in a futile uprising against the King's judgement.

Through it all, through all the disinheritance and forfeiture, I had waited. I waited for the King to summon me to explain my own investment in the plot that nearly killed him; my knowledge of events. Anticipating Henry's declamation of a more personal punishment became a wearing drag on my spirits when I was ignored. When I requested an interview, to know sooner rather than later, I was refused. I was acknowledged at Court, but only by an inclination of the King's head, his cool eyes surveying what my next plot might be. My future hung over my head like the mythical Sword of Damocles. Every night, while I imagined its fall, a fatal blow, Henry remained as silent as a hunting owl, and I was too proud to make a scene, to accost him and demand my rights as an innocent widow. I thought it would have entertained the Court immeasurably. I had too much dignity.

Denied an interview, I wrote petition after petition, showering the King with them, demanding the return of my dower rights, demanding the items of personal jewellery and plate that were mine and had always been mine. I sent my petitions to the royal apartments, to await the King when he met with his Council, to be there before him when he knelt in prayer in the chapel at Westminster, to be there beside his plate when he sat at supper. I would not allow him to forget that he had a cousin whom he had made destitute.

'He'll probably lock you up to shut you up,' Dickon suggested.

'At least I will know what he intends. This constant not-knowing is heavy on my heart.' I eyed him. 'It should be heavy on yours too.'

'How should it? Everyone knows I had nothing to do with the plot, and since our brother Edward is all things magnificent to the King, why should I worry?' He smirked, his spirits recovered. 'You could throw yourself at the royal feet. Edward might pick you up even if the King doesn't. He'll keep you in black silk.'

'And they might both walk over me.' I could not forgive Edward. I could not ever see myself forgiving him. 'Can you imagine the sanctimonious crowing of the Court if I kneel before Henry of Lancaster? I will not.'

'You don't need to do it in public!'

And so I wrote again. I requested at least the restoration of the wardship of my son. Was I not fit to care for him?

In your mercy, my lord, in your understanding of the need of a woman and a widow to have her son's future in her own hands . . .

There was no mercy.

I entered my chamber after Mass, casting off black veil and gloves, handing my cloak to one of my waiting-women. It was the coldest January I ever recalled. I wondered how Richard was faring in Pontefract. No one spoke of him and I did not dare. Dickon lounged along a window seat, long limbs stretched, yawning, aping, had he realised it, Edward at his most annoying. He watched me as I walked to a small coffer that had been placed for my attention just beside the fireplace.

Light from the flames flickered, bringing the enamelled hounds to life, as if they would spring into action at my command.

'What is it?' Dickon asked, sitting up as I crouched beside it.

'I have no idea. I'm surprised that you have not already investigated.'

But there was a royal seal on the latch. Breaking it, I lifted the little domed-lidded casket, and placed it beside Dickon, who shuffled his legs out of the way, suddenly interested, as I opened the lid.

'Does the King send you money? Perhaps he is thawing towards you.'

There was a note inside, clearly not written by Henry but at his behest.

Here for the hand of Constance, Lady Despenser, is the sum of thirty pounds in gold and silver, found to be in possession of Thomas, Lord Despenser, when taken prisoner on board ship.

I lifted the leather bag, which chinked with the coins.

'It was with him when he was captured,' I said.

'But not enough to buy his life.' Dickon took the bag and weighed it in his hand. 'I know Thomas was not well liked, but I'd have taken his money.'

'Would you?' I asked, surveying the youthful features which could hide a multitude of resentments. 'It's blood money. Thirty pieces of silver.'

'It's more than I ever see in one place. If you do not want it, give it to me.'

I took the bag from him and replaced it in the coffer.

'I have a need for it. A better use than to line your pockets, little brother.'

'You would not miss the odd coin.'

'Oh, but I would. Go away, Dickon, while I think.'

'Bribery, is it?'

'Who's to know?'

I sat and thought of the value of this gift. Henry was not closed to my circumstances after all, but his silence was a constraint in itself. Driven by a need to be free, I acknowledged that I needed help, and there was only one obvious source.

To do him justice, Edward came within a day of my summons.

'Edward.'

I was cool but not hostile.

'Constance.' He bowed, expression unreadable. 'I expect you need something from me.'

'Yes.'

'Why would I be amenable, whatever it is? You have cast me in the role of enemy.'

'Sometimes a woman has a need to negotiate with the enemy.'

'But the enemy does not always need to comply.'

I lifted the leather bag from the coffer and shook it gently to advertise the contents.

'Sometimes the enemy can be persuaded.'

'How much?'

'Enough. I think that you owe me at least one favour.'

Within two days I was escorted into the presence of my cousin Henry. My father on one side, my brother Edward on the other. A fine trio of questionable allegiance, the Lancastrian collars of 'esses' glinting a mockery on three breasts. My coin of thirty pounds had passed from my hands into Edward's as a sweet bribe. If it could buy me forgiveness and mercy it would be well spent, even though it was an amount I was reluctant to give.

So here we were, in one of the audience chambers, servants, couriers and courtiers bustling in the background, Henry making it as uncomfortable as possible for me. Before me, small and vulnerable, my hands on their shoulders, stood Richard and Elizabeth. I would make every appeal I could lay my hands on. This was for them, for the Despenser inheritance. *Control your emotions*, Bishop Henry Despenser had advised.

We made an appropriate obeisance. My children mirrored our actions, well trained, watchful. I felt Elizabeth tremble under my palm, and pressed a little harder to reassure. Henry nodded. He was like a cat with a nestful of mice. Not exactly hostile, not playful. His claws were sheathed but we all knew who had the power here.

'Well?'

The Duke of York stepped forward. 'My daughter has a request, my lord.'

'The problem with your daughter, sir, is that I doubt both her honesty and her innocence.'

'If you were in such severe doubt about her loyalty, perhaps you would already have incarcerated her, my lord.' My father, at his formal best, had all the weight of a royal uncle. I was impressed. I kept my eyes lowered in subservience. Edward on my right said nothing at all.

'It is still in my mind to do so.'

'You have taken everything else of value from her, my lord.'

'It was deserved. It is what is expected for a traitor's widow.'

'Is there nothing I can say in my daughter's defence, sir?'

'Nothing that would persuade me to exonerate her.'

There was no moving him. Well, I would do it. With much grace, I sank to my knees, pulling my surprised children with me.

'I am here to beg for your mercy, my lord.'

He was not impressed. Irritably he gestured for me to rise.

'In God's blessed name stand up, Constance. And your children. They look terrified. I do not eat children, whatever you tell them.' He smiled grimly at them. 'I appreciate the pretence to call on my mercy, but they should not be here.' He gestured to some passing esquire. 'Take them to the window. Feed them, talk to them, entertain them. As long as they are quiet.'

Looking startled, the squire chivvied them away. I watched as he lifted them to sit on a window seat, then sat beside them. From somewhere a platter of sweetmeats arrived.

'What do you want from me?'

I stood. How could he not know? Had he not read my letters?

'I have written, my lord.'

'As I am aware.' He gestured to one of his servants who came forward, bearing a whole package of letters. They were mine. I could not tell whether he had actually opened them and read them. 'Tell me in your own words.'

I did not hesitate. This was what I had worked for.

'I ask what any woman and widow in my position would ask. Restoration of my dower rights despite the forfeiture of the Despenser estates. Custody and wardship of my two children, Richard and Elizabeth. They are too young to be parted from me.' I placed my hand on my belly, hoping that he would not prove cold-hearted against my final plea. 'I carry another child for my dead lord. I need to raise them as loyal subjects, in knowledge of royal mercy.'

'A specious argument. I cannot argue against that.'

Well, it was not hopeless so far. I continued:

'I ask for restitution of the jewels and plate that were mine during my marriage. I would ask for restitution of some manors that my son will inherit. I acknowledge my husband's guilt. I ask that it will not be visited on his children or his widow.' I swallowed. 'If you need proof of my loyalty, it is that I am here today, with my father and brother to speak for me.'

Henry visibly sighed.

'Do you stand for your daughter, my lord of York?'

'I do, my lord.'

To Edward: 'And you will tell me she had no part in the plot.'

'None to my knowledge, my lord.'

'A very pragmatic answer, Rutland. But then all your answers are so. I will consider it.'

'It would not be right that my sister live in penury, my lord.'

I felt like reminding him that he had received thirty pounds from me without any sense that it would reduce me to penury.

'So you will not keep her on your charity. As you do your younger brother.'

'I will if there is no alternative. But I would rather the proud name of Despenser be considered worthy of a royal pardon.'

'The treasonous name of Despenser is worthy of no such thing.' Henry surveyed me, his chin tilted. 'You would not consider taking the veil, I suppose. It would solve a major problem for me.'

'No, my lord. I would not. Nor would it be appropriate for me to wed again, with this child in my belly.'

Edward intervened before I could say more.

'We appreciate the need for time for you to decide on Constance's future. But it would be to all our advantage.'

'And how is that?'

'Constance will be a burden to no one if she receives what should be hers.' He slid a glance in my direction that held a command that I remain silent. 'Her gratitude would ensure her loyalty, and that of her offspring for all time.'

'Which would be a miracle worthy of Saint Thomas Becket himself.' A pause. Clearly he did not believe a word of this. 'I have an invasion of Scotland to consider.'

'Then it would be good to leave a grateful and loyal Court in London, my lord.'

'As you say.'

Henry turned and stalked to the window, where he spoke soft-voiced to my children before looking out in the general direction of Scotland. Edward now nudged me into furthering my own plea.

'If it please you, my lord . . .'

'No more, Constance! I have heard enough.'

Driven by my conscience I said: 'It is not for myself but for my younger brother, Richard of Conisbrough. His annuity from King Richard, his only source of income, has come to an end. Would you consider restoring it? It would mean little to you, and so much to him. It is only one hundred pounds a year.'

I held my breath. Henry walked back. 'Very well, I will restore some of your property so that you have an income of your own. I will restore your son and his inheritance to you. There was never any doubt in my mind that your daughter would remain in your care. Further, I will consider an annuity for your brother.' All a mark of favour that turned my thoughts upside down. Why had Henry been so generous? And as if he read my thoughts: 'I have treated you with generosity. It will please me if you keep your nose out of my affairs. Spend your time on your estates when they are returned to you. As your brother said, it will be to both our advantages.'

Victory bloomed warmly beneath the detested livery chain. I had what I wanted. I would have to thank Edward, I supposed.

'I kneel at your feet in gratitude, my lord.'

Instead he came even closer, so close that I could read the disfavour in his eyes. Placing a hand on each of my shoulders, he leaned to apply a cousinly salute to first one cheek and then the other. His grip on my flesh was hard, his lips cold. There was no affection here. It was done to make an impression, so that all the Court would know.

'There is no need. I won't demean your pride further. Sufficient to say, in the eyes of the Court, you are restored to my good graces, Cousin Constance. Your King accepts your apology and welcomes you back into the fold. All I ask is that you will be a loyal subject.'

'Indeed, my lord. You can rely on it. You have all my gratitude.'

Although he looked askance, he stepped back, releasing me. It was over. I pulled Edward away from where the King and the Duke began to talk of troops and armaments for the march north.

'Now what?' he asked, looking wary.

'King Richard, of course.'

'Shh. Why would you risk being overheard, when by your profession of loyalty you have just persuaded Henry that you have no interest in Richard's future?'

'What are you going to do about him? Are you planning a rescue attempt?'

'No.'

'Are you going north with Henry for this Scottish campaign? You could find an opportunity to visit and see his circumstances.'

'I could. I might. But I will not launch an ill-advised rescue. Stay out of this, Constance. Count the blessings that you have just achieved.'

'It seems wrong that we have abandoned our true King.'

'Not wrong. Just—'

'Just pragmatic. I know.'

No use belabouring him when he would not be moved. Edward was shallow. Untrustworthy. But he had helped to restore some semblance of dignity to me.

'My thanks, Edward.'

'Anyone would think that I was returned to your sisterly affection, along with your dower and your jewels.'

'Anyone would be wrong.'

His smile was sly. 'You won't have to put up with me much longer. I'm not for Scotland with Henry. I am being sent to Gascony. I am appointed Governor of Aquitaine. I'll remake my fortune and my reputation.'

'I should congratulate you. At least the weather will be more congenial.'

I swept up my children and departed. There was no hope for Richard and there was nothing I could do about it. As for Henry, he might have promised restitution but to what extent had been made craftily unclear. I thought his promises might just be empty ones, to allow him to escape from an uncomfortable confrontation. After all, he owed us nothing. As for Edward, he might revel in his new position as Governor of Aquitaine, but as I interpreted it, he was to be sent as far away from the English Court as possible. I wondered if it had crossed his mind that this was a promotion with a bed of thorns attached to it.

But for now I was alive and I had my freedom and a royal promise. Within the hour the Court would have heard that Constance of York had been enfolded in the royal bosom, the royal lips saluting her treacherous cheeks. No one would dare slight me now. Nor was I in fear of my life. To have breath was to have hope.

Chapter Twelve

I was granted little time to luxuriate in the success of my ingratiating performance. On a morning in the following week, finding Joan at my door in a new state of anxiety, I pulled her into my private chamber away from my women. When distressed she could not be relied upon to be discreet.

'Now what?'

The dust stirred up by the Revolt of the Earls was refusing to settle. I suspected that she had been weeping.

'My brother.'

'Your brother is dead and beyond retribution.'

How callous it sounded but patience was a costly entity. Henry had yet to fulfil his promises to me, and if he was taken up with arrangements for his Scottish campaign, my needs might be swept aside for some time.

'I have more than one brother, if you recall,' Joan remarked. At least I had roused some spirit in her. 'It is Edmund.'

I recalled him, vaguely, almost a decade younger than I, I supposed. A dark, wiry youngster bidding to become as handsome as all the male Hollands. And now the new Earl of Kent after his brother's death, except that the title and the lands had been declared forfeit. He was as disinherited as I.

'Isn't he still in Ireland? Wasn't he left there with a royal presence to cow the Irish, when Richard returned to deal with Henry?'

I had no interest in him. Nor could I imagine why he would cause Joan distress.

'Yes. No.' She actually wrung her hands, her frail fingers winding together, then releasing to re-clasp around her rosary. 'Yes, he was left in Ireland. I presumed he would be safe there. But now he has come back to England. Because of Tom's death.'

'Why would he do something so foolish? There's nothing for him to inherit.' And not the best move for him to make in the circumstances. Which Joan confirmed:

'He has fallen into the King's hands. He landed in Liverpool and was taken prisoner as one of the renegades, which he never was. I am told that he is in the Tower awaiting Henry's pleasure.'

'And it may be Henry's pleasure, before he leaves to impose his will on the Scots, to make an example of him with an axe to his nape.'

Joan blanched, a gleam of moisture in her eyes. I sighed. I should not have said it. But who knew what revenge our new King would take? I tried to soothe her.

'Was Edmund close to King Richard? He was much younger. If he lived only on the fringes of Richard's Court, then Henry might not feel compelled to make an example of him.'

The tears now became rivulets, until she mopped at them with her sleeve.

'But Richard had an affection for him. He gave him an annuity of one hundred marks as a much-loved King's nephew.'

Which could seal his fate. He would certainly have already lost the annuity into Henry's coffers, as Dickon had lost his.

'I cannot help you,' I said. 'Henry will not listen to me again. I think I have used up all his mercy. Have you asked the Duke?'

'He says to leave well alone, until the King decides to release Edmund. But I am afraid that he never will. Or worse . . .'

I caught myself up before I sighed again, an image leaping clear into my mind of Tom Holland embracing his sister, soothing her fears. There was much affection in the family. Watching Joan's strained features I realised that she would mourn her brother until the end of her life. To lose another one would be worse than heartbreaking. Because I had no experience of such emotion did not mean that I was totally cold and without compassion. I took her hand and drew her towards the fire, aware that she was shivering.

'You must not fear the worst,' I said.

'How can I not?'

'Because there is always hope. The Duke will not come to your aid. Which leaves Edward.'

Joan looked doubtful. 'Will he be persuaded?'

'We can but try.'

The brightening in Joan's sad face unpredictably touched my heart.

With a groan, probably produced for my benefit, Edward took up his habitual position, legs stretched before him, at my fireside. His tunic was almost as unappealing as the one now belonging to Ralph Ramsey, but without the glitter. Considering the weight of chains and clasps, he had come from some Court function.

'How is it that you are so indolent but can be Master of the Royal Game,' I observed. But in truth, on the hunting field or at the tournament, there was no man who could rival Edward for energy.

'I match the needs to the day. Now I have to recover from a morning spent at Henry's beck and call and a chamber full of vociferous petitioners. I would rather hunt boar than listen to endless discussions over what to do with Richard's little Queen Isabelle. Keep her and her dowry here in England or return her to France. Her father the French King is demanding that she return but Henry is reluctant to hand over so much useful money. But you did not call me here to talk about Isabelle's woes. What do you want now?'

I told him.

The groan became a snarl that was genuine enough.

'How many more requests must I take to the King? My knees are worn out with grovelling. I see him flinch as I approach.'

'I hadn't noticed much kneeling. Who else should I ask? He has decided that you are his friend, so we'll make use of you, before you depart for Aquitaine.'

'I'm no friend of his. Keep your friends close and your enemies closer.' For once Edward was plain-speaking. 'I know exactly why I am in royal favour. I dare do nothing to disturb that delicate foundation. He needs all the magnates he can get on his side so he tolerates me.'

'Good. Remind him of your support at the coronation. Of our father leading him to the empty throne. And then persuade Henry to release Edmund Holland. As you say, he needs all the friends he can get, even if they only pay lip service. Here's another magnate to win to his side. Look at all those Holland sisters of his, married into magnate families. It will tie Henry into a slew of unenviable alliances.'

Edward yawned again. 'It will please me when this country is settled down into peace.'

'What if it never does? Will it even settle while Richard is still at Pontefract? Very well, I won't talk of that. Get Edmund Holland out of the Tower and then Joan will stop weeping over me.'

'*You* persuade him, now that you are dear Cousin Constance again.'

'I am only dear Cousin Constance in public. He has seen enough of me. Just do it, Edward. How old is Edmund Holland? Barely more than a boy. His head on London Bridge will not benefit Henry to any degree. Ask him to show compassion and the House of York will take him to its bosom once more.'

'What do I get in return?'

'My goodwill. I have no money.'

Edward snarled again, but silently, as he thrust himself from his chair and left.

It was I who snarled when Henry proved to be less good than his word. January had barely slid icily into February when he saw fit to grant me a paltry number of goods belonging to my husband, together with items of jewellery and plate regarded as my own in his lifetime, most of them inherited by me from my mother. Henry's promise had been vague but I had expected more than this. Where was my dower, that was indubitably mine?

'What use is this to me?' I entered Joan's chamber without courtesy, driven by justifiable anger.

'What has displeased you now?'

She was standing before a fitful fire in spite of the billowing smoke as February winds shrieked round the towers of Westminster. If I had bothered to look carefully, I would have seen a smile on her lips in a moment of sheer pleasure that had nothing to do with my appearance. But I did not look, too taken up with Henry's treachery.

'Henry has restored to me a handful of goods worth the magnificent sum of two hundred pounds. And that's not all. I have returned to me various pieces of inferior Castilian plate that I would happily dispatch to the smith for melting down, and jewels that I will never wear. Their settings are so heavy they would drag me to my knees.'

'At least you have got them back. Isn't that what you wanted?'

I swept that aside. 'I need land and an income. I need the return of the Despenser manors that will belong to my son. I need my dower. Henry promised restitution. I do not call this restitution. I call this mealy-mouthed offering a humiliation. Of what use is two hundred pounds? I knew his promises were empty ones when he made them.'

'You could petition him again. He is never unwilling to listen to a reasoned argument . . .'

'Holy Virgin, you sound like the Bishop. Never. I will not. And if Bishop Despenser expects me to plead his case, he will live in disappointment. He can find another fool to beat mercy out of Henry, for I will not.'

'Constance . . .' Joan raised a hand in the direction of the window embrasure.

I became aware of a man standing there, and immediately regretted being so outspoken in unknown company. Would it not pay me to keep a lock on my tongue? Henry might have ears behind every tapestry, every screen. One word out of place and the Despenser inheritance might slide for ever into Henry's treasury. I swept the man with a glance. He was tall and slender, conspicuously dark-haired, and not without a degree of presence. He did not slouch like Dickon. I was surprised to note a faint curve to his mouth as he acknowledged my less than elegant fury, which annoyed me even more.

'And who are you?' There was neither grace nor greeting in the challenge.

Joan opened her mouth to reply, but the man stepped forward to silence her with a glance. He bowed. Quite a beautifully extravagant bow, truth be told, the feathers ornamenting his high-crowned cap sweeping Joan's polished floorboards.

'I am Edmund Holland.'

A Holland. I allowed a more searching recognition to move over him. So this was Joan's brother, late a reluctant inhabitant of the Tower of London.

'I am Earl of Kent, stepping into my tragic brother's shoes,' he added to interrupt my ill-mannered survey, his beautifully modulated voice at odds with my sharpness, 'if the King sees fit to restore the title.'

Here was composure, certainly. And confidence writ deep in Edmund Holland, who had the build and poise of a swordsman. There was the look of now-dead John Holland about him, a self-awareness, a latent authority. Even an awareness of his own importance. I wondered if he was as driven with ambition as his uncle. If so, he would soon put himself in the way of danger in this troubled reign, but then he was of no interest to me. I had no memory of him at all, except to note, cynically, that here was all the physical beauty that had passed Joan by.

'Have we met?' I asked.

'Some years ago, Lady Constance. It seems that you do not recall.'

He had all the courtesy that I had abandoned. 'No. I do not recall.'

'But I remember meeting you. I am fortunate.'

I was unsure of his meaning, and not inclined to discover.

'I will leave you to your family reuniting.'

Joan was smiling again as I strode from the room.

For just a moment I was sorry. For a moment I felt a twinge of guilt for my discourtesy. For that moment I felt more isolated than I had ever been in my life.

In the grim light of a late dawn, the four little bells attached to the corners of the shrine of one of our greatest kings, Edward the Confessor, rang out miraculously. More loudly than if rung by a human hand, so that the arches of Westminster Abbey reverberated with the sweet sound. The monks about their daily offices sank to their knees in terror and amazement. Baseless rumour spread, fast as a raptor's flight, soon to be confirmed by fast-riding courier.

Richard of Bordeaux was dead. Richard, one time Richard the Second, King of England, no longer drew breath. The news flooded the Court, into every corner, every corridor, every chamber, like a swarm of summer gnats.

'Have you heard? Is it true?'

Most pertinently: 'Whose malign hand helped him to depart from this life?'

And: 'Are we talking murder? And if so . . .'

It was alive on every tongue. It took shape in the royal chapel after Mass when the priests whispered, and in solars where women threaded their needles with sharp comment; in the kitchens and butteries where the cooks slapped the skillets onto the fires to fry chitterlings in onions and garlic. From noble tongues to the lowest of the cleaners of the privies, there was speculation and shocked horror. Accompanied by many godly commendations and some infernal damning, here was a death that would not go unrecorded to its grave.

No need for Edward to visit Pontefract to discover the health of Richard of Bordeaux. No need for me to consider anew how to arrange Richard's escape, even if the only choice for him was a flight to Scotland or France, to wait for better times.

Richard was dead.

All we had hoped and planned for was at an end. The plotters were dead and so was Richard.

I shut myself in my chamber, in company with bitter regret and loss. All I had not felt when Thomas died swept over me now; a desolation that brought me to tears, cold as the stones when I knelt to offer up prayers for Richard's soul. Henry was now King with no one to challenge his grasp on the throne. All we had planned and fought and died for had been obliterated by some foul deed in Pontefract Castle.

I would be there, this pregnancy permitting. I would be there as witness when Richard's body was brought from Pontefract to London. Despite the frequent nausea of those early days of my pregnancy, a nausea that not even tincture of St John's Wort in a cup of wine could conquer, I would not stay away.

'It will be a boy,' my women assured me as I retched over a basin. 'You must rest. It will not be good to mingle with the crowds.'

Yet mingle I would. How had Richard died? I knew what the King had said. I did not know the truth, nor would we ever, but I would bear witness to his death. Another cup of St John's Wort was pressed on me.

'It is also good at warding off madness,' I was assured.

'How fortunate that I do not suffer from madness,' I said, but I drank anyway.

'Why bother?' Dickon asked.

'Because it is important to me. He deserves some dignity at the end.'

'At least he has not been cast into a ditch at Pontefract, unhallowed and forgotten.'

Which I had to admit had some truth in it. Nor could I fault the ceremony with which his return to his capital city was encompassed. The once-sacred body was carried in solemn procession to St Paul's on the twelfth day of March where Mass was sung for the dead King's soul. Henry attended and joined the rest of the pall-bearers to mark his cousin's passing. I stood with the ranks of the nobility that saw a need to be there at this end to a royal life, even if he were King no more.

A silence wrapped us round, raw like ice-crystals spangling winter foliage. And yet there was a strange acceptance, as if this was the rightful end, the seal placed on Lancaster's usurpation. There could be no peace for Henry as long as Richard lived and as long as there were those who would espouse his cause. Now all were keen to view his body and acknowledge the death, even if they hid their thoughts on the manner of his passing.

At Henry's command, Richard's face was exhibited from forehead to neck. Still fair, even at peace, but his flesh was leached of all colour, as waxy as the candles that surrounded him. Perhaps thinner than I recalled, but there was no evidence of violence to his person. No true sign of starvation, no sign of outrage waged against him. Those who had thought to see wounds and scars, or any sign of ill usage, were to be disappointed. But starvation or smothering would leave no wounds.

As for Henry, his expression, hard and shuttered, was untouched by neither guilt nor remorse.

The Mass was long. I was unwell, nausea hovering unpleasantly. I thought of requesting Joan to accompany me to escape the incense that clogged my throat.

'*Libera me, Domine, de morte aeterna in die illa tremenda . . . Deliver me, O Lord, from eternal death on that awful day when the heavens and earth shall be shaken and you shall come to judge the world by fire . . .*'

I could not form the words. I needed air; I needed to sit. My head felt light with the dread words. Although the Requiem was almost at an end I feared that I could no longer withstand the emotion that filled the space around me, fear of embarrassment adding to my woes. I tried to direct my mind to the corpse so magnificently displayed. It was wrong that a man so young should be dead. How could it be that it was by his own hand? Henry had said that Richard had refused food, had deliberately starved himself to death. I could not believe it.

I focused on Henry whose eyes were downcast in grave respect.

Richard had been murdered, I would swear it. It may not have been by Henry's own hand but it would have been by his command. He was as guilty as if he himself had applied the pillow to Richard's unsuspecting face.

I should feel gratitude towards Henry. After my outburst of anger, he had finally relented to grant me a list of Despenser manors worth over one thousand marks. And then, the most astonishing recognition of all, I was granted custody of my son Richard. With his wardship came possession of most of the Despenser lands, for me to administer in my son's name until he came of age. I was suddenly a wealthy widow, more than I could ever have wished for. With Henry's patronage I was no longer a piteous figure cast on the charity of others.

Why had he decided to be so inexplicably generous? It was not through my doing. Perhaps I owed it to Edward after all. Not that I considered Henry generous: I still did not have my dower restored to me, as was my right.

The space around me seemed to press down so that perspiration prickled along my brow, uncomfortable beneath my veil. Darkness closed in and I felt the ground uncertain beneath my feet. My breathing was shallow, uneven.

'*Blessed Virgin . . .*'

As the voices of the Requiem faded and the incense choked every sense, a hand closed gently over my arm, cushioned by the thick velvet of my cloak, to give me support.

'Do I escort you out, my lady? I think some air would aid you.'

A man's voice. Was it one of the clerics? For a moment I stiffened, then breathed in, praying for deliverance from the black waves that seemed to race towards me, not caring who it might be who had seen my predicament. Even my worst enemy would be welcome. Even Edward.

'Before God! I wish you would.'

He extricated me from the crowd, slowly, carefully, supporting me discreetly all the way as he led me, weak and almost blind as I was, to the door and out into the cold air. It slapped against my cheeks, the perspiration cold along my spine, restoring me to the sense of what was around me, and I could breathe again.

The waves receded, the delineation of stonework becoming sharper.

'My thanks . . .'

'I can find nowhere for you to sit, my lady. But you might drink this.'

From the folds of his houppelande, Edmund Holland produced a small leather flask, presenting it to me. When my hands still shook, he held it firmly for me to sip the strong liquor. It made me cough, but at his urging I sipped again. The nausea was retreating like wavelets from a beach. I breathed in, more deeply.

'It is a relief to be here. I would not dishonour our recent King, but I would curse the priest with the thurible. The incense near choked me.' There was no need for him to know of my pregnancy. I did not seek compassion.

Finally, with all my senses restored, I turned slowly to look at my rescuer who was restoring the vessel to within the folds. Edmund Holland's face was a mask of severity, his voice low, without expression.

'I saw your distress, my lady.'

'And you came to my aid most gallantly.' I breathed in again, grateful that my balance was once more secure and my wits restored to me. I owed this man more than my thanks. 'I think I was not very courteous to you when we last met.'

'No, you were not.'

I felt my brows rise. 'I had received bad news.'

'And a restoration of inferior gold plate can excuse any ill manners.'

I could read no censure in the direct regard but I knew mockery when I heard it.

'No, it cannot excuse crude behaviour. I suppose you expect me to ask pardon.'

'Yes. When you are fully recovered. Until then I will merely accept that you were aware of your discourtesy. I am sure that you were. Perhaps you consider that your rank absolves you from good manners.'

It was like receiving a knife wound, gently delivered by a master, but lethal in its disembowelment.

With a slight bow, he turned and walked a distance, yet still within call, giving me a discreet space and time in which to recover fully, while I turned my back to him. What right had he to launch such an attack? And yet I could hardly fault him. Discourtesy was a demon I must face. I turned back to watch where he was engaged in conversation with an official clad in royal regalia, casting Edmund Holland into the shade, and yet I noted that his garments had undergone a distinct renaissance since I had last seen him. Fashionable, costly; I presumed that Joan had taken him in hand after his sojourn in the Tower. The patterned red and black of the formal houppelande beneath his fur-lined cloak became him very well and shrieked ostentation in the thick gold embroidery and furred cuffs. The royal official, seeing my interest, nudged him and nodded in my direction. I had obviously been a source of conversation.

Edmund Holland returned in leisurely fashion to stand

before me. I was on my guard, expecting a return to his evisceration of my character. Instead:

'Do you wish to go home, my lady?'

'Yes.'

'Then I will ensure your safety.'

His hand guiding me once more, without my permission, he led me to where the liveried retinues awaited their diverse lords.

'Shall I find my sister to accompany you?'

'No.'

'She might be glad of an excuse.'

'I do not need her now. My discomfort was a minor thing and soon remedied by an absence of incense and a too-strong dose of false regret from the congregation.' His hand fell away and I expected him to leave me with my retainers. I must indeed make amends. 'I am sufficiently recovered to ask pardon for my churlishness,' I said.

'Your apology is accepted. Anger can reduce us to words we regret, as I know to my own cost, and doubtless as you do to yours.' And before I could think of a reply: 'Do you suppose he was murdered, my lady?'

It was a question I had not expected. I looked at him, seeing no guile. What I did see was a keen intelligence.

'Yes. I am convinced that he was. Richard would no more starve himself to death and thus abandon his crown than I would attend this tainted Requiem in sackcloth and ashes.' I was in command again, my head clear, my thoughts clearer, and I had no intention of offering a diplomatic lie to one of the Hollands. His openness was a breath of fresh air. 'I am Constance. We are close enough related for you to presume with my name. And if you are going to discuss Richard's murder in this public arena, it should definitely be Constance. And I will call you Edmund.'

The dark eyes were hooded, and then opened wide so that I felt drawn in to his thoughts, if I permitted it. 'So who murdered him, Constance?'

'If you mean by whose hand, I know not. However it was done, it was with skill to leave no mark of violence. One of the royal guards I expect, under precise orders, or one of Henry's household. I swear our King will know. How advantageous for him to have Richard dead.'

'Do you suppose that the King will allow him to be buried at Westminster? You have your finger on the pulse of this place far more than I.'

I shook my head, relieved to experience no disorientation. 'King's Langley, I expect. Out of sight, out of mind. He'll have no thought of setting up the tomb of a royal martyr under the very nose of Lancaster.'

'Richard's tomb in the Abbey is already constructed.'

Indeed it was. A fine edifice as memorial to King Richard and Anne of Bohemia.

'Which will not sway Henry one inch.'

He glanced at me, as if considering his next move. Here was a man who did nothing carelessly. 'I think that you encouraged Rutland to speak for me with the King,' he said.

'How do you know that?'

He laughed, his dark features hauntingly illuminated. 'Nothing magical. Joan told me.'

'It is nothing.'

'It is everything to me.'

'It would not have done to have left you in the Tower. It made Joan unhappy.'

'But I am still in your debt.'

What a trivial exchange of words, and yet I felt there was nothing trivial about it. It made me feel that I must be on my guard.

'A debt which you have repaid by rescuing me,' I responded lightly, coolly.

In response Edmund Holland took my hand and raised it to his lips in a formal salute. He released me immediately as I pulled my hand away.

'I will continue to serve you. Do I summon you a litter?' he asked.

'No. My horse is here.' I pointed to where a Despenser groom stood and exchanged opinion with others of his status.

'Are you fit to ride alone? I will ride with you.'

'It is no distance.'

It was in my mind to refuse. I had been astonished at my reaction to his salute, when it was a mere conventional recognition of a family connection, albeit by marriage. I needed no other escort than my own groom, but then, in a moment of pure indulgence, I nodded my concurrence, watching him as it took him no time to discover my mount and his own, whereupon he dismissed my groom, helped me to the saddle and rode at my side. All with supreme efficiency. He had a masterly air about him, but then, when did the Hollands ever not?

'What will you do now?' I asked him, discovering that it was no mere polite enquiry. I wished to know the answer.

He turned his head to look at me. 'What do you advise? Do I remain here to wager on winning the King's interest?

Do I take to the tournament fields of Europe and win myself a fortune? Or do I go crusading and put my soul right with God? I imagine your advice will be pertinent.'

I wondered if there was cynicism in the listing of possibilities. It seemed to me that Edmund Holland knew exactly what he would do now that he had achieved his freedom. Yet I would give him my advice.

'Stay here at Court,' I offered promptly. There really was only one path for a man of ambition. 'Offer your services to Henry. As we have seen, any loyalty to Richard is now redundant.'

My escort turned his gaze to survey the road between his horse's ears. 'But can I do that with a true heart? There is blood on our new King's hands. Blood that is difficult to excuse. So much of it that it drips from his sleeves. Holland blood, too.'

Was he so squeamish? I was disappointed in him. My reply was sharper than I had intended.

'As there would have been dripping from our hands and sleeves if the Revolt of the Earls at the Epiphany had gone full term. We were as savage in our plotting as the King was in the outcome. And it has to be said that those who died did not do so at Henry's hands. You might question whether he would have stopped the executions – I doubt that he would – but were we not intending to kill him and his sons? There's no point in squeamish deliberations over whether to become loyal to Henry now that the future is writ clear. I thank the Blessed Virgin every day that Henry proved himself merciful to me, as he has been to you. So this is my advice, Edmund Holland, for you to take or reject. And I think your sister would say the same. Make yourself indispensable.' I felt my mouth twist, but I said it anyway. 'My advice is to watch and learn from my brother Rutland. He will show you how it's done. He smiles and bows and offers duty and service. What is in his mind I cannot guess, and neither can the King, but his miming of a perfect servant is faultless. And, while you are becoming indispensable to Henry, don't forget to remind the King that there is a title and estates to be restored to our name, and yours.'

'Sage advice.' His brows arched beautifully as he tightened his expensively gloved fingers in his reins. 'Sadly he'll not be quick to reinstate a Holland. Henry has already taken some of the Holland estates for his own. He claims that they were rightfully his as part of the Lancaster inheritance.'

'Which is patently not true. But you can petition for the rest, as you must for the Earldom of Kent.'

'As I must. Or look out for a rich wife.' He guided me through a raucous crowd of apprentices who were celebrating King Richard's death in bucolic style, a crease forming between his brows, his voice less mellow. 'By God I'll need one. There are three surviving Holland dowagers, all with a claim on the estates. I am beggared before I begin.'

'Ignore them,' I advised callously.

'How can I? I have a duty to them. They have a right to an income as widows.'

'Then if you are iron-bound by duty, you must petition Henry, and explain your chivalric commitments. Who knows? You may rouse his compassion for these beleaguered women.' I shrugged my disinterest. 'He can only say no. In which case it had better be the rich wife. Do you have anyone in mind? You could always look across the sea to some French or Italian heiress who needs a well-born husband. It would be a better plan, all in all, than going crusading. A holy war could end in your death. The rich wife might not be to your taste, but she's unlikely to creep up on you with a dagger against your ribs in the dark of the night.'

Edmund Holland laughed aloud, a bright sound that made men and women turn their heads. 'Such a simple remedy for an overwhelming problem. As I thought, Constance. Full of good advice.'

Helping me to dismount, he escorted me into the palace at Westminster where he gave me over into the care of my women.

'Thank you,' I said. 'It was not necessary, but I appreciate your riding with me.'

'I will visit and ask after your good health.'

'There is no need. And you can always ask your sister.'

'So I can. Yet I will come to see with my own eyes.'

There was a strong will, interwoven with all the inbred appeal that came so naturally to him. All the desire to please and be pleasing that Thomas had lacked.

He is just a man intent on making his way in the world, I thought.

No, he was not. There was none of the brusque outspoken clumsiness of Dickon. None of the sly self-satisfaction of Edward. None of the callous self-will of the late Thomas Despenser. I lingered to watch him as he walked away.

'I hear my brother rescued you from the deluge of pomposity,' Joan remarked on her return from the Requiem.

'Yes. I was overcome by all manner of traitors saying their farewells to the King they had betrayed.'

'I expect Edmund kept you good company.' She sat with her feet near the hearth and sipped from a cup of spiced wine that I had refused.

'He was amenable enough.'

'He has ambitions.'

'Do not we all?'

Midsummer 1400: Cardiff Castle

I gave birth to a daughter with all the travail that I recalled from my past confinements. Agonising but quickly over. I was fortunate, said the midwife who ruled my chamber when I began my labour. Not all women were so blessed. So my daughter came into the world, a sturdy child with wisps of light brown hair. I thought she had no resemblance to Thomas or to me. A placid infant, I handed her to her wet nurse and the young woman employed to rock the cradle.

Did I have any affection for her, for Richard or Elizabeth? If I did I did not know how to show it except in physical care. Did I regret it? How could I, since familial affection was not something that I had learned at my mother's knee. My children were not embraced and kissed except by their nursemaids, but, conscious of my duty, I would ensure that this child be raised as a true Despenser, a proud if flawed name, related by blood to the King. One day she would be much sought after as a well-connected wife for some great magnate. Such a scrap of life to carry so much hope. I named her Isabella, after my mother, for there was royal Castilian blood in her veins too.

Fleetingly, in my heart I wished that I had given birth to another son. I would not willingly burden either of my daughters with the restricted quality of life that I had experienced, but there was no use in repining. A strong-willed wife need not necessarily be without influence.

A month after my ordeal, after a churching when I donated

candles to the Altar of Our Lady, I was thus purified, restored to my place in society, and on my way back to Court. It would not be good policy for me to be absent too long.

Chapter Thirteen

August 1402: King's Langley

Had we not had enough of death?

Death stalked us. Not content with winnowing its way through sundry Plantagenets, Despensers and Hollands, the reaper was to strike again at my family. Not that it was unexpected, nor was it due to untimely violence against us. As the sultry summer days moved from July to August in the year of 1402, the remains of my family gathered to lay to rest the body of Edmund of Langley, Duke of York, and to pray for the calm repose of his soul.

'A blessed release,' Dickon announced.

As perhaps it was, the pain that had hounded him for so long robbing him of any enthusiasm for life. In the end he had become too frail to do more than offer silent loyalty to King Henry.

It was a well-attended affair as the earthly remains of Edmund Plantagenet, last remaining son of King Edward the Third, were placed in the tomb that already housed those of our mother, Isabella. The Duke's will had been most explicit.

This is where he would lie, in the richly sculptured edifice of alabaster and black marble, adorned with heraldic shields, all set within the arches of the Church of the Dominicans at King's Langley where he had been born. Who was I to interpret the whims of the male Plantagenets?

Did we mourn?

Not noticeably, though we were all clad in black magnificence, sweating in the heat as we sparkled with gems and gold thread. It was the end of an era, the curtailing of a generation. The future was in our younger hands now.

The consequences were on the whole predictable. I allowed myself to speculate as I assessed those who had journeyed to King's Langley. My brother of Rutland, with whom I had exchanged few words, and those frigidly polite, since the Epiphany debacle, had now stepped into our father's shoes as Duke of York. From the costliness of his garments and the weight of bullion on collar and cuffs he was enjoying the benefits of his new rank. The gleam in his eye was not the product of filial tears. Joan, shrouded in sombre veils, became a youthful, valuable and childless widow, with a whole new future of possibilities lying in wait for her. Dickon, head bent in false solemnity, was doubtless untouched by the death of a man who had refused to acknowledge him privately although he went through the required motions in public, while I found it difficult to mourn a father who had rarely been moved in my direction by affection. The Duke's death changed nothing for me. I was still a traitor's widow and seemed, surprisingly, destined to remain so until the King willed otherwise. My father's death was an irrelevance. As I watched the straight spines and bent heads of the mourners, I felt isolated from it all, as if my path into the future were an indistinct track through shadowy woodland.

I shed no tears, moved more by anger than by grief, for what was it that fixed birth and death, these two inevitable boundaries in life? Nothing but the malicious weaving by the gods of a new tapestry, gods who rarely had our best interests at heart. The Three Fates, so beloved of the Ancient World, were arbitrary in their control of birth, of life and of death. Clotho, Lachesis and Atropos span and wove and snipped with merciless delight, with no regard for the pleasure or ambition of their victims.

Which merely added to my restlessness.

For were these arbiters of our fate not women? And women with power to inflict their desires, while I had none. I had no role to play outside my own household, nothing to exercise my mind and my ambitions beyond the pages of an account book and the willingness of my steward to allow me into his world of estate management. He would rather I kept to stitching and playing the lute, neither of which I did well.

Thus the lot of all women, to be governed by men. When it happened, as it undoubtedly would, my hand in marriage would be disposed of, against my will and my choice, by the political machinations of King Henry. I was surprised that no match had been mooted already, to place me under the legal control of one of Henry's magnates who would enjoy my wealth and my name. Until then I must dedicate my life to the Despenser estates and castles in the name of my son. I had desired their restoration to me, but it was not in my nature to bury myself in a domain of charters and rent rolls and reluctant tenants who discovered every excuse not to pay what they owed.

Meanwhile Joan mourned, dry-eyed behind her veils, as much as was seemly.

'You should weep,' I advised her as the royal gathering dispersed and we were left standing beside the sharply carved tomb, dust motes shining in the dim light. 'Your next husband might not be so kindly.'

'My lord Edmund was kind to me,' she admitted, 'although I bore him no son.'

She placed her hand on the marble as if in a final wifely caress.

'He could hardly blame you if you were rarely intimate. And I would be grateful if you would fold back your veils. It is like talking with a spectre.' And as she did, without demur, we moved slowly away towards the door-arch where sunlight spilled in. 'Henry will have you wed again before you can draw breath.'

Colour, briefly, touched her cheekbones. It had to be said that the dense black did not become her pallor. 'It is already under discussion, and my lord Edmund only just interred. Lord Willoughby of Eresby is suggested. Baron William Willoughby. He is a firm supporter of the King, based in the north, I think.'

'Is he interested?'

'Interested in a Holland? Of course he is. The King is keen to reward one of his supporters. Lord Willoughby will snap me up.'

'And to his good fortune. So it will be Lady Willoughby. A step down from Duchess of York.'

A little smile touched her pale mouth. 'Ah, but there are advantages: William Willoughby has only thirty years to his name, which might make up for my loss of marital rank.'

Halting, she turned and eyed me with distinct speculation. 'Treason aside, it is a surprise to me that there has been no marriage arranged for you.'

'It is a matter for consideration for me too,' I admitted.

How could it not be a gnawing concern that to my knowledge no man, titled or commoner, English or foreign, had shown any interest in offering for me as a wife? It hurt my pride that I was unsought. I knew not whether to feel relief or chagrin at being so undesirable.

'You cannot blame them.' It was as if Joan could read my thoughts. 'I suppose that the taint of treason might dissuade many.'

'And my Plantagenet blood is of so little value?'

Joan flushed a deeper red.

'Forgive me. I am in a mood to be dissatisfied. Let us talk about you instead.'

'I thought that after the child was born, Henry might have a plan for you,' she persisted. So too, I had thought. It was now two years since I had given birth to Isabella. 'Henry connived at his sister's marriage to Sir John Cornewall,' Joan observed, beginning to walk again. Elizabeth of Lancaster was another cousin and Huntingdon's widow; Sir John Cornewall a close friend of Henry, a formidable soldier and exponent on the tournament field. 'I expect he thinks it will keep her from under his feet.'

'Do you say? Well, it seems that I am to remain firmly under Henry's feet.'

'But you are not content, are you?'

'Content?' I replied without thought, simply to stop her prying. 'Of course I am content. Why would I not be?'

'Do you not love your infant daughter? I must come and visit your nursery.'

'You will be welcome. She is at Conisbrough with Richard and Elizabeth.'

'Do you not love her?' Joan asked again.

I regarded her with some compassion. It was her dearest wish to carry a child.

'As much as I love all my children. Love is not an emotion that has had any place in my life.' Realising that she was in a mood to commiserate further at my obvious lack, I stopped her. 'I will pray for a good outcome for you, and that your new husband fills your womb within the first year of your marriage.'

But Joan would not be distracted. 'And I will pray that you will find a husband who is rich and ambitious and has some measure of affection for you.' She thought for a moment, then, with a twist of a smile for the incongruity of such a prayer: 'And a man who is willing to let you go your own way.'

'Does such exist?'

I thought of those I knew. The men who frequented the Court. Those who were here now to pay their respects whether genuine or false. I would choose to marry not one of them. For what manner of man would I choose?

The figures in the windows, fair and richly clad in their stained glass, stared down at me in solemn displeasure of my thoughts on the occasion of an interment, or looked heavenwards in pious indifference to my plight.

I looked across at Edward, who had returned from his royal appointment as Lieutenant of Aquitaine for this burial, Joan's gaze following mine to where he stood within the excellent company of King Henry and two of his younger sons, John and Humphrey. Sleek and affable, it would seem that the life in Gascony was an advantageous one clad as he was in costly Aquitainian fashion. There was a general burst of laughter now that the need for gravity was past. Edward was offering an opinion on some matter that took their interest, and yet . . .

'Speaking of contentment . . . My brother is not content,' I remarked to Joan as a groove appeared momentarily between his brows, despite the laughter. 'He should be more than satisfied. His reward for turning evidence has been astonishing, even for a man with royal blood in his veins.' I glanced at her to see if she would react to my lack of discretion but she did not. She knew where the evidence had come from. In the past two years Edward had emerged from the disaster smelling of sweet clover rather than the rank pungency of the latrine. Royal patronage lay on his shoulders, thick as the open-edged garment of black damask velvet that brushed the tiles as he moved. Keeper of North Wales. Lieutenant in Aquitaine. Who was closest to the King apart from the royal sons, whose lives he had saved? Now with our father's death, as Duke of York he had acquired supreme status as well as the royal regard.

'Do you not speak with him?' Joan asked.

'Not unless I have to. He pursues his own path. And while he is in Gascony there is no need to do so. You have no cause to love him either.'

Edward turned his head, as if he felt the weight of my regard. We had had no conversation since his return. Then without any recognition, he returned his attention to the King, their heads close in some exchange of opinion.

I frowned. 'I would almost say that Edward is plotting again.'

'I won't deny it. I see my brother is bidding for royal preferment too.'

Joan nodded towards the dark figure, neatly attached to the royal coterie. Had he taken my advice, so carelessly offered? It seemed that he had. He looked up and bowed to Joan, and then to me, before giving his attention back to the royal matter in hand. For the briefest of moments I recalled his concern for me, so long ago at the Mass for King Richard. Now he had none, nor was it necessary, for my moments of weakness were past. Clearly he no longer had any need for my advice or my company.

'You are not content, are you?' Joan had asked.

'Of course I am content,' I had replied.

No. I was not.

Returned to Westminster, because I had no desire to go elsewhere, unexpectedly disgusted at my weakness, I fell into a melancholy induced by helplessness as the days at Court with their proscribed events and formality unwound before me. Was I destined to spend my life as a widow with my paternoster beads and my needle? I was young, I was clever, I was educated, but I was bound about with Plantagenet shackles. Even the Court held no attraction for me. I felt as dry and desiccated as the corpse we had interred at King's Langley.

If I were a man I could ride into battle. I could accept a royal office, as Edward had done, and administer some far-flung province. And I swore I was capable of it. I could go on pilgrimage. Could I not do all of that? A pilgrimage was the obvious choice for a woman in my position, with the state of her soul to be redeemed. But to do so would be no fulfilment, travelling the pilgrims' route in prayer and piety. I burned with ambition. I burned with a desire that was physical.

It was the opinion of many that I had no cause for dissatisfaction. Restoration of the wardship of my son had given me virtual control of the Despenser properties. I had a choice of accommodations. My financial situation was excellent. It was, in the opinion of many who saw Henry's open-handedness as a weakness, more than I could have hoped for. Nor had I given up on persuading Henry to restore my dower rights. I tapped my fingers on the lid of the coffer that contained my writing implements. I went to the lengths of picking up a pen. Why not bend my mind to writing yet another petition to demand the return of my dower properties?

To my lord King Henry from his cousin and loyal subject Constance.

But I threw it down almost as soon as I had picked it up, driven to prowl the room. Why was I not satisfied? I had enough income for my comfort. My children were safe and in good health. I had no burdensome husband against my will whom I could not love . . .

Ah . . .

I shook my head. Such a path across thorny terrain held no interest for me.

But once planted, even in such infertile soil, the seed could not be ground under my heel until it died. For there was the truth of it. I had twenty-seven years to my name but I had never known love. I had neither sought it nor received it. Even Joan lived in hope of her new husband.

I seized my lute, struck a chord, and sang.

'Take thou this rose, O Rose,

Since Love's own flower it is,

And by that rose
Thy lover captive is.'

I dropped my lute on a cushion with a grimace of impatience. Joan would smile and weep over such sentiments. I was unmoved. And yet my rooms here seemed so empty, so unlived in. So desolate. They echoed with emptiness.

As if to remedy it and smooth the anguish of my thoughts:

'My lady.' A knock on the door. A soft-footed servant. 'You have a visitor, my lady.'

'Who is it?'

'My lord Edmund Holland, my lady.'

'To what purpose?'

'He does not say, my lady.'

I would not meet him here. For no reason that I could fathom, I said: 'I will come to the hunter's chamber.' A little audience chamber attached to my dead father's accommodations with huntsmen for ever tracking a dappled hart in the stitched forest tapestry.

Any remnant of emotion was fast removed. I knew not what he wanted, but he must wait on my convenience. I summoned my women, selecting an over-gown the colour of ripe cherries and a new caul of finest linen to confine my hair, until I stopped, my hands still on the heavy silk. Was I selecting garments to make an impression on a man whom I had no need to impress? I dismissed my women and retained the severe garments I had donned at the beginning of the day. Edmund Holland would have no interest in what I wore. I stalked in unaccommodating mood to the encounter that I was already regretting.

He was waiting, seated at ease in company of the hunters

and their quarry. Which of the two was he? I wondered inconsequentially. Hunter or prey? It was not an easy life for a man, hampered by lack of lands and title and with a name for treachery, to make his way at Court, although he seemed to be attaining a foothold, however uncertain. Now he rose to his feet at the sound of my footsteps.

'I will go, if this is not convenient to you, my lady. I would not disturb you.' The voice was unmistakable. So was the elegance and the steady, confident regard. 'I was told that the Duke of York was here.'

So he had not come to see me at all. I became brisk, unfriendly.

'No, he is not. Is he not with the King? Enjoying his new title?'

'No, my lady.'

'Then try the mews. I imagine Edward will be saying farewell to his favourite hawk before leaving for Gascony.'

I did not understand why he had not asked one of the servants. Any one of them could have informed him of Edward's absence. Then why was he here? Was it to see me? I could see no reason for that either.

'I will look for him there.' He bowed. I thought he would leave. 'You have my condolences, my lady, on the death of your father.'

We had slipped back into a formality. I felt it on my tongue, keen as a disappointment, sour as unripe fruit.

'I do not need them. It was not unexpected.'

'And yet you were his daughter.'

'You are labouring under a misapprehension if you believe that our family was – or indeed is – tied by bonds of mutual affection. We are ignorant of such softness.'

He bowed again at my indifference, as if he accepted it.

Suddenly, I did not want him to leave.

'I see that you are smiled on at Court,' I said.

'I took your advice to make myself a frequenter of Court circles. It helps that I am thought too inexperienced to either manage my own affairs, or to be a dangerous insurgent.' He smiled briefly, but it did not reach his eyes. 'No one who has lived in Ireland, which is a hotbed of such, can remain ignorant of malpractice.'

I liked the saturnine air that sat lightly on him.

'To be a King's friend pleases you, then.' I matched him, malice for malice. 'As it does my brother.'

'It must. I need his patronage. I need the restoration of my estates, so I cannot afford to merge with the tapestries as just one more participant in the hunt.' He gestured to the flamboyant company that rode around the walls in pursuit of the deer. 'Henry appears to bear me no animosity, so I live in hope. My coffers are not bottomless. Indeed, their contents are already severely compromised, so that I am forced to exist on royal charity, as well as being dependent on my sister's interfering hand in the garments that I can afford. Humiliatingly, there is little in my coffers but dust and moths, until Henry decides to be forgiving.'

It was expressed without emotion.

'I am sorry for your moth-inhabited coffers,' I found myself replying. 'But don't reject Joan's sisterly ministrations out of hand. No one noting the depth of velvet on your houppelande would consider you anything but a man of means. I see she has you well in hand.' I had no compassion for my brother Edward, for his everlasting impecuniousness. Why should I have any thought for Edmund Holland?

'I'll not talk about money to you, my lady. Enough to say that my three surviving dowager Countesses of Kent continue to remain alive and well, their demands on the Holland estates still constant and heavy. If I had hoped for the early death of any one of them, I am doomed to disappointment.' He shrugged lightly, a slight smile robbing the comment of callous intent. 'So it behoves me to become obsequious and win Henry's recognition with a seat on the Royal Council.' A gleam appeared in his eye. 'Or I could hope for some skirmish between Henry and those who question his right to the crown. Are not the Welsh under Owain Glyn Dwr posing a threat in the Welsh March? To fight on a battlefield would win the King's favour.'

'Then I wish you good fortune. And that you don't die in battle.'

I felt an infinitesimal stroke of concern against my heart, although why I could not discern. Was this not simply a light-hearted exchange?

'I have no intention of dying in battle, or in any other circumstance, until I have achieved what is mine by right. I am in pursuit of a glittering future.'

He bowed again. Approaching, he saluted my fingers, as he had once before.

'God keep you, my lady.'

No, I did not like the formality.

'Once you called me Constance,' I said, for some reason irked that he had withdrawn from me.

'So I did. And will do so again.' The talk of death and ambition was overturned with one of clever enticement. 'Or perhaps even Constanza, when the mood takes me. Yes, I will call you Constanza.'

'You will do no such thing!'

My reply was immediate, but the sombre eyes lifted to mine.

'Why not?'

'No one calls me Constanza.' It had been the name of my mother's sister, and I had been called for her. I had no desire to be addressed as Constanza by anyone. It endowed my name with far too much intimacy for my liking.

'It has an air of drama that becomes you.'

'That is nothing but a foolish nonsense.' And yet: 'When will the mood take you, Edmund Holland?'

'Who is to know? Adieu, Constanza.'

It was said almost as a challenge. I refused to respond to it.

'Adieu, Edmund Holland.'

An inconsequential meeting. I still did not know why he had come. I regretted when he left me. I regretted not changing my gown and veil.

I was a foolish woman, cast too much into her own company.

Early May 1403: Palace of Westminster

Almost a full year had passed before my brother returned from Gascony, when the first days of May were encouraging us to put aside our heavy winter damasks, to pack the furs with rosemary against the moth, and to array ourselves in summer silks. I had not seen him since the burial of our father as there had been no need for him to return to England, but now, in the spirit of forgiveness, I decided that it was time that I precipitated a reconciliation. I was twenty-eight years old. I could not remain immaturely at odds with him for ever.

Edward was dressing for a royal audience when I was shown

into his chamber, a body servant arraying him as my brother raised a hand in a sign, undoubtedly arrogant, for me to wait. I watched with amused awe as his servant clothed him in each chosen garment, Edward shrugging into a short tunic, the tops of the sleeves padded to enhance his shoulders in Aquitainian style. How long would it take the long-suffering minion to close every button that stretched from neck to hem? The whole was completed by short leather ankle-shoes pulled on over sleek hose. A gold chain was hung around his neck, a variety of rings pushed onto his fingers and a brooch attached to his felt cap.

A nod of thanks and the servant left us, while I walked round my brother, assessing from every angle.

'Well?' He looked over his shoulder.

I thought he had gained a little weight, but not enough to detract from the overall magnificence.

'Impressive! Gold buttons, too.'

'Which is my purpose. Are you come to welcome me home?'

Edward embraced me and applied a brotherly salute to my cheeks. It seemed that he was of a mind to be amenable despite the clouds that had never quite gone away. But then Edward was always clever at disguise.

'You look prosperous.' I fingered the sleeve of his tunic, admiring the close-woven cloth. 'With a distinct air of French fashion.'

'Appearances can be deceptive.' His friendly tones vanished as if I had stamped on his foot. 'The campaigning in Gascony has all but beggared me.'

I thought he was exaggerating. His garments denied any beggary.

'No more than Henry's demands on me as Richard's

guardian,' I replied lightly. 'I have been ordered to secure the Despenser castles at Caerphilly and Longtown against the Welsh. Where do I find the funds to do that? I resisted as long as I could but when the five royal demands arrived at my door, one after another in consecutive weeks, I had to make a minimal attempt. Henry is in debt and has no sympathy for anyone else in similar circumstances.'

Edward's glance was unpleasantly speculative. 'As I recall, with the wardship of Richard in your keeping, you are an extremely wealthy woman.'

'That's as may be. And I am grateful for it. But it does not run to coating the walls of Caerphilly and Longtown in gold.'

His shoulders twitched into an unmistakable denial. 'Your debts are in no manner comparable to mine, and I see few paths out of the morass.' He was abrupt, abrasive, turning the conversation without finesse. 'I hear much about the progress of Owain Glyn Dwr, attacking the Welsh March and running the Marcher lords ragged.'

I allowed him to do so. 'All true. I expect Henry will send you to bolster his efforts against the Welsh prince. Our King might even find the means to pay you, if parliament is willing to raise the taxes.'

I thought he would jump at the chance to discuss the plans for the coming campaigns, but Edward would not quite meet my eye.

'What is it?' I asked. 'Is something wrong?'

'Not a thing. I am home and I will set myself to make my mark. If it be in the Welsh campaigns, then I will place my sword at Henry's disposal.'

'I wish you well.' I tried hard. 'And it is good to see you back in England.'

'I will remember that.'

His answering smile was enigmatic, and one that I did not quite like. But although our reconciliation had not been wholly satisfactory, the black cloud had muted to shades of grey. There had been some meeting of minds, however shallow.

We were settled at the Despenser house in Aldgate, the whole Despenser household, the children in a state of permanent excitement that drove their governor and servants to despair. Built by some long-dead de Clare lady, it had been returned to me as part of Richard's inheritance, and it was more suited to family life than the chambers in the Palace of Westminster. It pleased me to have the children there under my eye, the girls being little more than infants.

'Will we go and see the lions and leopards in the Tower?' Richard asked on every occasion that my path crossed with his. This morning it was when we broke our fast with the main officers of my household. It was a movable feast, after we had heard Mass, with a simple meal of bread and cheese and ale served to my steward and priest and to the clerk of the kitchen. I considered Richard of an age to be present although his sisters still remained in the nursery.

'Yes.'

'When? When can we go?'

'Soon.' It was not a visit I relished. The caged animals, restlessly prowling or utterly somnolent, were too reminiscent of my days shut up there with Thomas, afraid for our lives. But I capitulated when Richard, with all the importunity of his six years, opened his mouth to make a further demand. 'We will go tomorrow.'

As Richard, his voice echoing in a shriek of joy, departed to inform his sisters, his feet clattering on the steps, a messenger arrived to offer me a document. From Henry, recognising the seal. What it was I had no idea. Perhaps merely a request to attend some formal Court function now that the new Queen Joanna, a Princess of Navarre and Duchess of Brittany whom Henry had married in February of this year, was in residence. As a royal cousin he might wish me to join the Queen's household. Mildly curious, I broke the seal, unfolded the document. It would be an interesting experience, and I would probably accept.

I smoothed the document.

My hand stilled.

This was no invitation.

Employing all my willpower, I curbed my fist from crunching the parchment, seals and all. I kept my breathing steady, my face without expression, my fingers pressed lightly.

I looked up at the messenger, who was waiting with the patience instilled by his position. In the distance I could still hear Richard's expressions of glee, as if to hammer home the blow that had just been struck at me by Henry in his wisdom. In his deplorable self-serving lack of integrity. Richard. The Despenser heir. He was mine to raise and nurture. His lands and estates were mine to supervise until he came of age. Thomas might not have engaged my emotions but Richard was the boy who, as a man, would fulfil the Despenser ambitions. I would raise him well and with pride in his dead father. It was my duty; it was my desire. Who would know the importance of family and heredity more than I, a daughter of York?

'My lady?' I realised that I was staring at him, my expression less than amenable, and the courier had become unnerved. 'Do you have a task for me? My lord the King said that I might be at your disposal in the circumstances.'

'How considerate of him.' My apparent serenity amazed me. 'I have another message for you to carry. If you will find the Duke of York, I would like him to visit me here, as soon as is possible.'

He bowed. 'Certainly, my lady. I will say that it is of utmost urgency.'

I went to my parlour to await my brother. Rage was a red flag that billowed and snapped in a howling gale.

Edward came.

I remained seated.

There was no warmth of greeting or embrace today. He knew why I had asked him to come to me. At least he had done so without too much delay.

I held out the document from the King.

'I won't ask if you were ignorant of this.'

'No. I regret it.' He took it from me, turning it over. There was no need for him to read it.

'Regret?' I asked. 'Henry awarded Richard's guardianship and wardship to me. It was promised that such powers would remain in my hands until my son came of age, as is proper and correct. Henry considered me perfectly capable of managing the estates and my son's future marriage.' My throat was dry with the enormity of what these two men had accomplished between them, at my expense. 'And now I learn that the grant of wardship has fallen into your hands. All of it. The wardship.

The control of the Despenser lands and estates. The control of my son's future.'

He did not deny it. How could he, when here was the proof in his own hands? As if it burned his flesh, he handed it back. I took it but let it fall to the floor between us, where it lay, a dangerous legality to burn and divide us. All that Henry had returned to me had been wilfully seized and reapportioned. Even this Despenser house in Aldgate, this room, where I sat to receive the instigator of my ignominy, was no longer mine to use.

'Did you petition for this?' I asked. 'Do I presume that it was you who persuaded Henry to reverse the grant of patent?'

'Yes.'

'And you told me nothing of your little conspiracy. Not one intimation!'

'No.'

'You knew when I last saw you. On your arrival home. And you said nothing.'

'I had no wish to fend off you and your arguments.'

'Fend off?'

He sat, although I did not invite him to do so, his hat and gloves clasped loosely on his knee. 'Here is the situation. I am in debt. You knew that. Your son's wardship will go some way to solving the problem.'

'I knew that selfishness was engrained in your bones, Edward, but even I could not have envisaged this level of self-interest. You have enriched yourself while beggaring me. You have robbed me of my son. You are despicable.'

'You really don't understand, do you? Or you choose not to do so. My service to the King in Gascony has put me in debt to the tune of one hundred thousand pounds, with no hope of paying it off.'

'So you went begging to the King.' My son's wardship in exchange for the debt Henry was unable to pay.

'That is the truth. Henry was not unwilling.'

'I would like to have been informed personally. Not by a servant with a letter.' I rose to walk behind him, where I thumped a fist down onto his padded shoulder. 'How could you do this? I know we are ambitious for power, for wealth, for status. At least I had my son's Despenser interests at heart. You have no one's interest but your own. You killed my husband and now you would rob my son.'

At last. I had pierced his magnificent self-confidence. He surged to his feet, letting hat and gloves slide to the floor. His tone was no longer smooth and sanctimonious.

'Do you not know the state of my debt? I am drowning in it. I have found it necessary to sell and pledge all my gold and silver plate. By next year I will be eating off earthenware from my kitchens. Next I will find a need to mortgage my land to pay my men-at-arms. Is that worthy of the Duke of York? Before God, it is not. The Gascony expenses exacerbated the whole situation. Henry owes me. He was willing to endow me with Richard's wardship. If he expects me to serve the crown in Wales against Glyn Dwr, he really had no choice.'

All so simple. So easily explained.

'You could spend less on your clothes and your jewels. The ruby pinned to your hat,' – I nudged it with my foot – 'is large enough to kill a man at twenty paces if used as a slingshot.'

'It will hardly pay another week of the services of my escort, much less my men-at-arms.'

'You have stabbed me in the back, dear brother.'

Meeting of minds? There had been none. I could never have guessed what vicious little scheme was afoot between Edward and Henry, that they should have made their own arrangements so effectively, without any consideration for me. Well, I should have suspected it. Edward was entirely lacking in principle where his own ambitions were involved. I was reduced once more to an all but penniless widow, still without even my dower rights.

'It is unfortunate that you did not choose a wife who could have brought you an income to suit your rank,' I accused.

'Indeed.' His voice had instantly cooled. 'Beatrice of Portugal would have suited me down to the ground.'

It was a betrothal made and broken before Edward was nine years old, the Portuguese heiress becoming betrothed instead to the son of King John of Castile. Further illustrious suggestions had also fallen through: a Visconti betrothal, a Valois bride.

'Does Philippa realise that you would have exchanged her for a better-endowed bride? Or even a younger one capable of carrying an heir for you.'

Philippa de Mohun had lived twenty years before Edward was born. His reason for wedding her was as much a mystery as any, that one of the most eligible knights in England should wed a younger daughter of the Mohun family with no land and no dower of any real value. Perhaps it had been love. I felt my lip curl at the incongruity of it.

'My relationship with Philippa is not your concern.' Edward stooped, all lithe energy, to pick up hat and gloves, easy control restored. 'Do you want my advice?'

'No. Not unless there is any redress for me.'

'There is none, and you'll get my advice anyway. Petition the King again for your dower rights. He will, I expect, be feeling guilty. I doubt he will refuse, whatever his financial strictures.'

'Thank you, Edward. I value your timely advice.' We faced each other, hostile as rats in a barrel. 'Perhaps you can inform me. Where is it that you wish Richard to live? Does Philippa expect him to join her childless household? And what of me? Do you wish me to vacate these premises immediately?'

'I think we can leave Richard where he is with his mother for the moment. I give you leave to stay in the Aldgate house.'

'You cannot believe my gratitude. I will enjoy being dependent on my brother's charity.' I walked to the door and held it open for him. 'I will tell Richard that you are now his guardian. And since you are, his burning desire is to see the lions in the Tower. I will tell him that you will arrange to take him. You will enjoy it. Watching caged creatures struggle to escape their bonds.'

'Your wit is always a pleasure to observe.' He bowed. 'I will not see you destitute. God keep you, Constance.'

'I think that I despise you more than any other man.'

'It is unfortunate.'

He left me to retrieve Henry's document from the floor, outraged as I realised that knowledge of my humiliation would spread around the Court faster than a summer wildfire. Meanwhile I was driven to speak to my son. He stood before me, face solemn, eyes wide. My demeanour unnerved him.

'You must listen to what I have to say, Richard.'

'Yes, madam.'

'You must listen carefully. Do you understand?'

'Yes, madam.'

'You are Richard Despenser. When you are full grown you

will be Lord Despenser. The Despenser estates and lands and castles will all be yours, because you are the heir of your father who is dead. Do you understand?'

'Yes, madam.'

'Until you are grown, your uncle of York will administer your land. He will keep it safe for you and in good heart. But it is yours, not his. It will never be his. When you are grown, you will step into your father's shoes and become Lord Despenser. Until then you must obey your uncle of York but he will be kind to you.'

I felt my hands curl into fists.

Richard considered this. 'How much must I grow, to step into my father's shoes?'

I drew him close. 'Until your head reaches to my shoulder.'

'Will it take me long?'

'Some years, but one day you will be old enough and tall enough to take the land back from your uncle. That is all you have to know.'

I would repeat my admonition to him every year as he grew. His inheritance was Despenser and Edward merely held it in his ward.

'Yes, madam. I understand. And I will grow. Can we go and see the lions now?'

I took him, of course, acknowledging that Edward would never find the time. What to do with a boy of six years, who knew nothing of the battles for power and wealth, at which he was the centre?

As we watched the beasts prowl their cages, tearing apart gouts of bloody flesh flung to them, before falling into a depressed somnolence, I considered whether it would be in my interest to berate the King for what he had done. I had been well betrayed and thus it would give me enormous satisfaction, but it would make no difference. Why would I invite public rejection? It would be more politic to respond with cold acceptance and send a petition instead, for infuriating as it might be, I had perforce to take Edward's advice. I would write a petition before these unpleasant proceedings could be swept aside. I deserved my dower restored; it was the least I should expect after Henry's breaking of his legal agreement. Meanwhile, I directed my women to collect up the children to escape this miasma of rotting flesh and animal dung, of the hopelessness of captivity. Richard would be satisfied for a little time.

'Constanza.'

The recognition was instant, as he knew it would be. I turned slowly, knowing by some inner sense that I must be careful with my response. I might not understand the jolt of pleasure that pricked my emotions into life, like an ill-jabbed brooch pin, but it was impossible to deny it.

'Edmund Holland,' I replied with no evidence of the turmoil that set my heart beating as if I had enjoyed a fast run in one of Edward's hunting expeditions. I was all light insouciance. 'Now what might you be doing in the Tower's menagerie? Have you developed an interest in elderly lions who barely rouse themselves from sleep?'

'I would do the same if I were caged day and night.' He offered them barely a glance. 'I might ask the same of you.'

'I have the perfect excuse. An importunate son.'

'And I have no excuse whatsoever, except perhaps for your captivating company.'

'You are flattering, sir.' He did not mean a word of it. Or did he? His confidence, I decided, was bordering on arrogance.

'Of course I flatter you. I have been sent by the King to inspect the state of the royal armoury in the Tower, but since I was told that you were here, I made a detour. The armoury will not go away in my absence. Henry expects the outbreak of a great conflagration and will be prepared. My appointed task is to count weapons in particular and armaments in general.'

'A fascinating task.'

'And one that any squire could accomplish just as effectively.'

He walked with me, out into the relief of the fresh air, to where our horses and travelling-litter for the girls awaited us.

'Will you journey with us?' I asked, for what reason I knew not. 'You could abandon the armoury for the day.'

He shook his head. 'Keep my King waiting? I dare not.'

I masked the regret, expecting him to bow and be on his way, except that he turned to me, taking all my attention.

'I see worry on your brow,' he said as Elizabeth and Isabella were lifted into the litter, Richard mounting his horse. 'Will you tell me what troubles you?'

'No.'

The habit of keeping my own counsel was too deeply engrained, even to open my thoughts to this man who invited me to do so. I could recollect no man ever doing so before.

'But something has disturbed you. Do I detect your brother's fell hand?'

'Why would you say that?'

'I imagine he often ruffles your feathers.'

'Yes. He does and he has. But I'll not tell you about it.'

Which he accepted with a faint smile. 'Do you wish me to take him to task for you?'

It seemed to be a perfectly serious request, without the flippancy that Dickon would have used. I tilted my chin.

'Are you considering throwing down your hood and issuing a challenge, on my behalf?'

'If you wish it. I think, given the Duke of York's reputation, he might beat me into the ground, but I would hold your name on my tongue with my dying breath.'

Ah, there was the humour behind the stern facade.

'I'll not ask such a sacrifice of you.' To my astonishment I stretched and touched his hand where it clasped his belt. 'There is little value in challenging Edward as long as he has the King's ear.'

He covered my hand with his, turning it, carrying it to his lips so that he kissed my palm.

'When you have confidence in my talents, I will be your true chivalric knight.'

The severity had been restored. What an unnerving man he was. I resented being so unsettled.

'I am not aware that I need a chivalric knight.'

'That is because you have not yet been awoken to the fact.'

I resisted such a thought, regretting encouraging him. What use had I for some mythical knight-errant to ride to my rescue? There were enough men of courage and valour in my own family, and not one of them could be relied on. Why would Edmund Holland be any different? I would fight my own battles against my brother Edward.

'Nor will I awake, as you so poetically put it. What use have I for such?'

'You will discover when I am gone.'

He released my hand and stepped back, our conversation come to an end it seemed.

'Why? Where are you going?' I asked before I could stop myself.

Helping me into the saddle he shook his head. 'To fight for King Henry, if rumours are true. The Percys are about to set the north in flame.'

Bowing, he walked back towards the Tower, and I watched him go until he climbed the steps out of my view. I did not understand why I felt the need to do so.

Edmund Holland had talked of making a name for himself on some distant battlefield, earning fame and financial reward as his grandfather Sir Thomas Holland had done when taking valuable French prisoners at the Battle of Crécy. The opportunity came faster than anyone would have thought. It took all our menfolk to a clash of arms when the growing hostility between King Henry and the Percy family came to a violent head. Henry prepared to march north and west to make contact with his son Prince Hal on the Welsh border, so preventing Sir Henry Percy from joining forces with the troops of Owain Glyn Dwr. Edmund Holland rode with them.

When Joan and I stood with the royal household of women to wish them success in their venture, I recalled bidding Thomas farewell when King Richard's campaign took him into Ireland, but my heart had been left untouched, where it should have been engaged in solicitude. Husbands who left for war often did not return. Now, in this brave rallying of forces I owed no marital duty in God's eyes to any man. I swept the melee of men and horses, surprised that I was able to pick out no banners proclaiming the familiar lions and fleurs-de-lys that would belong to Edward, Duke of York.

Edmund Holland came to make his farewell to Joan, very recently become Lady Willoughby, who hugged him with sisterly fervour but refused to weep over him. 'God keep you,' I said when Edmund had been released, a farewell such as I might have bestowed on the least of my household as they fulfilled some errand for me. But he had been kind to me, so that I would not wish to see him ride to his death or injury.

The lightest of feathers stroked across my heart.

'God give me a strong arm in battle,' he replied, signing the cross on his breast.

'And bring you safe home.'

'More than that.' He bent his head, considering. 'I would like to think that if I impress King Henry sufficiently, he will restore my title and my lands. Pray for me, Constanza.'

Ignoring the birth of interest in Joan's eye as she registered his use of that name, I replied much as she would have done.

'There is no need to ask. You will be in my thoughts.'

For a long moment his eyes, always serious, held mine. 'I would like to think that you meant that.'

'I do not lie.'

I did not think that I had ever promised to hold any man in my thoughts and prayers.

'Light a candle, then, in my name, when you pray to the Blessed Virgin.'

But I knew that his thoughts were already far from me. He did not even foresee the possibility of death while I was suddenly too well aware of this sudden twist of fate, to take such a number of these men from us. Many who drew their swords on the battlefield would not live to tell the tale of their heroic feats of strength and skill.

I watched him ride out, with so many other familiar faces, armour bright, Holland pennants proclaiming his lineage even though he had yet to achieve the title for himself. For me it was a new experience, and not a pleasant one, to care for someone. I did not even understand why I should be so troubled. Caring had invested in it a depth of cruelty that I had never envisaged, and certainly did not want.

And no – I looked back over my shoulder once more as I made my departure. My brother Edward's heraldic motifs were not on display. I wondered why they were not flying, as usual, at the forefront of the banners, and why it was that Edward should not be riding out with the King's forces on so vital a campaign.

Chapter Fourteen

The battle, for it could not be avoided, was held on the twenty first day of July, on the flat fields to the east of the town of Shrewsbury in the west. We worried, waiting for news. King Henry was hard pressed but emerged with victory; Prince Hal proved himself a valiant fighter on the battlefield but would carry a bitter memory of that day in a scar that would mar his features until the end of his life. Henry Percy was slain, his body suffering dismemberment, the ignominy of all traitors. As for Edward, if he had been present, I fleetingly wished him a painful, if not necessarily lethal, encounter with a sword, a suitable punishment for wheedling my son Richard's inheritance out of King Henry.

And what of Edmund Holland? I tried not to think of him, except that his loss would cast Joan into a further pit of grief. For myself I denied any such concern. But when the affray was over and the King returned to London with some celebration, a note was delivered to me.

In thanks for your prayers. They were most felicitous. If you need proof of their power, and of my eternal gratitude, I trust that you will be present at the thanksgiving that King Henry will make at Westminster.

Edmund Holland

How could I not be there? A full Court ceremonial in the Great Hall, attended by every magnate who wished to distance himself from the Percys and be lauded as loyal to the Lancastrian crown, fur and damask and jewels rivalling the gleam of the candles. What they lacked in solemnity was provided by the Mayor and aldermen, with a handful of regalia-clad priests to dispense their blessings. And throughout it all, Edmund Holland stood at Henry's right hand with the heroically wounded Prince. Edmund had indeed taken the eye of the King who now led him forward to present him to the expectant Court, raising a hand to still the conversations.

Edmund, thus being presented, surveyed the ranks with stern dignity. I found myself almost holding my breath at the latent power in that unmoving, unsmiling figure on the dais. It was as if his feats on the battlefield had hardened him, hammering out a sharp ambition as a smith would create an edge on a fine sword.

King Henry addressed us. 'I would present to you Edmund Holland, a man known well to you all. His family has not been the most notable for its loyalty despite its illustrious heritage. But here we have a man who fought at my side at Shrewsbury, where he proved time and time again his courage under attack. He is worthy of his name, following in the footsteps of his grandfather who was brave on the battlefield and even braver to wed Countess Joan of Kent.'

There was a rustle of laughter. It was well received. Edmund inclined his head, his face pale beneath the campaigning bronze in reaction to what was to come.

'In recognition of his service to me and to my heir,' – Henry nodded towards his son – 'it is my pleasure to restore to Edmund Holland the title and the lands appertaining to the Earldom of Kent. Raise your cups in toast to Edmund Holland, Earl of Kent. Today, sir, the inheritance is yours.'

The toasts were made, Edmund surrounded by a congratulatory crowd, while I felt a sense of rightness at this achievement. The rebellious Hollands were reinstated, recognised, drawn back into the fold. Edmund, magnificent in his new authority, had achieved his life's ambition and the reign seemed set fair for the future.

In a clear memory, from what prompting I did not know, I recalled the dice still in my possession, but I had no desire to try them. I was becoming a loyal subject, wooed and won by Henry of Lancaster with his sense of justice amidst the joyous clamour of the raising of cups of wine.

I began to make my way through the chattering nobility, intent on giving my own recognition of the inheritance, when certainty and celebration were laid waste for me. A young page, all sharp elbows, found his way to my side. A message was delivered, brief in its telling but one that cut to the heart. Without thought, I abandoned the scene of Edmund Holland's glory and took horse to the house in Aldgate. His achievements were cast aside in the need to return to the Despenser household.

It was a silent place as I entered, as if the dread that had accompanied me on my brief journey had already come to pass. My breath was short, throat dry, perspiration unpleasantly clammy along my spine beneath my Court robes. And here was my steward, the lines on his face evidence enough of the imminent disaster that awaited me.

'Am I too late?'

Did we not all have experience of death that crept and struck without warning? This was no expected demise on a battlefield from sword and arrow or trampling warhorse. This was a terrible domestic tragedy, suffered in so many households. It made it no better for me.

'No, my lady. But we think not long now . . .'

'Where is she?'

'In the nursery, my lady.' He was whispering. 'The little maid seems comfortable there. I will take your cloak . . .'

Not waiting, I ran up the stairs, through the shadowed chambers to the room where my daughter lay. Eyes wide open, Elizabeth did not recognise me.

'What is it?' I demanded from one of my women who crouched by the bed.

'A fever, my lady.'

'Has the physic seen her?'

I knelt beside my daughter, smoothing back the matted hair.

'Yes, my lady. He says it is not the plague – which we knew anyway.'

And indeed there was no rash on her fair skin, merely the intense flush of a heat, her breathing difficult. I questioned them. They had given her hyssop in wine for the hard cough that racked her poor tormented body, which was cooled with cloths steeped in rose water. There was no need to take my women to task; why would I rail at them when they were doing all they could? Had they not loved Elizabeth?

Her final breath came as the day drew to a close, soft as pillow-down.

'It was all so fast, my lady. We could do nothing.'

Such a wanton cataclysm of death to strike at the heart of my family. And now Elizabeth. All we could do was arrange her burial in the Church of St Mary in Cardiff, where the Despensers held sway, with an inscription to allow her some immortality. It was a sad little cortège, without panoply for she was only a child. She had not quite yet reached her sixth year and had known so little of life, yet I made it clear to all who might take note of us on our route that here was a Despenser daughter. Her small coffin draped in the silver and red quarters, the gold fretwork and the *bend sable* overall proclaimed her proud lineage. At least she could go to her rest with all the recognition she deserved as her father's daughter.

After which I had no desire to return to Court although I retraced my steps to the Despenser house at Aldgate. There I remained with Isabella and my household, in mourning, Richard sent precipitately to Edward's London property for his health and his safety. If I returned to Westminster and the Court, what would I do there? I did not know. I did not understand how this one small death could chain me to inactivity. This small death touched me more than all the rest.

There were others who had different plans for me. Within little more than a month of Elizabeth's burial, in the early hours of the morning before we had even celebrated Mass, I was in receipt of a request to join the household of Queen Joanna. I resented the interference although it was not a surprise. The Queen had appeared to me to be possessed with a degree of compassion as well as strong will. Perhaps she sensed my isolation. As a woman who had been forced by French politics to leave her sons behind in Brittany, thus arriving in England with only her two daughters, she would know the tribulations of family partings.

The messenger who delivered the invitation waited for my reply. Or was it a command? It would not be beyond Henry to insert me into the Queen's household, my days taken up with royal demands and formalities, to ensure my future loyalties.

'Yes, I will come,' I said, more to rid myself of him than with any enthusiasm for the position. I would probably regret my concurrence.

'An escort awaits you now, my lady.'

I could see no need to hurry. I had neither the energy nor the inclination to jump to the royal bidding. I was not polite.

'Tomorrow is soon enough. I will make my own arrangements. Dismiss the escort.'

He departed, looking askance as if he would rather not deliver this refusal. And returned with a brisk knock to the door, pushing it open before I could invite him to enter. But it was not the messenger.

'My orders are to escort you now,' said Edmund Holland, Earl of Kent.

'Why would you be here in Aldgate to escort me? Is the Earl of Kent reduced to obedience to so menial a task?' I was all haughtiness.

'My sister thought you would be reluctant. She thought you might reject the offer out of hand, and then regret it.'

'Your sister is all too busy about my affairs. I will make my own decision. I told that officious little messenger that I would accept, but I will come in my own good time.'

All my old ambitions seemed to have died a precipitate death.

It baffled me how Elizabeth's death had drained me of all that had once mattered so much.

'Then I will wait.' He sat, crossing his ankles as if he would wait for ever. 'How long does it take a woman to get ready?' he enquired as if consumed by interest. 'The Queen expects you forthwith. Your coffers can follow tomorrow with your women. You are to come now with me.'

I disliked his peremptory tone.

'I am not dressed for Court.' My fine wool houppelande was high-necked, undecorated, suitable for mourning but not to associate with the gaudy creatures of Queen Joanna's household.

'You look perfectly acceptable to me.'

I felt I was being hounded. As indeed I was. There was a conspiracy here. And yet I had to admit in a small corner of my mind that to return to Court would have its advantages. Here in the Aldgate house I felt like a sick raptor, moulting and ill-tempered, enclosed in a cage away from its fellow inmates of a lively, chattering mews. It was time that I stepped once more into the environs where events happened and were discussed.

I would not admit such an inclination to this authoritarian escort.

'Henry need not fear me. I am not inclined to plot and connive. I have seen the error of my ways.'

'Henry will be pleased to hear it. Do I inform him, or will you? Perhaps you would like to send for your cloak and hood. There is rain on the horizon. Or do you wish me to do it?'

'Becoming Earl of Kent has gone to your head,' I snapped. Then I remembered. 'Forgive me. I did not offer my good wishes on your achieving your true inheritance, or your success on the battlefield. You must be proud. It was not any want of appreciation that rendered me so desultory . . .'

My words halted, fell into silence. I remembered the page's warning and its terrible aftermath.

Edmund stood, mischief suddenly wiped clean. 'You received news of your daughter's illness at the reception.'

All washed back over me, a fast unruly tide that became a deluge. I covered my face with my hands as if the imprisonment of my fingers could contain the grief that surprised me with its virulence. The pain in my heart was a physical hurt but I would not weep.

I heard his footsteps. Then felt his arms come round me and I in my weakness rested my forehead, lightly, against his shoulder. Just for a handful of seconds, when my whole world became centred in the encirclement of his arms. My breathing, already compromised, became more difficult; the beat of the pulse in my throat was unbearable.

Before I pushed him away.

Except that he did not allow it, instead using the flowing sleeve of his tunic he dried my cheeks of the tears that I had been so determined not to shed, holding me still when embarrassment would have made me turn away.

'She was so young,' I explained, unable to escape, unwilling to explain.

'And her loss is a cruel one.'

'I feel an insidious guilt that I could not prevent her death.'

'It was God's will. You cannot carry the blame.'

I stiffened beneath his light touch. 'I regret my lack of control.'

'It has been a trying time for you.' Before I could deny it, he leaned and placed his lips softly on mine. The lightest of kisses. 'Now go and make your dispositions with your women and I will take you to the Queen.'

It was a shock, robbing me of an easy refusal. Thus I became a member of the Queen's household. Not an onerous task nor one to which I could not quickly become accustomed. Queen Joanna was an easy ruler of those who surrounded her.

'I will visit you,' Edmund had said on delivering me into the ranks of the Queen's women.

'There is no need.'

I already regretted what I saw as my weakness. I would live better without pity. It was a relief that the Queen received me with no more than a nod of acceptance. It was a strange experience, to be met with understanding, even if it was unspoken.

As for the Earl of Kent's token commiseration, best not to think of that. Best not to think of my unwarranted reaction to him.

Edmund Holland began to haunt my days.

'What is this?' I asked, the package lying on my hands like an altar offering.

'A gift,' he said.

'Why? It is not the day of my birth, that I must celebrate.'

'I do not know the day of your birth.'

'Nor is it New Year.'

'As I am aware. This is in the manner of a wooing.'

It was the last statement I would have expected. An embrace when I was in extremis was one thing; this was quite another, and regrettably I laughed. It sounded harsh, drawing attention from the Court women who until now had had their heads bent in gossip over some mindless stitching. Fortunately the Queen was not of their number.

'I have no wish to be the recipient of a wooing.'

My weakness at the Aldgate house, I assured myself, was a momentary lapse. I needed no one's shoulder to weep on. I needed no man's kisses.

'No? I recall how soft your lips were. In spite of the tears, which were entirely acceptable in the circumstances.'

I had no wish for such recall. 'I do not give you permission to woo me.'

'I don't need your permission. Merely your acceptance of the gift. Open it.'

I loosed the soft leather covering to expose a pair of beautifully embroidered cuffs, edged in the finest lace. I could not help but be impressed.

'They are exquisite.'

'I brought them home from Ireland.'

I ran my fingertip over the incomparable craftsmanship.

'I knew that one day I would meet the woman to whom I would wish to present them,' he continued.

'It would be indiscreet of me to accept.'

'Not necessarily. If it displeases you, so that I cannot woo you openly, then I will do so in secret.'

His smile, one so rarely seen, had great allure, a Holland trait. Had John Holland wooed my mother in similar fashion? I wondered. I could understand why she had succumbed. But I was made of stronger stuff.

'If it is in secret, how will I know that it is a wooing?'

The smile vanished at my deliberate perfidy.

'Because you will know me, and you will know the value of my words and actions.'

He bowed and left me still holding the cuffs in their leather wrapping.

And woo me is exactly what he did. Oh, he was persistent, showering me with items that the beloved might acceptably receive from her lover without arousing too much gossip or scandal. Except that he was not my lover and I did not think that I was his beloved.

Edmund Holland kept his page well occupied. Over the coming weeks I was in receipt of a brooch, a mirror, a belt, a purse, a comb, a pair of gloves. None of great value, but all proclaiming: *You are my chosen one.* I received them, admired them and placed them in a coffer, unnerved by the whole experience. I might be baffled but it was enough to draw the interest of the royal ladies when the page approached.

'Whom have you drawn into your net this week, Constance?'

'No one, to my knowledge.'

'Are they all anonymous?' They peered over my shoulder in the manner of inquisitive doves in a dovecote.

'Nothing but a mischief-maker, I expect. Who would be foolish enough to send me lover's gifts?'

I would lie wholeheartedly, eager to deflect suspicion. I thought on balance they agreed with me, and indeed there was nothing to suspect. Except:

'Isn't it the same page every time?' they smirked.

'I have not noticed.'

I felt a flush of heat in my cheeks, but when Edmund Holland and I were in the same room, he greeted me as distantly as any man of my acquaintance.

I did not know what to make of him. In truth I had never been wooed before. Trivial as the gifts were, I was overpowered by them. I had received formal offerings from my family at New Year as was customary, but such gifts were entirely predictable. A bolt of rich cloth, a pair of paternoster beads, an enamelled cup with a lid. Had I ever received a personal gift from Thomas? Not that I could recall, since there had never been any wooing between us. No carefully chosen trinket. Not even a badly chosen one, I admitted. Since our betrothal had been a youthful affair, any gifts – and they escaped my memory – had probably been chosen as suitable by his mother.

This shower of lover's trinkets was very personal. It was very deliberate.

Even more confusing, what did he want from me?

In contrary fashion, I resisted him, acknowledging that I was becoming too dependent on the pleasure that the gifts brought. Edmund Holland's appearance at Court was infrequent for he appeared to be engaged in royal business, but when he was not there, I looked for him. The gifts meant nothing, I chided. He had been kind after the death of Elizabeth. These items were only symbols of his gratitude for my prayers and the candles I had lit – not that he would have known of those – that had brought him through the battle at Shrewsbury without harm. Of what importance were lover's tokens?

But then, I did not think he was merely a kind man. An ambitious one, as were all the Hollands. Was that the root and branch of it, of his solicitousness? But there was no logic in such a path. I would not be influential in bringing him to anyone's notice. I would not promote his career. More like I would taint him with the whiff of treason that clung to me and my brother. Nor was I sufficiently wealthy to draw his attention. I was no desirable heiress.

'Why would you even consider becoming closely acquainted with Constance of York?' I asked him with uncomfortable directness when an occasion presented itself. 'It will do you no good.'

'It is not a choice for me,' he replied.

Which was no answer at all.

Since I could see no way forward, and since I refused to examine my own emotions on this matter, I decided to put a stop to it. When a Holland page approached with yet another neat leather-wrapped package, causing some merriment, I took it, placed it in the small travelling coffer I had deliberately to hand, and handed the whole back to the youth.

'Return these to your lord.'

'Yes, my lady. Is there a message?'

'There is no need for one.'

He would understand. I had returned all his gifts. Tucking the coffer under his arm, the page departed, while I decided that all I felt was a wave of relief. But here was a point of interest, and one that dried my throat. Would he take me to task for my gauche return of the collection? Or would he merely make use of the rejected items to lure another more susceptible female to his side?

To my chagrin he did neither. There were no more gifts. Edmund Holland bowed with cool grace as if there had been nothing between us. The whole episode of the gifts was ignored as if it had never occurred.

Which forced me into an explanation of my churlishness, under a pretence of walking beside him to Mass:

'I could not accept them. It was not appropriate.'

'Then I will save them and my affections for a woman who considers them appropriate. And who does not allow me to kiss her when she has no intention of returning my admiration. Or accepting my gifts.'

Which put the whole blame on my shoulders. I was furious with him, with myself.

'You should not have given them to me.'

'Why not? It was my wish.'

'It was not mine.'

'Then there will be no more.'

I hastened my footsteps to enter the chapel in the wake of the Queen. It was ignoble of me, and I regretted it, but I had achieved what I had set out to do. Any intimate relationship between us was thoroughly severed.

Tell me the name of a woman who is satisfied when she is no longer acknowledged?

I wanted . . . But there was the crux of the matter, the grub in the core of the perfect fruit. I did not know what I wanted, and how I had come to this impasse, I had no clear idea. This rift between us was my own doing, and now, perversely, I wished that I had not rebuffed him so forcefully. I lived with Edmund Holland's deliberate distancing, suffered it, until, infuriated by it, I decided that it behoved me to put it right. I misliked the chill in his eye when it infrequently settled on me. I discovered that I desired his kindness, his attention. I craved the chivalric admiration of a handsome man who sought me out in a crowd. But how to attract a man with some subtlety?

I had as little experience of giving gifts from the heart as I had of receiving them.

Thus I asked the only possible source of such skills, the women of the Queen's Court, when we were sitting in the scented arbour of the rose garden. I kept my voice light, unconcerned.

'What would you give to a man, to catch his interest?'

All eyes were turned to me.

'Could this be the man who gave you gifts and who has now apparently stopped? Has he abandoned you?'

So they all knew. The page no longer came hovering with packages.

'Possibly,' I replied.

The results were frivolous, with much laughter. A book. A hanap with jewelled stem and cover. Some item of horse harness. A pair of gauntlets. A virgin on Saturday nights. They were either ridiculous or as unimaginative as the gifts I had bestowed on Thomas.

'You are no help at all.'

'A hound,' said the Queen, smiling over the stitching that she did for appearances' sake. She took as little pleasure in it as did I. 'Or even better, a pair of hounds, if he is a man who enjoys hunting. They will bring you to mind every time he takes to the field and he can praise them for running well after the quarry.'

A better suggestion than most.

I sought out Dickon who was watching a contest on the tilt ground. His fortunes had taken a turn for the better since the King had decided to make use of him, sending him to

Herefordshire in the Welsh March to command a small contingent of men in keeping Glyn Dwr at bay. He had fought in the Battle of Shrewsbury, escaping without too much damage, but with no distinction as far as I could ascertain. Was it lack of aptitude or lack of opportunity? He had not emerged as one of the group of young men frequently found in the company of Prince Hal, but his taking command in his own name had at last given him a maturity as well as a ribald soldier's vocabulary. He dreamed as much of military glory as did Edmund Holland.

Now I found him where the thud of horses' hooves, the clash of metal, the raucous calls of praise or ridicule provided a constant backdrop. As chance would have it, he had a hound at his knee, and was pulling on its ears to its obvious delight.

'Can we find somewhere quieter?' I asked, dropping to one of the rough benches beside him. His fellows, owners of the stridency, melted away with sympathetic glances in Dickon's direction and some questionable gestures.

'No. It's a tilt ground. It's always noisy. What brings you here, Constance?'

'I need a hound.'

'What sort of hound?'

'I care not. But one with better breeding than that one.' It was slobbering over his shoes. 'I need a pair of them. Such as would be of value to a hunting man.'

Dickon twitched a shoulder. 'Edward is your man. He eats, breathes and sleeps hounds.'

Which I knew, but I had no intention of making myself either obvious or grateful to Edward. I ignored the suggestion.

'This is a small task, Dickon, that is within even your capabilities.'

'Nice to know I'm appreciated.' He thought for a moment, watching the distant clash of arms. 'Do I bring them here, to Westminster?'

'No. Or yes.' I had not thought of the practicalities of presenting them. 'Find out where Edmund Holland might be, and send them to him.'

'Why?'

'I owe him a debt. I will write a message. Send the groom who will accompany them to me first. And I want it done quickly. I want it done today.'

I never had much patience. Dickon twitched his agreement even more extravagantly.

'Who pays for them?'

'I do. And yes, you will be reimbursed for your efforts. Particularly if you go now. Try the royal kennels first.'

Dickon loped off. Indeed, I could not imagine him on a battlefield, but this task would not be beyond him.

The pair of hunting dogs was duly dispatched, although I never saw them. I paid a remarkably high price, and with the costly creatures I sent a note lacking any sentimentality but one which was intended to placate.

With regret for my less than gracious response to your generosity. The Earl of Kent has need of hunting hounds. I trust that these creatures will be acceptable.

I would not dismiss out of hand the idea of a chivalric knight.

Constance Despenser

There. Brief and specific. I would never sign myself Constanza. I had done all I could to right a trivial wrong, but one that had lain heavy on my conscience.

Returning to my chamber to change my gown for a formal

reception for some foreign personage I could not recall, I found the familiar page on my doorstep, an equally familiar travelling coffer tucked once again under his arm.

'Lady Constance Despenser.'

I held out my hands. I knew what was in it without lifting the lid.

'The message is: You will know what is in it and who sent it, my lady. And I am to ask for a reward for carrying it so far. It is very heavy.'

'It is not heavy.' I held it in one hand to prove my point. 'And you are impertinent. Tell your lord he can reward you.'

Were we now back on level ground in the gift-giving? It may be so, but I added up the hours involved. These items had been returned to me long before the hounds could have found their new owner. Edmund Holland had taken the initiative here. Who was entrapping whom? How ridiculous this was. The last time I had been plotting it was to kill the King. Now I was reduced to luring a man with a brace of hounds.

Edmund Holland followed hard on the heels of his messenger, before I had even selected a suitably impressive gown for the Queen's reception. His trail had not been difficult for Dickon to sniff out.

'I am here to acknowledge the delivery of two limmer hounds.'

His bow was a perfection. I dismissed my women and the garment.

'Are they acceptable?'

'Perfectly. They will be admired as a superbly bred addition to any royal hunt.'

Was there amusement in his eyes?

'Excellent,' I said.

'When they grow,' he added.

'Grow?'

'An adult limmer hound should be about this high.' He gestured with his hand against his thigh. 'My new hounds are more this size.' He cupped his hands, describing a small bowl. 'I estimate that they are less than two months old. They have, as yet, none of the noble formation of their kind.'

Which made me laugh. Dickon had fulfilled everything I had asked of him. Except the obvious.

'I trust you will be happy to raise them.'

'Of course. Why did you send them?'

'I thought I had explained. I owed you a debt.'

'Yes, you did. But I would rather be your lover than a keeper of your hounds.'

It took my breath.

'I don't want a lover.'

'Then I will kiss you, and you can tell me when it might be that you wish me to become your lover.'

Still I resisted.

'I don't want the scandal.'

'I predict that scandal will tread on your hem, whatever you do, Constanza. When has it ever mattered to you what the Court says of you? As for me, it is bred in my blood and my bones.'

Edmund Holland was decisive. Before I could speak or even think, he took a step forward. Then another. When he folded me into his arms, I felt cherished. It was my downfall. My undoing.

Neither of us made an appearance at the Queen's reception.

I did not need a change of gown, from heavy damask to insubstantial cendal, impressive or otherwise. Were we missed? Apparently not. Against all my better judgement, I had taken a lover. I suspected, in moments of clarity, that it was Edmund Holland's intent from the moment that we met, yet at the end, who was seduced by whom was not clear to me.

Was I disappointed? How would it be possible for a woman to be disappointed when a new lover unclothed her with such exactitude, with such care for her pleasure, with such admiration in his hooded eyes and possessive smile? I had had no experience of it. It was a delight and an awakening, for I too had much to learn in the enjoyment I could offer in smoothing his tunic and undergarments from his shoulders and down from his thighs. I learned quickly, while his skilled hands, elegant, fine-fingered, knew every place where a caress could reduce me to a sigh.

If it touched my mind to wonder where he had acquired such skills, I found no need to dwell on it when my breath shortened and my flesh shivered. If it was only the burn of lust, I did not care. If it was the blackest of sins, for such it was outside the bands of marriage, I would embrace it. For the first time in my life, when I was able to think again beyond the progress of the moment from desire to fulfilment, I had compassion for my mother's lack of love in her marriage, and an understanding of her seeking solace in the arms of her own lover, John Holland. I found mine in the embrace of his nephew, and I had no husband to cuckold.

I lived in a world of heightened awareness of all around me, as if my surroundings were lit by the sconces of the finest candles in

King Henry's private chapel at Eltham. Contentment wrapped me around, a fur-lined winter robe. My feet were planted in a cloud of joy; my heart warmed into life as if I had drunk a cup of highly spiced hippocras too fast for good sense, the cloves and cinnamon and mace enhancing my senses to the exclusion of all but the man who had presented me with that cup.

Was this love?

If it was, it had crept up on me, without my knowledge, against my wishes, and all was new to me. It was like being led into a dance where I knew none of the steps, so I must make my way blind, dependent on another, or trip and be foolishly humiliated. I was a novice at such emotions, searching for appropriate words and actions that would be acceptable to my lover but would not expose my own vulnerability. For the first time in my life I lacked confidence. Nor did I enjoy the sensation of being less than in control. An unknown softness settled on me so that I was more tolerant, more forgiving. It was a weakness, which made me wish to resist, to seize back my own dominion over my life, fearing that Edmund had lit the fire of this love in my heart, only to extinguish it when the emotion had run its course. Was that not always the painful end of an affair? But oh, it was marvellous, too. I lived from hour to hour, until I saw him again.

At first I was cautious, even when he said that he loved me. How could I cast my pride so wantonly into the hands of any man? He could betray me. He might well decide, on an entirely male whim, that he had no love for me. No one in my family could talk to me about the lasting quality of love. No one had experienced it. How could I be different?

But my body was awoken to the magic of physical need, so

different from my nights of marital duty with Thomas. There had been no harshness in him but insensitivity had made him brusque, thoughtless. Neither his pleasure, nor mine, were in his thoughts when he fulfilled the deed to achieve a Despenser heir. At least when I carried his children he left me alone and sought out others to satisfy his lust.

Edmund satisfied his lust with me, while I learned the power of desire.

Why was it so different? Because he loved me. He cared. One day he would need a wife, a Countess of Kent. Once day he would need an heir. But not yet. Not today. Not tomorrow. I still retained the cynicism engrained in me since childhood but while this delight lasted, I would enfold it to myself and enjoy the experience. For yes, it was far more than contentment. It was a happiness with the purity of new honey dripping from a spoon. It was as clear and sparkling as the gems in the collar he gave me as a New Year's gift.

Edmund fastened it around my throat. It was not a livery collar, denoting service and duty and dependence, but a work of art for a man to give to the woman he loved.

'It is a symbol of my regard.' It was a very private gift-giving. 'Rubies will guarantee you health, wealth and wisdom.'

'And true love.' I knew my gem lore.

It was an old piece, a family piece. I could imagine Holland women from the past enjoying the weight of gold and precious stones against their collarbones.

'It becomes you.'

I found my mirror beneath my pillow. The collar was from a past age, even barbaric in its heavy carving, but it exuded power, so much that I felt a terrible sense of foreboding. I looked up at him, to find him watching me.

'You do not know me,' I said. 'A gift such as this is too particular.'

'I know you better than you can ever imagine. If you think I give this gift lightly, then *you* do not know *me*.'

'I doubt that I do.'

'Then you must learn. It is yours, with my love and admiration. When I am rich, I will give you another to cast this in the shade. Until then, own this, as you own my heart.'

A troubadour's words. Once, such sentiments might have made me retire from the lists, uncertain of how I should respond. Now they moved me beyond sense. How could I reject it?

Edmund then enjoyed removing both collar and clothing. I no longer resisted.

Every morning I awoke to an intense sense of anticipation. In the hour before dawn when the Devil was known to send temptation to prick and burn, my heart sang with hope for that day, and the next, and on into the unforeseen future. I had no doubts of Edmund's love for me. Did he not swear it? Did he not prove it? Nor did I doubt mine for him.

The years between us in age had no place.

Meeting was as simple as turning a page in my Book of Hours. I was a member of Queen Joanna's household. Edmund had become a respected member of the Court. The Court was our métier. When Edmund sang for the household after supper, it was primarily to me that he sang. When the minstrels struck up a dance, with whom should he dance but me?

'I am the lady's uncle by marriage,' he announced, the glint in his eye at odds with the solemnity of his delivery of this quaint relationship. 'We will dance.'

No one questioned us. Did they notice? Of course they did. What value discretion against the possessive light in Edmund's eye, but the Court women chose not to discuss my affair in my hearing. I imagined much was said when I was not present.

As I pulled on the gloves when we hunted, when I tucked the rose at the bosom of my gown, all the years of my life without love marched before me. They blurred, except when I wished to take them out and regard them with astonishment that I should have had no experience of this yearning to see and meet one particular man. His presence in a room heated my skin and dried my throat. I had an inordinate longing for his kisses. So many years had been wasted in a desert. An affectionless childhood. A loveless marriage. Now I was desired. Subtle, sensitive, elegant, he was the lover I would have dreamed of. I was enchanted by it all. Not even the harsh politics of the day could douse the flame that engulfed me. For the first time in my life it was difficult not to shout my happiness so that my voice echoed through the chambers and antechambers of the Royal Court.

I was besotted, yet I was not blind. I had too much experience to close my eyes to the faults of any man. As I too had faults. Edmund was driven and ambitious, as much as any member of my family. He sought gold to rescue him from the constant debt that indented the corners of his mouth. He sought Henry's recognition so that he might become one of the Royal Council. There was little difference between Edmund and my brother Edward. Or even Thomas. Except that there was that indefinable allure that made my heart beat faster when he entered a room. I was drunk on the sweet power of mead.

'I worship you, with my body and with my mind,' Edmund Holland said.

'I will love you until the day of my death,' I replied.

Certainly I was in no mood for conspiracy and plotting. All that had been laid to rest. Revenge against Henry, the planning of which had filled many of my earlier days, was put aside. How could it have been so important to me? It was as if it were part of my youth when I was naive and without true judgement. I had been punished by Henry, redeemed by Edmund's love. I had come into my own as a woman of experience.

A surprising kindness grew in me.

Which did not mean that my eyes were closed to the machinations at the Royal Court. Ambition was, after all, too deeply ingrained in all of us, to be wilfully cast aside.

As if in confirmation of my new loyalties, at the turn of the year, when everyone was in a gift-giving mood, Henry capitulated. Nor did he resort to an impersonal document but took me aside.

'Your husband was a traitor, and died as such, but in the spirit of New Year when all past conflict should be laid to rest, it behoves me to restore your dower properties.'

So simply said, so easily accomplished. So imperious as King to subject. I should warm with gratitude. Instead, as cousin to cousin:

'Is this in response to a guilty conscience, Henry?'

His face was grim, for the moment wiped clean of festive humour. 'There is no guilt.' He knew to what I had referred. Edward's gain at my expense continued to hang between us like a moth-eaten tapestry.

'No, of course there is not.' This was New Year and a time

of rejoicing. I would not cast a blight over it. 'I can only offer my thanks for restoring what is rightfully mine. It is the best gift I can imagine receiving.'

Henry managed to smile. 'We will do better together, Constance, when you do not snipe at me at every given opportunity.'

'I promise nothing.'

'I did not think that you would.'

'I will learn to guard my tongue.'

'If you do it will be the first time in your life. I would be everlastingly relieved if you write me no more petitions.'

I laughed and agreed, for indeed it was a gift of great satisfaction. At last my dower rights had been restored to me, the castles of Llantrisant and Kenfig in Glamorgan and properties spread throughout England. I might no longer have the Despenser estates under my hand, but I was no longer penniless, of no importance. I could forgive Henry, a little. It was a gift of great value to me.

But not the most eye-catching.

'That's new,' said Joan, returned to Court with the fifth Baron Willoughby who, a staunch supporter of our King and a Knight of the Garter, had recently been appointed a member of the Royal Council and was keen to make his presence felt. Now Joan, willingly abandoning her husband to affairs of state, had her gaze fixed on the collar.

'Yes.'

She stepped around me. 'Do I recognise it?'

'Do you?'

'I can tell you the inscription that runs around the inner edge, if you wish,' Joan said, peering closely, close enough to rub her thumb over the significant jewels.

'I know it for myself.'

It was prosaic enough, engraved on a multitude of notions of power or romance: *Amor Vincit Omnia.*

'It belonged to my grandmother Joan, Countess of Kent. It is a family jewel, not of great value, so never sold when their fortunes were at their lowest ebb, when her father was executed for treason. Can I guess how it came into your possession?'

'I imagine that you can.'

Joan's tone was uncommonly acerbic. 'He could have given you a far grander jewel if he wished to impress,' she speculated. 'I wonder why he did not.'

But I knew. Because I would refuse a more conspicuous statement of love. Edmund Holland was a clever man.

'Take care, Constance.' Joan clasped her hands together when I made no reply, her fingers tight-knit. 'I would not presume to give you advice. I doubt if you would accept it. But I see no happiness for you in this. Edmund needs a rich wife.'

'So he tells me.'

She frowned at me. 'Has he become your lover?'

'Yes.'

'You should know better. What can he bring to you but ultimate misery?'

'I foresee no misery. He brings me joy. The collar is just a gift, not a commitment.'

'He might break your heart.'

'I doubt I have one to break. And until he does, he owes me nothing. Nor do I owe him. We are not bound together with fervent promises or declarations.'

I would deny it to her. I would deny it to myself, while Joan abandoned me as a lost cause. I cared not. This was new and precious for me, and I would admit no fault, neither in Edmund nor myself.

'I worship you, with my body and with my mind,' Edmund Holland had said.

'I will love you until the day of my death,' I had replied.

Joan's warning slid from my skin, leaving no mark.

I was in no mood for insurgency, but others were, and dangerously so, in the incompetent hands of Maud, Countess of Oxford, mother of Robert de Vere, one-time favourite of King Richard, a man driven into exile by the Lords Appellant. For some inexplicable reason she believed, or claimed to do so, that Richard was still alive, in spite of all the evidence pointing to the opposite, but then Maud had a particularly sharp axe to grind.

I knew nothing of this new disturbance until Edward, in the capacity of his new office of Keeper of Carmarthen Castle and Lieutenant of South Wales, made it his mission to broach the subject.

'I take it that you are not involved in this ill-planned enterprise, Constance.'

'Then why ask me, if you think I would not be?'

'I have to know. I have to know if you are becoming involved in a stirring-up of new treasons. In which all involved will surely founder.'

'Then here is the truth. If I had been part of the plot, it would have been better organised. It might even have been successful. This attempt was a dismal failure.'

Countess Maud had involved herself in a conspiracy with a handful of priests to depose Henry by inviting a French invasion, rescuing King Richard and reinstating him, even going so far as to distribute Richard's white hart badge amongst those who were drawn in. The Duke of Orléans and the Count of Saint-Pol with a French army were to invade Essex.

'No one wants the French in control,' I said. 'What was she thinking?' The Countess had been arrested and sent to the Tower of London where she languished, praying for a pardon under the generous but inexplicable auspices of Queen Joanna. 'Does she deserve a pardon? I will have to hope that the Queen will plead for me if I ever get myself into similar difficulties – which I have no intention of doing.'

'Well, don't. Henry may not wage war on women but his blood is up.'

'Be at ease, Edward. I promise I will become involved in no conspiracies.' There had been enough blood spilt in this reign. But it reminded me. 'I could ask why you did not fight in the battle at Shrewsbury.' I waited, sensing a stillness about him. 'Or perhaps I should ask – on which side did you fight at Shrewsbury?'

'You could ask either question, but I doubt you will get an answer. Just don't get involved with any plots of Oxford's making.' He was abrasive, turning the conversation without finesse. 'What's this I hear about you and young Holland?'

I felt my hackles rise. 'What do you hear?'

'Nothing to your advantage.'

'You should not listen to empty words over a cup of ale.'

'Not listen? It reached me in Carmarthen by a gossipy royal messenger.'

I exercised my own deflection.

'Then the Court is short of more pertinent facts to talk about than my private concerns. Far better to discuss the progress of Owain Glyn Dwr. I expect Henry will send you back into Wales within the week to bolster his efforts against the Welsh prince. Our King might even find the means to pay you, if parliament is willing to raise the taxes.'

Which put an end to our exchange of family niceties. No, I would not become enmeshed in any insurrections. There was no longer any pretence that Richard was alive. His widow Isabelle had remarried in France, to her cousin the Duke of Orléans, which was proof enough for any who might need it. I hoped that she would find happiness. As I hoped that Joan would too.

Happiness had an effect I had not anticipated. It made me absurdly sentimental.

I would not consider my own remarriage. I was not so overcome with jewels and protestations of love that I lost sense of reality. Edmund needed a rich wife; what's more, his marriage was still in the King's gift. In spite of his newly restored titles and his pre-eminence on the field at Shrewsbury, he was still, by the letter of the law, within the King's authority and not able to choose the ultimate path of his life. Perhaps Henry had not completely forgiven the Hollands. Control of Edmund's future bride could enable him to keep that final royal fist wound tight in Holland family affairs.

Edmund might strain at the shackles, but he did not speak of them except for an oblique comment after a snatched hour of physical pleasure.

'We will live within the boundaries set for us. We will take enjoyment where we can. We will live and love to each other's joy. We will live and love now.'

And I would snatch at the joy while it remained to me, for I could foresee the future, as clear as my reflection in my mirror, when eventually Henry chose a wife for the Earl of Kent, a woman of wealth and status and a solid reputation, perhaps even a daughter of a powerful European family to consolidate an alliance. I would not be that bride.

I accepted the path of my own choosing, as his mistress. I would not sully his reputation, as I accepted that mine was well-nigh beyond repair. When did it ever harm a man to take a mistress? It was the woman who was the Daughter of Eve.

Chapter Fifteen

December 1404: Eltham Palace

It was my intention to travel with the royal party from Windsor, where the Queen had been settled, to Eltham, an easy journey by river and then road. Christmas, at the Court of King Henry, was invariably celebrated in these days at Eltham Palace, Henry's preferred residence. I received a letter, tucked inside my missal when I went to Mass on the morning of our departure. A single sheet of parchment, thrice folded, without seal or inscription. It rested under my fingers for the whole of the priest's unctuous liturgy.

Returned to my chamber, my coffers packed around me, I stepped through the usual chaos of departure to the window seat and unfolded the page. It was written in an unknown hand, without signature.

It would be wise for you not to travel to Eltham today.

Make an excuse.

Tell no one of this warning.

A stark warning, and there was only one conclusion that could be drawn. It must be that there was some perceived threat to the safety of the King and Queen. But who would make the threat and who would warn me to the exclusion of others? A dangerous letter to leave lying around, I lit the parchment in a candle at my elbow, and watched it fall into ash in a convenient silver bowl, dusting it from my fingers.

'We are ready, my lady.' One of my women gestured to the coffers. 'Do I order them to be taken below? We expect to leave in a half-hour.'

Should I heed an anonymous warning? I did not think so. Anonymous warnings were merely mischievous.

'Yes,' I replied. 'Bring the miniver-lined cloak and hood. Inform the royal party that I will be with them forthwith.'

We travelled by royal barge along the Thames, a regal party with Henry's younger sons and his daughters as well as the young daughters of Queen Joanna and my own Isabella. And then by cavalcade, a multitude of horse-drawn carriages and mounted escort towards Eltham. If anyone plotted our destruction, here was the perfect occasion to do harm to so many of the royal family. The letter had made me watchful. Should I have informed the Queen to whom I wished no ill? But all passed off in seemly perfection. Henry had a reputation for organising his travels with attention to every detail.

If anything snatched at my attention on that eventless journey, it was that our escort was larger and more powerful than was usual. The royal barges were accompanied by a flotilla of small craft, bristling with men and weapons. As for the cavalcade, before and aft and at each side we were hemmed in by smart soldiery on polished mounts, their weapons gleaming in the low sunshine. Did Henry foresee trouble, or was it merely a sensible precaution? Nor did we waste time, not stopping to receive the welcome of those who gathered at the roadside to wish us well. We rode on with nothing more than a wave of acknowledgement. Perhaps there was an unspoken air of tension cast over all.

Perhaps there was also a guarded exhalation of breath when Eltham opened its doors to us. The threat had, I suspected, not been a false one. If I considered anything for longer than it took to decant children to their appointed accommodations, it was that Edward did not travel with us. I presumed that he was still upholding his authority in Wales.

Any discomfort fast forgotten, Eltham Palace provided the perfect venue for the lavish and lively Christmas all expected. The King and Queen Joanna celebrated with enthusiasm, their household responding to the tone of hopefulness. The bloody events of the Battle of Shrewsbury were fading into the past, the Countess of Oxford's insubstantial plot was laid to rest. Owain Glyn Dwr might still be a danger, a furious wasp in the Welsh March, but he could be ignored until the new campaigning season in spring. Meanwhile the Court festivities awarded Henry the opportunity to keep a keen eye on those he did not altogether trust, while smiling over all. Edward had made his excuses from Christmas at Carmarthen Castle and made his presence known if only in the quality of his houseaux, the supple leather reaching to his thighs. Dickon, with neither military nor political position to keep him occupied, nor a wife to give him status, lurked uselessly on the edges of conversations. Joan was accompanied by Baron Willoughby and was in need of no compassion; there was a serenity about her, although there was no evidence that she was carrying a Willoughby heir.

To my carefully masked delight, Edmund Holland, Earl of Kent, was also present.

There was much dancing and playing of foolish games. The royal minstrels were overworked and breathless. The food was extravagant, a surfeit of roast swan and sculptured sugar confections, one cunningly carved into the moat and towers of Eltham Palace.

Edward invited me to dance, a sedate processional that required little effort and, unlike the carole dance, allowed the opportunity for conversation. I was reluctant. I had not seen him since he had warned me off meddling in any dangerous affairs. I considered refusing but thought better of it since it would not be politic to be at odds with my son's legal guardian. I might need to negotiate with him when the time came to discuss Richard's future bride. It was necessary to look ahead.

'To what do I owe the honour?' I enquired.

'To make a show at this interminable feast as the best-dressed people in the room.'

As we were. There were no signs of penury on Edward's well-clad shoulders, yet I thought he looked strained. Glyn Dwr must be running him ragged, but nothing new there. Perhaps it was shortage of money despite having my son's estates to drain. I felt the old bitterness rising in my throat. His houppelande, its sumptuous folds all but reaching the floor in deep blue damask with much gold thread, must have caused his steward to offer up prayers. The gem-studded girdle would have weighed a lesser man to his knees. But I looked again at the lines between nose and mouth, deep-carved, lines that were new to me.

'You look as satiated as a cat on the hearth,' he remarked as we came together in the dance, hands touching, sliding away.

'As I am.'

'At least dancing with me will prevent you lusting after Edmund Holland.'

'I do not lust.' I smiled with all innocence. 'Are you enjoying my son's inheritance? Those boots are not the work of a common saddler.'

The movement of the procession gave him time to rally his attack.

'Do you wish to be an object of pity? Of mockery? How can you preserve your dignity when you slide into bed with the Earl of Kent at every opportunity?'

I looked round at my fellow dancers in feigned astonishment. 'I see no pity. And there is no one here who would dare to offer me disparagement. We are not indiscreet. The Aldgate house offers us privacy when we have need of it.'

And was it not true? Edmund and I were most circumspect. Who was to know that the jewels I wore were Holland jewels? Only Joan, and she was discretion itself. Who was to know that we had spent an afternoon in intimate solitude, even here at Eltham, except for two of my most trusted women who would fear dismissal if they gossiped?

'If you think your affairs are secret, you are not the woman I grew up with.'

We separated. When we rejoined, Edward kept hold of my hand and pulled me aside, away from the dancers who simply re-formed around us.

His next words were not what I expected.

'I need your help, Con.'

I forced my lips into a smile, for the sake of any who might be watching, and patted his arm.

'Indeed? The last time you actually asked for my help, my husband was executed by a mob.'

'Well, that has no bearing on the present. You don't have a husband to be executed. Nor as I recall did I have to ask. In those days you were in the thick of the plotting from the beginning. False emotions have made you soft, Constance.'

'I'll not argue against it. If you had ever experienced love, you would know its power for yourself.'

Edward drew me further away, the grip on my forearm uncomfortably tight. 'Are you really content with all this?'

Uncertain of his meaning, I followed the sweep of his arm to indicate the music and dancing, the laughter and loud voices. The King and Queen receiving Danish ambassadors with regal grace, intent on promoting a marriage between one of the royal daughters and the Danish heir. Once I would not have been accepting of this Lancaster power. But now . . .

'I am content.'

'Where have your ambitions gone? Destroyed in the arms of a lover who will never wed you?'

It was an uncommonly sharp accusation, and not inaccurate, yet I would not rise to Edward's cleverly cast bait. His devious betrayals had destroyed any desire in me to be amenable, however deliberately chastening his accusation.

'And how do you know that? You are not privy to what goes on between us.'

'Henry won't allow it. Henry is self-serving and you're no innocent or wealthy bride for the Earl of Kent.' The habitual laconic persuasion in his low voice had vanished, replaced by an urgency that was raw. 'Even if you are willing to sink into

Lancastrian luxury, I'll not live out my days as Henry's lapdog, yapping his name in Carmarthen Castle to terrify the Welsh.'

'I thought you were well rewarded. You have achieved everything and more than you did under Richard.'

'Rank, titles, office.' His eyes narrowed on the royal party. 'But I'll never be Henry's heir.' So that is what he wanted. After everything that had gone before, the failure, the near death at the vengeful hands of the Lords, Edward still looked to the crown. 'We can do better,' he whispered, sotto voce.

His pleasure-loving features had hardened. I had not thought him so driven, nor could I understand what had suddenly resurrected this furious ambition. Nor could I see any role for me in his planning, whatever it might be.

'What do you want from me, Edward?'

He drew me further away into a quiet gallery where in daylight we might have enjoyed serene views of the moat, away from the constant stream of pleasure-makers. It was only when we had walked to the far end, where we would be unheard, where candles threw little light, that the tension rampaging in my brother was unleashed.

'I want an acknowledged role in government. I want to feel the reins of power, held tight in my own clenched fist. Henry allows no man's hand anywhere near them, except for his own sons. Prince Hal has already been blooded on the battlefield and is becoming a man of renown. Thomas is a born leader. And if it's not the royal princes dictating the future, it is the Beaufort half-brothers.'

'But that will never change.'

Surely he was not considering another assassination attempt, when the last one had failed so appallingly for all of us? I would not be party to it.

'No, it won't. But what if we change the family who rule England?'

I sighed. Once I would have listened but not now. 'Not again! No one will support you, Edward.'

He ignored the derision in my voice. 'No, they will not on my own account. But what if we support the conspirators who would make Edmund Mortimer, Earl of March, King?'

'Shh!'

This was treasonous stuff. I had had no idea his thoughts were moving in that direction.

'Why should we not, if we consider that the claim of Lionel of Clarence's daughter takes precedence over that of Henry of Lancaster,' Edward demanded, voicing a proposition that had obviously been uppermost in his mind.

Lionel of Clarence had been King Edward the Third's second son, thus his claim to the throne pre-empted that of John of Gaunt, Duke of Lancaster. Except that his only offspring was Philippa, a girl. She had wed Edmund Mortimer, Earl of March, thus her grandsons Edmund and Roger had a claim to the throne that was significant, some would say, far stronger than that of Henry of Lancaster, except that in a document attached to his will, King Edward the Third had disinherited his Mortimer descendants. Yet there were still many who would consider Edmund, the young Earl of March, to be worthy of a claim to the English throne.

Edward dragged me into a walk. 'We tried to remove Henry once before. Why not try again? And this time we will succeed. One of the reasons for our failure was that Richard remained in Henry's hands until his death. This time we could ensure differently. We could hold the one key player in the game.'

My thoughts were running rapidly.

'Can you not see that to hold the boy Edmund Mortimer under our control could ensure our success?' he asked when I did not reply.

I shook my head. Time had passed, times had changed, and those who might have supported a Mortimer claim no longer had the power to do so. Not even Joan, who was aunt to the two boys, had to my knowledge any interest in their claim.

'I see no hope of that,' I said. 'Hotspur is dead. Northumberland is holding onto power but is discredited with the King. Glyn Dwr has his own problems in Wales and I would put no faith in the boy's uncle Sir Edmund Mortimer, who has thrown in his lot with the Welsh. The Mortimer cause seems to me to be lost. Would you put your faith in a boy of so few years? I doubt he's any older than my own son. What's more, the Mortimer heir is Henry's prisoner, craftily ensconced in Windsor. Your wits are awry, Edward, to even consider it.'

'My wits are in excellent health. I have thought about this.' I had not seen such enthusiasm in him since before Richard's death. 'With a Mortimer King, and a young one, look at the range of power open to us. For me, for you, for your children. Glyn Dwr will never have power at the centre of government, even if he enforces his claim as Prince of Wales. Northumberland is too old and weak to bid for it. But *we* can have it.' He stopped walking to face me. 'This is why I need you.'

'No.' Before he could explain further.

'I need you to rescue the Mortimer heir and his brother from Windsor. There would be no suspicion in your visiting Windsor, or in speaking with them. You have sufficiently close connection with the royal household now that Richard is sharing his education with the younger royal sons.'

'You want me to rescue them.'

'Exactly. Get them out, dispatch them with an escort to the Despenser Welsh lands in Glamorgan. I'll do the rest.'

This all but robbed me of breath. That he should ask me, believing that I could even give it consideration after his previous betrayal. I would not. To trust Edward was as foolish as to offer my neck to the executioner's axe.

'I'm honoured that you think I can.' My reply was as dry as week-old manchet bread.

'I know you can. It will give you something to think about other than Holland's handsome face.'

'That's no way to persuade me!' I turned away from him, to lean on a window ledge and look down into what would have been the grey depths of the moat if I could have seen them. 'It's too dangerous. Do you really wish to vie for power with Glyn Dwr and Northumberland and Sir Edmund Mortimer?'

'Who's to say I need to? We can do this, Constance. With the Mortimer heir in our hands we can encourage the country to rise to his support. His claim is better than Henry's. We can make Mortimer King and our future is ensured.'

'Our future? Even if I thought there was any chance of success, I see nothing in it for me.'

'You are his royal grandmother's cousin. Your son Richard can be his close friend and confidant. I can't think of a better foothold for power. Will you do it?'

I shook my head again, unwilling to even consider it.

'Think about the advantages.'

'I see only failure.'

Edward was standing before me, his hands ungently clasping my wrists.

'There is so much to play for here in this game of chance and power, Con. Don't reject it out of hand.'

I felt as if I were being hurried along when I could not see the path beneath my feet. There were dangers, where we might all trip and fall. It was as if I were tipped back into my old life when conspiracy had been as easy as taking a breath . . . which dragged a thought into my mind. A thought that made me stiffen under Edward's grip. I had forgotten about it. Now it flared into a fully fledged fire.

'Did you send me the warning?'

'Which warning?'

'Not to travel with the royal party.'

'Why would I?'

'If you have usurpation in mind now, you might have considered a wholesale slaughter on the road to Eltham.'

'You are too suspicious. There was no plot to my knowledge. Did you not arrive here safely?'

'Which does not mean that a massacre was not in your mind. What deep deeds have you at your fingertips, Edward?'

'None. Other than the one I have laid before you.'

Which irritated me beyond measure. He was calm with conviction, and I did not believe a word he said.

'Well, you can't expect me to decide something so important at a Christmas feast, between the wine and the sweetmeats,' I said. 'I need to think about this.' Anything to put him off, to give me time.

'Don't think too long. It all needs to be put in place.'

When he released me, I walked smartly back along the gallery to the door.

'And Constance.' His voice carried to me, echoing strangely.

'What?' I did not look back.

'Don't speak of this to Edmund.'

'Why should I not?' Now I turned. 'He is the boy's uncle. If you are serious about this, would he not be the obvious ally for you, to hold your own against Northumberland and the Welsh when it comes to the sharing out of power?'

And why should Edmund not know? The Mortimer boys were his nephews, sons of his and Joan's sister Alianore. It concerned me that I was beginning to think about this plot, rather than reject it out of hand.

'The fewer to know, the better,' Edward urged.

It reminded me of the night we had conspired together to bring about the Revolt of the Earls. The well-furnished chamber, the costly candles, the meal of dishes much loved by Richard. Most importantly the gathering of my family and the Hollands, all intent on bringing down Henry of Lancaster. We had been so sure, so determined, so driven. We had our tenants at our disposal, and those in the country who would be roused to Richard's support, to fight for the crown. Now here we were, myself and Edward, in a gallery, little more than a corridor in the gloomy light, with nothing certain but a plot fomenting in Edward's ever fertile, ever ambitious mind. What could we two achieve? We had failed then, and we would surely fail now. I wanted to be no part of it. I would not ask who might be our allies in such a chancy attempt.

And then I remembered Edward, who was now warning me of gossip, informing Henry of the Epiphany plot.

'Since you know all about the truth being dripped into the wrong ears,' I accused.

He did not deny it. Without another word he led me back into the Great Hall.

'If this is to work, I need your help. And before you refuse me outright, take a look around you at the Court. What do you see?' I followed the line of his sight, then returned to study the severity of his expression as he spoke words that I imagined came from the heart. 'I am honoured now. My opinions are valuable now. And since my star is in the ascendant, so is yours. But what of the future? Look at them all, like carrion around a carcass. Beauforts and royal sons. Look around you, Constance. Love should not make you so very blind. If we have any ambition to enhance the House of York, we cannot afford to let sleeping dogs lie. Henry's health is not of the best. We must plot our future now, before it is too late. Think about it and tell me at Mass tomorrow.'

I resisted such a command.

'I can tell you now. My ambitions are dead.'

'Are you forgetting what is owed to your family?'

'Why not ask Dickon? Why not draw him into your plotting?'

'Dickon does not have the *entrée* to Windsor. You do.'

Which was as selfish an explanation of his wooing me as I could have anticipated. With barely a bow he walked away, leaving me alone. It was as if shadows, following me from the gallery, now closed in, despite the blaze of candles, as I absorbed all he had said, and a whisper of a breath breathed over my slumbering ambitions. I felt them stir as I climbed the discreet staircase to the upper minstrels' gallery where the singers were quenching their thirst between songs, and once there I did exactly what Edward said I should do.

What do you see? he had asked.

Below me, with an excellent view of velvet caps and opaque veils, I watched the movement of the Court, strangely foreshortened. There were the patterns, constantly shifting, that I recognised so clearly. Once they had so shifted and re-formed around King Richard. Now they merged and parted, vying for power, around King Henry. All the magnates, superbly dressed for this celebration, competing for the royal ear, for some particular sign of their importance, their hopes for a position, a title, an opportunity to show their prowess on the battlefield or in furthering royal policy. There was not one magnate present who did not wish to have the King bend his head to hear his opinion, his advice. With a glance in my direction, Edward walked across to where Henry sat, conversing with a purple-clad Bishop. He was received with a smile, an open-palmed gesture, and drawn into the conversation. Edward's position was secure.

Had I not had enough of treason and terror?

What would a new insurrection bring us? Power. Influence. Some vestige of control over a young and inexperienced ruler. My brother would enjoy that enhanced power. Would I not too enjoy my family's pre-eminence, my son at a Mortimer King's side? There would never be the chance of the crown, but energetic life in its shadow was not to be ignored.

But the risk . . .

I had not been averse to risk-taking when we arranged the Revolt of the Earls, but since then I had lost close friends, a husband. And I had found Edmund Holland. Did I want to step into the Mortimer circle of affairs? They were nothing to me.

What was it that Edward wished me to absorb from this

vantage point? When it happened, I immediately recognised that it was a change in the pattern that I had always known would occur as the years passed. The King's attention was taken. He stood and walked towards the group of young men who were gathering to choose their partners and begin a boisterous round dance. And at the centre was a quartet; there was no doubting their importance from their extravagantly furred garments to the imperious nature that lay on their shoulders. Henry's sons. The eldest, Hal, scarred but imperious. Thomas of Clarence, making a name for himself as a capable soldier. John of Bedford. Humphrey of Gloucester.

Here was the future.

And the two daughters, Philippa and Blanche. What of their future espousals? Unless they married overseas, the husbands of these royal daughters would also make a claim on royal patronage.

And there were the Beauforts, my cousins from an illegitimate liaison. They too were present. Henry Beaufort, newly created Bishop of Winchester, was the Bishop in full clerical splendour, even now offering some serious advice, by his expression. Then there was John Beaufort, Earl of Somerset, who stood, a watchful and loyal presence, the man whom we had deliberately not invited to be part of the Revolt of the Earls. Also Sir Thomas Beaufort, who had been in control of King Richard's imprisonment in Pontefract. A trio of powerful half-brothers on whom Henry could lean.

Standing deliberately on the edge of the crowd, for he had not chosen to follow the King, Edward's eyes lifted towards me. There would be no place for Edward of York, except as an ageing statesman, rewarded with control of the royal mews and kennels and perhaps the command of some light foreign enterprise, as the years progressed. The battle for power would be in the hands of the Lancaster sons, not the offspring of York. Edward did not even have a son of his own to make a way into the gilded group. For the first time in my life I recognised a cruel fear in my brother's face. I read it in the widened eyes, the skin pulled tight across the well-moulded cheekbones. Edward the confident, Edward the clever manipulator of men, now seeing his future in the inevitable isolation. It struck at my heart in a moment of sheer pain. I could not imagine my brother powerless and ineffectual, a travesty of the man he had been as he was ousted from power.

Once again I turned my regard to the crowd, out of interest, picking out Dickon, not one of the dancers. Twenty years old now, resplendent in garments that I had paid for, looking less like a badly wrapped package. Where did he stand in the shifting patterns? Still lacking land, lacking titles, lacking opportunity to show his worth. Had Henry ever paid him the annuity that had been promised? I thought not. There would never be opportunities for him with such royal blood jostling for position. He was old enough to be acquiring a wife, but where should he look? The past scandal should not be a blight to hold him back. The name of York should be enough to attract the attention of some aspiring family. I must remind Edward to begin discreet enquiries.

And then there was Edmund, whom I discovered directly below me, in some deep discussion with the new Queen. Titled with a proud name. But would he be able to seize and hold Henry's regard? I watched as, strolling, he joined the energetic group and was instantly swallowed up in the circling dance.

He would have to work hard to gain the money he needed. Would there be a place for him on the Royal Council? It remained to be seen.

I leaned my hands on the gallery rail to survey the whole colourful array. As the years passed, our ambitions were destined to be clipped, as neatly and effectively as Edward would clip the wings of one of his raptors. Now his stance on the periphery was deliberate, to make a clever gesture for me to read, a self-sought isolation. The house of York without power, without influence. I could see the day fast approaching when it would be not of his, or my, seeking.

If we rescued Edmund Mortimer, Earl of March, making him King, would not all our ambitions be renewed? Would I not have my revenge for my dead husband? But how great was the risk?

Later, Edmund came to my rooms, much as I expected, and collapsed on the floor at my feet. He had been dancing, although not with me. When he was settled with a cup of wine, I allowed my fingers to ruffle his already disordered hair. The light shone on his brow that was glossy with his efforts. A companionable silence developed, not the usual hot passions. Except that it was not companionable to my mind. My thoughts were very much my own and I could not dispel the churn of possibility left by Edward, like lees in the bottom of a cup.

There was a nudge against my knee. I looked down to see Edmund looking up at me, head tilted.

'You look mightily preoccupied, Lady Constanza, or is it exhaustion?'

'It will take more than one feast to exhaust me.'

'So what occupies your mind?'

Why should he not know what was in Edward's mind? I would be interested to provoke a reaction from him. Would he prove a useful ally, as uncle to the heir, the perfect conspirator? Yet something stopped me, perhaps a wariness, perhaps a fear that once known, this plan could not be swept back behind the tapestries of Edward's creating. Nor would I willingly put the burden of treason on Edmund's shoulders.

Yet I would be interested to know his reaction to what Edward was planning. So, in desultory conversation: 'I'm merely wading through the rumours afoot at Court.'

'There are always rumours. What is it this time?'

'A French invasion to give weight to Glyn Dwr's ambitions.'

'It's possible. What will the French get out of it?'

His eyes were closing with the warmth and his exertions. In profile his nose and cheekbones gave him the appearance of a raptor, his dark hair falling over his forehead. I took a chance.

'What is your opinion of the Mortimers?' I asked.

Which opened his eyes. Edmund pulled me down to sit with him, his arms around me so that I could lean. I had never had any man to lean on. It had a warmth that undermined all my thoughts.

'What about them?'

'Their claim to the throne through Philippa of Clarence. You are closer to them than most. The Earl of March being your nephew.'

Edmund's reply was laconic enough. 'Their claim is no closer than it has ever been, and as Henry's sons grow stronger, the Mortimers wane on the horizon.'

'What if someone saw fit to support them in their claim? Is it not viable?'

'It would be a dangerous and foolhardy move,' he said, 'but yes, one with much validity. If someone saw fit. And was rash enough.'

I stopped leaning, surprised at the force of his decision. I looked at him. 'Why dangerous?'

'Because however you like to argue it, the Mortimers do have a claim to the throne. They could be a serious threat. But Henry would resist. And Henry has an army, which might just cast England into civil war. Who would want that?'

'It is a claim through a female line,' I pursued.

'Through Lionel. Who took precedence by birth over Lancaster's father. Those two boys, my nephews, have the power to cause a devastating upheaval. I'll not support them. Why did you ask?' He sat up, his eyes narrowing. 'Is there a truth here, that someone would promote their claim? What gossip have you heard?'

'Nothing definite, except that there is much discussion of their right to rule, supported by Glyn Dwr and the Earl of Northumberland.'

'Oh, that.' I felt him relax again and yawn against my hair. 'But the Earl of March is not free to make the claim, nor likely to be. Best to leave well alone.'

I turned my face against his shoulder. Did Edmund have no ambitions for his nephews or for himself? It seemed not.

'I mislike the idea of turning this reign upside down,' he continued. 'I hope for patronage and promotion at Henry's hands. Why not? He has been generous. I see no value in instigating more disorder and bloodshed.'

'Would you not achieve your ambitions more effectively as uncle to the king, if Edmund of March were crowned?'

'With Northumberland and my Mortimer brother by marriage pulling the strings? It's possible but I'd not wager my non-existent fortune on it. Why are you asking? Has something been mooted, that such a plot exists?' he asked again since I had awoken some element of suspicion in him.

'No. I think that most opinions mirror yours. Better Henry and the young princes than the unknown of a Mortimer King with the Welsh using him for their own aggrandisement.' If my conscience was awoken at speaking so great a falsehood, I smothered it beneath the demands of necessity.

To my relief, Edmund appeared to be satisfied, stretching his length along the floor, his head in my lap. But then his fingers encircled my arm, much as Edward's had done, pulling me down closer so that he could watch my face, reading every nuance as he said:

'Don't do it, Constanza.'

'Do what?'

'Whatever it is that clouds your most beautiful eyes. It's not worth it. You have earned your redemption. Don't be persuaded by those who would use you, then abandon you to face the outcome. If it's the Mortimers who interest you, they are seen as a danger to the King and so are well guarded. I see no good outcome there, whatever it is you are thinking.'

He was stern, uncompromising in his judgement. I managed a soft laugh.

'I will not be persuaded into any nefarious conspiracy. Even if anyone was unwise enough to try.'

'I don't trust your brother of York.'

'Who does?'

'Promise me that you will not.'

Promise me . . . How easy it was for men to mould women to their desires, whether physical or moral. It stiffened my resistance.

'There is no need for your concern,' I replied.

Did he read my subterfuge? If he did, he made no comment, merely: 'Then I must trust your good sense.'

He pulled me down to his mouth, so that I never did tell him. His kisses were sweeter than any plotting. But later, as I lay beside him, absorbing the pure elegance of his features, enjoying the softening in sleep of the austere lines of jaw and mouth and fine bones, Edward's request came back to haunt me, as did Edmund's denunciation. In which direction should I step, and who would persuade me?

Would it be Edmund? A lover who had given me a gift of inestimable value. I might not doubt his love, but his ambition was of true Holland proportions, seeking promotion and Court position at Henry's disposal. He would not risk his present security in some half-formed plot, nor would he willingly put me in danger. All he saw was imminent disaster.

Or would it be my brother, knit to me in blood and bone and marrow and sinew; by past experience, who loved himself more than he loved anyone else? Who had sought me out because I was of use to him?

In the past I had prided myself on my own clear-sightedness in choosing where to put my favour. I had believed in insurrection to restore Richard, but Richard was dead. The Earl of March's claim to the throne was a living entity.

I slid from the bed to pour a cup of wine, choosing a stool beside the ashes, sipping as a further thought drove sleep from me. Would I make this choice purely at the behest of another?

What of my own desires, my own ambitions? I disliked the notion that I would be pushed in either direction because Edward or Edmund demanded it of me. All my life I had followed a path of my choosing, as much as I was able. What did I want now? I could retreat into intimate comfort with Edmund, or I could make a stand for the power of York in a new reign.

It did not make for an easy night. I had risked my life once. I could not deny my role in bringing about death and bloody destruction once. Perhaps my moral stance had been altered by love and redemption.

Love or ambition. Which was the more powerful? To achieve one would undoubtedly destroy the other.

I attended Mass, where I had conversation with Edward. Since this was twice within the space of two days, it would seem to any interested observer that we were at last reconciled as, imprinted with patterns of red and blue and gold from the stained glass, we knelt to honour the raising of the host by Henry's priest who spoke eloquently of loyalty, of honesty, of obedience to God and the King.

'Have you made your decision?' Edward asked when the ceremony had come to its end with the blessing, God's grace hanging delicately over us with the clouds of incense. Deliberately I did not answer, making the sign of the cross, rising to stand at his side but my eyes still on the altar with all its gilding and jewels, the sculpted figure of Christ's agony. I seemed to be surrounded by death. Would I not dishonour God if I encouraged Edward in his treason?

'You must have seen what I have seen, from your vantage point with the minstrels. The cliques developing around Henry,' Edward said. 'We belong in none of them.'

'Yes. I understand your concerns.'

'What hope for us as the royal cubs become wolves? The Beauforts are already well entrenched. Will you help me?'

No. The one word formed in my mind. I felt it hot on my lips, but I did not speak it, and Edward absorbed my reticence. I slid a sideways glance. He was watching me, hawk-like, unsure of my response.

'Help me to rescue the Mortimer boys,' he urged.

I stopped at the door, looking back at the crucified body of Christ, shimmering in the fading light as the priest began to douse the altar candles. There was blood on the hands and feet where the nails had been hammered in, blood from the wounds at His side, as blood marked Henry's soul; the blood of Thomas Despenser, of Thomas Holland, of John Holland. Of King Richard. Revenge was a powerful motive if I were to become enmeshed in Edward's plan. Our dead deserved a memorial, perhaps in the making of a new Mortimer King.

'They have the right,' Edward said against my ear. 'The boy has the right to be King. We did not save Richard. We let him go to his death at Henry's hands. We can save the Earl of March.'

Would it ever all come right? Only God knew. For the first time since entering the chapel I looked directly at my brother, remembering the changing patterns of power within the Court that boded ill for us. And there had been Edward standing on the edge, Janus-faced, looking forward and back as the god of ancient Rome, the god of beginnings, of gates, doorways, passages and endings too. I knew how Edward wished to see the future. Would I help him to open this door and enter this passage to what was to me an uncertain ending, but one that might with careful planning achieve all we dreamed of?

What could I lose? Edmund Holland's face, severe in reproof, imprinted itself at the forefront of my mind.

'Constance . . .' Edward banished the vision for me, and I recalled his fear that he would lose all that he had striven to achieve. A keen protectiveness pushed me finally into a decision.

'Very well. I will do it.'

I thought I detected a sigh of relief as he said: 'God be praised! And my thanks.' He leaned to salute my cheek but I remained aloof, stepping back.

'And my reward?' I asked, aware that his breathing had returned to a measured rhythm. 'You realise that you must appeal to my mercenary nature.'

He flushed slightly. 'Of course. Gold chains or land?'

'I'll take the land.'

I would at least ensure that my daughter was well dowered. It struck me that as yet I did not know what it was that I was committing myself to. I had agreed with no knowledge of the burden he would put on me.

'So what is it that I have to do?'

'Come with me and I will explain. I promise it will not be beyond your skills. You might even enjoy the conspiracy.'

I had made my choice. I had rejected Edmund's advice and walked into the net of Edward's making, for better or worse. And, I admitted, it was for my own desire. The temptation to be involved was too great to reject.

As a result of Edward's rapid outlining of his strategy, after the Christmas festivities were done, the mummers' costumes packed away for another year, I accompanied Richard when he returned to Windsor. An entirely innocent visit of a mother with her only son, who was being given the rigour of an education within the royal household. Humphrey, the youngest Prince, was fourteen years, so older and it might be hoped wiser, but Richard benefitted from the royal tutors, both on the practice field and in the pages of his books. He was enthusiastic about swordplay, if not his ability to write legibly.

In the chilly emptiness of the Windsor wall-walk, the January wind whipping our cloaks and my veils, I asked him about Edmund and Roger, the Mortimer boys, the sort of question that any mother would ask. He was quick to respond, finding their company enjoyable. Much of an age, they shared lessons, and practised their skills together with bow and sword. It was clear from Richard's open answers that he regarded them as friends, with much competition between them, rather than as royal prisoners, which they undoubtedly were.

And then to the pertinent information.

'Are they kept under lock and key?' I asked my son who saw no guile in my interest.

'No, not during the day.'

'What about at night?'

'Their door is locked.'

'Is it guarded?'

'Yes.' He gave a rough shrug. 'They are considered to be a danger to the King. All they are interested in is swordplay and the hounds. Edmund has his own hawk.'

It was a trite comment, picked up from somewhere.

'How do you know they are locked in?'

'I tried to get into their room once,' he confided. 'Roger had promised me a knife that he did not use. He said the hilt was carved into a dragon, and that I could have it. But I was sent away.'

Which was proof enough. But how stringent was the guarding?

During my stay over two nights I made myself aware of the supervision of the two boys, that the door to the Mortimer accommodations was indeed locked every night, but it was a light guarding. The lads were quiescent and well mannered with no reputation for rebellion. Over the years the surveillance had become a mild one. I discovered where the keys were kept during the day when the boys were at large. It would be possible for a well-bribed servant to lay hands on them. It should be possible to create an opportunity for escape.

More urgently I made contact with a locksmith in Windsor. Coin changed hands with promises of more when the arrangement was complete.

Satisfied, I said farewell to Richard.

All was set in place.

On my return to Westminster, Edmund was awaiting me. I wished he was not.

'He has been haunting us, my lady,' one of my women informed me, nostrils narrow with disapproval as she relieved me of cloak and heavy travelling veil, constraining my pleated hair as tidily and quickly as possible into a jewelled caul. 'He has called every day in your absence.'

'Then I will see him.'

I wished I could refuse. I wished I could order my woman to make an excuse, any excuse. Engaged as I had been in what would become a hotbed of treason, I had no wish to face him now, being too weary for subterfuge. I raised my hand to summon her back, to change my mind and send a message that I was indisposed, but that was a coward's path. I knew not why he was here, nor what was so urgent, but I must receive him and accept whatever it might be.

The one fear that ground in my belly: had he guessed what I had been doing? It was a foolish fear; I should rejoice at his coming.

'My lord.' I curtsied.

'My lady.' Edmund bowed.

Still, before my women, we kept up the appearance of family acquaintance. While wine was brought, we talked of the Court's expected move to Kennington, the good hunting to be found there, the Welsh raids that continued to harry the March, but however eloquent he might be, I could see that there was a restlessness about Edmund. Not disapproval, but a tension that clipped his words.

The servant departing, the door closed, I smiled.

'There is an urgency about you,' I said.

Edmund pushed the cup of wine aside, stood and took me by the shoulders, lifting me from my chair. His fingers were hard on my flesh. His eyes held mine.

'It is done.'

Did he indeed know? My heart shuddered. Did he know my purpose in visiting Windsor? He would assuredly damn me for my involvement. But of course he knew nothing. How could he? I tried to discern disgust or recrimination in his eyes, but I could not. I swallowed against my suddenly dry throat. This was all compounded, not by guilt, for I felt none, but because I had deceived him. Unless Edward had gossiped, the conspiracy must still lie between the two of us, and surely on this occasion Edward could be trusted.

'What is done?' I asked lightly, keeping my breathing even.

'What have I desired more than all else?'

'The King has invited you to join the Royal Council,' I suggested.

'No. What made you think that? Has he said anything to you? Or has Edward?'

'No. Neither Henry nor Edward discuss royal policy with me.' I realised how much I missed it, the endless shredding of Court policies, but at least I was breathing more easily now. Edmund knew nothing about how I had spent the past days. 'Something has occurred to please you,' I said.

He kissed me gently on the lips. 'Guess again.'

His solemnity was compromised. I riffled through the possibilities.

'You have been given a military command.'

'Constanza!' He shook me, his eyes alight. 'The King has at last agreed to my marriage.'

For a moment I was baffled. Then a sudden cool breath touched my nape, like the panicked flutter of a bird's wing in a trap, but I commanded a faint smile.

'And who will be the bride? Does Henry have a suitable wife in mind?'

How calmly curious I sounded when my world was crumbling beneath my feet. Was this to be the future, as I had feared, and so soon? Some wealthy and important bride who would restore the Holland fortunes and give Edmund the power that he wished to achieve. What of me? I would be abandoned, the shadowy mistress, consigned to the very edges of Edmund's life. A woman to visit when occasion allowed, when he recalled and had a brief desire to renew old passions. Or I would be banished from his life completely.

I had acknowledged this, accepted it, but not yet. Not yet.

'Is she English? I asked.

'Of course she is English.'

'And who is she to be?'

'Being flirtatious does not suit you.'

'Flirtation is the last thing on my mind. You have just informed me that you will marry.' I felt an edge of frustration rise up in me, as sharp as a blade, yet strove to keep a smile of understanding redolent in my voice. I would never admit my own frailty, not even to Edmund Holland. 'Wives and mistresses do not sit well together,' I said. 'I foresee a parting of the ways between us, my dear heart.'

His grip gentled, and slid down my arms to my hands in a smooth caress, pinioning my hands together between his own.

'My wife is whomsoever I wish to wed, as long as she is a subject within the King's dominions. So wed me, Constance. Be my wife.'

I regarded him in silence.

'Have you nothing to say?'

I could think of so many things to say. The impossibility of it. How unwise it would be, for him, for me. I would bring him no advantage despite my Plantagenet blood. Those who had mocked Joan the Fair Maid of Kent for marrying below her station, when she chose Thomas Holland, would equally mock Edmund Holland in nailing his Holland pennons to the soiled reputation of Constance Despenser.

His hands gripped harder.

'Be my wife, Constance.'

I took a breath. Why would I even consider marriage? I had no good experience of such as a state. Why would I chain myself once again to the whims and ambitions of a man I barely knew?

'Yes. I will.'

It was said without any difficulty at all. An acceptance writ in shining gold. Because even I knew that marriage to a man of birth and title granted a woman far more freedom and opportunity than was allowed to a spinster or a widow. I did not wish to be a mistress until age spoiled my face and limbs, and my lover turned from me to younger attractions. And I loved him. I realised that I was smiling.

'I will marry you,' I repeated as if he might have misunderstood my first acceptance.

There was no misunderstanding. 'I will make you a woman of pure reputation.'

'I would deny any man's ability to achieve that. But you may try.'

I could not believe the joy that surged in my breast. In that moment it rivalled all ambitions.

Edmund was not the only man to be awaiting my return.

'Well?' Not even a greeting from my brother. His regard was quizzical. He had thought, I realised, that I would return with a refusal.

'It can be done,' I said.

'Will you do it?'

'I will do it. It is all in hand.'

Chapter Sixteen

February roared in as if it were March, crisp and cold when the high winds finally fell. Excellent hunting days lay ahead, but today Edward and I were hunting for a new King. All was arranged; all it needed was a nod from Edward and I knew what I must do. For this was our planning: within a matter of days the Mortimer heir would be safely ensconced in the Despenser fortress in Cardiff while the Court at Kennington, enjoying the good sport provided for the hounds and raptors, was only just being awakened to the threat to the crown. I had made my maternal excuses for a visit to my son at Windsor, as had already proved to be so easily accepted. I would not be questioned.

With a retinue stronger than might be considered necessary if anyone cared to assess the number of armed men who would accompany me, I hoped that Edmund might have gone hunting with Henry and the Queen. Lost in love I might be, but I had no wish to explain the purpose of my journey to him.

He had not. There he was, on the shallow flight of steps, next to my waiting-woman who was holding my cloak and hood and gloves. I dismissed her, handing my gloves and hood to Edmund as I fastened my cloak, concentrating on the pin of my brooch so that I need not meet his eyes. I would just have to make the best of this farewell. My heart pattered within my bodice.

'Are you hunting, my lady?' he asked. 'If you are, you're late. They left a half-hour ago.'

'No.'

The brooch was giving me some difficulty. Anxiety made me clumsy.

'Where are you going? Did I know you were leaving Court?'

He took the brooch from me and fastened it himself with clever fingers.

'No. I'll not be gone long,' I said. 'I will be at Windsor for a few days.'

I began to walk towards where my escort waited, needing an escape. He would damn me for what I was doing, and what would I do when the plot was complete? Throw myself on Edmund's mercy? Had I really agreed to Edward's instructions without seeing their repercussions? It felt as if I stood on the moving ground of a quagmire. One careless step and I would be swallowed up. Edmund had asked me to wed him, all I could have wished for, and here I was, casting it all into jeopardy.

'You saw your son only recently.'

I glanced up, forcing myself to meet his regard. His expression was unreadable.

'And I will see him again. I am told that Richard is unwell, with a fever. It is my duty to see that he is given the best treatment.'

'So you need to be there.'

'Yes.'

He angled his chin, brows formidably level. 'Why have my suspicions suddenly been given a boot in the groin?'

'I don't know. Why should they? Why should a mother not visit her son?'

'No reason at all. Except that I don't believe one word you have said.'

I raised my chin against the sudden pain that he should brand me false. Even more that he should have every reason for not believing me. I was lying to him, because I must.

Before God, this was no bedrock for marriage.

'I might be more willing to accept your reason for this departure,' he added, 'if it were a frequent occurrence for you to show such maternal concern.' He handed to me my hood, then my gloves, which I donned, briskly efficient, before turning to grasp my horse's bridle. 'What are you doing, Constance, that you are not willing to tell me?'

Noting that I had become Constance, I halted, spinning to face him. There was no love in him today. I could not afford for there to be in me.

'Stay out of this, Edmund. It's best if you do not know. There is no place for you in this.'

How cold I sounded, how unapproachable.

'But I will know. What have you got yourself into?'

I had already said more than I wished, and was unwilling to place the burden of truth at his feet. It would bury a knife in the heart of his love for me.

Edmund kept his distance. This would be no intimate parting.

'You asked me about my Mortimer nephews,' he said. 'They are at Windsor. Tell me this is not about my nephews. Tell me that this is not some devious conspiracy by your brother.'

He thought I was so vulnerable. He believed that I would simply obey any dictate that my brother cared to make. Did he not realise that I had my own opinions, my own ambitions? No, he did not know me. He knew only what I had allowed him to know.

'What if it is?' I did not deny it now. Nor did I lower my chin. There was an anger simmering in him, as there was in me, but the fault was undoubtedly mine. How could a man love a woman who refused to be open with him, who lied and lived by deceit? I did not deserve love after all, and here I was in the act of demolishing the gift I had so unexpectedly received.

Edmund had brought all his intellect to bear on my sudden departure.

'Oh, I see it all. You rescue them and make Edmund Mortimer King. The York family seizes power in his name.' How wounding his words. How damning.

I replied, matching emotion with cold calculation:

'Are we not all ambitious? You would seek patronage from Henry. We would seek it elsewhere.'

'I'll not deny it. But why did you not tell me? Are you the woman who shared my bed and accepted my offer of marriage? I do not know you.'

His repetition of my own assessment was bitter indeed. The ice of desolation filled my veins, leaching into my voice. 'No, you do not know me. And I am sorry for it.'

Edmund's reply was all fire. 'Was it Edward? Did Edward warn you against telling me? What did he think I would do?' The anger was building with every question. 'Did he warn you that I might tell the King and have you all arrested?'

An inconsequential shrug that shamed me, yet I met the condemnation in his eye. 'The fewer to know the better.'

'And you did not trust me enough to tell me.'

'If you recall, I asked your opinion.'

'You denied that you had fallen for Edward's plotting yet again.'

'I make my own decisions.'

I moved to mount my horse, my limbs stiff. This was a brutal farewell, his words following me.

'Anyone of any sense would see that an escort of this size and military strength is more than required for a short journey to Windsor.'

I indicated for my groom to help me into the saddle. I could not ask Edmund, although he came to stand at my horse's head, holding the bridle. He had not yet finished with me.

'Did you know that this is not the only plot that Edward has put in hand in recent weeks?'

So I was not the only one to harbour suspicions about the journey to Eltham.

'I have heard that there was to be an attempt on the King's life on the road,' I said carefully. 'Which did not materialise.'

'And the one at Eltham itself? By paid assassins?'

I did not know. My silence answered the question.

'A ludicrous venture, to climb over the walls at Eltham during the Christmas festivities. Did he tell you of that? I doubt he intended to climb the wall himself. His assassins would kill the King.'

'How do you know?' I whispered, sufficiently shocked.

'Does it matter?' He drew a gloved hand across this mouth. 'I see from your face that you didn't know. But I doubt it would have made any difference to you. You are up to your neck in his vile enterprise, whereas I was foolish enough to believe that you would deal with me with honesty and honour. I thought that your days of blood and treason were long gone.' For a moment he studied the floor at his feet, before once more searching my face, his eyes expressing all the conflict I had created in him. 'The woman I see you truly are, prepared to carry out York's bidding without question, does not fit well with my integrity.'

'But that's the problem, Edmund.' I could not defend myself, but I tried. 'This is treason. I would not burden you with it.'

'How noble of you.' His sarcasm bit deep. Then his voice changed and his hand was hard on mine as I gripped my reins. 'Don't do it. For the love I have for you, I beg of you, don't involve yourself in this.'

'Do you have no compassion for your nephews?'

'Yes. All the compassion in the world, but I see no future for them as the pawns of Glyn Dwr and Northumberland.'

'Edward will stand for them.'

'Edward will stand for himself.'

His fingers tightened until I winced with pain. 'Don't, Constance. If you love me, abandon this scheme. If you would wed me, step back. It's not too late. You were fortunate to be restored after the Epiphany affair. If you are involved in this and fail, Henry will show neither compassion nor mercy.'

I wrenched my hand free. 'Henry will have no compassion! Does that matter so much to you?' A rage struck from nowhere. 'Henry killed your brother. He killed your uncle.'

'As I recall, it was the townsfolk of Cirencester and Pleshey who have blood on their hands.'

'And Henry was not in agreement?'

'They plotted to kill him.'

'And now you will be the perfect loyal subject.'

I hated the taunt in my voice, yet still I made it.

'We have to make a choice in this life. I choose to make my fortune with the man who has the kingdom in his hand. What point in bemoaning the death of King Richard? Or of Tom and John Holland? It will not bring them back. This is where we are. Henry is King. Don't ignite the flames of bloodshed and loss again.'

I stared at him, the man I loved and who loved me. The man whose love I had just wilfully destroyed.

'I cannot retreat from this because I have given my word,' I said. 'I will release them, send them on their way, and then I will return to Court. I can promise no more.' I swallowed hard. I was not born to beg. 'All I ask is your tolerance. I don't ask for your complicity, or your forgiveness, merely your silence until I return and all is in hand to dethrone Henry. We can't have Richard, but we can have the next best thing.'

'You are implacable! How can I dislodge an idea when it is buried in your mind?'

'You cannot.'

He released me, then released my horse and strode away, before swinging round to say: 'I petitioned for my freedom to ask a woman I thought I loved to wed me. It seemed that I made a mistake. How could I wed a woman who dives into the first pool of treason to lap against her toes? You were right, Constance. I do not know you.'

He walked on. When I stretched out my hand in a gesture of utter despair, he did not see me. He did not look back when I turned my horse in the direction of Windsor. No time for wallowing in self-recrimination.

February 1405: Windsor Castle

After Compline, before the household went its separate ways with the priestly benediction for our quiet rest, I held out my hand to Edmund Mortimer who saluted my fingers and bowed, while their habitual guard shuffled in impatience.

'Goodnight, my lady. God keep you.'

'I wish you good rest.'

'And to you too, my lady.'

'You might find this of value if your mind will not settle. These pages will be particularly comforting. Look . . .'

I opened my missal at random. The boy was polite but uninterested. The guards yawned their boredom while I stepped closer with the open page, running my finger at random as I whispered:

'Do not undress or retire. Await the signal. I know not the time but it will not be late.'

'Why?' His lips soundlessly formed the word.

I could have explained but to what purpose? I must rely on their obedience after years under surveillance.

'It will be to your advantage,' I said.

Eyes brightening, he nodded, fortunately not without understanding.

'I will be sure to take this sage advice, my lady, and read carefully.'

He took the missal, turning to smile at his guard. 'We are ready.'

I could not believe that all should have unfolded as smoothly as a bolt of new silk, waiting for me to shake it out. I had been made welcome at Windsor as a frequent guest. My son Richard, feverless, welcomed me without any degree of surprise, supporting a maternal embrace with stoicism. The Mortimer boys had been willing to eat supper with me, enjoying news from the Court. John and Humphrey were still at Kennington with Henry and the Queen as far as I knew. There was no interest expressed in Constance Despenser coming to meet her son and being entertained by the Mortimer heirs.

Now I retired, taking Richard with me.

'Come and tell me how your education progresses,' I said.

But once in the chamber provided for me, leaving him to prowl the room, turning over any objects that took his interest, I considered my own participation. If I could achieve their escape, all well and good. They would be long gone before their absence was discovered. But where would suspicion lie when their door was opened on an empty chamber come the morn? My presence here was obvious; pleading innocence or ignorance would be futile. There was only one outcome here. I must go with them. It would ensure their safety and mine.

I looked at Richard who was sitting cross-legged on the floor, inspecting the blade of his knife, holding it up to the light. He must come too. I could not leave him to Henry's mercy. If this escape was successful, my days of acceptance at Henry's Court were at an end.

I had said I would return to Edmund. That I would not put myself in danger. Had I truly believed that I could simply declare my ignorance when Henry's Mortimer prisoners disappeared at the time that I was in residence? I had always known that I must be a physical part of their flight to the west. I hoped that Edmund would forgive me. And if he would not . . .

Closing my mind and my heart to the great personal loss

I had set in motion, I could not deny a tingle of excitement that spread through me, a welcome return. It was long since I had enjoyed such anticipation, such a sense of danger to be accepted and overcome.

'Richard.'

He looked up.

I crouched beside him so that our eyes were on a level.

'I expect you are good at keeping secrets.'

'Yes, madam.' He looked suddenly wary.

'Can you keep a very important one?'

'Yes, madam.'

'Then this is what you will do. Go to your room. Dress as if you were to go hunting. Collect the heaviest cloak you have. Then return here, as silently as you can. If anyone questions you, tell them that you need to speak with me before I leave tomorrow, and that you have a gift for me, wrapped in your cloak. No one will question that. Say nothing more to anyone. Can you do that?'

His eyes glinted in the candlelight, as if it were a game. He was on his feet and halfway to the door.

'Gently, Richard. We must not draw attention.'

He was gone, closing the door quietly behind him. I must trust him. I could not leave him here to bear my guilt.

Now for my own preparations. In a leather pouch beneath my pillow were keys on a ring, new, unused. I sent for Richard Milton, an esquire of Edward's who had accompanied me. He did not have to ask what it was that he should do. By the time Richard had returned, booted and cloaked and excited, the keys had changed hands and Milton was on his way.

'Did anyone question you?'

'No, madam. Where are we going?'

Why should I not tell him? 'To Wales. To your lands there, in Glamorgan.'

'Does my lord Edward know?'

'Yes.'

He cocked his head. 'Do Edmund and Roger come with us?'

'God willing, they do. And now we must wait.'

We waited, senses stretched for any untoward noise of commotion that would signal my failure. Until a light scratch of a knock on my door. I moved to listen.

'It is time, my lady,' said Richard Milton.

I opened the door. 'Are they released?'

'They are, my lady. They await you by the wall in the outer bailey.' He looked at my cloak and hood, and at Richard at my shoulder. He did not have to ask, a man well chosen by Edward. 'I will go and procure two more horses.'

'What of the guards?'

'Unharmed but well trussed up and hidden in the cellar. They were induced to fall asleep with a dose of belladonna in their ale. They'll recover, but we'll be long gone.'

We followed him down the silent stairs. There were no servants; all were asleep or quiescent with the promise of a small coin, yet my heart was thudding. In every movement, every shadow, there lurked danger. What could I say if we were discovered? It would be impossible to be plausible if found at this hour in this company. Blessed Virgin grant us anonymity.

A little group awaited us in the outer bailey, dark shadows against a darker backdrop. There were horses standing quietly, my armed escort at their heads to muffle any noise. Would I be prepared to trust the future of these boys to Milton? And my own safety? I had no choice. The conspiracy, for good or ill, was under way. For a brief moment Edmund was there, in my head, hot with condemnation of me and my untrustworthiness. Too late for that. He might be my lover but he was not my master, nor would he ever be. I turned my thoughts to what needed to be done, without delay. At least there was no moon.

'My lady?'

'Let us go.'

We led the horses towards the gate which opened at some given signal. We mounted, a tight-knit group. I looked back over my shoulder. One cry of alarm and all would be undone. We would all be prisoners.

Then we were outside the gates, into the town.

We must ride as if our lives depended on it. As indeed they might.

'Do we follow the plan as discussed, my lady?'

'We do. We ride west. As fast as we can without the horses foundering.'

I looked at the young Earl of March and his brother. 'Today you will be free.'

Following Milton at a steady pace, at last I allowed my mind to return to what might be. If all fell out as we had planned, perhaps Edmund would join me and we would push the Mortimer claim to its true fulfilment. Perhaps he would forgive me in the end.

I could not look so far ahead.

We rode hard and fast. No one was following us, although at intervals I left men behind to keep an ear and eye trained. We had to pray that there would be no discovery and news would not reach the King until we were far beyond his vengeance. As dawn began to break behind us, we rested, then rode on, the boys displaying a tenacity, despite their youth. We had accommodation arranged this night in a friendly house. Milton would leave us, probably at Bristol, to take ship to France, then Flanders, to whip up support. The Despenser tenants had already received advice to arm themselves in preparation. Edward had assured me that Glyn Dwr and Sir Edmund Mortimer had promised their aid. We must make the best time that we could until we were out of Henry's long reach. He had proved that he could move with unnerving speed when danger threatened his crown.

The Mortimer lads rode silently with a dedication, Richard determined to show himself as their equal. I rode with my heart in my throat, thankful that the weather was good, the roads free from mud. We made good time.

'I will keep an eye on them,' Milton assured, riding beside me.

'They think it is a grand adventure.'

'Let them continue to think that.'

But I knew it could end in death. I had to keep my mind set on what would be. I dare not worry about what might be following us.

We rested overnight at Abingdon and were under way almost before dawn. The boys were pale and tired but there were no complaints, merely an exhausted acceptance. Rain drenched us before we had covered a handful of miles, but we continued to keep up a steady speed. There was no word of our being followed, but at some point Henry would know and have sent out the warning that we were to be apprehended.

'How far are we from Bristol?' I asked.

'Not too far, my lady.' I thought Milton was being optimistic since the lads were listening. 'We'll skirt through the forest around Cheltenham.'

I nodded. 'We'll be safer when we cross the River Severn.'

It became a talisman. If we could cross the river, then Wales would be within our sights and we would secure this bid for freedom. I would not express my fears. Every muscle was tense, even as the miles vanished beneath our horses' hooves.

We rested briefly for a mouth of bread and a cup of wine, not even dismounting. Then on again, the rain clearing but the going hampered by mud that clung and squelched. Until our serjeant-at-arms, who had dropped back a little way, rode abreast and signalled for me to stop.

'There are horses following, my lady.'

'Merchants?'

'No, my lady. A larger group than that, moving faster and more organised. I sent one of my men back.'

'Let me know when he returns.'

Regardless, we pressed on. And then the serjeant returned to my side.

'Tell me the worst.' I could read it in his face but I strove for calm.

'We think the pennons are those of the Earl of Somerset.'

I imagined them: lions, fleurs-de-lys, a portcullis, the heraldic symbols of my cousin John Beaufort, Earl of Somerset, Henry's half-brother.

'He's brought a considerable force, my lady.'

Bad news. The worst news.

'Can we outrun them?'

'We can try.'

'Then let us waste no time.'

The forest hampered us, the low branches, the uneven terrain, the thick, sodden undergrowth that encroached on the paths followed by Milton, but it would also hamper the hounds on our trail. Hiding was impossible. The boys were tiring, the horses were nearing the end of their stamina but still we pushed on. If only we could reach the Severn. We could cross and take refuge, but my mind repeated again and again that it was too far. Too hopeless.

'They're overtaking us, my lady.'

It was a grim warning that intensified with the loud command.

'Halt!'

And with it reality faced me. I would not be ridden down like a doe to be torn to pieces by the pack. I would stand my ground. I would negotiate if I could. Would it be possible to sway John Beaufort to allow us to continue? I could hold out little hope but I would not surrender without trying.

At a gesture from me, we turned to face the hunters, my men creating a protective circle around us, but it was a matter of minutes before we were surrounded.

I had no personal experience of the carnage of battle, of vicious death, of the monstrosity of blows delivered, of bodies hacked, of the spilling of blood from terrible wounds. I had no knowledge of the nerve-shredding shrieks of wounded and dying men. The tales of such events, told by the victors, full of honour and chivalry, did nothing to prepare me for the horror of what I witnessed that day, when I forced myself to watch the outcome of what I had started, denying the nausea that rose in my throat as blood and torn flesh spattered the hem of my cloak. I was in no danger, but the soldiers of my escort were fair game, outnumbered and overwhelmed by a force of greater skill. Flight had been our only chance, not battle. Death came to some who protected me.

'Tell them to stop, to lay down their arms,' I ordered Milton whose voice would carry more strongly than mine. And as he bellowed our surrender, I urged my mount to the edge of the clearing where the Earl of Somerset, my cousin through the blood of John of Gaunt, sat his horse and waited for me. All fell silent around us apart from the snort of winded horses, the groans and oaths from the men wounded in my cause.

I sat and simply looked at him, sickened to my soul, my cloak dark with rain that had soaked through, and on through the rest of my garments to my skin. I would not apologise. What was there for me to say? All I could see about me was the mist of failure, and the consequences of the terrible choice I had made. But here was no moment for weakness. I must bargain for the lives that were left.

'Well met, cousin.' John Beaufort oozed animosity.

'I wish I could say the same.'

'You've caused us a great deal of trouble, Constance.'

'Legitimate trouble, John.'

'You couldn't hope to win.'

'Who told you of our flight?'

'What matter? Whatever your plan, you are foiled.' And no, it did not matter. We were captured and the blame was irrelevant. 'My orders are to take you, the Mortimer boys and what remains of your escort, back to Westminster. The King will be waiting for you there.'

I inclined my head in acquiescence. 'So we are not to be chopped down and our bodies hidden in the forest.' It was impossible to swallow the bitterness of defeat.

'Hardly. Since when did the King stand so barbarously outside the law, even when his enemies deserve it? Although he might make an exception in your case. You are a persistent thorn in the royal backside.'

Now he dismounted, helped me to slide to my feet and bowed before he took my hand and led me a little distance away where we could speak with some privacy, but what more was there to say? There was nothing that could incriminate me more than this – action that spoke louder than words. I flinched as my feet squelched and sank in the ooze of the forest floor.

'What were you thinking?' Somerset rounded on me. 'Or was it York who put you up to this?'

It was so easy to blame Edward. I found myself leaping to his defence even though he did not deserve it. He had made the rod for his own back.

'Why would you think that?'

'I thought you might have had more honour. I thought you might have seen the value of remaining loyal to Henry, even if your brother is blind to it. If Henry executes the lot of you, you will only have yourself to blame. You will have to throw yourself on his mercy.'

'Again.' I glanced up at him, determined to open every pathway. I placed my hand on his sodden arm. 'How strong are your own loyalties, John?'

He showed his teeth in a grimace.

'Strong enough not to throw in my lot with the Mortimers and the Welsh rebels.'

'But you were a loyal subject of King Richard. As were we.'

'And now I am a loyal subject of my brother Henry.' He laughed softly. 'I don't care how persuasive you are, I will not allow you to go free. What a schemer you are.'

'What is scheming to some is justice to others.' I allowed my hand to fall away. 'I have no money to bribe you.'

'It would not be enough.' I read compassion in the gloom of that rain-drenched forest.

'Will he execute me?'

'I don't know.'

'The Mortimer boys?' I looked over to where they stood, surrounded and disconsolate. Suddenly I was weary to the bone. If they met their death, the blame would be mine. 'It would be the best excuse Henry could snatch at, to remove them from the scene.'

'No, he will not. Nor your son.'

'Do you swear it?'

But he would not. He could not so commit himself.

'We must begin our journey back. By the Rood, Constance, you are your own worst enemy.' And then as he dragged me back to the horses and helped me to remount: 'Is Edmund Holland involved in this?'

I thought of Edmund, of his warning, his fury when I would not listen, his abandonment of me.

'No. The Earl of Kent is as loyal as you. He is entirely innocent.'

But there was blood on my hands and on my conscience.

By the time we reached Westminster I was tired to the bone. When John Beaufort helped me to dismount, I could barely stand.

'Where are you taking them?' I asked, seeing the boys herded away, stumbling after so many hours in the saddle.

'We have a chamber for them. They will be cared for.' He looked me up and down. 'Are you ready to meet the King now?'

'I would rather change my clothes.' I could not imagine the impression I would make. My hair was damp against my cheeks and neck, my linen coif shapeless, my cloak and skirts were splattered with mud, and worse. The fur of my cuffs clung unpleasantly to my wrists.

'Henry cares not what you wear.'

I followed him, every footfall a clap of doom. No, I did not suppose that he did.

Henry, as neat as an illuminated letter in a Book of Hours, rendering me horribly aware of my own deficiencies, ignored me as I was led into the brilliantly lit chamber, but nodded to his half-brother.

'Thank you, John. It was well done.'

'Do you wish me to stay?'

'I don't fear for my life.'

'Perhaps you should. But she has no weapon.'

'Nothing but her mind and her heart. Weapon enough.' And at last to me, his regard sliding over me: 'Sit down.'

I sat, my skirts clammy around my legs. While he poured and handed me a cup of hot spiced wine I pushed back my hood. My hair had come loose from some of its pinnings to fall onto my neck. This was one of Henry's private chambers. I was relieved to see that there were no guards, no audience for my coming humiliation.

'Drink.'

I did not need the encouragement. I drank, grateful for the warmth that might bolster my courage.

Henry sat also. It could have been a reunion of friends after a long absence, a cousinly conversation. He steepled his hands, elbows on the arms of the great chair, but, when I expected him to begin a thorough condemnation, he continued to sit in silence, waiting. I could not wait.

'What do you wish me to say? You know what I have done. There can be no denial. All you have to do now is pronounce judgement.'

He sighed.

'Why, Constance? Or do I need to ask?'

I gave the simplest statement I could without the involvement of ambition and personal dreams. 'You should not be King.'

'How many times do I have to hear that? Do you truly care about the strength and legitimacy of the Mortimer line? Or is this merely another exhibition of York's ambitions? I can't believe your brother is uninvolved. You would use those boys for your own ends.'

All delivered in an even voice as if he were discussing the state of the crops. But this was treason and I was in fear of my life.

'You would lock those boys up, forcing them to spend their lives as prisoners. They deserve freedom.'

Henry made no attempt to justify his actions. 'The bloodshed is on your shoulders, Constance, and yours alone,' he continued. 'The men who served you died because of your tinkering with the succession. You had no right.' Suddenly his regard was fierce. Here was the condemnation. 'You even put your own son Richard's life at risk in this ill-judged venture.'

'I dared not leave him behind. I accept my guilt.'

My voice seemed to come from a great distance. Every word I uttered would incriminate me further.

And then, swift as a dagger-thrust: 'Who set up the plot, Constance?'

I refused to answer. The old loyalties to my brother tightened.

'I don't suppose it was Edmund Holland. His feet are set on a path to becoming a great magnate at my Court. He has too much to lose.'

'Edmund Holland is innocent,' I said, the least I could do.

'Whereas you have resurrected death and suspicion at the centre of my Court. What happens to Milton now, the man who followed your orders? And the locksmith who could not resist your bribe?' His expression had become bleak, his voice abrasive. 'Shall I tell you what happened to your locksmith? I cut off his hand. It betrayed me by being in concert with your treason. Then I cut off his head. His death and the manner of it will make a worthy memorial to those who flout my authority.'

I drew a breath.

'You escort will be punished, but not by death. They followed orders. But Milton will die.'

'I am sorry for it.'

Henry stood and walked around me, to come to a halt at my side so that I must perforce look up. 'What value is that? Your regrets have robbed men of their lives.'

'And what part did you have in robbing King Richard of his?'

His face paled as if I had drawn his lifeblood.

I lifted my chin. 'What of my son? He has no guilt.'

'I have yet to decide.'

And because I must face it: 'And what of me? You have me at your mercy.'

For the first time his banked temper was evident as he walked behind his chair and drove his fist into the carved back of it.

'Death. The penalty for treason is death.'

'You forgave us once.'

'A mistake of vast proportions.'

'Which you will not repeat.'

The cloud over me was as black as an encroaching storm.

Henry showed his teeth. 'Oh, I will take no responsibility for shedding your royal blood, cousin. I'll not have it on my conscience. I shall send you before the Royal Council. They will decide if your treachery is worth an execution. And I warn you, I will not argue the case against it if that is their decision. You can stand before my Council and argue your innocence if you dare.'

I could imagine it. The hot desire for revenge of the magnates who made up the Royal Council. Henry would make me stand before them and receive their judgement.

'You would not!'

It stripped me of all my pride. Would he throw me to the lords in the Royal Council, a gout of flesh to the hounds after the completion of the hunt? There were so many who would once again enjoy an opportunity to drive their daggers into

York flesh. Ambition and success made enemies. We had much experience of it.

'I would, Constance. As you will learn.'

He walked to the door, opened it. 'Take her to her chambers and lock her in.'

'What will you do with the Earl of March?' I asked as I passed him. If he read a plea in my eyes, in my voice, I could not prevent it.

'The Council has already decided. He and his brother will be placed in the care of Sir John Pelham in his castle at Pevensey. There will be no more plots to rescue them.'

Chapter Seventeen

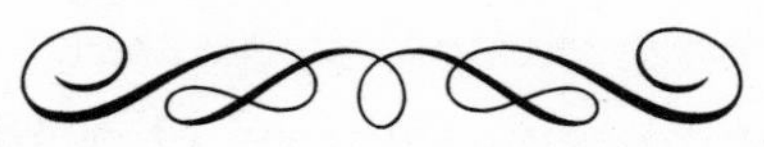

February 1405: Westminster Hall

Bright in my mind, unbidden, came memories from the past. The personal attacks against Edward by Henry's first parliament, the howl for vengeance, and here was Henry preparing to subject me to the same horror. Henry had decided, in his regal wisdom, to make an example of me. I was brought to the Great Hall, a guard on either side, to stand before the great lords of the realm, the ranks of eyes focused on me. If the intention was to cow me, to shout my insignificance in this vast space, it was successful. I was a prisoner, at their mercy like any condemned animal. Except there would be no mercy. I was guilty. I must accept and bow my head to the inevitable.

Braziers lit for warmth, the taint of rancid herbs rose from satins and furs to smother my senses while Henry took his seat at the head of the table. I would not look at him, knowing that, notwithstanding my own culpability, this was a deliberate ploy to intimidate me and send a message to the ranks of would-be rebels throughout the country. If I, the King's own cousin, were to be punished with an execution, it would deliver a hard message to all those who might consider another conspiracy, another plot. I would not be allowed to escape justice. If Edward's culpability could not be proved five years ago, mine needed no hard proving. The leniency after the Revolt of the Earls would not be repeated.

A desire to laugh rose in my throat. How had I ever expected mercy when Somerset had caught me in mid-flight in company with the Earl of March? Perhaps I did not deserve mercy. Someone must pay for the deaths of those who had fought for me; there was no excuse that could exonerate me.

That knowledge sank its teeth into me, my blood as cold as my feet in the soft shoes I had put on. It was February and the Great Hall was so chill that I could see my breath in soft puffs of air. The massed Councillors were muffled in their furs, damply shuffling on their seats in discomfort. Perhaps they hoped it would be a short meeting, with no other business but my condemnation. My hearing might be brief and very final.

From where I was told to stand at the foot of the table, I looked round, masking terror beneath a perfect confidence, my face still. Some would say that it was arrogance, but I was of rank equal to that of the man who faced me, who wore the crown. Emotion was forbidden as I assessed the company summoned to bear witness to my downfall.

There was Edward, robed and magnificent, head bent in some discussion with his neighbour. And Edmund, newly come to the Royal Council, stern-visaged, hair as black as a crow's wing, a frown in his eyes as he studied the carved angel hovering on the opposite roof beam. My heart clenched at his lack of acknowledgement even as I accepted the inevitability of it. A woman accused of treason could not expect friendly overtures, even from a man who was her lover. Who had once been her lover.

And then when I had all but given up any hope, he turned his head, his gaze resting on my face. All I could read there was rejection. He had warned me and I had ignored his warning.

I looked away from him, as if I were unmoved.

To my right sat John Beaufort, Earl of Somerset, who had been my undoing. Sir John Pelham who had been given control of the Earl of March. And then all the other faces that I knew so well. Sir Roger Winterton who as Henry's friend would damn me out of hand. There was no compassion to be found here. I could expect none and thus must fight for my life. But would anyone fight for me? Would I be forced to face the prospect of my death alone on this day? There was only one means of escape for me. It was risky, it was unprincipled, but it might be my only hope.

At last I looked at the King. Beside him sat his heir, Prince Hal. I bowed my head in acknowledgement of Henry's regard. I did not smile. I thought I would never smile again. My face was frozen into immobility.

Henry had already begun his campaign against me. He had kept me solitarily confined for four whole days, during which I was allowed no visitors, only a serving maid, not one of my own women, to answer my personal needs. I did not know if any asked to see me. Thus he had isolated me in my comfortable prison, allowing the fear to build without comfort or advice. But it had given me the opportunity to prepare for this ordeal. My appearance was one of thorough preparation, all traces of my flight and humiliating return obliterated beneath damask and sable and fine linen. If I were to be condemned, there would be no doubt in anyone's mind that I was royal. Pride must come to my aid.

A murmur, a rustle of silk. So we would begin. There was no seat for me: they made me stand to face my judges and their justice.

'We are met here on this auspicious day at the behest of our King to celebrate the defeat of this heinous plot against his state, and to enquire into the attempt to take the Earl of March and his brother from the royal household and deliver them into the hands of one of our most dangerous enemies, the Welsh rebel Owain Glyn Dwr.'

The accusation was made by Sir John Pelham. Who better to choose than such a keen legal mind? Unctuously smooth, the accusation rolled on in its dry legality.

'The plot was foiled at the hands of one of our number, the Earl of Somerset.' He bowed to John Beaufort who remained unmoved. 'Lady Despenser is brought here to answer for her part in the despicable conspiracy to tip this country into the horrors of renewed civil war. A situation we have already faced and defeated. This is even more worthy of our contempt since the lady is the close cousin of the King. She is here in our midst to await our sentence on her.'

He drew a breath as he turned to me while I felt the weight of displeasure from every lord and cleric in the hall. With such a burden of sin against me, how could any man have compassion? And all of it true.

'Here are the charges against you, my lady.'

They were read out, brief and succinct. I mentally absorbed each one.

Treason. Subverting the loyalty of the royal household at

Windsor. Creating the means of escape for Edmund Mortimer, Earl of March. Spiriting him away to the Despenser lands in Wales where my tenants were already armed and ready for rebellion. A proposed alliance with Owain Glyn Dwr and the Percy Earl of Northumberland. An invitation to the French to send troops. Sir John's knowledge of the plot was superb. I wondered how it had become so detailed. It was also quite damning, raising a sharp-tongued discordant jangling of comment and accusation from the Lords. I doubted there was one voice offered in my favour.

Then all lapsed into silence. They were waiting for me. I had not realised.

'What is your reply, my lady? Can you invalidate any of the accusations?'

It was in my mind to remain silent. To deny my complicity by my absolute denial of their authority to judge me. Let them do their worst, but they would get no cooperation from me. Yet how could I stand in silent denial without making a mockery of my situation? I had been caught truly red-handed in the company of the Mortimers and there was the Earl of Somerset who could testify to it. I had employed the locksmith. It had been my coin that had bought the silence of the guard. My involvement was as clear as if written in blood on the stones at my feet. I wondered what had happened to Milton. Was he already dead?

My only hope was Edward. Would Edward protect me? Would he leap to my defence, as any wild creature would stand between death and its young? But what could he say that would not incriminate himself?

I must accept the responsibility for it. Silence was not an

option for me. I raised my chin, becoming aware, in that moment of defiance, that Edmund was watching me.

'It is true,' I replied with a clarity which must reach every ear. 'I helped the Mortimers to escape from Windsor. I knew of Owain Glyn Dwr's part in the scheme.' But I would not shoulder the blame for that which I had not known, the worst of the scandal. 'I was not aware of the invitation to French troops. I would never concede to that.'

It would not save me, but it needed to be said to put a single feather in the scale against the weight of my guilt.

Sir John merely wafted my feather aside. 'Regardless of your ignorance, this is treason, my lady.'

'Yes, it is treason.'

'The penalty for treason is death.'

'Yes. It is death.'

How easy I was making this for my accuser. I had no arguments to make to add to that feather. The scales were tilted outrageously against me.

'You do not even have mitigating circumstances for your involvement, my lady. The Mortimer boys are not of your direct blood. This was interference, to further your own ambition, to harm our lord the King.'

I could sense the shuffle of agreement.

'No. I have no blood connection except a distant one through my own cousin Philippa of Clarence.'

'It does not assuage your guilt.'

The nails into my coffin were being hammered more firmly by the minute. It astonished me how calm I could remain under such an attack with the outcome so clear. Would I be so controlled if I had to step onto a scaffold and face the axe? I might be tested to that ultimate fate.

I shivered a little beneath my furs.

Sir John had turned to the King and bowed. 'It seems that we need no more time to decide this unfortunate case against Lady Despenser, who has given her assent to her involvement. Do we give judgement, my lord?'

Now I bit down on that harsh surge of panic. Would no one speak for me? Edward, chair pushed back, was studying the toes of his shoes beneath the table. Edmund had his eyes on the King.

Again the evidence against me was repeated in all its horror.

'You instigated a plot to usurp our King, my lady. You were involved in negotiation with our enemy the French to send troops. You were in league with the Welsh Prince to invade the border. The evidence stands for itself. Have you nothing to say, my lady?'

Why repeat this evidence again and again? Momentarily I closed my eyes against the incriminations and willed my brother to speak for me, to drop some small word to my credit, or I would assuredly meet my death. My tongue refused to form the words in my mouth. If I spoke out, I would damn him too. He could not save me without admitting his own guilt.

Sir John leaned forward, one palm flat on the table, as if commanding me to speak.

'Were there others in the plot with you, my lady?'

So here it was, like the gentlest slap against a cheek to bring a sleeper into full wakefulness. So that was what they wanted to know. There was an urgency behind the soft question.

'If you will tell us, it may be that the King will show some leniency. It is thought that you, a woman, would not have been alone in this. How could you have negotiated the alliance with France and Glyn Dwr alone? Who worked with you, my lady? Who was it who inveigled you into taking part?'

They were offering leniency. They would pardon me if I betrayed Edward. It was as if my lips were incapable of parting. I could not, dare not, reply.

Sir John cast a glance, in no manner innocent, towards my brother.

'Perhaps I should help you, my lady. There have been rumours that the Duke of York was not unaware of this plot. Is that true?'

The resulting silence could be sliced and chopped with a blunt sword.

'Is it possible, my lady, that his grace the Duke was the instigator? That he used family loyalties to win your compliance? He would need someone with unquestionable entry to the royal household at Windsor. Your son was there. You were the obvious choice. Is that how it was?'

Before I could respond, there was movement on the dais beside the King, when Prince Hal rose to his feet and spoke out.

'It seems unlikely, sir. A mere empty rumour. I will speak for York who has been praiseworthy in his service to the crown in Wales over recent months, working at my side to keep the rebels in check. I detected no treason in him.' The Prince's face was as implacable as his father's, and even though his voice still held the light timbre of youth, the wound granted him a malevolence with the banding of light from the upper windows. Nor was he satisfied but continued to turn the knife in the wound he had just created. 'Why would he be involved in so nefarious a scheme, risking the King's displeasure? I would say that the Duke has no involvement in whatever his sister chose to do. Lady Despenser has, unfortunately, an unenviable reputation.'

So young and ignorant. Or so damnably manipulating.

And I felt the first ripple of anger. The Prince would ride to my brother's protection, praising him to the heavens, but would condemn me in the same breath. Some might question my brother's veracity since he had a reputation for treading his own path, but would they grant me leniency? To my left Edward's face became creased by a smile of studied charm as he too rose to his feet. Of course he would take the praise and none of the blame. The anger within me became a fury rising up to all but choke me when Edward replied, bowing to the King.

'It pleases me that my loyalty to you is recognised, my lord, by your gracious son. I will continue to serve you to the end of my days.' His eyes slid to rest on me. 'I deny any rumour of treason.'

Complete and utter hopelessness was there in that vast space, to press me down to the slabs of worn stone. I should have expected it, but why did it hurt so much? Edward, the one source of affection in my growing years, who had encouraged me, laughed with me, saved me from loneliness. Once I had thought we were the closest of friends, that I could trust him with any of my hopes and fears. He had supported me through a loveless marriage and the previous treacheries. Now he had urged me to participate in his plan for York greatness, before so casually denying me.

I could not look at him, those familiar features that had called on my family loyalty and duty and then abandoned me. I was choked with ire. And fear. With hot terror. Who could I trust? He had destroyed the only firm foundation of my young life. He had cast my affection, albeit mired in past treasons, into the gutter and stamped upon it.

I had always known his ambition, his putting self before loyalty to a cause. His glib and smiling tongue that hid a rapacious desire to wield power. I had always known, but I had not expected this.

Or perhaps I had, which made the hurt course through me with menacing power. The candles shimmered before my eyes so that my balance was all but over-set, so that I must clench my fists, my nails dug hard into my palms, the physical pain bringing me back to the present. But Edward's attention was no longer on me. He swung round to address the gathering which seemed to me to be hounds baying for blood. He stirred them further.

'Lady Despenser was alone in this plot, my lords. Through her wide connections she was able to create the release of the boys. Hers is the blame. Who knows what powers she had to make contact with France and the Welsh traitor? Hers is the cupidity. She has no reply for the accusations. Therefore, my lords, we must consider her punishment for—'

'No.'

A single clear word that clove through the utter repugnance now directed at me. I could not, would not, take all the blame. If no one would speak for me, then I must protect myself. I would stir up these dusty, opinionated, pompous lords. I would shock them to their embroidered boots.

'No,' I repeated. 'I was not alone in the plot. I was not the instigator. How indeed would I hold negotiations with France or Glyn Dwr? I have not the power or the connections to win them to a conspiracy.' I ran my tongue over dry lips, for here must be my confession. 'Yes, I arranged the escape of the Earl of March. I paid the locksmith and bribed the guards. But I deny full complicity. It was my hand, my money that opened their door of captivity for I believed that they deserved freedom. Why should they remain incarcerated for the rest of their lives?' It sounded virtuous to my own ears, and perhaps there was some truth in it. 'I will admit my fault, my treason if you will, but it went no further than that. I would *never* invite a French army into England.'

Edward's reply was ingratiatingly formal. 'So who is to blame, my lady?'

I had come so far. I would put the blame where it should lie. I would not be so betrayed. Anger drove me on. I could not contemplate that Edmund had been as silent as a grave. No one had come to my rescue.

Never having felt so alone under the blind eyes of the carved angels and the all-seeing, all-assuming eyes of the lords, with more than a hint of drama, and quite deliberate in its execution, I pointed an accusing finger as I spoke the unforgiving, and perhaps unforgivable, words.

'I had no part in the devising although I aided the outcome. My brother the Duke of York devised the plot and laid it out before me.'

Edward's eyes, unfathomable, for the first time lifted to mine as Sir John responded.

'I would suggest to you that the Duke of York makes an easy target, my lady. My lord Prince Henry has spoken for him.'

'If there is treason here, he is the perpetrator.' There had been a sneer in that smooth voice, which made me add, when

I had not intended to: 'It is not the first treason that York has planned, in which I had no part. Are you aware? For I have been made so. There was a conspiracy to assassinate the King on the road to Eltham for the Christmas festivities. He would be waylaid and left dead in a pool of blood.'

Henry did not look altogether surprised.

I would make them sit up, all these sanctimonious lords.

'Why should you not believe it? Oh, it was a dangerous proceeding, but there were contingencies. If the attack failed, the walls of Eltham could be scaled by assassins.'

Eyes widening, Henry looked round as if for confirmation. 'We have heard naught of this. Do we believe it?'

I saw Edward's face set a little around his mouth. So I had discomfited him and I enjoyed it. But the sneer of Sir John Pelham was joined by a smirk. As for Edmund, he sat silent and motionless, as he had since I had first entered this chamber.

'And perhaps if that was unsuccessful,' Sir John added, 'our lord the King would be murdered at his prayers, or at his bath? There are so many possibilities for an imaginative mind.'

A murmur of laughter. They did not believe me. Better to blame a woman, steeped in original sin, than one of their own.

But Henry, not inclined to laugh, raised his hand for silence. 'I think, my lord of York, that you must answer this accusation.'

Edward stood again.

'Indeed, my lord. Most willingly.'

'Did you know of this plot to rescue the Mortimers?'

'Yes, my lord. I admit that I did.'

There was just the slightest hesitation of breath in the room.

'So you were involved.'

'No, my lord. It was never my doing. I fear that Lady Despenser is mistaken.'

'If you were aware of it, why did you not make it known?'

It seemed to me that Edward's skin had paled but his reply was immediate. 'I never thought it would happen. How could a woman have the power to create such havoc? If I was wrong, my lord, I ask forgiveness for my lack of judgement when dealing with my own sister.' He bowed to Henry. 'Lady Despenser was quite capable of such an upheaval to the peace of our country.'

'And the plan to climb over the walls of Eltham, your grace?' Pelham persisted.

'Do I look as if I would?' He spread his arms in pure display, as vain as any popinjay. 'As if I could. Lady Despenser is misinformed.'

Laughter fell on him as a blessing. He was superbly and expensively clad from his soft-crowned hat with its costly jewel to his scarlet leather shoes, a man of means and today a man of leisure. It spurred me into personal confrontation, when I had vowed that I would not.

'Why would you have to climb yourself, Edward, to achieve the murder you desired? It would be possible for you to pay someone to do so, while you remained innocent. As you claim your innocence here today by naming me the sole transgressor.'

My use of his given name, when he had been so deliberately formal, made this more than personal. But Edward sighed, superbly theatrical, addressing the magnates as if he were a mummer of great skill, and I recalled him donning costume and mask to act out some dramatic scene in Twelfth Night festivities. St George or the Devil himself. His words were a cold dousing of my anger:

'Here is the truth of it, my lords. I knew about the plot. My sister asked for my compliance, which I refused. It was I who forewarned King Henry of it, knowing of what my sister was capable. This allowed my lord Somerset to take steps to stop it. As for this accusation of assassination, I deny such a felony.'

Sir John addressed the King. 'Is it true, my lord, that you received warning of the plot from his grace of York?'

Henry was cautious in his reply. 'I received a warning, certainly, when I was at Kennington, news that the boys had gone, which enabled me to send my brother of Somerset to check the flight of Lady Despenser. The source was unclear but it came by royal courier and thus I presumed it came from my own household.'

Edward smiled self-deprecatingly. 'I sent a messenger. Perhaps the source of my warning went astray, my lord. Or perhaps my messenger met up with your courier who, under the royal seal, carried the news for both that the boys had been secreted out of the castle.'

So horribly believable. His soul was as black as hell, as dark as any winter's moonless night.

'Then we are left to judge the truth of this as it stands.'

Sir John addressed the chamber as a whole, palms raised to appeal to their sense of rightness, so that I saw it all emerging in their rapt demeanour, a spell cast by my brother. They would send me back to my chamber. They would deliberate in my absence and declare me guilty. My brother's reputation might be far from spotless, but I knew that not one of his fellow Councillors would condemn him on my word, not with the Prince speaking out for him and the King oblique in his comment.

I swept the room with a glance that was a challenge. There were few who would meet my gaze, perhaps from embarrassment, and those who did mocked me. Except for Edmund, who finally took my stare and held it. I could read nothing there. Long ago I had given up all hope of his aid. Edward's rejection and Edmund's deliberate isolation merely threw me back on my own devices. So I would seize the only course open to me, dishonourable as it might be judged by these self-promoting lords. I would stir this moribund gathering to life at the point of a sword. Astounded at my own audacity I spoke out, addressing the King.

'I will not be found guilty of complicity on my brother's words, my lord. The guilt does not fall at my feet alone.' I took a breath to demand what no woman had ever demanded. 'I ask for a judicial duel, my lord, to prove my innocence. To prove my worth against that of my brother. I challenge his grace of York to a duel.'

Which stunned the room. Challenges were issued by the throwing down of caps, resulting in a heated exchange of opinion. I had resorted to force of arms.

'A trial by combat, my lady? So you will take up arms against his grace?' Sir John queried as if he could not believe his ears.

There was the laughter again, perhaps in relief, while I, committed now, vented my scorn, my sneer a mirror of his.

'I ask for a champion to come to my aid and fight in my name.'

Silence. Not even an indrawn breath. All I could hear was the rustle of some bird above my head, perhaps a dove that had become trapped within the Hall. I was trapped too but I would fight for my rights before the law.

'Is there no man here who will come to my aid as any knight errant to fight for his lady's honour? Is every man here so certain of my sole guilt?'

My breathing was shallow as I willed just one of the lords to commit himself in my name. I tried not to notice the curl of Edward's mouth; it hurt too much. As for my own champion who had once promised to be the most chivalrous knight when I called on him – would not Edmund offer his sword in my name? If he loved me, he would come to my succour, in some token knightly gesture, despite my admitted guilt.

I could see only his profile turned from me; elegant and austere and closed to me.

He would not. Whatever the rumours of our relationship, he would not spread further news of it, as we might spread sweet herbs amongst the rushes for mocking feet to tread upon, and I felt cold once more replacing the heat of my anger, spreading from my head to my hands, the rings on my cool fingers becoming loose. This was the man who had offered me marriage and the worship of his body. He too was abandoning me so that he would remain anonymous and without shame.

'Will no man offer his sword?' I asked again, my eyes fierce, my voice echoing in the still air.

'I think there is none, my lady.' I flinched at the pity in the King's reply. 'Your honour has become a questionable entity.'

And then there was a movement at the door where some squires and pages had collected while their lords were so engaged, and a figure strode forward, to stand beside the table at Edward's left hand.

'I will answer the lady's challenge. I will fight as the lady's champion.'

A light voice. A smoothly innocent face.

'I know not your name,' I said, heart leaping but not in relief.

'I am William Maidstone. I am a squire to his grace of York.' He bowed to the assembly. 'The lady should not go unchampioned.'

'There is no need,' I said. He was so very young and no doubt suffering from his first dose of chivalry.

'There is every need. I challenge his grace of York to a duel.' He drew his sword from his scabbard. 'Now or at a time of his own choosing. May I be called to justice if I fail to prove the lady's innocence.'

I did not know him as one of the many young men of Edward's household. I could have wept. This brave boy, this foolish boy, who had barely grown his first beard. He would fight for me, and would surely be beaten into the ground. My brother might be thickening around the waist but he was a knight who could ride second to none and wield a sword and lance with skills he had learned before this boy was even born. I could not allow William Maidstone's defeat to compound all the other disasters of this day.

I raised my hand to halt the challenge. But William Maidstone's voice rang out again. He was caught up in the moment, his face flushed, his voice unsteady in his enthusiasm.

'Will you meet me, your grace, and we will prove where the truth might lie? I swear your sister would not disparage your reputation without good cause.'

As I thought: a severe case of courtly love from a youth brought up on the tales of King Arthur's brave knights, even at the expense of risking his own office of squire with my brother. The boy's face was aglow with it, the foolish adoration. To my horror, Edward drew his sword from its gilded scabbard that I had once worked for him over a long winter. I could not be responsible for this boy's death or maiming, even though to refuse his championship would dent his pride. He would recover from that.

'I accept your challenge.' I heard Edward, unable to believe that he would do so. But his own honour hung on it.

'Will you fight now, your grace?'

'Why not? There is space for me to defeat you speedily enough. Why not here?'

Edward was already pushing back his chair, the grating of wood on stone harsh, but no less harsh than the outcry from the assembled lords, caught up in the drama as the squire and his lord prepared to do battle.

'Why not? Because it is not my wish that this unwarrantable challenge should proceed further.' A new voice. The King had stepped down from the dais to stand between challenger and challenged. 'I refuse the challenge and its answering. There will be no combat here, no bloodshed. I have heard the evidence and I will make the judgement. Take Lady Despenser back to her accommodations. I will give my decision on the morrow.' And because there was some compassion within him: 'Take this not to heart,' he said to the squire. 'Your bravery is noted and my refusal is no comment on your stance on this. My lord of York, I will be grateful if you wait on me tomorrow after Mass. I will settle matters to my own satisfaction.'

And thus I was led out of the Great Hall. At the door I stopped, and before the guards could chivvy me along, I turned my head and looked back to where I knew he was sitting. Edmund Holland, already standing, bowed to me. It meant nothing. It meant everything. His silence throughout had been a condemnation. In the end, how effortless it had been for me to destroy his love.

Another night in which I did not sleep. I remained seated by the window, watching the dawn break and winter light gradually fill the room. Slowly my surroundings took shape. The outline of the bed, a coffer by the wall. The figures on the tapestry emerged, all familiar to me. But my mind and thoughts remained rigidly centred on that one certainty after Edward's betrayal: Henry would demand the ultimate punishment. There was, it seemed to me, no future for me to envisage. All hung on Henry's whim and the persuasive tongue of my brother, my brother who would meet with him after Mass only to reiterate that he bore no guilt in the Mortimer affair. I had learned the hard lesson, again and again, that Edward was not to be trusted. He was as lethal and slippery as an eel that refused to be caught to be cooked, escaping the cook's hatchet, to slither beneath the door. He would bargain for his own life but not for mine.

As for Edmund, silent, reproachful, I refused to allow any vestige of him to creep into the shadows of my room. If he had tried to see me, I would have refused. What could I say to him? I could imagine what he would say to me. Edmund's wordless denial had been as wounding as Edward's vocal rejection.

Stretching out my hand, I touched my fingers to the livery collar that lay, gleaming softly, on the coffer beside me. I would never wear it again, unless I took it to my execution in a gesture of hopeless defiance. Where would I face my end? Now this I could envisage. On Tower Hill? I found myself hoping that Henry would allow me more privacy, but privacy was not the design behind the public execution of a traitor. I would be put on show, a royal pawn to ensure the loyalty of a restive country. Constance of York, Lady Despenser, a royal traitor. I hoped the chroniclers made good comment of my courage in adversity.

My mind slid inconsequentially. Had Thomas died with courage? Had he shouted for mercy when his gold coins were rejected as insufficient to save his life? I did not know.

I had a visitor. A light footstep following the rattle of the key in the lock.

'Don't lecture me,' I ordered as she walked into the room, the door closed behind her by the guard who stood outside. After my behaviour at Windsor, Henry had given trenchant orders. This time I had neither key nor gold nor a willing locksmith.

'I would not,' Joan replied, taking a seat to face me. 'How did you know it was me?'

'Who else would come and visit me in my ignominy?' The bitterness in my voice appalled me. 'Who would be allowed past the guard but a woman?'

'Well, I thought you might need my company. If you will snap at me I will go away.'

'I'm in no mood for gossip.'

It horrified me that Joan's kindness should be rewarded by no more than a snarl of rejection. There was no kindness left in me.

'Then I will sit quietly until you decide to speak to me.'

Which she did with habitual ease, hands folded in her lap, still little more than a grey outline against the dense mass of the wood panelling. She had not removed her cloak, although she had pushed her hood back from the padded roll that confined her hair. How dissimilar we were, Joan in all her complacency while I seethed with inner rage, yet still she had chosen to come to me in this black hour before my sentence was pronounced.

'At least you haven't brought me one of your cats for company.'

'You do not know what I have in a basket beyond the door. Cats make good company when one is in distress. Do I bring it in now?'

'No!'

I saw the glint of her teeth in a smile. 'But no, I haven't. I doubt you will be here for long.'

I was aghast and must have shown it, despairing that, after a sleepless night, my control was compromised.

'I did not mean death!' she assured.

Perhaps she had. But her furious denial made me laugh, shaking me from my melancholy. I stood, then cast myself onto the cushioned window seat beside her. At close quarters she looked well. I suspected that she looked far better than I.

'It was the worst thing that you could possibly have done,' she said. 'Had you no sense of what the outcome would be?'

'Apparently not.'

I shrugged, reacting as my sleeves shifted against my cold flesh. I was about to receive the lecture after all and resented it. It was one thing for me to admit it; it was quite another for Joan to coat my guilt with a further layer.

'I never did like your brother, however hard he tried to get under my guard,' she stated. 'I certainly did not trust him.'

But I had, when I was young. Or at least I had closed my eyes to his faults. He had been the certainty in my life while I had been smitten with admiration for a glorious older brother. I was a poor maker of choices, a poor judge of character, it seemed. Even after his terrible volte-face over the Revolt of the Earls I had let him back into my affections, because, with shared delusions, shared dreams that would never be fulfilled, Edward remained the one fixed entity in my life.

'I will not be believed, will I?' I said.

'I doubt it. Your reputation is tarnished.' She smoothed the soft kid of her gloves on her knee, her eyes lowered to the task. 'Beyond reclaim. My husband said I should not visit you.'

'So why are you here?' And when she made no response: 'Edmund warned me not to become involved.'

'Of course he did. You should have listened to him.' Now her eyes rose to mine and I read disparagement there. 'If you will risk the scandal to share a man's bed in intimacy, you should at least be willing to listen to his advice out of it.'

'Henry will see Edward after Mass and hear his weasel words,' I told her. 'I doubt I will have to wait much longer.'

'They're casting wagers that your brother will be showered with royal grace and allowed to go free, in spite of his questionable past.'

'A woman is of no value whereas Edward has proven indispensable.'

A silence fell and stretched until I broke it.

'Why have you come, Joan?'

'I'm not at all sure.' She cast the gloves onto the seat between us. 'Why did you do it, Constance? Was my brother's admiration not enough for you? Your restored dower lands, the health of your children?'

It would be enough for Joan. It seemed that it was not enough for me.

'Henry broke his promise. My son was given into Edward's care.'

'Was that a motive to plot his downfall? You were not forced into another marriage against your will. You were allowed the freedom to manage your dower properties. You were invited to Court. Your children were well sponsored. Why did you do it? Surely that would be enough for any woman of integrity.'

Integrity. Edmund had used that word when he had rejected me.

'You always were contrary,' Joan continued in combative style. 'Your father said that you were born under a directionless star, streaking across the heavens without control.'

Joan risked a hand on my arm. 'I think Edmund cares deeply for you,' she admitted.

I shook it off. 'He was not noticeably keen to ride to my rescue. It took a mere squire to offer to become my champion.'

Which urged Joan to her feet.

'Would you expect him to make such an exhibition of himself? It was an outrageous thing to do, Constance. To issue such a challenge, even when your guilt was self-evident.' Clearly someone had been enthusiastic in drawing the details for her. 'What did you expect? A battle to the death in Westminster Hall, with you posing as the innocent damsel to be rescued, to be carried off on horseback to some romantic Avalon? It would have been worthy of a poor mummers' play, and badly acted at that, with all parties held up to ridicule.'

I would not bow before her scorn.

'I had thought the man who had offered me marriage would wield his sword in my honour. Or some such romantic nonsense. I was obviously not worthy of it. Except for some youth in the fit of lustful longings with songs of chivalry occupying the space between his ears.'

But Joan had caught only one word.

'Marriage?'

I stared at her.

'Edmund has offered you marriage?'

'Why not?'

'I had not thought . . .'

'That he would ask me? He has.'

'Have you accepted?'

I read shock and not a little bafflement on her face.

'Yes.'

'Does he have Henry's permission?'

'Yes. The King has granted him the freedom to wed any woman of his choice.'

'I'll wager my paternoster beads he had no thought on it being you!'

'Why not? It will tie Edmund to him, a marriage to a royal cousin.'

'Well, I wish you good fortune.'

'Except that Edmund's chosen bride will lose her head before they can exchange vows. Besides, he has changed his mind in the face of my iniquities. And how can I blame him? You should be relieved that you will not have me for a sister.'

'I am so sorry.'

To my discomfort, Joan sat again, enclosing my hands in hers, until I stiffened, so that she released me with a sad grimace.

'I offer you consolation and you reject it. There is no hope for you. But whether Edmund has or has not changed his mind, you have to face Henry. It is time you made ready.'

So as the sun rose late, in a fit of remorse I allowed her to help me dress in sombre wool and pleat my hair beneath its veil, confined in a gilded caul. I was silently glad of her company.

I observed myself in the hand mirror she held for me.

'I will go to my destiny as a royal daughter.'

'You do everything like a Princess. That's the problem. Don't antagonise him. And don't even consider wearing this.' She lifted the Lancaster livery collar from where it glowed with baleful intimations on the coffer and slipped it into her sleeve. 'It would be a travesty and would win you no friends.'

'I think I have done quite enough to antagonise everyone. I will receive my doom with silent grace.' I hesitated before admitting: 'I did not realise the true horror of battles. I cannot obliterate the memory of the carnage when we were caught. I think that it will live with me for ever, and that I deserve whatever punishment Henry doles out to me.'

I refused to acknowledge Joan's arched brows. In truth, I was in fear.

I was escorted by a single silent serjeant-at-arms, considered sufficient to ensure that I would not escape, for who would aid me? It was two hours after noon so I presumed that Henry had had his conversation with my brother. If he was as slickly sincere this morning as he had been yesterday, I decided that he would have sat at meat with Henry at noon with no retribution hanging over him. Redemption was becoming second nature to him.

The room into which I was bowed was a small antechamber with no furnishings of note and no source of heat, perhaps deliberately chosen to impress me with Henry's generosity in seeing me at all. Why not simply send me to an even colder dungeon in the Tower? What need for this liberal spreading of further family anguish for either of us? The walls were bare and marked with damp, the fireplace empty and long swept clean.

I tried not to respond since the movement of my veils would reveal what might be interpreted as terror. I should have worn a tight-fitting wimple that would give nothing away. How long would it take to give this judgement?

'Do I come with you?' Joan had offered.

'I will face my fate alone,' I had replied.

So here I was. And to my surprise, here was Edward, too. Dressed as finely as I yet with far more ostentation, in vivid Venetian silks. In contrast Henry looked as if he might have just returned, with dust on his boots, from the hunt.

I acknowledged them both with an inclination of my head such as I might have given to an enemy. Then I curtsied to my cousin and ignored my brother although I slid a glance in his direction. I could read nothing in his stance or his expression, but he was not shackled as a traitor.

Hands locked on his belt, Henry addressed us both in a voice that could scrape away the skin. It was privacy that had dictated this choice of venue.

'I might have hoped that my cousins of York would give me loyalty. I grant you that it was an uneasy start, but I treated you with leniency. I restored your lands. I enhanced your positions at my Court. I gave you, Edward of York, power that befitted your abilities. You repaid me with insurrection.'

'I have sworn my loyalty to you, my lord.' Edward was still adamant.

'And probably broken your oath more times than I know.'

'I have worked tirelessly for you in Wales.'

'I acknowledge that, but I have heard enough. What is it that you want from me, Edward? Power? A place at my right hand? You have as much as a man with four sons can give. Is it money that you want? I cannot give it. My own coffers are to let. You have my admiration of your skill in handling men. Yet still you are not satisfied. We have already discussed this. I have given you the wardship of your nephew. You know I can give no more.'

So they had already held their meeting, which gave all the appearance of being a stormy one, nor had issues been laid to rest between them. I for the moment was superfluous.

'You are an able man. I need able men. My sons will need able men.' He drew a breath, a ragged inhalation as if it gave him pain. 'This is my decision. In the certainty that you had some connection with the Mortimer plot, despite the lack of evidence, I will exercise my power to punish you. I am sending you into Sir John's Pelham's hands at Pevensey where you can decide what it is you wish for, and the value of your life. I must be God's own fool to pardon you yet again, but I cannot quite believe that behind that atrocious damask there does not beat a heart that is worth winning. I cannot afford to have your head, although some would say that I cannot afford to let it remain attached to your proud neck. Perhaps it is a weakness in a King, but I have had enough bloodshed in recent years. I hope that you will learn loyalty from Pelham.'

And I, control abandoning me, laughed aloud at this debasement. So Edward would not escape with his skin totally intact. He would suffer the humiliation of imprisonment. It was a laughter fully edged with contempt, of which I was not proud, but I felt he deserved every hour he spent under lock and key.

My brother bowed, realising that argument was valueless. All he asked was:

'How long, my lord? To give me hope through the hours and days, while I prove my loyalty.'

'As long as I see fit.'

Edward was dismissed. Not once did he look at me. I turned my head to watch him go. Until Henry sighed.

'What do I do with you, Constance?'

'Execution?' I suggested.

'Is that what you think you deserve?'

'I admitted my guilt,' I said, my voice as featureless as the walls. The laughter was a thing of the past. 'Since I was apprehended in the company of the Mortimers, all the evidence would prove that I was more involved than my brother. Joan fears for my life. She has become an excellent judge of character.'

'Then her reading of your character will not be flattering. But Joan does not know me as well as she thinks she does. I admit to having considered it. It would rid me of one unpredictable cousin that I can well do without. Unlike your brother, you have no value to me. Is that too cruel?' His lips thinned, his brow furrowed as if he were still caught in a dilemma. 'You can neither lead an army nor sit on my Council nor oversee my parlous finances. Thus the weakness of being a woman. Your death would not be detrimental to my reign. This is the third time you have swum within my pool of disloyalty.'

He studied me. I looked back at him. It had hit hard. Was he trying to terrify me into obedience? I was of no value. There was only one solution I could think of, however much I might despise it. It would be better than death.

'I could marry one of your loyal followers.'

It was the only offer I could make. My blood was a cold stream at the thought of yet another loveless marriage, but at least my blood would still be in my veins.

'You could, but I know none who would take you. You are not wealthy enough to attract an important husband. Your reputation does not stand you in good stead; you have lost the esteem of any man of fine sensibilities. Who would be willing to take you on as a wife, unless a dose of royal blood in your children was paramount? Your past might suggest that you would add hemlock to a husband's pottage if he displeased you.'

I swallowed. 'You could send me to a convent.'

Blessed Virgin. I prayed that he would not.

'Ha! I would have to spend more money than I have to found a chantry to persuade any self-respecting Abbess to take you.' A quick strike of anger lit his suddenly weary face. 'Why did you do it?'

How often had I heard that question? How often had I found an unsuitable answer? I simply shook my head.

'I have shown you leniency,' he continued, 'but now you have been the cause of the deaths of too many men. None of it need have happened. I won't ask again if it was your brother's influence. I am sure it was, but that's no excuse and I know full well that I can trust neither one of you.' He flung away, the few steps it took him to the further wall, then back again. 'I have decided.'

I held my breath. I forced myself to meet his regard with neither plea nor defiance.

'Kenilworth,' he announced.

One of Henry's great fortresses in the Midlands.

'Is that where I will die?' Better than in public on Tower Hill.

'Not unless you take a fit of the ague or the pox. I'll not have your head, cousin. Edward to Pevensey. You to Kenilworth. Your brother Dickon is under my eye, playing the role of perfect courtier in the hope that I will promote him. That should keep the York family in check for the foreseeable future.'

'Imprisonment.' I repeated the word, savouring it in my mouth. I could not quite absorb what he had just said. 'So I will live.'

'To my detriment. Any decision otherwise will be with God.'

I felt the blood, now even colder, drain from my face.

'I thought you might at least be thankful.'

I could barely speak. All my senses were held in suspension, closing in on me. It was only then that I could admit how deep my fear had been that Henry would take my life. I felt a hand close on my arm.

'Your face is as white as new snow. You won't faint, will you?'

'Certainly not.' I buried my teeth in my lower lip.

'For a moment I thought you might astound me by proving to have a range of human emotions.'

'No, Henry,' I managed to reply evenly as the blackness receded. 'I have none. I am as you see.' He freed me, as if to touch me was anathema. But then, as relief swept through me, I remembered. An unpleasant doubt crept through my mind on silent feet. 'Richard was sent to Pontefract. He failed to live long enough to come out of Pontefract except in a shroud. Why would Kenilworth be different for me?'

Henry looked affronted. 'I'll not starve you to death.'

I would live. It seemed that I would live after all.

'How long will you keep me there?' I was echoing my brother, so was not surprised by the response. But there was a lightness in my breast.

'Until I think you might enjoy your freedom without stabbing me in the back. Be thankful.'

I considered. 'And my children. My son? He will be without guardianship, with Edward imprisoned.'

'I will ensure that he is well cared for, in my wife's household. I will visit neither his uncle nor his mother's sins on his head unless he shows your traits too strongly. Your dower lands will become my property, of course. I may at least get some benefit from your betrayal. It will help pay for my campaign against Glyn Dwr.'

I could expect no less. Kenilworth. So I would not be kept in penury. It was more palace than castle since my uncle the Duke of Lancaster had put his lavish hand to the private living apartments.

'And my daughter Isabella?'

'In my magnanimity I will allow her to remain with you. She is very young to be separated from her mother.'

'May I receive visitors?'

'Within reason.'

I would not be totally isolated, but who would visit me was beyond my imagining.

At last I curtsied, deeply, because he deserved my recognition. 'Thank you, my lord. You have my gratitude.'

'I wish I believed it. I will arrange an escort for you.'

As I walked towards the door, his voice followed me.

'I thought that perhaps you would wish to say farewell to your brother. You will find him waiting for you. My serjeant-at-arms will take you there.'

I stood, head bowed. Henry had arranged this, an unpleasant little touch of malice to end the day. This would be the first time that Edward and I had been alone together since the abortive plot, since he had sworn evidence against me before the Council. Without reply I allowed myself to be escorted, and there he was, in yet another unused antechamber, even colder than the one where Henry had made his judgement. At the sight of him, when I stood before him, my escort retreating to the wall, I was empty of all but memories and an anger that shook me.

'I have nothing to say to you, brother.'

'Did you expect me to leap to your protection? When it would have incriminated me?'

I tilted my chin. 'No. In all honesty I should have known what to expect. But I thought that you would not so publicly brand me a traitor and a liar.'

'You accused me of the assassination attempt.'

'You denied me.'

He raised his hands palms upwards. 'It is done, Constance. It is behind us. Is there no reconciliation in you?'

'No. There never will be.'

A grin lightened his expression into the handsome visage that everyone at Court would recognise. 'We're not dead, nor will be until the span of our heartbeats determines the end of life. He'll let us go eventually, you know.'

'You, perhaps; I think he'll happily forget about me. I am to go to Kenilworth.'

'I know. At least you won't have to listen to Pelham's lectures on your lack of opprobrium.' He tilted his chin to match mine. 'Do you despise me utterly?'

'Yes.' I considered. 'Yes, I think I do.' I gestured to the guard at the door who had been an interested party, except that there had been nothing to hear. 'I am ready to go.'

'Farewell, Constance.'

I could not reply. My guilt was self-evident but his betrayal had been unmerciful, while my hopes of marriage to Edmund Holland were buried in a grave of my own making.

Chapter Eighteen

Winter 1405: Kenilworth Castle

What does a woman do with her days, incarcerated at the royal will in a royal fortress? The moments of time hung like rotting fruit on a winter's bough. My life became enclosed within walls and though I was free to order my own life within their confines, Henry's watchful household and resident guards prevented my stepping beyond, not even to ride beside the mere. I could watch the comings and goings of servants and couriers, of those merchants and craftsmen who delivered goods, of smart retinues of liveried soldiers. I could admire the freedom beyond the walls, acknowledging all the time that there was none for me.

Luxury was mine, for Kenilworth had enjoyed the indulgent hand of John of Gaunt. Unnumbered chambers with efficient fireplaces that did not belch smoke, a Great Hall and dancing chamber if I were in a mood to dance. Unnumbered beds with hangings and tapestries, woven and stitched with skill in the Low Countries. My own waiting-women, my own possessions to keep me company; all had been restored to me.

My daughter Isabella. My life and my days were my own, but still I could not leave.

Even the news from the Court and the travails facing Henry seemed to be distilled into the merest drops of dew. It felt to me that I was simply existing, suspended in a silken cocoon which wrapped me around in soft luxury just as it pinioned me in hard containment. No chance of plotting here, no knowledge even of what might benefit from my interference, which was exactly what Henry had intended. Here at Kenilworth I was involved in nothing other than what I might eat, when I might visit the chapel to give thanks for my life, which intricate pattern I might set my needle to. I was not allowed to correspond.

Occasionally I wondered: what was Edward doing in Pevensey? I would wager that he had at least persuaded Sir John Pelham to allow him to hunt.

Meanwhile I withdrew into my own world. Too cold to walk in the gardens where the plants had retreated into autumn hibernation, I read and stitched and played the lute, but not songs of love. I played more games of chess than I could count, the only plotting that I was allowed. I laughed with the visiting mummers and sang with Henry's minstrels. I read the stories of King Arthur to Isabelle but she was too young to understand. I attended Mass.

By the Virgin, boredom struck hard, every day more difficult than the last. I would welcome anyone with some erudite conversation. The priest's offerings were little more than homilies on the importance of clasping a life without sin to my bosom. He sent me yawning to my bed after supper.

Had not Henry promised to allow me visitors? Probably in a moment of weakness. I had little hope, and as the weeks crawled past with agonising slowness, I gave up. Would it be like this for the rest of my life? I had thought myself a woman of strong will, but loneliness gnawed at me. I might keep a perfect semblance of acceptance, occupied from dawn to dusk, but who was to know my mind?

I did not think about Edmund. I would not. I banished him during my days, but my dreams were beyond my control.

The first intimation was the half-grown grey kitten that scampered across the floor of my chamber and vanished behind a tapestry, whether from fear of, or in pursuit of a rat I did not know. And then a voice, beyond my door that was ajar, raised into giving some sort of command.

Joan.

I was shocked by the intensity of that moment of sheer pleasure. Desperately short as I was of a conversation other than the climate, the mould on the walls in the old keep and the state of my soul, Joan was more than a welcome guest.

The anonymous servant bowed. 'You have visitors, my lady.'

My heart jolted again, my embroidery sliding from my knee to the floor. Was it possible that Edmund had come with her? I stood to face the door. Careful. Be careful. Nothing has changed between you since that day he abandoned you to Henry's justice. Be grave and circumspect, for have you not proved that you do not need him? Love has a finite quality when it is ignored and betrayed.

I considered my clothing, picking embroidery threads from my sleeve, wishing I were arrayed in more than a plain houppelande and a linen coif – for we kept no formality at Kenilworth – but too late for that now.

'Constance. There you are.'

Joan approached, her hands held out in greeting.

'Joan. Your gift gave you away. It's chasing vermin behind the arras.'

There was that gentle laugh that hid a frequently sharp tongue. 'I brought it for company for you, not as a mouser. You have to win it to your affections.'

'I will do no such thing. I dislike cats. I am not so desperate.'

Oh, but I was. My heart had sunk with a thud as Joan's companion stepped into the room in her wake. Even worse, it seemed that my second visitor had read my response. He smirked.

'Sorry I'm not Edmund.'

It was Dickon.

'Joan said I should come,' he admitted.

'So you were not persuaded through love of your sister.'

'No. It would be good policy at this precise moment to keep in with our cousin Henry.'

'Of course it would. But I will not persuade you into rebellion.'

'I can see the opportunities for myself,' he replied. 'But for now I am the most dedicated subject.'

He subjected me to a rough clasp. I expected that Joan had ordered him to do so, since I might lack for human contact and so be encouraged by a brotherly embrace, which touched me, but as soon as I could extricate myself, I stepped back to survey him. Dickon was no longer a youth, but a grown man. There was a solidity, even a quaint dignity to him. But was that only a facade? I still suspected that beneath the wool and leather that encased his broad shoulders there was the old restlessness, the perennial disgruntlement. Momentarily I wondered what man he would become. He was no soldier, and, I thought, no diplomat. What were his gifts? Perhaps he would become merely a trustworthy servant, one day taking his seat on the Royal Council, although I did not think that Henry would ever value his advice. Dickon was a ship driven by strange winds. If Henry would give him a title and land he might settle into loyalty.

'Has the King decided to espouse your cause?' I asked, since I detected a contentment about him, usually absent.

He replied promptly. 'He is heavily involved in the marriage of his daughter Philippa to the King of Denmark, probably next year when she will be eleven years, of an age to travel. It is mooted that I accompany her to Denmark as part of her official escort.'

So at least one member of the York family would keep the name prominent in Henry's mind. 'And will Henry pay for your clothing and jewels so that you might make a good impression?' I eyed his garments, which were less than impressive after the long journey.

'I hope so.' There was a sudden glint in his eye. 'I think he will knight me before I go.'

I smiled at his pleasure. 'Tell him you would like a title at the same time, as well as the annuity that he promised you but never paid.'

A servant bought wine, and so we sat, conversing about those we knew. After a successful campaign in the north to demolish Percy power, the Earl of Northumberland being forced into exile in Scotland, Henry was once again tied up in campaigning against the Welsh prince Glyn Dwr, suffering bad weather and significant loss, eventually retreating from the field. When I expressed little interest in Henry's victory or defeat, Dickon turned the conversation adroitly to the personal.

'Richard is thriving in the Queen's household. Edward is making the most of his little sojourn with Sir John Pelham.'

'I do not care if Edward burns in the fires of hell.'

'He says he dislikes Pevensey,' Dickon continued. 'He says it's like living in purgatory with no hope of redemption.' He grin widened. 'But he is making good use of his time.'

I raised my brows. Of course he was. 'Has he found some kitchen wench to admire him?'

'He is writing a book.'

I laughed. How could I not? 'A book?'

'About game and hounds and hunting and some such.'

Joan hid a smile, entering the exchange of news. 'We hear that he has found a noted French work of erudition about the chase. We think he is copying most of it into his hand to pass it off as his own.'

How apposite of Edward. 'And if he dedicates it to the King, he will buy his release quicker.'

'To the Prince actually. He will dedicate it to Prince Hal.'

Which reminded me of the Prince leaping to Edward's defence to my cost.

'Ha! I doubt then that Edward will stay long in purgatory, since Prince Hal was so impressed with his efforts against the Welsh. Edward will be received back into the angelic choir before we can blink.'

They stayed with me overnight, Dickon leaving us in peace after supper.

'Are you happier with your new husband?' I asked.

'A woman can't complain.'

'I could. Are you carrying a Willoughby heir yet?'

'I will let you know when I am.'

There was no disguising the sadness that touched her soul as she turned the exchange into other channels, but wherever our discussions took us, there was one question I did not ask, that I had no intention of asking. In the end, with suspect insouciance, Joan provided the answer.

'Edmund says—'

'I have no interest in what Edmund says.'

'But still I will tell you. He is in good health.'

I did not reply.

'He is busy.'

Everyone was busy except for me. Even Dickon. Even Edward was putting pen to parchment in his prime interest of hounds and hunting and how to impress the King.

'So the Earl of Kent is also making a name for himself with Henry,' I observed.

'Yes.'

'Henry had no suspicion of Edmund, as their uncle, of being involved in my Mortimer escapade.'

'Apparently not.'

'Nor of you, as their aunt.'

'I am above suspicion.'

'How fortunate.'

'Edmund has begun to step into our father's shoes, extending his powers as Justice of the Peace in the south. He has also been given a command under Prince Thomas in the royal fleet.'

'Excellent.'

Joan refused to be deterred although her voice had become acid.

'He made a name for himself off the coast of Normandy, and at some engagement against the French at Sluys.'

'How gratifying.'

Which ended any confidences until Joan prepared to leave on the following morning, on the way to one of her husband's northern properties.

'Take the cat with you,' I said.

'I doubt I can find it.'

Her groom helped her to mount and she gave the command to depart.

'Joan . . .'

She reined in, looking down at me with a little sigh as if she knew what I would say.

'Tell him . . .'

But what could I suggest that she tell him? If he could not come of his own volition, I did not want him. Even Dickon had managed to find his reluctant way to Kenilworth.

I shook my head. 'Tell him nothing at all.'

'Then you will become a lonely old woman.'

'But it will be my choice.'

When she had ridden out of calling distance, Dickon at her side, I wished I had not been so proud.

Henry had, in his appalling tolerance which I found little less than a humiliation, given orders that I might be allowed, under strict guard, to ride in the environs of the castle. I would not thank him, but it added greatly to the quality of my life, even though our riding, with Isabella, was of a sedate nature.

Sometimes, under metallic grey skies, wrapped in furs, we took out the hawks to fly at the wildfowl on the mere. It was a relief to view the majesty of the rosy sandstone walls from without rather than from within. When the sun managed to shine, it looked less of a prison.

Returning on a dank morning, my features half frozen by a brisk wind and a spattering of rain, I was alerted before I even rode into the bailey. He had arrived a little time ago and rather than wait inside had seated himself in a sheltered patch of desultory sunlight on the steps, accompanied by the kitten that was growing into a sleek cat. It was purring under his hand.

For a moment I sat on my mare and regarded him, as he regarded me. The perfect influential magnate and King's friend, Edmund Holland, Earl of Kent, his dark magnificence enhanced by a velvet chaperon and a sable cloak. His gauntlets, cast aside on the step, offered enough gilding to rival my new altar cloth.

He stood and swept me a bow as if I were the Queen herself.

I dismounted, any reaction to the mere sight of him effectively quashed behind the need to twitch the damp folds of my gown into seemly order, smooth my veil, and issue a range of instructions to my escort, none of which was essential. I thanked my groom, supervised my daughter being lifted to the ground. Only then did I turn to him. I would not appear too needful of his company.

I could have run into his arms.

'My lord Earl.'

'My lady Despenser. Good day to you. I wondered when you would see fit to notice me.'

'How could I not?' I gestured to the pennons that proclaimed his estate, the three golden lions on their red field snapping as the wind flirted with them. 'To what do I owe the honour?'

'The honour is all mine.'

He bowed superbly again, without expression. He was as clever at dissembling as I.

'Was there something you wished from me? I cannot imagine what, since I am, at this present time, free to grant no favours for anyone. Perhaps you have misconstrued the extent of my influence, when incarcerated in the King's fortress.'

In some spirit of what could only be trickery, he bent to pick up the cat that had been weaving around his ankles, placing it into my arms. It had decided to accept me; my reciprocal tolerance being low, I handed it promptly to Isabella, who proceeded to stroke it once more into a purring frenzy.

Meanwhile I waited, unable to step past the moment when I had issued my challenge against Edward, and my lover had turned his face from me. Nor could I forget his condemnation of me as I set out for Windsor and the abortive plot. Love had proven to be such an ephemeral commodity. It added another layer to my bitterness.

'I am here to relieve the tedium of your hours,' he said, ignoring my lack of appreciation for his arrival. 'Joan advised me that I should be made welcome. And that you were short of company.' His dark brows became a solid bar but whether from amusement or annoyance I could not deduce. 'Perhaps my sister was incorrect after all. Do I leave immediately? I will go if you wish it.'

I almost dispatched him. Instead, but with no noticeable warmth: 'I have no control over who comes here.' Then added: 'Some days I would welcome the Devil himself.'

'I can be better company than the Devil.'

I heaped silent curses on Joan's head. She had made me an object of pity. Still I did not move, even when the horses were led away and Isabella, clutching the cat, darted off in the wake of her nursemaid.

'That was not the only reason for my visit.'

'Then come and take a cup of ale.' How equable my invitation. 'You can enlighten me. Joan says that you are busy about the King's business. And your own, of course.'

I turned to lead the way, leaving him to follow. Instead, with some neat adjustment of pace, he matched his steps to mine.

'I have discovered a love of the sea and naval campaigns,' he said.

If he thought my offering him ale was a sign of my thawing, he was mistaken. But why was he here? Our marriage agreement assuredly lay in the dust beneath our feet.

'I should be honoured that you found the time between one expedition and the next. I expect Prince Thomas finds you invaluable. Just as Prince Hal appreciated the loyalty of my brother Edward in the Welsh campaign. How fascinating that the men who cross my path find it so easy to earn royal patronage.'

The old spark of anger shook me. Better than complaisance. It made me feel alive again.

'I have not found it difficult. Moreover I enjoy the sea.'

'How fortunate for you. So what are you doing here, on dry land?'

'I am keeping in touch with old friends.'

'I am honoured to be placed in so illustrious a category. I think I have not many.'

As soon as we were out of sight of my women and the servants, in the shadowed environs of the entrance hall in the old keep, I found my forearm taken in a grip that seemed far from friendly.

'Release me.'

'I will not. I can read you like a page of a missal, Constance. You think I should have taken up your challenge.'

I tugged ineffectually. 'It had crossed my mind.'

'You think I should have leaped to your defence, to be your knight in shining armour, exchanging public blows with Edward for the gratification of all present. Can you imagine trial by combat between Edward and myself, the whole Court eager to cheer or jeer? Whoever emerged the victor, your name would be sunk in the mire. It would have done no good, and made us both the object of even more scandalous predictions. As a point of conversation to be dissected over supper, it is still alive and well. Furthermore,' – he pulled me to face him – 'I suspect that Edward would have beaten me well and truly, and you would still have been shut up here until Henry sees fit to release you.'

'I know I should not have done it,' I discovered myself admitting under such an unexpected flurry of criticism. I resisted his hold but he would not let go. 'But what should I have done? Accept the full weight of the evidence that I and I alone was at fault? If fury drove me to immoderate lengths, then I make no excuse, and your berating me makes the hurt no less.' I tugged hard but to no avail. 'You made your disapproval clear to a blind man, and then you left me to fend for myself.'

'You were quite capable of arguing your own defence. You didn't need me.'

'And you were intent on keeping Henry's good faith. You have all my admiration, Edmund. A truly marvellous sleight of hand. Our King has not decided to suspect you of being complicit then?'

'He might, but he is not saying. You were caught, so you take the blame.'

'Is that all you have come to say? If you would care to release me we will forgo the cup of ale and you may leave. I could ask why you did not come sooner. Perhaps you have the best of excuses. Treachery could so easily rub off on you; like limewash from a whitened wall, once applied it is difficult to remove.'

'Even you should see that it's difficult to drop in on a friendly visit when engaged in a naval sortie against the enemy.'

I admired his patience, even as I could see that it was wearing thin.

'Then go back to sea, Edmund, if it gives you such satisfaction.'

'You'll not dismiss me so easily.'

All my Plantagenet arrogance rose to the surface. 'Oh, but I will. You have said all that needs to be said, and I have no wish to hear more. My being Henry's prisoner does not make it obligatory for me to listen to condemnation from a man who was once my lover.'

Edmund promptly transferred his grip to my shoulders.

'No, it is not all I've come to say. And by God, you will listen. I disapproved of what you did. Why would I become involved in so ill-managed a scheme? But, my beautiful but frustrating Constanza, I love you no less. I have no idea why. There must be easier women to love.'

He kissed me on my lips.

My heart might thud with the unexpected words, my lips might burn at the unexpectedness of the salute, but my reply was unforgiving. 'I don't want your love. I don't need it. I expunge you from your offer of marriage. Is that why you came? I'll not hold you to it. And I will not be manhandled!'

'I swear you do not know what you want or need.' His second kiss was quite as firm and peremptory. 'I am here because I wish to be here. I recall the days when my love was all you could ask for. Here it is, freely offered.' He released me. 'Now walk with me.'

I stood, as rigid as a statue.

'We will walk,' he reiterated. 'It would be more dignified if you simply gave in and did what you were told. I have no wish to drag you, to make you an object of interest to your household, but by God, I will if necessary.'

Thus prompted not to argue the point, we walked in the gardens, my anger gradually quieted to a low simmer, my women and the guards at a distance. Since I could think of nothing to say that had not already been said, I paced beside him, a significant space between us, in unfriendly silence. I had not enjoyed his shaming of my choices. The muted show of the remaining autumnal flowers made no impression on me. The summer songbirds were silent in the cold; the scents were of foliage in decay. The keep still loomed over me, its intimidating bulk fast erasing any remembrance of his kisses.

'Your brother is petitioning for his release,' Edmund said, taking up an innocuous path. 'He says he is much troubled by heaviness of spirit.'

'And is Henry listening?'

'I think he is of a mind to be forgiving.'

'You surprise me.' I slid a glance. Was that why he had come? A bearer of good news, that Henry was softening towards me? But there was no hope in the stern set of his mouth. 'Not towards me, I presume.'

'You could try sending a petition.'

'I have sent more petitions to Henry than I ever thought possible in a lifetime. He could light every fire in Eltham Palace with them.'

In the shelter of some clipped bushes, stark in winter gloom, we halted. Edmund surveyed the mist-girt landscape.

'Once I asked you to wed me. And you accepted. Where do we now stand?'

'Apart from in this benighted spot? Let us walk on. My feet are frozen.' I walked away. 'Where do we stand? I know not. Except that we are unwed and will continue to be so.'

I had rejected him. Edmund refused to be rejected.

'Why?'

He followed me when, in painful honesty, my face turned away, I gave the reply that I must give:

'I have just offered you the right to retreat from a union that you no longer find acceptable.'

If I expected him to laud my sacrifice, I was mistaken. Edmund ignored it.

'When I am away from you I think of you constantly,' he said, swiping at some dying plant with his gloves. 'I wonder what you are doing, that perhaps you should not be doing. I miss your conversation. I admire your courage and your dedication when you have a cause to fight for. I love you, Constance. I don't want you as my mistress. I want you to carry my heir. Marriage is a way to make it all permanent and legal and beyond the scope of gossiping tongues. Who would object to the uniting of two great houses, Holland and Plantagenet?'

His response baffled me. 'I could remain here for another decade. Of what use to you is that? Would we communicate by letter? It's no way to achieve an heir.'

'I could move in with you.'

I caught a glint in his eye.

'Which I suspect would have Henry appearing with an armed escort at Kenilworth's door, to remove you.'

'Why would he care?' He took my gloved hand and drew it through his arm. 'Let us go back to the beginning, before we were struck down by this ill-fated attempt to change the succession. Will you wed me, Constance?'

'The circumstances are not auspicious.'

But I did not withdraw my hand.

'If all things were equal, would you still wish to be my wife?'

'Are you renewing your offer?'

It was impossible to take in. This was not what I had expected.

'Yes.'

'Do you love me enough to consider marriage to a woman condemned for treason?'

'I would be a fool to propose marriage if I did not. But do you love me enough to accept?' He hesitated, but only momentarily. 'Are you courageous enough to put your life into my hands?'

I looked at him. He looked at me. The wind was cold around us, but there was an unnerving warmth enveloping my heart.

'Yes,' I admitted. 'Against my will, I love you.'

'Then we will marry.'

'No, no!' I pushed him away. 'Henry won't allow it,' I repeated. 'You will risk all you have gained through his patronage. He can strip an office from you as fast as he awarded it in the first place.'

'Then we will make our vows without informing him. My grandmother, Countess Joan, has provided me with an excellent precedent.'

The warmth that I had fought so hard to dispel became more intense.

'Are you proposing a secret marriage?'

'Why not?'

I knew immediately what he had in mind. He came of scandalous stock.

'I doubt your grandmother would approve. She would not have us layer scandal on scandal.'

'Countess Joan never retreated from scandal when in pursuit of her manifold ambitions. It did her no harm. Are you less confident than my grandmother? We will wed. And then I will persuade the King of the value of releasing you.'

I was breathless, drawn along by such determined planning. He was so sure, so persuasive, holding out an enticing future on the palm of his hand.

'I can think of no value that he would recognise.'

'. . . and then when you are free we will announce our marriage to the Court and to the world.'

It was like trying to untangle a sad mass of embroidery silks. 'All I can see is disaster,' I replied. 'Better to withdraw from this, Edmund, and take a bride without complications.'

Which he chose to ignore, driving on as if I had not spoken. 'As my wife, I can argue more strongly for your release. If you are not my wife, I have no right to involve myself in your future. You must see that. And so will Henry.'

'I have neither money nor reputation. Henry has taken my dower lands again.'

'You have beauty and birth. You have my heart. The only question is: do you have the courage?'

He was offering me marriage. He was offering me love and admiration. He would work for my release. Was this truly what I wanted?

'Well? Are you, without precedence, lost for words?'

We should wait. Why wed now when an imprisoned wife was the last thing Edmund needed in his bid for fame and glory? It was a wooing in a freezing, windswept garden: no good could come of it.

I placed my hand on his arm.

Why would he choose me now, with all the difficulties that it entailed, when I had offered him his freedom from a proposal he should probably never have made?

Edmund was not finished.

'If my love has no value to you, send me away. If it does, then wed me. Now. Before you can change your mind.'

It was not an offer I could resist.

'I have lost all feeling in this wind. I accept. Let us discover somewhere warm and do the deed.'

Where should we commit this act? Discretion suggested some dusty cupboard in the kitchen regions where we would be undiscovered. Pride pointed to the Great Hall, built by my uncle of Lancaster, for celebration and festivity, where Henry himself sat to dispense justice when he was in residence. The fact that the vast space echoed around the four of us was of no moment. It pleased me to challenge Henry in his own domain, the winter light making the best of the vast windows. Still we needed candles to illuminate the proceedings, meagre as they were. The magnificence of our chosen chamber suited the moment, even though we still wore our boots and cloaks. Why waste time in donning finery, when there was so little time at our disposal?

We had a need of witnesses. One of my waiting-women and Edmund's serjeant-at-arms, both of whom looked either aghast or ablaze with the potential scandal. To any onlooker who was curious, we could have been indulging in a brief conversation before one of the fireplaces where a fire had been hastily lit, an occasion of no moment. Such a marriage had no place for priest or holy blessing, merely an exchange of intent. I thought of the rule-flouting Countess Joan of Kent exchanging similar vows with Edmund's grandfather, a man she loved. I could do the same. A marriage *per verba de praesenti*, frowned on by Holy Mother Church, despised by priests as a crude clout against their authority, but legally binding if witnessed and consummated.

'On this day, until death separates us, you are my wife.'

'By my words here spoken, you are my husband.'

No more. No less. Nothing further was required of either of us. All duly witnessed, Edmund rewarding them for their presence and their silence with a coin.

Did I miss some poetic declaration of love? I did not. Edmund's hands were warm and sure around mine. He had come to me in my captivity. I was his wife.

'Now we will make our union true, my beloved Countess.'

He kissed my hands and then my lips.

Leading Edmund to my private chamber, I could not believe that I had allowed myself to be drawn into this legal commitment, but we celebrated our marriage in fine style, for pleasure as well as legal necessity, after so much time apart, eventually for him to fall into sleep, leaving me to study his half-averted face. He was so familiar to me, but each detail was suddenly clear, as if drawn in by a monkish scribbler with pen and ink, on the border of a manuscript. The thin blade of his nose, the fall of his hair over his forehead. A scar, gained in some distant skirmish, which merged with the lines at the corner of his mouth that deepened when he smiled. The weathering of the sun, fading immediately into the tender whiteness at the hollow of his throat. The dark lashes, soft on his cheek, contrasting with the firm chin that announced a will of iron.

He opened his eyes, as if catching me in the unpractised art of spying, and I felt a flush rise to my cheeks, my temples, my hairline.

'Do you like what you see, my wife?'

'I see a man of more integrity than I can lay claim to.'

'I see a beautiful woman who is now my own.'

Leaning, he kissed my lips, so softly, then rolled to rise and dress. Disappointment strong in me that he must leave, I was conscious of his every movement, every breath, every stretch and flex of muscle and flesh as he reclothed himself. I loved him. I had loved him for a long time. This was more than physical desire – it was an intertwining of souls – and now I was forced to admit it for myself.

I smiled at the foolishness of romance in my turn of thought.

'What are you thinking?' He was pulling on one of his boots.

'That I love you.'

'And there – I thought you would never say it.'

'I think I have only just come to the realisation of it.'

'A venison haunch, long in the roasting, is often the best and most tender on the platter.'

I laughed. So much for poetry. But it was an analogy that pleased me.

Edmund Holland, my husband, departed with due formality and no outward signs of our nuptials. Except for his final murmur against my cheek.

'I will speak for you with the King. When he releases you, I will come with drum and shawm, pipe and sackbut. I will announce your release with trumpet and rebec.'

My brother, with no great fuss, was released from Pevensey, his lands returned to him as he was restored to royal favour and the King's Council, all enhanced by an annual income of two hundred pounds. Such the price of treason for a man who had the allure of a stoat approaching a fear-struck coney. His book on all matters of hounds and hawks and the skills of hunting was named impressively *The Master of Game*, to be finely bound and dedicated to Prince Henry. Even in captivity Edward had had his eye on what he might salvage for his future advancement.

I was not released.

Thus the world continued to move on its allotted path, but without me. My marriage made no difference to my life. It was as if it had never happened.

The promise of trumpet and rebec hovered over me as insubstantially as a distant dream. The instruments themselves kept silence.

Chapter Nineteen

June 1406: Westminster Palace

I returned to the beating heart of the Royal Court. Henry released me.

When hope was a dead leaf on a bough, I had what I wanted. A full six months over and above the time it took my brother to inveigle his way out of confinement, Henry had sent for me to return from exile. So here I was restored, where Joan embraced me and insisted on playing mediator as I stepped once more into the Court environs with all its eddying interests and ambitions and snapping occupants.

Here I would be reunited with Edmund. I would be free to acknowledge him as the man I had wed with vows legally taken. I would see him again, with no more hiding, no more pretence. Pardoned and restored, I would take my rightful place as cousin of the King, and as Countess of Kent. My blood sang with the anticipation of it, masking a faint edge of disappointment. There had been no shawms or trumpets. None of the promised fanfare. Edmund, it would seem, was not even aware of my release.

'You had better make a suitable obeisance to Henry,' Joan said, expertly threading her way between courtiers. 'As long as you learn from past encounters, and watch your tongue.'

'I have learned conciliation. I have learned patience.'

'I think you might need both of them.'

I thought that there was a tightness indenting the corners of Joan's lips, the vestige of a frown, but then she moved on, leaving me to step back into the world I had left. It was much like performing a well-known dance, the movements returning with ease, the ebb and flow of who must be recognised, who could be ignored. The shifting alliances of the court nobility were familiar, the faces around the King much the same, but there was a distinct change in the mood of the gathering. We might tread the same measures but all was uncertain underfoot, as when ice melts in spring and begins to crack, to the danger of those who risked testing the surface. The Court, so it seemed to me in that moment of my rebirth, was not at ease, the magnates circling like raptors around a suffering King and an ambitious heir.

As for my own re-emergence into this power-hungry society, one false move on my part and all could so easily be shattered. I was restored, but I knew how precarious my status. Henry had been most lenient, but with so much deceit in my past, I must not challenge this leniency. My curtsey before King Henry was of the lowest, a perfect courtly obeisance, while my demeanour could not be faulted as that between subject and King.

Henry raised me up, and as his hand gripped around mine, his face softened into a smile, but his eyes were taking heed of every nuance in this public reconciliation, as I masked the shock of his appearance. Henry was undoubtedly ill. Hair close-cropped, it emphasised his gaunt features, his hollow cheeks, the greyness of his skin. Nor was standing easy for him. We would never see Henry on the tournament field again. I wondered if he was capable of leading his troops into battle. The three years since Shrewsbury had wrought such a terrible change. I almost felt compassion.

'My lord. You have given me my heart's desire.'

'Welcome, cousin. At last you are returned to us. We are pleased to see that your months in Kenilworth have worked a miracle.'

We both understood each other very well. I could feel the eyes of the Court watching every step, every gesture, straining to hear every word.

'I am most grateful that you should invite me to be here, my lord. I deeply regret the concern I have given you in the past.'

'You astonish me. New feathers, Constance?'

'As you see, my lord.' I lowered my eyes self-deprecatingly. 'They have flourished during my seemingly never-ending exile. I will prove to you that I am your most loyal of subjects. I have learned the hard lesson you imposed on me. The depth of your generosity has been more than my heart's desire.'

I did not lie. Henry had again restored my dower lands to me, all my goods that had been confiscated, even going to the length of a sum of fifty-six pounds to cover my expenses of resettling in London. It had almost unnerved me, but then Henry, as ever, had his own reasons for winning my subservience. I had yet to learn what they might be.

'Have you learned the lesson?' He drew me forward into the inner circle. 'Can I trust you not to forget it, if the occasion arises?'

'You trust my brothers, my lord. You reward them with your favour and patronage. Why would you not trust me? I am a reformed woman.'

Did I mean it? I thought that I did. My future had a brilliance as Countess of Kent, furnished with love and respect; my position at Court enhanced by the man who had come to Kenilworth to wed me. I would never tread the path of revolt again.

'Is such redemption possible?' Henry was looking beyond me, addressing Joan.

'I will vouch for it, my lord,' she replied with crisp consonants.

His smile held an element of disbelief.

'Your brother of York is invaluable to me,' Henry said. 'Perhaps I can encourage you to be reunited with him. I understand the rift between you.' Of course he did. Henry knew full well that I had not plotted alone to rescue the Mortimers. How adept he was at using his knowledge to bring men to his side. And women, too. 'I suggest it is time to step across that chasm you helped to create, for the good of the realm. I can use both of you for the defence of the kingdom; even you, Constance. Your castles in the Welsh March are strategically vital to me. Your future loyalty has been heavily bought.'

Such a clever demand on my sense of duty and my worth. And there was Edward, strolling through the throng with Lancaster livery collar a-gleam, smiling at me as if nothing were amiss between us.

'I will not have my Court rent with family dispute.'

Henry's final admonishing, the steel fist within the doeskin glove, as Edward, my hand formally on his arm, steering a path, acknowledging and being acknowledged on all sides, which made clear to me how easily my brother had stepped back into a position of pre-eminence since his return. Aware of eyes following us, if the Court hoped for some entertainment other than the staid Danish ambassadors they would be disappointed. I turned my smile on Joan who was watching me with fierce warning in the set of her mouth. Yet I could not resist.

'You did not visit me, brother.' As soon as we were out of earshot of the gathering I removed my hand from his arm, but the smile stayed in place.

'I was not at liberty.' Edward's smile was equally pinned with diplomatic expediency. 'But you know that. Combative already, Constance? You have been at Court less than an hour and already you find fault.'

'I have been here since last night if you had made the attempt to discover. And I am never combative. You have been at liberty since the turn of the New Year. And as you were the one to put me in Kenilworth Castle in the first place, I thought you might at least have come to ask after my good health.'

'If I had appeared at your door you would have hurled a pottery ewer at my head.'

'I might well. I might still do so. Fortunately there is none to hand here. Henry might claim poverty but the vessels that I can see are all of gold.'

Edward grunted a laugh. 'Do you wish to sit?'

'No. This is not a conversation to be taken at ease. You were about to explain to me why I saw nothing of your heraldic devices approaching my door at Kenilworth.'

'I decided it was best to devote myself to royal service.'

'Of course you did.' I patted his arm in understanding.

Not even an apology. I surveyed the crowd, taking note that Edmund was not present. 'And have you been successful in your bid for royal patronage? Working so hard as you clearly have?'

'Can you doubt it? I am as close to Henry as I ever was with Richard. He has restored all my lands to me. It may be news to you, but it is rumoured that Henry will make me Constable of the Tower of London again. It was an office I regretted losing in the aftermath of the usurpation.'

'Impressive,' I murmured.

'It is most impressive. A symbol of his restored trust in me.'

This was getting us nowhere. Edward had a smooth answer for every eventuality. I took a cup of wine from a passing servant, and sipped. In truth I did not know what I wanted. Anger still nipped around the edges, yet it was a relief to exchange opinions again.

'I hear that you have taken to writing,' I said, allowing my tone to express fulsome astonishment. 'How much did you copy from the original?'

'Copy? Most of it, of course.' He was still candid when it suited him. Perhaps he hoped to win me round by admitting to some sleight of hand. 'It is the most excellent description of hunting by Count Gaston de Foix. How can I better his magnificent *Livre de Chasse*, when he writes with the hand of an expert? But I've added my own comments and experience, and will continue to do so. It is not yet complete. When it is, it will be the most admired treatise on the art of venery and all that the chase has to offer the skilled huntsman. And, of course, as you might have surmised, dedicated to the Prince.'

'Excellent policy. You have not changed.'

'No, I have not. And neither have you, although what your

present ambition is I am uncertain.' He took my wine cup and finished the draught. 'One day I expect you will forgive me.'

He was so confident. So smoothly assured. I felt like striking him with one of his own much-lauded hunting weapons.

'Only when I think you deserve forgiveness,' I said instead, matching him with voice and tone. It was the one question I could never answer and had feared to ask, but here with the opportunity, ask it I would. 'Tell me this, Edward. Would you have allowed me to go to my death if Henry had decided to embrace the full weight of the law against me as a foresworn traitor?'

His brows drew together infinitesimally. I doubted anyone would have noticed, except those who knew him well.

'Now that you will never know, dear sister.'

Much as I had expected; I would never know, could only speculate. If my safety and his ambition hung in the balance, I would like to think that he would come to my aid, but I could never place a wager on it. It added a gloss of sadness to my spirits, and I turned away.

'It's good to see you again, Constance.'

Now that I had not expected. I did not think that I believed him.

'I am still deciding on a reciprocal thought. I am finding it difficult.'

He laughed. 'I will leave you to your indecision. Do I tell Henry that we have made peace?'

'You may tell him whatsoever you wish to tell him, Edward. As I am sure you always do.'

'Smile, Constance. Look as if the betrayals of the past are behind us.'

I smiled. 'They never will be.'

I watched him as he returned through the crowd, awed anew in spite of everything by his impeccable sangfroid. Edward had the remarkable facility of survival against the odds. Then I was free to rediscover Joan and to ask.

'Is your brother not at Court?'

'No.'

Which was more than a disappointment. I had accepted his absence from Kenilworth, knowing that his time was not his own, but what woman was content with being ignored? I wished that occasionally he had placed my interests before that of his ambition. But that was a foolish hope, and I knew better. I did not yet know a man who would consider his wife or lover to be important when a campaign was afoot.

'He is at present with the fleet, to my knowledge,' Joan added. 'Constance . . .' She was tugging at my sleeve with surprising urgency. Perhaps I was inept in hiding my disappointments after all, for she was frowning at me. 'There's something—'

But there was an interruption. The Danish ambassadors had arrived, smiling and fulsome, glittering with official regalia as they were received by Henry and the Queen and the young bride, Philippa. Toasts and words of well-wishing were exchanged.

'It is a good match,' Joan said, abandoning her previous thoughts. I thought that she sounded uneasy but I could see no reason for it.

'Without doubt. Will Edmund accompany the escort? He was present when Philippa was first contracted to wed. I know that Dickon expects to be one of their number.'

I could see Dickon mingling with the body of courtiers, exuding a distinct air of confidence. His new knightly honours sat well on his surprisingly handsome and less angular figure. But Joan was not interested in him.

'I think Edmund is not appointed as one of the escort. It is expected that he will remain at Court when the fleet returns.' There was a breathlessness about her. 'I will be relieved when this is over. Why are such receptions enough to make you wish that you were buried somewhere in the country?'

Her tone was unconscionably sharp, but I was not the cause. I turned to follow the direction of her regard. Together we watched the approach of a small entourage, decidedly not Danish.

'Who is this?' I asked. Someone new come to Court, Italian I thought, by the cut and extravagance of their garments. If the Danes were ostentatious, these visitors were doubly so.

I was aware of Joan taking a breath before announcing: 'It is Madonna Lucia Visconti.'

Visconti, a foremost name in Court circles as rulers of the Dukedom of Milan. One of the Visconti sisters had wed Lionel of Antwerp, my uncle, in a fatally short marriage, so here was a woman of some importance, and certainly of presence. I was not the only one to watch her approach.

'So she is unwed,' I said.

'Yes.'

'Is she looking for a husband amongst Henry's sons?'

'Too old for that, I'd say.'

'Since when did age work against a useful alliance?'

Now that she was close enough, Madonna Lucia proved to be typically Italian in colouring, a dark-haired lady as far as could be judged beneath her jewelled coif, sallow-skinned with well-marked brows and a fine nose. But not a young woman. I considered that she was older than I. Was this not the Visconti daughter who had once vowed to wed no one but Henry, on meeting him during his days of exile?

'She is very beautiful, if your taste runs to dark women.'

'She is also very rich, whatever your taste.' Joan was acerbic. 'She is on offer with a vast dower, so it is said. Seventy thousand florins, if the gossips are to be believed.'

It was a sum to entice any man.

I watched as Madonna Lucia was ushered towards the royal party where she was made welcome, presented to the ambassadors as an honoured guest.

'She is well received,' I remarked.

'Any woman with all those coffers of gold coin would be. But I think they do not look to her for a royal marriage.'

'Then who?' I surveyed the audience with some amusement. 'Every unwed lord in this room stares at her as if she were a plum tartlet and he a starving beggar.'

Joan looked away. 'I know not. All I know is that I need a stool to sit on. My shoes hurt. Will you come with me?'

Having done all that was necessary to make my return a matter for public debate, and since Edmund was somewhere on the high seas, I had had enough of the stiff formality. I began to make my way towards the door when a young page loped up and bowed before me. The King wished to make me known to the most recent visitors. I complied. It would not take long and would be in my interests to pick up all the threads of Court life in that self-important knot of Italianate magnificence. It was uncomfortable to realise how little I knew of recent events.

Joan was uncommonly anxious. 'I should tell you, before Henry does—'

'Tell me later.'

And once again I was practising my role of grateful cousin returned to the warmth of the royal breast. I was in a mood to please and be pleased.

'May I present my cousin, Constance, Lady Despenser, newly returned to Court. We expect that she will remain here and help us to celebrate this alliance. You are already well acquainted with her brothers.'

I curtsied to the ambassadors whom I recognised. To the Queen who regarded me with discreet suspicion. I smiled at Philippa, making all the requisite hopes for the future happiness of the young bride in Denmark. It was all most gratifying. Now I could retire. But Henry had drawn the Italian lady forward; he addressed her.

'Madonna. You know Baroness Willoughby, of course, but not my cousin Lady Constance Despenser.'

We both curtsied.

Here in this Italian lady of such repute was a fine elegance as well as vast wealth. I wondered why she had not wed before now. Perhaps some childhood alliance that had come to naught with the unexpected death of the betrothed.

'I have been absent for some months, Madonna,' I explained with careful subtlety. 'In the north, at my lord the King's request.'

'I am newly arrived too,' Madonna Lucia explained. 'Since my marriage contract with an English nobleman was arranged last month, my lord the King has invited me to make my home here until the date of the ceremony is formalised. It pleases me to accept, to become known to the English men and women who are acquainted with my betrothed. Of course I will make my home in England after my marriage.' She laughed lightly, an attractive sound, showing good teeth. A wave of heavy musk perfume enveloped us as she shook out her sleeves with a sleek ripple of fur. 'It is such a shame that my betrothed is not here today, but he is, I understand, at the beck and call of the King. Is that not the phrase, when he is frequently absent?'

She smiled openly around the group that nodded its concerted approval. 'I am certain that you will enjoy your stay at Court, my lady. To whom are you betrothed?'

Was it not the obvious enquiry for me to make? I heard Joan's intake of breath.

'Of course, you may not know.' Henry nodded his satisfaction. 'Madonna Lucia is betrothed to wed Joan's brother, Lord Edmund.'

'The Earl of Kent,' Madonna Lucia added. 'I will become Countess of Kent when the knot is tied. I anticipate it with joy.'

The words dropped, catastrophically, into my mind like hailstones into a still pond, to melt and dissipate, leaving barely a ripple on the surface but a deep cold below. My breathing was compromised; so was my reply as I struggled to discover suitable words.

'Lord Edmund.' I glanced at Joan as if expecting her to deny it. I saw her throat move as she swallowed but there was no denial. With no choice at all, I gathered my wits and my words of congratulation. 'I wish you every good fortune in your marriage, Madonna.'

It did not seem like my voice, my words.

'Indeed.' Madonna Lucia beamed, her features bright with

an inner light. 'It has all been negotiated to the liking of my ducal family in Milan.'

Breath leached from my lungs.

'I did not know. News does not always reach Kenilworth as fast as one might hope or expect.' In that moment of absolute horror I summoned every element of control – of voice, of face, of pride. 'I wish you well, Madonna. I am sure that my family have already done so.'

'They have been most welcoming.'

I dared not looked round the little group, afraid of what I would read on more than one face, when my intimacy with Edmund Holland had been the subject of much rumour. I could not bear to read pity, or malice. It was a blessing that no one knew of my marriage; no one but Edmund and myself were aware of that legal bond. But Joan knew of our closeness. That Edmund and I were lovers. Her discomfort at my elbow suddenly acquired a life of its own.

She should have warned me. As a friend she should have warned me.

But why did the reaction of others concern me?

It was Edmund who filled my mind. How could he exchange vows with me, then in a second breath negotiate a betrothal with a Visconti heiress? I would have said that it was false, that the man I loved would never take so cruel, so insensitive, a step. It could not be true, except that the forthcoming marriage was verified by both bride and King.

Betrayed. Abandoned. Rejected. The ugly words echoed and re-echoed in my mind. I had been cast aside like a furred cloak, once handsome but now worn and not quite fashionable. All the trust I had placed in him, believing that his love for me was as deep as mine for him. I must show none of my desolation. I would give none of my family even the smallest hint that this marriage hit me so keenly. I would accept this blow as if none of it mattered.

'Perhaps you would agree to visit with me, Madonna?' I invited her.

'I would like that, my lady. You can tell me what you know of my betrothed. I am keen to learn.'

'I will be happy to do so.'

The words all but choked me.

How I retired from that audience with composure intact I would never know, unable to find suitable words to express the utter dismay of such a discovery. I had found the words by the time the door of my chamber was closed. Joan, of course, had followed me. I dismissed my women, standing in the centre of the room, my hands fisted at my bosom in the folds of my houppelande.

'I do not wish to converse with you.'

'I am sorry.'

I rounded on her. 'Why could you not tell me? How could you leave me to learn of his betrothal in the public arena of the Court? Every man and woman there would rejoice at my discomfiture. Constance of York cast aside for an Italian fortune.'

Joan merely took a seat.

'I was unsure if you were still lovers.'

'Perhaps you had hoped that it had died a death, born of rabid treachery and distance? It would not do for a Holland to be associated with such a scandal.'

Joan ignored the sneer through long practice. 'I thought that Edmund's future might no longer matter to you. I am so sorry. It might have been for the best if any feelings had lapsed.' She looked at my face. 'Am I to understand, from your tirade, that he is still your lover?'

'I certainly understood that he was. It seems that I was wrong. What Edmund might believe is an entirely different matter. I did not think him so immoral as to make promises to one woman, and then to another, at the same time.'

'So what is it that Edmund has promised you?'

I was all but breathless with the shock, but I knew when to ignore her questions. No longer able to face her, I stood at the window, looking out with unseeing eyes at the carved pinnacles. Did she not realise how cruelly distressing this news was for me? That I had been so wantonly betrayed was as savage as the tearing pains of childbirth.

'By the Rood, Joan. You would leave me in ignorance before the Court and have me humiliated.'

'I would never humiliate you. I thought all was over between you.'

'You thought that my relationship with Edmund was a trivial moment of lust, destined to evaporate as soon as I was shut away. You hoped that was so.' Swinging round to face her, I opened my hands, to let fall the voluptuous skirts of my houppelande, flattening them so that the swell of my body was more than evident. I rested my jewelled hands, fingers widespread, on my belly. 'You were wrong. And I am truly shamed.'

The folds of my houppelande had covered all trace of how I had spent at least one night of my captivity. I was carrying Edmund's child.

Joan stared in disbelief.

'Oh, Constance.'

'Oh, Joan,' I mocked.

'Why did you not tell me?'

'Because I had no intimation that Edmund intended to wed one of the Visconti.'

'Were you expecting him to wed you?'

Reading the disbelief in Joan's face, wishing I had said nothing at all, I shrank from telling her the truth. A woman so scorned was an object of worse than pity.

'I am expecting nothing, other than this child. All the scandal of this babe will be swept away, behind the tapestries of the York household. Are they not clever at such niceties? My brother's birth owed more to John Holland than to my father.'

'You won't make a scene?'

'A scene? Why would I? If I even contemplated it, who would be the only one to be damaged? Not Edmund Holland! As my mother's daughter I am cursed with a lustful disposition and an unfortunate illegitimate child. I'll not willingly bring such condemnation down on my head. I have had a lifetime of disfavour.'

I knew we were both recalling my challenge to my brother, when I had felt a rampaging desire to shock everyone, the Court, the King, Edmund of Kent. I had been betrayed. I had been betrayed again. But I would be no martyr in this sorry relationship.

I would make no scene.

Joan sank her teeth into her lower lip.

'How long?' she asked.

'Six months.'

'You'll not hide it much longer.' Ever practical. 'Do I tell Edmund that you know of his betrothal?'

'Why not? I would be the only one at Westminster in ignorance if I did not know. Just don't try to excuse him to me.'

'I will not. After all, he was not bound to you through more than—'

'Sins of the flesh,' I finished the thought for her.

'I swear there was never hope of more, Constance. You must have known he could never wed you.'

'Go away, Joan,' I dismissed her.

'You deserve my compassion.'

'I do not ask for it. And don't speak of this child to your faithless brother.'

When the door closed with a light click I was weightless with loneliness.

I needed to know . . .

Had he ever loved me? I had thought that he had. He had stolen my heart, and I had been a willing victim of so effortless a thief.

Had he been forced into the Italian marriage by Henry? I had seen no evidence of forceful persuasion. And if that were so, surely Edmund would have either pleaded a previous commitment, or come to me. He would have told me. It was the action of a knave to leave me to discover his perfidiousness for myself, in the most shaming of circumstances.

That was what I needed to know. Had I been seduced by a man who was flagrantly cruel and did not deserve my love?

But I must wait, for until he returned I was bound by silence. Never had I found it so difficult not to rage.

It was not long before he returned. Edmund Holland, Earl of Kent, newly betrothed to Madonna Lucia Visconti, to be the recipient of a handsome, well-connected bride and a vast dowry, returned to London.

Edmund Holland, husband of Constance, Lady Despenser, *per verba de praesenti.*

Edmund Holland, father of Lady Despenser's soon-to-be-born child.

Would I seek him out, or wait for him to come to me? Ah, but who would he visit first? Madonna Lucia or his legal wife? I was not of a mind to wait. Where would a newly returned naval commander be? Reporting to the King, of course.

Alerted by the sound of male voices and much laughter, I came upon a scene of domestic harmony, drawn together for their own enjoyment to appraise a brace of new hounds, alaunts by the look of them, a gift to the King from the Danish bridegroom. The audience chamber, often the venue for dancing, had been transformed into a wholly masculine preserve, discussing the merits of various hounds, about which diversity Edward was entertaining his audience with an ooze of charm and expertise.

Superfluous to this male audience, I stepped no further into the room which had King Henry at the centre, fondling the head of one of the sleek Danish creatures; Prince Hal, stroking the wings of a superb goshawk on his wrist, perhaps another gift. John Beaufort was there, my captor with a possible foot in many camps, being wed to Margaret Holland, sister of Edmund and Joan. Henry Beaufort, Bishop of Winchester. Edward, master of hunting and political intrigue.

And there was Edmund, suave and polished, skin bronzed

from days at sea, his hair longer than when we last met. His eyes were alive with his successes. He was all that I recalled, even his voice holding that recognisable quality of stern dignity, of occasional humour and a distinct authority. My heart leaped with that recognition, before I ordered it to be still.

Edmund was speaking. 'I have two limmer hounds ready and trained to hunt. My huntsmen tell me that they are now in their prime. I've had them since they were young so can vouch for them.' He was addressing the King. 'I would be pleased to give them to you. You keep me too busy to use them as often as I would wish, so they don't earn their keep.'

A hand gripped my heart, even though this trivial betrayal could never compare with that of his proposed marriage. He would give away my gift to the King, to curry favour.

'I'll take them.' Henry's agreement was prompt.

'I've seen them,' John Beaufort said. 'Fine animals. Sleek heads and a good colour, and more trustworthy than these beasts. I'll take them off your hands if my brother will not.'

Henry grinned. 'Too late, they're mine.'

Cups of ale were handed around. Henry and Edmund shook hands on the deal.

'Do you ever make use of wolfhounds?' Prince Hal asked, passing the raptor to one of the mews servants.

'I have. In Ireland,' Edmund replied. 'I have run with them to marvellous effect.'

'I hear they're chancy beasts.'

'Only if you are a wolf.'

There was laughter and Henry's hand closed around Edmund's arm, pulling him even closer into the royal circle. My heart jolted again at what I was witnessing. Here was acceptance. Here was a well-paved road to power opening at Edmund's feet. He addressed Henry as a friend, without formality. How affairs had moved on during my absence, Edmund using all his skill to make a name and a place for himself. I could not fault him. I admired him; I could even wish him well in his ambitions. All he needed was a well-born, well-connected and well-dowered wife to walk beside him. A wife who would enhance his future. I understood with terrible clarity why he had accepted the betrothal to Madonna Visconti.

But that understanding of his need did not destroy the rage that afflicted me when witnessing that little scene of camaraderie and the careless disposal of my gift. What of me? Was I not worthy? Why go through a sham marriage if he had no true intention of keeping those vows?

Unable to answer any one of the questions, I was driven to retreat. Facing him in this company would achieve nothing, but face him I must.

When Edmund Holland stepped into the cool splendour of St Stephens's Chapel, alone, I was already standing there, at the foot of a painted angel, its wings spread wide. Of course I was there, knowing exactly the time and place he would arrive, in this first hour after noon. Had I not arranged this meeting? Borrowing a reluctant royal herald, I paid him to don his regalia and carry a message, one that I knew Edmund could not ignore. King Henry wished to discuss a campaign in the west with him.

Edmund would be disappointed.

The vast space of gilded and painted masterpieces closed round us. I moved from my protective angel and saw the moment of realisation on his face that this appointment was fraudulent. He would speak with me, not the King, and I had no interest in campaigns in the west.

This had been my choice; better to conduct this conversation in public, where emotion could not rule. All could be decently aired between us in the House of God. Servants and couriers came and went around us with barely a glance. Although it was a sacred space, it was also a place of much coming and going, and we were simply part of the Court's daily life when Henry was in residence. Acolytes tended to candles and incense burners. Priests went about their affairs of worship. In the far corner, beneath the vast painted figure of St George, I espied a Bishop, accosted by some courtier who was expressing his desires with dramatic gestures.

My communication here with a man of my own family would be perfectly anonymous.

Combed, burnished, hunting wool and leather exchanged for damask, fur and gold chains for his proposed meeting, Edmund Holland, newly created Knight of the Garter, was magnificent against the equally magnificent backdrop of King Edward the Third's chapel. I could read nothing in his face as he turned and saw me, nor in his behaviour. The Earl of Kent bowed to me as if I were an acquaintance. I curtsied, a discreet swish of expensive skirts that told nothing of the pattern of my thoughts.

But here he was. The man who had seduced me and whose seduction I had relished. The man I despised. The man I still loved in the distant reaches of my heart. Acknowledging him, as if this were a chance encounter and not part of a thoughtful scheme, I was the true personification of regal tolerance.

Interested in how he would address me, I allowed him to be the first to speak.

'My lady Constance.'

'My lord Edmund.'

So that would be the pattern of it. How nervelessly formal we were. Once he would have enjoyed removing my garments, one lace, one clasp, one layer at a time. Now he remained within a lance's length of me. Did he expect me to throw myself onto his breast and plead for his return? I waited, motionless, hands clasped lightly, my eyes on his. If I had ever needed the proud Plantagenet and Castilian blood of my parents, it was now. His hands rested on his jewel-set belt, an item of considerable value, and of Italian craftsmanship, I thought. Undoubtedly a Visconti gift.

'You will have heard the news,' he said. At least it absolved me of launching an accusation as if I had been playing the spy or, even worse, pretending ignorance until he deigned to tell me.

'Yes.'

'Of my betrothal.'

'Of your betrothal.' I lingered on the word, creating a soft sigh of regret. 'I have met the bride. Engaging as she is, I still admit to some surprise.'

'I owe you an explanation.'

I made a little space, stepping aside as two clerics manhandled a box of books between us, struggling with the carrying poles as the weight of the box threatened to over-set them. Then:

'Why would I need an explanation?' I allowed my smoothly plucked brows to rise infinitesimally. 'Although I have to say that I was not aware that you were free to enter into a betrothal.

Was I mistaken? I am sure you will have good reason for offering your hand to this Italian woman.'

Edmund matched me, in coldness, in moderation. In pure arrogant assurance.

'It was politically expedient.'

'Ah . . .' My sudden appearance in his path had not undermined his poise to any degree. 'And was it your choice, to make this politically expedient move?'

'It was an alliance promoted by the King.'

'Of course. I suppose that I might be aware of the value of being in league with the Duchy of Milan. My uncle Lionel, Duke of Clarence, took the same step before his ill-fated death. I advise you to eat and drink with care when you sup with the lady's family but I am sure that you are well versed in the methods of the Visconti to remove those they find irrelevant.' Another infinitesimal pause. 'Is there monetary value in this match?'

Now he hesitated, but only fractionally. He was well in command. 'You are aware of the financial restrictions that have been an ever-present burden on me.'

'Which Madonna Lucia's considerable dowry will go far to alleviate.' How light my tone, how understanding of his predicament. How damning in the softness of my replies. 'This is most fortunate for you, Edmund. As it is for the heiress, in achieving a husband who stands so highly with the King. I understand that I must compliment you on becoming a Garter Knight. Your offer of the hounds to Henry, by the way, was an excellent stratagem. Henry could never refuse such an offer of hunting dogs. I did not realise that my gift to you would hold such value.'

I heard his sharp inhalation. 'You are not making this easy for me.'

'I have no intention of making this easy for you.'

'Then I will make all plain. Our marriage was never tenable.'

'And were you not aware of this obstacle, whatever it might be – for I am not altogether enlightened – when you petitioned me for my hand? I recall your being astonishingly persuasive, yet you now claim it was not *tenable* when you made those vows. In the presence of witnesses, too.'

'We both accepted that there were . . . difficulties.'

I took a step closer, to keep this between ourselves if anyone had any interest in us. I noticed that his fingers were white as they clasped the gilt filigree, firm enough to crush the delicate links. 'Why did you do it? If these *difficulties* were so overwhelming for you, why did you offer me marriage? At best it was . . .' I sought for a word. 'At best it was unkind. At worst it was of a deceit beyond belief.'

'It was appropriate at the time.'

'Until Madonna Visconti and her gold florins appeared on the scene.'

I caught the anger, the flash of high colour across his superb cheekbones.

'Perhaps you were overcome with the romance of the moment. You promised me a full set of minstrels to announce my return to Henry's Court as your wife.'

'I need a wife with a spotless reputation.'

'You knew my reputation at Kenilworth. And who is spotless? Not you, it seems. Do not tell me that you need a wife of rank and status. My rank is comparable to any woman at this

Court, certainly to that of a Visconti. I am Plantagenet. Would you argue against that?'

'No.' For the first time his gaze slid from mine. His voice softened. 'You are royal and incomparable. You always were. You always will be.'

But I was not to be flattered into compliance.

'I know why you abandoned the vows you made to me. I can even understand why you might. What I can never forgive is that you did so, leaving me in ignorance. Leaving me to learn of your defection through gossip and innuendo. Fortunately for me Henry made all plain so that I did not have to experience, in my ignorance, the humiliation of honeyed words of regret from well-wishers. And now you inform me, so very politely, that I am not fit to be your wife; that I was misguided in ever believing that I could be. I despise you for that, Edmund.'

He was pale, his gaze now returned to mine was stark. 'I can only apologise.'

'For what? For ensnaring me into a marriage that you will not recognise?'

'If you will.'

'How legal was our marriage, dear Edmund?'

For here was the real issue, for both of us.

'Legal, if you intend to hold me to it.'

'Of course it is. It was legal for your grandmother when she wed your grandfather. Her second marriage to the Earl of Salisbury was declared void by His Papal Holiness because of this previous marriage *per verba de praesenti.* Her marriage to your grandfather was witnessed and consummated, as was ours. If it were not so, your Holland descent would be illegitimate, dear Edmund.' I showed my teeth in a little snarl. 'What would you do if I challenged your new Italian betrothal?'

He looked away, and I thought he would not answer, but he was merely gathering his reserves to deliver the final blow, with all the savagery of any knight on a battlefield.

'If you chose to do that, I would deny there was any understanding between us. I would say that your imprisonment unsettled you, making you prey to desires that never existed between the two of us. That my visit to you was out of nothing but a friendship, which you mistook. I would say that there was no marriage. I would defy you to produce evidence to the contrary.'

How ruthless he was prepared to be, but I replied in kind.

'In effect you want me to hold my tongue, or risk your public repudiation. How demeaning it would be for me to produce a servant to bear witness to my honesty. And yet I might even do so, rather than be forced to my knees to accept what is a blatant lie.'

His eyes were as hard as slate. At least I had roused some emotion in him.

'I hope it does not come to such unpleasantness between us. We were both raised in a political world. We both know what it is to be faced by conflicted loyalties that force us to change sides.'

'If you mean that we both know what betrayal looks like, then yes.'

Taking two steps away, he waited until a little covey of self-important ambassadors had stalked past, chains jingling, jewels glinting in the candlelight; then he returned, his face stern, as if before a priest with the need to confess.

'I loved you, Constance. I love you now. I will love you

until the day of my last breath. What I cannot do is follow the dictates of my heart. I owe it to my family, since the Hollands have been brought so low, to make a mark on this reign. I owe it to the Hollands who have gone before me. I need royal approval and I need a bride who will bring me wealth. What I do not need is a wife who will for ever be a subject of gossip and rumour.'

'You knew about the gossip and rumour when you wed me. Were you overcome by the force of your love?'

His face was as pale as the costly candle wax, burning on every altar. 'How can I deny it?'

'And Madonna Lucia had not then been held out by Henry as a tempting morsel for you to pick up.'

'No.'

'But now you have tasted the rich flavours of royal patronage,' I added to his superbly reasoned argument. 'It is a heady brew from which you cannot abstain.'

'I have done ill by you. I acknowledge it. But never believe that it is through lack of love. My admiration for you is beyond question. All I can ask is that you understand and perhaps one day can forgive.'

He took my hand, unwilling as I was, and pressed his lips against my palm, before similarly impersonally saluting my lips. Was this deliberate declaration of love intended to rouse the same memories in me? That I would forgive and forget in a spirit of noble altruism? I would not. I would be no martyr for Holland promotion. When he sensed no response in me, Edmund's hand fell away and I read a flash of regret, but whether true or feigned I could not guess. It no longer mattered.

He bowed. 'You have every right to remain silent.'

'What more is there for me to say to you? I find it hard to envisage your admiration when your thoughtful explanation has done naught but magnify my mortification.'

'Then that is your loss, for it is honest admiration.'

He bowed again and walked away towards the distant door in the wake of the Bishop who had also completed the business of the day, doubtless with more satisfaction than I could claim.

In that moment my loss became a solid thing with weight and dimension and texture. I breathed it in with every breath and with it came fear and grief. It was as if I could see a wall being built stone on stone to separate us, all my hopes for the future being dashed to their death against it. My eyes and throat were dry. As dry as the dust scattered on the surface of a coffin. The memory of his salute on my palm burned like a foolishly clasped brand. Was the culpability mine? Only in that I had trusted him too much. I had allowed myself to be enticed by fine words that held no meaning.

'My lord . . .' I said to reclaim his attention, for there was still one matter between us.

He stopped, but did not turn. And in the end I could not do it.

I could not tell him about the child. I wanted no more kind consideration. He had left me with increasingly visible evidence of our final meeting when we were man and wife. I would have to endure the unendurable; the scandal of a child born with no recognition from its father.

I stood there without plan, without recourse, unmoved by this exuberantly decorated masterpiece around me, the work of the best carpenters, glaziers, workers in stone and wood that England could produce. Not even the doves and eagles with their gold-edged wings awoke a response in me. The painted and gilded elephants demanded no adoration of the skill to produce them. I turned away from the painted gaze of King Edward and Queen Philippa, my severe grandparents, beneath the great east window. Even gentle Philippa condemned me for what I had done.

When a hand cupped my elbow, I turned swiftly, angry at such familiarity.

'You look lost.'

I forced my muscles to relax, my mouth to smile.

'Lost?' I had no wish to speak with Dickon, full as he was with his knighthood and the pending visit to Denmark, but was unable to extricate myself, and so as so often I resorted to stark levity. 'How could I be lost when I have spent the whole of my life at Court? There is nothing here to surprise me.'

'Who was that? The man you were talking with?'

Edmund had just disappeared into a throng of choristers bustling through, intent on discovering somewhere discreet to practise some new setting of a chorale. I let my eyes rest on where he could no longer be seen.

'Merely an acquaintance. A man of no importance.'

It was hard to speak those words, but it was the truth.

'Then come and talk to me. I need you to find me a wife. Someone rich and titled.'

I dragged my mind back to the present. 'Why me?'

'Because everyone else is too busy about his own affairs. You're my last hope.'

It was not complimentary but at least it would engage my mind. 'And do you have any particular woman in mind?'

'No. Her age and beauty – or lack of – are irrelevant. I need a wife with powerful connections.'

The irony of Dickon's demand could not be ignored. Was this not the ambition of every man within these walls that resounded with so much past victory and anguish? One of the choristers had begun to sing in a high register, clear and clean and heart-wrenching in the plainsong, the acoustics shivering with the pure tenor notes.

It made me shiver, too, as if my heart were breaking. Love had kept me fine company. Now it was the passion of rage that stirred my blood.

Chapter Twenty

Autumn 1406: Conisbrough Castle

'Holy Mother, in your divine mercy, come to my aid!'

My breath was short, my labours to push the child into the world were protracted and hard. How could I have forgotten such pain that gripped and tore and robbed me of my dignity so that I cried out in extremity? Dame Edith, my midwife, who coiled strings of coral beads round my neck, pressing draughts of fenugreek, spurge laurel, flax and fleawort on me, wiped my brow with a lavender-soaked cloth.

It was a season when all was amiss; when winds howled around the thick walls and six buttresses here at the great keep of Conisbrough, yet it was as warm as midsummer so that winter layers of wool and fur, already lifted from their coffers, were laid aside. Every day the clouds banked and loured, but it did not rain. And then it did, so that the roads were awash and the crops stood ruined in the fields while mould grew on the newly baked bread in the clammy dampness. Still the winds blew from the west, dislodging jackdaws' nests into the chimneys so that the cook blasphemed when fires smoked and his junkets were coated in speckles of soot. The new brewing of ale became rancid in the barrels and was fed to the pigs. They said that there were strange stars to be seen in the heavens. The season was not at one with itself.

Neither was I, and Dame Edith was growing anxious.

'God's Blood, I remember nothing of this travail,' I said, when I had breath to speak.

My flesh was racked, my body subsumed in agony through the dread hours of night, when all was threatening, into a new dawn. Still there was no blessed result and all was on fire. I gripped the wrist of the wise-woman, skilled in herbs and potions, who had been sent for when Dame Edith's knowledge had failed. Mistress Margery, with a reputation for arcane skills, worked at my side with a tough dedication but without compassion.

'Can you do nothing?' I demanded.

'I am doing all I can.'

'It is not enough.'

'It's in God's hands.'

She was anointing the mound of my belly with oil of violets, the pungent scent filling the room.

'And you lack courtesy.' My whole body felt to be under siege from hellish torment.

'All women are equal when in childbed.'

'All men are equal when they are absent,' I said in bitter humour.

I did not want this child that merely put a mark on my solitude and my disgrace and my crass belief that Edmund would stand by his vows. This was the second time that I had given birth without the benefit of a husband's grace, but at least Thomas had been dead. Edmund was merely wooing elsewhere.

As the pains tore at me with relentless fervour, all thought was obliterated, except one – would this be the end of my life, failing to give birth to a child I had not wanted? I snatched at any remedy.

'Do you not have some saint's girdle, to give me ease with a miracle?'

'I do not. I have no truck with saints' girdles.'

'If we were at Westminster, we could borrow their sacred girdle, dropped by the Blessed Virgin from heaven. The monks swear by its efficacy.'

'As any man would, to keep a woman quiet. What do they know? We are not at Westminster.'

'Blessed Virgin, have mercy!'

'But we can try this.'

I watched Mistress Margery tearing parchment into tiny pieces, dropping them into a cup of wine, stirring with her not over-clean finger.

'Will you poison me?'

She presented the cup to my lips, lifting my head. 'Drink.'

I did and all but choked on the draught, pushing it away.

'Finish it. Here are the sacred words of the Holy Mother. The Canticle of the Blessed Virgin Mary. *Magníficat anima mea Dominum. Et exultavit spiritus meus: in Deo salutari meo,*' she intoned. 'If you drink them, they will imbue you with the Virgin's strength.'

So, beyond arguing, I drank again. As the hours passed, I was conscious only of autocratic admonitions to pray to God, for assuredly his succour was needed. 'Tell me,' I croaked over the petitions of my women, barely recognising my voice. 'Is there a danger?'

Mistress Margery was whispering in my ear. 'It may be that the child will die.'

My instructions were issued without any thought from me as I clenched my fingers in the sleeve of her tunic. 'Save the child.'

I knew not what she did, merely giving myself over to the kneading fingers, the anointing, the constant background of prayer. And then a rush of effort that drew all strength from me.

A cry. A weak whimper reminiscent of a kitten. Then silence. Followed by some murmuring from my women. The wise-woman leaned over the bed.

'The child is alive. You too will live, I expect. Give thanks, my lady. It is a miracle, with or without the girdle.'

'Is it a son?'

'You have a daughter, my lady. Girls always fight harder for life, in my experience.' I was honoured now with respect. 'She is small but she is in no danger. We will care for her but you must rest.'

The detritus of birth was removed, my shift changed, the bloodied sheets tidied away, the foetid air sweetened by the sharp tang of rosemary.

'Let me see her.'

Her face was still flushed from the energies of birth, her eyes tight shut as if to block out the world that had taken her so long to enter. Emotions in abeyance, except for relief that it was all over, I handed her back and fell into sleep. Until I struggled into wakefulness – how many hours later? – to the sound of my door opening and closing, and then a conversation, a voice I had not expected to hear.

'Is the child strong?'

'Yes, my lady,' Dame Edith replied. Mistress Margery had taken herself back to her usual haunts.

'And Lady Constance?'

'She will be all the better for a good sleep. The days have taken their toll.'

'Is she in any danger?'

'No, my lady. There is no fever.'

'Has she seen the babe?'

'Yes,' I said, disliking the discussion going on around me as if I were not present, either in body or in mind. 'She has.' Bringing the conversation to an end. As I turned my head, there, coming into my line of sight, was Joan. After our vituperative parting I had resigned myself to a rift, yet in my heart I knew that she was the only one who would come.

'You are late for the event itself,' I said, signalling for more pillows, shocked at how indolent I felt. 'Good to see one Holland face, at least.'

'You are fortunate that I am here at all.'

I struggled to sit up and took the cup that she presented as she sat on the edge of my bed, wiping with a square of linen at the perspiration beading her upper lip in the heat of the room.

'You could even thank me.'

No, she had not entirely forgiven me.

'So why are you here?'

'I am on my way to join William in Silsby.'

Conisbrough was not too far out of her way, but far enough. 'Thank you. I am grateful.' Suddenly, acknowledging a need for this small offering of human kindness, however much it might baffle me, I felt the bite of tears, before blinking them away.

'Bring the child,' Joan ordered, offering me the opportunity to regain some equilibrium.

'She looks like any other child.' I wiped my eyes on the sheet.

'I am come to admire my niece.'

'And report back to your brother?'

'Yes. If you will not tell him, then I will. He should know, and one day his child might need her father's recognition. I suppose that Edmund has not come here because you intimated that he would not be made welcome.'

Joan would have no sense of the tenor of our parting.

'He has not come because our paths have separated.'

Joan nodded. 'I think it is excellent news. Edmund must be circumspect in his dealings with you. Madonna Lucia will be a more willing bride if she does not know of the past.' The wet nurse entered, my daughter clasped to her bosom. 'Give her to me.'

I watched as Joan took the child into her arms, as if she had a lifetime of experience.

'I think that you would love her more than I ever will.'

Joan had failed to quicken; her expression as she smoothed the babe's cheek was one of great tenderness.

'Then let me take her. I'll tell William that I have had a miracle birth and that he has a daughter.' She smiled at me with a well of sadness. 'I fear that I will never have a child of my own, and here you are with a daughter that is more of a burden than a blessing.' She transferred her smile to the child. 'Have you chosen a name?'

'No.'

'She has the look of my family.'

'Did you not believe me? That the child is Edmund's? I am no whore.'

Lightly chiding, she clicked her tongue against her teeth. 'I believe you.'

'Well, I won't call her Joan. Not even for your grandmother.'

Joan placed the child in my arms. 'She needs a name. She needs to be baptised, although she looks healthy enough.'

'It will be tomorrow, here in the chapel, where I was baptised.'

I looked at my daughter without the stress of birth on her features. I could see no resemblance to the Hollands except for the dark curls of hair, visible beneath her little coif.

'Well? What will it be?' Joan nudged me. 'Philippa, after the old Queen? Joanna, after the new one?'

My daughter opened and closed a hand into a fist, catching the edge of my shift. Perfect fingernails, and there was a strength, but she was so vulnerable. I would not let her suffer for my sins. She was in effect a legally born daughter and I must speak for her. The realisation came as a throb against my heart, that with Edmund's abandonment, this child had a true demand on me. Gone were the days when I could afford to be driven by selfish desires. Here was my duty, my obligation. In that sardonic moment I accepted that perhaps here was the road to my redemption. I looked up, tempted to tell Joan of my marital status, but the babe's breath caught and she began to cry. The moment was gone, a fleeting temptation, fast abandoned.

'Hush.'

When I stroked my fingers over the little cap she instantly quieted, which brought a chime of recognition of my past children, as well as an amazement within me. I smiled. For some reason she had touched my heart.

'Do you realise how close you came to dying?' I asked. 'How close you came to killing your mother?' She snuffled and, in the manner of all young creatures, fell suddenly into sleep. 'I will do all in my power to ensure that your life is an easier one.' I kissed her brow, knowing the name I would choose. Not a Plantagenet name but a Holland one. 'Alianore. You will be Alianore.'

Joan placed a hand on my arm. Her sister, Alianore, the mother of the two ill-fated Mortimer boys, had not long departed this life.

'Thank you,' she said, as suddenly tearful as I had been. 'I would not have suggested it.'

'When is the marriage to take place?' I asked as if it were of no consequence.

Joan made no pretence at misunderstanding. 'At some time in the New Year. After the celebrations and before the onset of Lent. Will you tell him of this child?'

I must, of course, in my new spirit of responsibility. And yet . . . 'No. And you must not. Now that you have set your mind at rest that I am alive, I'll not keep you. Go to William.'

Her regard was a condemnation. 'You have lost him, Constance. Set your mind to it.'

Could I accept that I had lost him, irretrievably and for ever? I thought that I had, after our severing of all ties at Westminster, but he said that he had loved me. Were we beyond healing? I had borne him a daughter, a legitimate daughter. It was not in my nature to retreat before the enemy, and before God Edmund was not my enemy.

'I will never set my mind to it.'

'Then I pray that the Holy Mother will give you peace, for I see no hope of it.'

Why did I not tell her that we had exchanged vows? Why would I not inform Edmund that he had a daughter? Because

I could not bear to see condemnation in Joan's face, or dismay in Edmund's. I was not yet strong enough.

Joan, in her wisdom and to my annoyance, was not yet finished with me, delivering a parting shot as she opened the door. 'You should be thankful.'

'Thankful? What maggot in your brain persuades you that I should be thankful that I am put aside for a Milanese woman with more gold than wit?'

Joan's soft mouth was a line of disapproval. 'I don't defend my brother. Nor do I know what was between the two of you. But this I will say. He has done you the great service of allowing you to understand what love between a man and a woman can be. You should be everlastingly grateful to know how it feels to be moved by desire, by passion. It is not vouchsafed to all women. I would not reject such knowledge out of hand.'

The attack brought me up short. I should have read in it a mirror of her own unawakened capacity for carnal love but I replied without pause, without kindliness.

'I would reject it. My weakness has shamed me.'

'Then I will pray for your immortal soul,' she said with bitter derision. 'It seems that prayer is all I can do for you.'

'I do not need your prayers.'

The door closed on Joan's silence, broken only by the whisper of Alianore's sleeping breath as she lay in my arms.

On the twenty-fourth day of January in the year of 1407 the most public marriage of Edmund Holland, Earl of Kent, with Madonna Lucia Visconti, aunt of the present youthful Duke of Milan, compared notably with his most private one with me. An ostentatiously royal event, it was held in the short cold days, after the New Year festivities and before the Lenten restrictions on performing the sacrament of marriage came into play. It would be an occasion to lift the combined heart of the Court, although mine was enclosed in perpetual ice. The bride glowed with satisfaction at her ultimate victory, at the age of thirty-four years, in capturing a husband who had lived for a mere twenty-three. King Henry clung voraciously to his health and encouraged the match.

Wrapped in furs and velvet hoods, but not swaddled as to hide the wealth of gold chains and heavy jewels that gave off a cold, frost-like glitter, the Court made its fractious way across the Thames from Westminster, complaining at the need to re-form at the much-decorated church door of the Augustinian Priory of St Mary Overie on the south bank.

I was there, my mood uncertain.

'It might be better if you were not,' Edward advised.

'Better for whom?' I was keeping my eye on the water that, puddled on the boards of our craft, was seeping into the soft leather of my shoes. 'These shoes are ruined.'

'Then you should have worn wooden pattens.'

Edward had taken it upon himself to accompany me and, feeling the need of some familial support, I had done little to persuade him against it.

'Better for all concerned,' he continued, picking up the conversation, as he stepped up beside me, counting the remaining coins in his palm after paying the boatman. 'I swear that rogue has fleeced me. But as I was about to say – watch your tongue, Constance.'

I walked on ahead of him, surveying the gathering ranks. 'I know how to make a good impression at a royal occasion.'

'I recall you issuing a challenge to mortal combat when you were not best pleased with me.'

Slowing my steps, I tucked my hand into his arm. 'Today I am best pleased with everyone.'

'Even Edmund?'

I caught the speculative look. What did he know of my past with Edmund except for an unfortunate liaison which gave me a child? Nothing at all. He would never even guess at the terrible mistake I had made.

'Constance . . . if there is anything I can do . . .?'

'About what? I am delighted with the prospect of this marriage. I will smile serenely and wish everyone well, particularly Edmund and Lucia.'

He pulled me to a halt, as if he must get some thought off his chest before we went further.

'Did you expect him to wed you?'

I met his gaze steadfastly enough. 'Why would I expect any such thing? We merely enjoyed a chivalric interlude.'

'I know he was your lover.' And when I stiffened: 'Perhaps you hoped that he would forsake the Milanese woman . . .'

My hand tightening on his stopped him. 'No. This is the marriage that the King wants. Edmund too. I had no hope. What could I bring to the marriage bed of an ambitious man?'

Delicately, there was no mention between us of the child. Edward knew of her existence but nothing more. He had never asked me the name of Alianore's father, but he had guessed.

So we joined the august throng at the church door with its intricate carvings and elegant arch. My appearance too was elegant, sleek and groomed, but Edward's question had stirred my thoughts to less than elegance. Today Madonna Lucia would become Countess of Kent, while I, however hard I might fight against it, was engulfed in a wave of raw fury, as hard-edged as the Visconti gems that encircled the bride's throat.

As the bride and groom arrived, as well muffled as the rest of us, one thought still teased at my mind. I was the one person here present who could put a stop to this union. I could speak out, declare my own interest. I had no proof without witnesses standing beside me to account for the deed, but I could swear on my royal name that Edmund and I had exchanged vows as his grandparents had done. He had wed me, and in good faith I had allowed it.

The voices from the crowd, rich with anticipation, clamoured in my ears but could not drown out the thought in my head.

Would I even consider demanding to be heard?

To do this would humiliate Edmund, and his bride, destroying this sacred event through a mean, self-serving act of revenge. I would tear what remained of my own honour to strips, to be consumed as rank meat was devoured by winged predators. My love for him was now transformed to spite, though he was my husband by legal right.

'What would you do if I challenged your new Italian betrothal?' I had asked.

'If you chose to do that, I would deny there was any understanding between us,' he had replied.

My tongue clove to the roof of my mouth as I focused on the woman who was enjoying being at the centre of this ceremonial, resplendent in a high-waisted over-gown of Italian silk, the sleeves of her under-gown buttoned tightly to her fine wrists, the epitome of Italian fashion. Her braided hair was enclosed in a sable hat embellished with a gold feather that curled to caress her tinted cheek, proving that she was not beyond artifice. Merged discreetly into the noble crowd, I watched as she lifted her face to speak with Edmund, her skin catching the light, her eyes bright with happiness. She was not in her prime, but the prospect of marriage at last had placed a gloss on her, a sheen of beauty that masked any imperfections in the lines of experience and age, of some discontentment. Once she had been put forward as a bride for Henry himself when he was travelling in Europe. She had given her heart to him, so it was said. Now the times were different and she was of an age to see value in any marriage to a young and handsome man of good birth.

As for Edmund, he had flattered his bride in his choice of garment, as Italianate as hers, the sleeves of his tunic long enough to sweep the floor with their dagged edges. The soft kid boots reached to his knee. Hatless, his dark hair gleamed in the fitful sun.

I could look no longer. I found Edward standing next to me once more, taking my hand and pulling my arm through his. I thought it was not in companionship, despite my earlier rejection of any plan to cause a stir.

'I don't trust you.' He answered the frown I turned upon him. 'Whatever you are planning, don't do it.'

'Why not?'

I was ashamed at the anguish that shook me, the overwhelming desire to reclaim what was legally mine.

'And rock the royal barge so that we all fall in the Thames and drown? Our past sins have been forgiven, Constance, but not forgotten. Let us keep it that way.'

My brother turned to stare at me. 'If you ever loved him, if you love him still. If you have any thought for his future good, you will remain silent. See what this marriage will do for him. It will be the making of him. Anything you do will surely break him.'

How the truth hurt.

'But what of me?'

'What of you? We are a selfish brood, my clever sister. We always have been. But sometimes you need to put your emotions and ambitions aside.'

'As you have done?' I retaliated. 'Have you ever put your ambitions aside for any man or woman?'

'No. Nor will I. But you are better than I will ever be.'

His arm tightened on mine, anchoring me to his side as if I were weak and needed support rather than a measure of his determination to restrict my actions. His hand gripped mine. But I would not allow it, even as my heart yearned for some comfort. I must stand alone.

'Release me.'

'You have no claim on him, Constance. Only an affair of some sentiment that must be rejected.'

I turned my head to look at my brother, as he had turned to look at me. 'You have no idea what my claim on him might be.'

And I saw horror bloom in Edward's eyes as he read what had, in that moment, been unspoken between us.

'Don't tell me that you have wed him, in some appallingly clandestine arrangement.'

I raised my chin. 'I will tell you no such thing.'

'Promise me you will do nothing.' His voice had become urgent.

'The days of your demanding promises from me are long gone.'

Edward freed me but still stood close, as I turned my attention on Edmund, awash in his heraldic achievements on breast and sleeve. If he knew I was one of those come to stand and shiver through the ceremony, he made no response to it; the congregation here-present to witness this sham marriage did not even merit a glance from the Earl of Kent. Glossy and shining, he drew all eyes when the King took Madonna Lucia's hand and placed it in Edmund's. The royal blessing was thus given.

While through it all I held my lips tight-closed.

The priest was beginning to speak: Henry Beaufort, puissant Bishop of Winchester, brought to preside over this royal occasion in all his episcopal gold and purple. I felt my muscles tense as he began the office of marriage, his words carried away by a stiff little breeze as the ribbons on his mitre fluttered. Edmund and Lucia replied. Henry nodded with approval. They would soon be wed.

Henry beckoned to a page who approached, bearing something that glinted gold on a cushion, which he presented, on his bended knee, to the bride who touched the gift and smiled her thanks.

'What is it?' I asked Edward, who from his height had a clearer view than I.

'Two gold dishes,' he whispered. 'Worth a small army on campaign. From a King who professes poverty at every turn.'

This was a gift indeed, making it a matter for no debate that here was a marriage much desired by the King and that Edmund was a much-favoured courtier. If I had seen it writ large when they had discussed the merits of hounds, I was forced to acknowledge it even more keenly now in this gift of royal gold. He had been drawn into the sacred inner circle, accepted and absorbed, awarded wealth and patronage, a Court *entrée*. If I claimed my rights as a lawful wife, all would be undermined, cast into scandal and unpleasantness.

'Do you understand now?' Edward asked.

Speak or remain silent. My final opportunity before the priest made the sign of the cross and declared them duly wed.

Edmund turned his head to look at his bride and he smiled. It was a smile that I remembered so well, full of admiration. And as the sun slid momentarily from behind a cloud, the Visconti jewels gleamed on her breast, in her hair, on her fingers; a King's ransom to fill Edmund's coffers.

With all my will I forced my tongue to remain still. I forced my feet to remain unmoving when it was in my mind to push to the front and intercede with an unbelieving Henry Beaufort. I forced myself to allow the vows to continue. Until, with a ripple of shimmering movement from the congregation, they were complete.

I had waived my own rights as a wife in my public acceptance of a new alliance.

'And now we will go and celebrate and pretend that we are all joyous.' Edward's touch on my hand was kindly, gentle even, bringing me back to the present. And when he took hold of my arm again I did not resist but followed the newly wed couple to the Bishop of Winchester's Palace where the doors were flung back and all were made welcome to the great feast and festivity, to the music and minstrels and rich dishes with Edmund and Lucia seated in marital splendour on the dais. Edward took it upon himself to have me sit beside him.

'You are being remarkably solicitous.'

My self-possession was restored despite the hollow space beneath my bodice. My voice sounded surprisingly emotionless.

'You deserve it. You were very brave.'

I did not feel brave, but there was no anguish now, merely a strange calm that had taken possession of me, for all had been decided, my future made clear. Nothing could be done to alter what had been witnessed between Man and God, with the support of all concerned. The priestly vows had taken precedence over my own claim. I could do nothing to invalidate it, when the bridegroom was in full collusion, and to what purpose? All it would do was create a storm that would sweep us all away. I had made my sacrifice.

Our cups were filled, we were invited to raise a toast, King Henry wishing them a long and happy life, and a fruitful one. I raised my cup with the rest of the throng.

And for the first time throughout all that long, tragic morning, Edmund's eyes sought and held mine. He had known throughout that mockery of a marriage service that I was there. Without doubt he had feared what I would do. Now here was such a moment of connection, to bring attention to neither of us.

And I knew what it was that he wished to say as he raised his goblet and drank.

Thank you.

That was the meaning of his bright stare.

Thank you. You have given me my freedom to become the leader of men I can be. You had the power to destroy me. You chose to smooth the path to my future.

It almost brought me to my knees. We had had a commitment

but one that must surely be ended by the simple expedient of my remaining silent for the rest of my days. In that one meeting of minds I had no doubt of his love for me. I could not hold him back and shackle him to me. Thus I raised my goblet and drank to their mutual happiness. It was done. Lucia was toasted as Countess of Kent.

'I will drink to your future happiness too, Constance.' Edward's smile was a twisted affair.

'There is no happiness.'

All my life I had plotted and conspired. I had sought attention and recognition. I had striven for power for my family whatever the cost. I had not turned aside from bloodshed and murder. If I had been a man I would have been accused of gluttonous ambition. All was at an end. That incredible gift of love had been stripped away as callously as I had plotted the death of my cousin Henry. There was no happiness. This was to be my penance.

There was still one matter that must be broached.

Between the minstrels' offering and the start of the dancing, I sought out Joan, who was of course present to see her brother happily wed. Her expression was as warily speculative as Edward's had been throughout the whole proceedings.

'So you are speaking to me today.'

'Yes. I want you to do something for me.'

'And what is that? I won't do it if it harms my brother.'

'Of course it will not harm him.' I said what I knew I must say. 'I acknowledge that I was at fault. I was not gracious when you visited me at Conisbrough.'

'Is that an apology?'

'You know it is.'

She kept me waiting.

'Do I have to kneel in penitence?'

'It would be good for your soul.'

'Consider it done.'

'Then I forgive you.' She kissed my cheek. 'What is it you wish me to do?'

'Tell Edmund. When you can find him alone, tell him he has a daughter.'

'Why don't you tell him yourself?'

I was not sure why I would not. Perhaps because I was not in command of my emotions as much as I could wish. Or because I did not wish to see the denial of her in his eyes.

'I cannot. Will you do it?'

'You know I will.'

January 1407: Westminster Palace

The door to my chamber in the old palace being left ajar, Edmund Holland entered with the softest of knocks. Perfectly composed, surrounded by all the familiar furnishings, redolent of lavender and rosemary that just failed to disguise the hint of damp and mould, I remained seated as he entered.

His appearance closed a hand around my heart and I lost my breath. There it was, the old reaction, not dead at all but merely in abeyance until I was taken by surprise. Now it stole out to cause a constriction in my throat, perhaps as St George must have swallowed when he had spied the dragon on his horizon. It was a discomfort to which I must grow accustomed. This would be a final meeting between us with any vestige of intimacy, any future ones being held at a courtly distance. Edmund was here for one purpose only, as my message delivered by Joan had had only one end in mind.

I did not smile, merely sat and watched him approach. Cruel perhaps, but guilt was not in me. I might have seized my new burden of conscientious duty but it was beyond me to accept repudiation by a lover with a meek heart.

Edmund bowed and removed the soft felt hat, jewel-pinned and feather-trimmed, another detail that I must learn to forget. He too was unsmiling. He did not speak as I absorbed his appearance, his garments, the familiar features, this morning imprinted with arrogance. He had not enjoyed the news imparted to him by Joan, but I was in control again, determined not to be seduced by the appeal that had once ensnared me.

'I am honoured that Joan's message persuaded you to visit me.'

My voice was clear, as emotionless as cold winter sunshine.

'Yes, it did. And here I am. You do not have a high opinion of my sense of honour if you thought I would have ignored such news.'

'Once I had the highest opinion of your honour.'

'Much has changed between us.'

There was a touch of temper about him as well as arrogance. Even in the short time since his marriage, it seemed that he had grown into his new authority. The title sat lightly on his shoulders like a velvet cloak cut and sewn to his order, no longer merely an impressive houppelande borrowed from his brother, one that he had yet to adapt for his own use. He was Earl of Kent in his own right and his own power with an heiress for a wife. I did not offer him my hand, nor did he presume that I would. Nor did I invite him to sit.

'You can hardly be surprised at my questioning your veracity,' I said. 'You rejected me for an Italian fortune. I expect you will receive the dower eventually,' I commiserated with deceptive kindness.

I knew of the careless talk circulating like wildfire through the antechambers of this vast palace, that there was no Italian fortune in the lady's coffers. Madonna Lucia would not be the first bride whose family broke the betrothal promises as soon as the union was complete and she could not be sent home with a quick annulment in her hand.

Edmund's response was short enough. 'There will be no problem with the dower. Perhaps we should attend to the purpose of this meeting. We have a daughter. I have a duty to her.'

'Indeed.' We might have been discussing the sale of a horse where I held the upper hand. And yet I needed Edmund's compliance; my daughter needed it. 'If you choose to take that duty on your shoulders, of course. Your most recent wife will assuredly disapprove.'

Edmund ignored the prick of my verbal dagger. 'Why should she? Illegitimate offspring are not uncommon. The King has a bastard and the Queen has not banished the boy from the Court or her household. They say she has a fondness for him.' There was a deep furrow between his brows. 'I have no intention of broadcasting the birth of this child. Nor I think will you. But why do we argue? You have called her Alianore.'

'Yes. Do you wish to see her?'

'Yes.'

Still I did not move. I had not even offered him a cup of wine. Instead I asked the questions that were at the crux of this meeting. It irritated me that I was a little breathless, but I doubted he would notice.

'Will you recognise her openly?' I asked lightly. 'She is your legitimate daughter, if our vows at Kenilworth were honest ones. I was certainly under the impression that they were.' I smiled at him with false insouciance.

Edmund replied with severity.

'To all intents and purposes the child is not my legitimate daughter, since our vows have been superseded.'

'Is that a legal argument?' Now I moved, walking past him to open the inner door for him to enter the room beyond before me. He was so close that his garments brushed mine, but I did not touch him, rather stepped back. 'His Holiness the Pope rejected such a legal premise in the case of your grandmother.'

'Too late for that, Constance.' The furrow on his forehead deepened in annoyance. 'You attended my marriage at St Mary Overie and raised no objection. You drank to the felicity of the bride. You know that to broadcast our exchange of vows now will be of no weight unless you wish to drag us through the papal courts as my grandfather and grandmother did. I don't advise it. It will do neither of us any good. And here's the difference. Whereas my grandparents fought together to win the papal judgement, I will not. I'll not support you if you make a mockery of my marriage to Lucia. I'll repudiate you, publicly if I must.'

And because it hurt, an unexpectedly blinding flash of pain, my dignity slid a little, letting savagery reign.

'You have made a whore of me, Edmund.'

'You made it of yourself, long before we ever exchanged vows. Did we not both flout convention and sin, in a storm of lust?' Anger flared in him to match mine. 'I do not think either of us harboured regret for what passed between us, but it is necessary to reassess the future. To accept brutal reality.'

Brutal indeed. By the Blessed Virgin, it hurt. Perhaps because it was true.

'Of course.' I walked across a sunny anteroom with no more conversation, dignity once again captured and pinned tight, as I would pin a veil to withstand the snap of wind on a battlement walk. I opened another door into the small chamber where Alianore was now accommodated, the tapestries leaping with rabbits and small dogs and exotic birds. No huntsmen and red-toothed hounds here. Our daughter lay in her crib while a nursemaid, who had been gently rocking her, rose to her feet and curtsied. When she had left the room I lifted Alianore into my arms and introduced her with a terrible flippancy.

'This, my lord, is Alianore, your four-month-old daughter. Alianore, this is your father, the Earl of Kent, even though you have never seen him and will rarely see him in the future. Indeed, he might not recognise you in public, so this is a momentous event for you. You must remember it.' Alianore crooned and sneezed before burying her face against my throat, her fingers clutching at my veil. 'Do you think that she is impressed?'

Although there was an element of colour on his cheeks, he did not rise to my baiting. Instead he studied the child, but did not offer to take her from me. He had no experience of young children. I returned, deliberately, to the crucial question.

'Will you, in law, recognise her as your daughter?' I asked.

'I will acknowledge her in my will. I will make provision for her.'

'And until then?' As if I were mildly interested, when truly the idea appalled me. What man ever made a will until he lay on his deathbed? What I desired was a formal recognition now. Nothing about Alianore's future as a Holland daughter must be left to chance.

'I won't deny her, if that's what you mean.' Which could be a clever ploy of promising nothing at all. 'I have brought her a gift. My squire will have given it into the safekeeping of one of your women.'

'Is it so large?' I enquired.

'No, but needs careful handling. An enamelled and gilded hanap.'

'Thank you. Truly imaginative. Is it perhaps Italian?'

'Yes.'

I smiled again at his sudden discomfort. Obviously a costly item that had come into his possession with Lucia. 'My family is awash with hanaps. My uncle John of Lancaster gave them at every opportunity. But I will not gainsay it. I will ensure that Alianore knows that her father gave her a newly acquired enamelled and gilded cup to commemorate her birth.'

To do him justice, he worked hard to avoid the barbs.

'She looks healthy.'

'Would I not care for her? She is all I have as a memento of our most agreeable liaison.'

'Constance . . .' His brows snapped together.

Enough of my annoyance. It was unworthy of me. Had he not made the effort to come here and make his daughter's acquaintance? He would not deny her. Accepting that it was all I could ask, I replaced Alianore in her crib and walked from the room, gesturing that he should follow me as the nursemaid returned, turning to look at him in that still sun-filled anteroom, the beams making a chessboard of the floor but unable to thaw what was within me. We were two combatants, on opposing sides.

'I think we said all that might be said the last time that we were here together at Westminster in St Stephen's Chapel.'

'When you did not tell me that you were carrying my child.'

'No, I did not. How remiss of me.'

'I loved you.'

That I had not expected. 'And you do not now love me?'

'I doubt I will ever be free of you.'

Nor would I be free of him. Love had overpowered me. Love had made a fool of me. Love had enticed with all its glamour, before it allowed me to fall from a great height.

'You make me sound like some uncomfortable affliction,' I suggested.

'Never that.'

I shook my head, drowning in regret. Although I had sworn I would not, I asked him anyway: 'What will you do now?'

'I will promote my career as Admiral where it seems I have a talent. I will serve Henry well – and his son after him.'

'You will make your fortune extorting huge ransoms from captive French commanders at the same time as you build a dynasty of lawful children.'

'Is that not what every man seeks? I will restore the Holland family to the King's right hand, where we should be. We should never have become involved in insurrection. I will make amends through good service and wise counsel.'

He sounded imperious, older than his years. How easy it was to fall into old patterns of converse. It would be so simple for the past to be swept away, allowing us to talk as if there were no rift between us, but I walked towards the door, opening it so that he must leave. Even then he surprised me as he donned his hat and gloves.

'What will you do, Constance?'

It was a question that I had pushed aside. All very well for Edmund to plan strategies to win high renown as Admiral, to make a name as counsellor to the King and his son. I would never be entirely forgiven or trusted. There was no role for me, either as a self-confessed traitor or as a woman.

'I am superfluous,' I announced.

His brows rose. 'Where is your ambition? I cannot believe that it is dead.'

'Indisputably it is. Dead in a flight from Windsor to the Welsh March. Dead in my brother's betrayal. Dead in all those endless months I spent in Kenilworth. Dead in your marriage to Lucia Visconti. I expect I could find more nails in the coffin of my hopes if I looked closely, but I have accepted my faults and the price I have been forced to pay. I can afford no ambition. I have a fatherless daughter to raise.'

I tried to say it without bitterness. It seemed that I succeeded, for Edmund laughed in disbelief.

'Do you take the veil?'

'I do not.' My reply took no thought.

'Will you then sit here at Westminster and plot revenge?'

I stilled for a moment to think of this. There was no chime within my heart for vengeance, no heat, and even if the best dish of revenge was served cold, I was not moved to cook it.

'On whom would I be avenged and for what purpose? My

brother Edward is impregnable. I cannot blame the King for my own choices, I have accepted that. You are beyond my reach and I'll not disrupt your marriage.' I hesitated, then said: 'I'll not take the veil, but I'll not wed again.'

It surprised me. I had made it: that first true statement of intent since Alianore had been born. Until now I had been swept along by the mill race of events, even when I had presented myself at Edmund's marriage in a spate of fury. It had not been of my own volition but of necessity, because to absent myself would have been a cowardice. Here I felt that I had taken up the direction of my life once more, with some vision of the future, some desire for the course in which my life might run. It was not an unpleasant sensation.

'So you will stay here.' Edmund dared to address me with compassion. 'Or will you wall yourself up alone in one of your dower properties?'

My reply was short. 'I doubt I'll be allowed to. Henry still talks of sending me to my Welsh estates, to preserve a strong front against the Welsh rebels. That will be my role, for the good of England. I will become a fervent champion of the King. York in support of Lancaster.'

'I doubt your ambitions are as dead as you tell me. They are as alive and well as are my own. I expect you'll soon be plotting the most advantageous marriages for your children.'

Another arresting moment which almost made me smile. Beneath the handsome exterior there was a hard cynicism that would carry Edmund Holland far in the politics of the Court. Trust no one. Keep one's thoughts close. Seize every opportunity. He would make a name for himself and perhaps for the glory of England. He would have been a worthy mate for me, except that he had proved to be as self-serving and duplicitous as my brother.

I might have damned him for it, but I knew in my heart that I was no better.

'I will be a spider in Lancaster's web, spinning heartily for his advancement,' I replied.

'It's a good image, but I don't necessarily believe you.'

'What you believe, Edmund, is no longer of any account.'

My reply perforce created between us the sharp tension of an irrevocable ending, one that could be tasted, even though Edmund Holland was chivalric enough to kiss my hands, my cheeks and then my lips. They were cold kisses.

'Farewell, Constanza. I did love you. I wish that we had met in more felicitous circumstances.'

'Perhaps it was the tragedy of it all that brought us together.'

'Perhaps it was.' He halted momentarily, as if against his better judgement, before pushing the door wide and stepping beyond.

'Edmund.' I followed him, hating that I must beg. 'Promise me that you will not allow her to live unrecognised.'

'I promise.'

I had done all I could.

He ran lightly down the stair and for the briefest moment I stood there, listening to the fading of his footsteps. Some of the wounds were healed but not all: I might accept the reality of it, but the abrasions of a squandered love were still sore within my breast. I had lost him. He was not mine, and in my damaged emotions I made my final farewells. Here was the man who had had, in his possession, the key to open up my heart, my life, as if he were releasing the lid of a coffer to display a glittering array of gems. Now the box was tight locked again, and I would encourage no one to unlock it. I did not think the contents would ever see the light of day again.

And I realised: he had kissed me, albeit chastely, in farewell but not once had he touched Alianore to mark her as his own. It was as if the intimacy between us, fated lovers as we had proved to be, had at last been sliced through, Alexander hacking apart the Gordian Knot of my malingering emotions. Strangely it was a relief.

My mind began to work again. Here now was my immediate ambition, for I was not born to be idle. You will spend your days plotting the marriages of your children, Edmund had intimated. And so I would. Returned to my chamber I mixed ink, discovered an unused piece of parchment and a pen, and began to write lists of possibilities, scoring through those where I saw no value.

It did not have the immediacy of riding through the night from Windsor with John Beaufort hard on my heels; it did not make my blood throb with excitement and fear, but it would be a worthy future for my mind to espouse. I would tie my children to the most advantageous families in the land.

My son Richard, Lord Despenser, was nearing eleven years and ripe for the making of an alliance. Which families were pre-eminent at the Court, and would continue their supremacy into the next reign? The Beauforts were as close to the King as any; my cousins now legitimised. I noted names and drew lines, calling on my wide knowledge of cousins and their offspring of a suitable age and lineage. I would paper over the treacherous cracks in the Despenser family's history, perhaps with Eleanor Neville, daughter of my cousin Joan Beaufort and her husband Ralph Neville, Earl of Westmoreland, a mighty power in the north since the recent decline of the Percys. And as Joan Beaufort was sister to the King, her daughter might be perfect as a Despenser bride.

Then Isabella. She was only six years old but older than I when wed in name to Thomas. The Beauchamp Earls of Worcester were a family to approach. I doubted they would reject an alliance with a young bride with royal blood in her veins.

I steeled myself against the old grief of Elizabeth's death as I closed my eyes, seeing the tapestry of connections that I was stitching. Had I not, for much of my adult life, been at the centre of a tapestry of treason, drenched in blood and death? I had stitched with my own hands and intellect to undermine and destroy. In my mind's eye I could see each interlocking stitch, the interplay of colour and vibrancy. There would be no redemption, no forgiveness for me in its creation, even though it had never come to pass. But now, all traces of that old tapestry consigned to the past, I would create a new masterpiece of benign loyalty.

Dickon must be my priority.

I wrote down a name, an obvious choice for my young brother. I had been thwarted over the Mortimer disaster, punished for my involvement. Here was a possibility that would stir the mud at the bottom of the pond for any number of the major fish swimming there.

The two Mortimer boys, now spending their young years in the fortress at Pevensey, had a sister, Anne, an unwed sister, the perfect age for a bride. If Dickon were to wed Anne Mortimer – now there was an alliance made in heaven. If the Mortimer claim to the throne ever came to anything, Dickon would stand in their midst by blood and marriage. A marriage made in hell, some might say; a marriage of possibilities, I would reply, enjoying a return of the old delight in intrigue.

I put down my pen, but then on impulse I pulled forward a clean sheet and began to write while the mood of conciliation and even conscience had me in its grip.

To my lord Edmund Holland, Earl of Kent,

I regret the tenor of our parting. I was neither fair nor generous. I need to remedy that, for you gave me a gift of great worth that I have only recently come to accept, which is the knowledge of love. I did not know what it was to desire the presence of a particular man, nor had I ever been moved by emotions, to both give and receive pleasure. My heart did not know how to respond in its beat at the sound of a well-loved voice. Now I know all of these things, however painful they might be in your absence.

I will never love again, but at least I will not go to my grave in ignorance of the selfless glory that it can bring. You have my assurance that the fire of love might settle to a mere flame as the years pass, but I doubt it will ever be extinguished.

I remain, as ever,

Constance, Lady Despenser

Joan would be proud of me. Not the poetic flowering of a troubadour I acknowledged as, gently, I put down the pen, folded the sheet and wrote Edmund's name upon it, sealing it with wax, pressing the indentation of my own seal. I had learned the joy of love. The value of it. But it was also dangerous. I would live without it and conspire for the future.

In a sad little reflection I accepted that no one would ever again call me Constanza.

Chapter Twenty-One

April 1408: Cardiff Castle

I had no anticipation of what would await me. No prescience of events far beyond my control. It is not given to many of us to foresee the future, which is a blessing in itself. I had ridden in from a circuitous tour of our outer defences, inspecting barbican, walls and postern gateways, questioning my steward closely about the state of the water supplies and the refurbishment of the crenulations where time and weather had brought dangerous erosion. The Welsh rebels and opportunistic French were not our only enemy. It pleased me to take my duties seriously. How active I had become in Henry's name.

I was not yet dissatisfied with the narrow pattern of my life.

I had been sent here to the Despenser castle in Cardiff, dispatched by the King in an effort to resist any further Welsh sorties into England. He had been kind in his request, but firm, and I had had no reason to refuse. A year later I was still in residence, having survived the terrible winter of frost and ice when rivers froze and animals fell dead from the cold. When the Earl of Northumberland began to rally his Percy retainers once more, calling on England to rise up against Henry, I had paid dutiful and pertinent visits to the castles at Caerphilly and Kenfig, Llanbleddian and Llantrisant, outlying fortresses but still susceptible to Welsh attack if allowed to fall into disrepair. These castles were Richard's inheritance. If I was lonely in my visiting, restricted by the limited vista of my responsibility, there was no one to know it but myself.

In the political arena Northumberland had raised the old cry of *King Richard is alive*. No one of either knowledge or sense gave it credence any more. The old Earl, attempting an invasion from Scotland, hoping to collect supporters from his hunting grounds in the north, was lured by false claims of friendship and killed on the battlefield at Bramham Moor, another death in the struggle for who should own the crown. Meanwhile Owain Glyn Dwr was in retreat. It seemed to me that at last Henry might be holding England fast in his mailed grip. England might just fall into a lasting peace.

But here, on this day in Cardiff, was a disturbance to the normal pattern of my day. The smart escort, now proceeding to occupy the bailey with its clamour and stench of overheated flesh of man and horse, heralded a visitor, and the blazon on the men-at-arms indicated who might have found his way to this wild border region. I sighed. Dismounting, I went to discover him, finding some difficulty since the great hall and immediate audience chambers were empty, until my chamberlain, clattering busily down the stair from the upper floor, informed me, with an air of disapproval, that our visitor had taken himself off to the nursery.

'He was most insistent, my lady,' he said.

'Has he been here long?'

'No, my lady. Just arrived. Nor does he intend to stay.'

'So why the visit?' No one chose to stay long, unless under coercion.

'He did not say, my lady.'

Lifting the door latch to the chamber, I discovered our guest crouched on the floor, entertaining my youngest daughter, making her and her nursemaid laugh at some shared joke. Isabella was curled on a window seat, clutching the sleek grey cat across her knees. A kitten no longer, Joan's gift travelled with us, secreted by my women unbeknownst to me, I suspected, since Isabella loved it inordinately. My elder daughter with seven-year-old dignity was considering whether to join her sister in the game, where Alianore, who was standing on her toes with barely a wobble, was trying to snatch a sparkling object, offered tantalisingly by our visitor, then hidden, enclosed within a tight fist.

When I closed the door my brother Edward looked across at me, but did not stand or turn aside from his teasing. His smile was not for me.

'Do you think this is for you?' he asked Alianore.

'Yes!' Alianore said. 'For me!' She snatched at the glittering prize, hooting with laughter when the fist again closed around it.

'Perhaps you must sing me a song, if it is to be yours.'

Abandoning the cat, Isabella crept forward, the temptation too great. 'I can sing for you.'

'So you can. I have heard you, little linnet. Perhaps I have a gift for you too.'

I might have been warmed by the scene, at the easy acceptance between this man and his nieces. Instead I resented it.

I resented him. What right had he to woo my daughters' affections?

'What do you want?' I interrupted, walking forward to rest briefly where Isabella had been sitting, misgivings rife. 'You have not been invited.'

'No,' he replied easily, 'but I thought I should come. Even uninvited or unwelcome. Hide your talons, Constance. It would be unwise to teach your daughters how simple it is for hostility to grow within a family.' His eyes were suddenly keen on my face. 'Don't shut me out. We should support each other.'

An observation I resented even more.

'What do you want from me? If it is yet another conspiracy, go away. You must find your willing pawns elsewhere. I'll not hold your cloak for you when you try to climb the walls at Eltham or Windsor, or wherever your next villainous deceits will take you.'

'I need nothing from you. Am I not a reformed character?'

I watched him offer Alianore a steadying hand when she tottered, suspicions building and rebuilding. There was a line between his brows.

'Is it possible that you have you fallen from Henry's favour?'

'I stand in the highest regard with Henry. You need not fear for me.'

'I don't. But it must be serious to bring you here.' I summoned a false smile, just a glint of teeth.

'I think so. But I thought I should also make the acquaintance of my niece, now that she is almost a young lady.'

He ruffled Alianore's curls, for somewhere she had lost her coif, unbalancing her so that she sank to the floor with a squawk. Whereupon he stood, caught her up and swung her into his arms. In a moment of weakness I was indeed cajoled and considered it regretful that he had no children of his own. He was not too proud to engage with a child who was not yet two years old, with as much affection as he lavished on his hounds and horses. Edmund had never done so. But the weakness was only for a moment.

'What do you want, Edward?' And then on a sudden thought, with a brush of concern: 'Is Richard in good heart?'

My son, now eleven years, was ensconced in Edward's household, learning all he must know as a page and at length a squire. It behoved me to trust that my brother was not teaching him the niceties of lies and treachery. I too, it seemed, was a reformed character.

'Richard is perfectly well, learning how to kill and prevent himself from being killed. He is growing fast, his appetite is enormous, and he needs a new horse if he is to fulfil his destiny on the tournament field. Or so he tells me. How did I never realise how costly an item in my receipt books a boy could be?' His eye slid away from my sceptical gaze, and back to my youngest daughter. 'She does not look like you,' he observed. He stood Alianore once more on her feet. 'The Fair Maid of Kent's beauty still breeds true, even though your daughter's hair is dark.'

'I can only pray that she has a more amenable temperament,' I said.

Edward took one of my hands, drew me to my feet, then closer when I still resisted, and brushed my cheek with his lips; but I stepped back, for I had sensed some concern in him, some unfathomable anxiety, stretching like a newly replaced lute string that must still be tuned. A shiver of awareness touched me. He was not here by chance.

'Tell me why you have come.'

There was fear in me now. I watched him inhale, lips tight-pressed. Then exhale. He delivered his message in three words.

'Kent is dead.'

It was stated so plainly, so directly, without warning, like a sword thrust from a master of the art, so that the pain came later, after the realisation that there was blood. My first thought was absolute. He could not be. He was still so young, in the prime of his health and strength. Beloved by the King, a Knight of the Garter, his status enhanced by his recent promotion to Admiral of the West. A formidable jouster and exponent of the arts of the tournament field, even rivalling Edward. Edmund could not be dead. How could he be dead when I had no sense of it?

'I thought you should know before some passing merchant told you, or a gossipy letter from Court,' Edward said.

Still, I shook my head in denial. It seemed that I could marshal neither my words nor my thoughts.

'There is no doubt, Constance.' Edward was stern. 'Why would I lie to you? It was in an assault on the Île-de-Bréhat off Brittany, in a naval campaign promoted by Queen Joanna.'

'I know where he was.' Had I not made it my business to know, even after we had parted, even though I knew there was no hope of a future for us? 'He had been given an independent command . . .'

Edward refused to allow me to wallow in disbelief. 'And it was a successful attack, except that he made a novice's mistake. He took off his helmet before the enemy was entirely dispersed, and a Breton crossbow quarrel took him in the head, leaving nothing for the surgeon to do but sew him into his shroud.'

I did not wish to imagine it.

Edward continued as if making a report to the King on the loss of one of his favourite commanders. 'He died instantly,' he said. 'His body is being brought back, to be buried at Bourne Abbey in Lincolnshire. I thought you would want to know.'

I did not need the minutiae of detail. I did not want it. But even worse, to my horror, I felt as little emotion as Edward in the telling. I could not grasp it. There was within me no sense of loss at all.

Edward was staring down at Alianore, who had decided to sit and examine the fine but dusty stitching on his boots, while Isabella returned to hugging the cat. 'Your daughter will receive no recognition from the Holland family. Did any one of them know of your clandestine marriage? Did you ever tell Joan?'

So Edward had indeed guessed after our charged conversation outside the Church of St Mary Overie. At least I need not dissemble with him. At last it was possible for me to reply in honesty although my blood moved as sluggishly as the still ice-bound stream beyond my walls.

'No. No one knows but you and me and two nameless witnesses who I doubt will ever speak of it now. What value in telling anyone since I bore witness to his marriage to Lucia, as if mine did not exist? As for this daughter' – I picked her up and wiped her hands with my sleeve – 'her father's death will make no difference. He promised to name her in his will.' I shrugged a little, accepting fragile reality. 'Except that I doubt he thought to make a will. How would he have anticipated his premature death?'

How unfeeling I sounded, taken up with matters of inheritance. I was impregnable to sorrow.

'If a man goes to war, he has a duty to make his will,' Edward replied with terrible certainty. 'But of course we never do. We never expect to die on campaign. Alianore will have no legal recourse to any Holland inheritance. I thought you should hear it from someone who cares for your well-being.'

'Do you, then, care for my well-being?' I kept my attention on Alianore. There were still so many wounds, and deep ones, between us. 'Don't worry, Edward. I will not weep on your shoulder.'

'I never supposed that you would, but it is there to absorb the tears if you change your mind.'

Edward proceeded to direct the conversation into events in Wales and at Court and the perennially worrying state of Henry's health, all the while carrying the burden of the exchange, thus allowing my mind to trace its own path. Edmund was dead.

When I could no longer bear Edward's facile attempts to cushion the blow, I turned my face away.

'You have delivered your news,' I said. 'You are free to leave when you wish.'

Edward bowed with ironic gallantry. It had after all been a ploy to allow me a little time and space. Then with careful fingers he pinned the brooch, which he had been holding all the while, to the bodice of Alianore's tunic where it glowed, its gems sparkling as red as blood in the sun that had, unnoticed, appeared to bathe the chamber in bright but cold light.

'You are a daughter of York, my child. You will lack for nothing and we will care for you. Even your mother, who never loved anyone in her life but herself, will protect you.' Above my daughter's head, he caught my eye, squinting in an errant sunbeam. 'Isn't that so?'

'Of course,' I lied without hesitation. 'I have no capacity for love. I am too selfish. I never have given my heart to a man and I never will. But I know how to protect my own.'

He laughed. 'Having a sister who is never ruled by unreliable emotion is a blessing. We will sup together later when I return from the fortifications at Longtown. Henry has sent me on a survey of the March.'

He walked to the door, leaving me standing with Alianore in the middle of the floor.

'Edward . . .'

He stopped, turned.

'Thank you.' I forced myself to say it. 'I would not have liked to discover it any other way.' And then because I desired to know: 'Is Lucia in mourning in widow's weeds?'

'Looking pale and dramatic. I fear she will not be a wealthy widow. He left nothing but debts, so they say.'

'What of her dowry?'

'Never paid. Her vast dower was all flattery and we were all taken in. I expect it's lining the coffers of her Visconti relatives.' His final glance was quizzical, warning me that he of all my family would sense my isolation here. His words confirmed it. 'I doubt you'll be here for ever. Henry will recall you to Court. You might even wed again, God save the man.'

There was a saturnine slant to his face.

I let him go, accepting that I must once again forgive Edward, since he had been gracious enough and understanding enough to grant Alianore the recognition that she lacked. She would be Alianore of York.

Alone, I watched her as she examined the jewel pinned at her shoulder. Edmund's only child. His heir, even if unacknowledged. I carried her to look out of the window, down into the courtyard where Edward's departing entourage provided much spectacle to entertain her. Isabella climbed to stand on the window seat at my side.

Edmund is dead.

The one phrase that remained as an echo of Edward's visit; I repeated it silently in my mind. Then again, meaninglessly, my lips forming the words. Why was I accepting of this death, as an event of such slight significance to me? Perhaps because I had lost him over a year ago at the door of St Mary Overie. And at the last, in these months in the solitude of my Welsh estates, I had finally come to a true acknowledgement. I was not the wife he needed even if I was the one he might have wanted. It was a political choice and I could not fault him in it. We had all made enough political choices over the years. A woman must bow her head and accept.

Alianore crowed when she saw Edward below, foreshortened, the fringing on his cap lifting in the breeze, ruffling with his hair. He looked up and, seeing us, bowed again and raised his hand in salute. While Isabella waved back and Alianore squirmed to be put down, with one hand I managed to unpin the brooch from her garment. Too precious for so young a child. It was a York jewel, which I recognised.

'When you are older, you will wear this.'

She did not seem to mind, her attention now taken with the ravens that were swooping low, their flight interlinked as if they flirted.

A group of minstrels congregated below to practise a new hymn for Easter as Edward's soldiery departed. Suitably plangent, the mournful harmonies awoke no answering response in me. Every feeling of which I was capable was moribund, nailed into a coffin that would be laid to rest in Bourne Abbey. Perhaps one day I would make my own pilgrimage there.

It made no difference to my life now.

Later, alone, when night had fallen and my chamber was shadowed, I lit a candle and lifted the small casket from the bottom of one of my travelling coffers. I lifted the lid. There was a familiar brooch, a pair of gloves, gifts of courtship from Edmund, suitable for a knight to give to his lady, gifts of little intrinsic value but all offered as a symbol of adoration. I lifted them out, recalling my lack of experience in courtship when I had received them: a mirror, a belt, a purse, a comb, embroidered cuffs. And the most precious of all, the archaic ruby-studded collar. When she was grown I would give them to Alianore, when she was old enough to understand that she was more than a daughter of York.

I had loved him, and I had to believe that he had loved me.

. . . your mother, who never loved anyone in her life but herself . . .

Shamefully, I had concurred. Edward would go to his grave believing me to be lacking either tender emotion or compassion. It would not do to destroy an illusion, one I had fostered all my life because it had proved to be the wisest policy. To reveal one's emotions only opened the possibility of rejection and heartbreak. I might hide it well but my heart had been broken.

Finally, at last, reliving the weakness that had made me consign this item to the coffer with all my past memories, I lifted out the letter I had never sent. The only love letter that I had ever written, still sealed with brittle wax as I had left it.

Where would I have sent it? My confessions were not such as I would wish to have fallen into Madonna Lucia's hands. Edmund had died without knowing my forgiveness and my abiding love. Smoothing the folds which had never been unfolded since the day it was written, refusing to reread it, I replaced it where it would remain. Tomorrow I would make arrangements for my priest to say Masses for Edmund's soul. And, because I was not without compassion, there was a letter I must write. Joan would once more be grief-stricken at the loss of a brother.

I made to close the casket but spied, rolled into one corner of the box in a screw of leather, the two golden dice that had cast King Richard's future and ours. Lifting them, I shook them in my clenched fist, the dull gold still emitting a baleful gleam. Dare I cast them now? If I did, was I skilled enough to interpret the message? Indeed, what question would I ask of them? I recalled the importance of three and six, the disaster of three and two. What would my future hold? Stability and happiness, or turbulence and grief?

Best not to know.

I threw them anyway, watching the dice fall on my lap.

Unseeing, I stretched out my hand and pinched the wick of the candle, plunging the room and the treacherous dice into darkness.

Edmund Holland was dead.

I would mourn him as was fitting. Already my face was wet with tears, for him and for my own unimaginable loss. I would now weep for him, alone, where there was no one to bear witness.

Acknowledgements

My thanks to Dominic Wakeford and the team at HQ Stories who launched my novel into the world with such enthusiasm for Constance and her family. I value, as ever, their dedication, their expertise, and their professionalism.

My ongoing thanks to my agent Jane Judd, whose calm presence, good advice and endless support are invaluable in all my moments of enthusiasm or uncertainty. I always rely on her verdict when she is the first to read my completed manuscript.

For all things technical and for the creation and care of my website, I must thank Helen Bowden and everyone at Orphans Press. I am constantly in debt to their technical know-how.

What inspired me to write about Constance of York, Lady Despenser?

Meet Constance of York, Lady Despenser, and her magnificently dysfunctional family in the reign of King Henry IV. A tale of medieval treason, tragedy, heartbreak and the personal cost of betrayal. Few families have come down through history with such a questionable reputation, and Constance not the least of them. Treachery, swapping allegiance with unnerving frequency, plotting murder and insurrection, they were a deviously cunning bunch, worthy of a soap opera. How could I not write about such a superb cast of characters?

Constance of York, Lady Despenser, Countess of Gloucester, granddaughter of King Edward III, stands at the centre of this family, the House of York.

Her father Edmund, Duke of York, the most ineffectual and impecunious of the five sons of King Edward III.

Her mother Isabella, a Castilian Princess, with a reputation for easy morals.

Her elder brother Edward, on the surface indolent and pleasure-loving, but driven by hot ambition and with a sly charm to match it.

Her younger brother Richard, damned with the taint of possible illegitimacy, who would ultimately meet his death by the axe for plotting against King Henry V.

Constance's husband Thomas, Lord Despenser, as able and as self-seeking as the rest.

And Constance? Tradition says that she equalled them in ambition and treachery, involving herself in every twist and turn of the conspiracies. History has damned her as a 'thoroughly bad lot'. Enjoying recognition at the vivid Court of Richard II, Constance could not accept the fall from grace that came with his death. Thus her life became vicious and unprincipled, devoted to revenge and restitution to the crown of those who might restore her family's influence.

But was her reputation as black as history paints it? Here is an opportunity to look behind the tapestries and spy into her life more closely. Product of an affectionless family, committed to a loveless marriage, Constance's life was emotionally barren. No victim, she chose to live in a man's world and involve herself in her family's treachery. That is until she fell in love. Here was offered the possibility of change and happiness. Unless Constance threw away her chances of fulfilment. Unless her lover abandoned her.

Here is a tale of thwarted ambitions and betrayed love. It highlights the influence that a woman could use, but also the restrictions on that influence in the medieval world. Constance was a woman of misplaced loyalties but must be admired for her steadfast support of those who demanded her duty. The ultimate betrayal by Constance's lover brought her heartbreak and loneliness.

How could I possibly resist writing about her, bringing her to life? Constance is not an easy heroine, but she makes for a formidable protagonist in *A Tapestry of Treason*.

And Afterwards…

Constance, Lady Despenser, sadly, for those of us who have come to know her, faded from history. She never married again. Perhaps she remained on her Welsh estates, perhaps she returned to Court. She died on 28th November 1416 in or near Westminster at the age of about 41 years. We do not know the cause of death. She was buried before the high altar in Reading Abbey.

Edward, Duke of York, continued to serve the crown with no more overt suggestions of treachery and some praise. He was present at the siege of Harfleur, commanding the vanguard on its march through France, but died on 25th October 1415 at Agincourt where he commanded the right wing of the English army. His bones were returned to England and buried in the church at Fotheringhay. He had no direct heir to inherit the title. His wife Philippa outlived him for many years and is buried in Westminster Abbey.

Richard of Conisbrough (Dickon) was eventually created Earl of Cambridge in 1414, a title that brought him neither land nor money. Disappointed, he became involved in a plot in 1415 to overthrow Henry V for which he was executed in August of that year. His motives remain under a cloud but it may be that he was intending to enforce the Mortimer claim to the throne once again.

Anne Mortimer, Richard's first wife, died in 1411 after only three years of marriage, soon after the birth of their son, another Richard, who would become the third Duke of York, of Wars of the Roses fame, and heir to both the York and Mortimer inheritance. Richard of Conisbrough's second wife was Maud Clifford, by whom he had no children.

After his execution he was buried in Southampton but there is no surviving tomb.

Edmund Mortimer, 5th Earl of March, died without a male heir in 1425. Richard of Conisbrough married **Anne Mortimer**, who became the Mortimer heiress after the death of her brother. After Richard's execution and the death of Edward of York at Agincourt, the ducal title passed to Richard and Anne's son, Richard. He became the famous Duke of York who wed Cecily Neville. Implicated in what was to become the Wars of the Roses, this Richard died at the Battle of Wakefield in 1460 but two of his sons, Edward and Richard, were to become kings of England.

Joan Holland, Duchess of York, had no children with William de Willoughby of Eresby, who died in 1409. She went on to marry twice more. Her third husband was Baron Scrope of Masham who was executed for his part in the same plot as Richard of Conisbrough. Her fourth husband was Sir Henry Bromflete. She died in 1435 at about fifty five years and was buried at King's Langley. Joan had no children from any of her marriages.

Richard Despenser was dead by April 1414, before he was twenty. He had been married to Alianore Neville, daughter of the Earl of Westmorland and Joan Beaufort, but he died childless so without a direct heir.

Isabella Despenser became heiress to the Despenser lands on the death of her brother and thus a valuable bride. She married twice, first to Richard Beauchamp, Earl of Worcester, and then on his death to his cousin, a more famous Richard Beauchamp, Earl of Warwick. The daughter of this second marriage was Anne Beauchamp, who married Richard Neville Earl of Warwick (the Kingmaker) and so mother of Isabel and Anne Neville.

Alianore of York married James Touchet, Baron Audley, with whom she had seven children. She made a claim against the Holland family that her mother had indeed married Edmund Holland, Earl of Kent, which would make her legitimate and thus the Earl of Kent's heir. The claim was rejected out of hand by the Holland family.

Travels with Constance of York, Lady Despenser

For those of you who might enjoy following in the footsteps of Constance – in person, by travel guide and history book, or by internet ...

Palace of Westminster

The royal palace which Constance would have known sadly no longer exists, a victim of fire. What a loss to lovers of medieval history it is, particularly St Stephen's Chapel, which was the creation of the best artisans of their day. Today we have only the Jewel Tower and of course Westminster Hall. This is impressive enough, constructed by Richard II, showing us what the rest must have been like if we could only imagine it.

Westminster Abbey

An essential visit for remnants of the medieval royal family. Edward III and Richard II as well as Henry V, all known to Constance, are buried here, as is Philippa, wife of Constance's brother Edward.

Tower of London

Always an excellent place to confine those who were a danger to the throne, even if it was not actually in a dungeon. The quintessential visit for medieval atmosphere.

Windsor Castle

Another of the royal palaces that Constance would have known well, where her fatal attempt to rescue the Mortimer heirs began.

Eltham Palace

Now famous for its Tudor additions and Art Deco splendour, there is little of the palace where King Henry IV and his Court spent most Christmas and New Year festivities. Still a place to visit.

Cardiff Castle

The original motte and bailey construction at Cardiff Castle, surrounded by its formidable walls, is a fantastic site to visit. It is easy to imagine Constance living there, wishing that she were back in the centre of political events in London.

Conisbrough Castle

This dramatic castle, with its eye-catching keep, in South Yorkshire is where Richard (Dickon) was born and where he lived as his brother Edward's tenant since he had no land of his own. It has an impressive position with views over the countryside, showing why it was chosen by the York family as its second residence after Fotheringhay.

Kenilworth Castle

The truly majestic power-base of the Lancasters in the Midlands where Constance spent her imprisonment at King Henry's pleasure. Its history spans the ages, from Norman through John of Gaunt's extensive building, to the work of Dudley to create a palace for Queen Elizabeth I's sojourn. Constance would have enjoyed the luxurious building put in place by John of Gaunt in the 14th century with its spacious rooms and wide windows, even if she was not in the mood to dance in the dancing chamber.

King's Langley

Little remains of the King's Langley palace and park built by the Plantagenets, but in the Church of All Saints there can be found the burial place of Edmund Duke of York and his wife Isabella of Castile. King Richard II was buried here temporarily until his body was removed to Westminster Abbey.

Tewkesbury Abbey

For those travellers interested in the final resting place of the Despensers, this magnificent abbey in Gloucestershire is a 'must visit' venue. Isabel Neville and her husband George Duke of Clarence are also buried here.

Fotheringhay

There is little left of the castle here, but the Church of St Mary and All Saints is a place of pilgrimage for those who are interested in following in the footsteps of the House of York. Dickon's son, Richard Duke of York, and his wife Cecily Neville, are buried here.